THE THRILLING LIBRARY:

Dr. Zeng ARCHIVES

BY

E. HOFFMANN PRICE, W.T. BALLARD & ROBERT LESLIE BELLEM

INTRODUCTION BY

WILL MURRAY

THRILLING PUBLICATIONS

2017

TABLE OF

CONTENTS

WILL MURRAY

THE FASCINATION with protagonists of Chinese or Asian origin among Western readers probably goes back to Sax Rohmer's immortal Dr. Fu Manchu. The Devil Doctor could hardly be classed as a hero, but he was the unquestioned star of the long-running series which bore his sinister name.

True Asian heroes followed: Charlie Chan. Mr. Moto. The Mysterious Mr. Wong. Some were so obscure that they have been forgotten. But they were all the rage after World War I.

Naturally, they infiltrated the pulp magazines. Not only Fu Manchu knockoffs like Dr. Yen Sin and the Mysterious Wu Fang, but lesser lights like A.E. Apple's Mr. Chang, Bedford Rohmer's Wo Fan, and Captain Lee Fredericks' Mr. Wong (no relation to Harry Stephen Keller's Mysterious Mr. Wong of the slicks). The Filipino sleuth of *Black Mask* fame, Jo Gar, also belongs on this list.

By the late 1930s, the sinister Oriental archvillain had gotten to be a well-worn if not worn out pulp-paper cliché. You couldn't give them away.

Writer Manly Wade Wellman recalled pitching a pulp plot to one editor around this time. "Once, doing something for Mort Weisinger (Better Pubs), I was stuck for a villain and said, 'How about a mysterious Chinaman?' And he cried, 'No, no, a thousand times no!'"

With the dawn of a new decade, the pulp publishers were struggling to come up with new heroes who would sell to the new 1940s generation of reader. Since Doc Savage was hard to duplicate, they settled for copying The Shadow, then at the height of his multi-media fame. They had been reinventing The Shadow since his inception, but now they were forced to be creative about it.

That is how the Thrilling Group of magazines came up with the Black Bat, and why Munsey Publications brought forth the Green Lama in 1940. The latter was an American millionaire who journeyed to fabled Tibet—where The Shadow purportedly received his mighty mind powers—later returning to the United States to battle crime tricked out in the emerald robes of a Buddhist lama!

Despite the apparent absurdity of the premise, the Green Lama went on to a distinguished career in pulp magazines, comic books and on radio. Go figure.

Which brings us to the obscure and recondite Doctor Zeng. The true story behind the creation of this unique hero may never be known this side of paradise, but we can assemble some of the pieces of the jigsaw puzzle.

Doctor Zeng debuted in *Thrilling Mystery*, in the juicily-titled novelette, "Fangs of Doom," during the period when the magazine's editors, under fire from censors, were hastily abandoning the old "weird menace" slant. The author was the remarkable Edgar Hoffmann Trooper Price, a former West Pointer turned practicing Buddhist, Orientalist, astrologer and contributor to *Weird Tales*, who by 1941 was busy writing pulp for publishers ranging from Munsey to Trojan. He had just concluded the Matalaa series for *Red Star Adventures*, where the byline Martin McCall concealed his true identity.

Created as a one-shot character, Doctor Zeng was an American who posed as a Chinese scholar in order to contend with crime in San Francisco's Chinatown—which happened to be E. Hoffmann Price's favorite haunt (he was living in the Bay area at that time). In actuality, Linwood Lawton becomes Doctor Zeng Tse Lin by the extreme expedient of plastic surgery. Clearly, he is a man on a mission. I'll leave his backstory for you to discover in the pages that follow.

Now I don't know if the Thrilling editors noticed the splash the Green Lama was making over in the pages of *Double Detective*, and so asked Price to go author Kendell Foster Crossen one better. Or if they had noticed that the hero of Street & Smith's 1940 revival, *The Whisperer*, had taken to assuming Chinese features as part of his crime-busting guise. But the notion came from somewhere. Regardless of those pulpy antecedents, Doctor Zeng was a true American original. Nothing like him had ever before appeared. Not until the advent of Kwai Chang Caine of TV's *Kung Fu* would his like be seen again.

American pulp audiences insisted upon Yank heroes. Almost every pulp magazine market notice stressed this. So it was pretty daring for Price to construct a hero who was, at least on the surface, Chinese. He also told a pretty adult story of what social consequences and restrictions Lawton encountered as Dr. Zeng. Perhaps the relentless success of the

Charlie Chan films, still going strong in 1941, had something to do with it.

And there it might have ended.

Before 1941 was over, we were at war with Japan. This made the Chinese, who had suffered a decade of oppression at the hands of the son of Nippon, our allies.

The Office of War Information was created in part to help propagandize the war effort. Several pulp writers, including The Shadow's Theodore Tinsley and The Spider's Norvell Page, joined OWI to help out.

During World War II, OWI issued mimeographed bulletins containing guidelines for editors and writers on how to produce popular fiction designed to bolster the homefront. Not far into the global conflict, OWI suggested to editors the idea of running stories spotlighting our Chinese allies, putting them in a positive light.

Almost certainly this directive inspired Thrilling editor in chief Leo Margulies to revive Doctor Zeng for *Popular Detective*.

For whatever reasons, Price was uninterested or unavailable. So the Lion of Standard turned to the California writing team of Robert Leslie Bellem and W.T. Ballard, then collaborating on the Jim Anthony novels in Trojan's *Super-Detective*. There, they toiled under the house name of John Grange. Their customary working method called for Ballard to dictate a first draft, which Bellem then polished for print.

When they brought forth their first Doctor Zeng tale, Bellem and Ballard went by the joint pseudonym of Walt Bruce. Perhaps this was to suggest two renowned pulp writers, Walt Coburn and George Bruce, who had gone on to Hollywood fame. The busy pulpsmiths did not merely revive Price's protagonist. They revamped him, giving Zeng a new American birth name, modifying his background to include a past scourged by the spreading Japanese menace, and bequeathing the artificial half-breed a new Chinatown headquarters, the Mandarin Emporium. Further, they Doc Savage-ized him in emulation of Jim Anthony, who was himself a Doc clone. Doctor Zeng Tse-Lin's name also acquired a hyphen.

The first Walt Bruce-bylined story was "Blood Cargo," in the June 1942 issue of *Popular Detective*. Five others followed. Where Bellem and Ballard lacked Price's sensitivity and insight into the Chinese community of that day, they make up for it in sheer pulpy entertainment. Because these tales were produced during wartime, expect a sprinkling of Nazis and like-minded villains.

Although market notices for *Popular Detective* listed Doctor Zeng as a regular feature (they typoed it as Dr. Zong!), the series ran only sporadically.

The last entry appeared in 1944, around the time Bellem and Ballard abandoned the Jim Anthony series. As Ballard told Ron Goulart in *Cheap Thrills*:

> "Bob Bellem and I wrote the character from its inception until I left California for Wright Field during the war. At the same time we were also doing a series about a Chinese. Doctor Somebody. I can't for the life of me recall the name... The stuff was pure formula and I did most of it on a dictaphone. I could dictate anywhere from thirty to forty pages a day."

And formula it was. The Thrilling editors loved their version of the tried-and-true pulp action pattern. In this case, in emulation of the Black Bat and similar Thrilling series, Doctor Zeng works with the obligatory police mentor/friend—in this case retired police captain Brian Carter. His young niece Ann provides the nominal love interest.

This series enjoys the distinction of featuring the last traditional pulp hero the Thrilling Group ever launched. It marks the end of the pulp era that began with *The Phantom Detective* magazine in 1933.

A final word on the origin of Doctor Zeng. I once asked E. Hoffmann Price about his creation. He told me that he had based Zeng on an unnamed Chinese teacher, adding, "I had not then my present Chinese associations."

Price went on to express ignorance that his quasi-Eurasian protagonist continued in other authorial hands, but was otherwise unmoved, noting, "I was a professional writer, not a fan."

Here is the entire Doctor Zeng suite. It belongs on your bookshelf next to Altus Press' three-volume set of the Green Lama. After you've read this tome, you'll no doubt agree with that hoary old saying, "They don't write 'em like that anymore!"

FANGS OF DOOM

CHAPTER I

THE MYSTERIOUS DR. ZENG

DOCTOR ZENG TSE-LIN looked as if he had nowhere to go, with all night to get there; yet he was actually in a hurry, and most of San Francisco's Chinatown seemed to know why.

"Doctor Zeng's looking for that man, Chow, again," shop keepers whispered. "Why doesn't he fire the one-legged fool?"

But no matter how many times his servant frittered away afternoon and evening sitting through a second and third showing of a western serial at the New China Theater, Doctor Zeng always forgave Lai Hu Chow. For the old reprobate was the one living link that connected Zeng with the mysteriously murdered parents he hoped some day to avenge.

Zeng, scarcely breaking his long stride, managed to avoid colliding with two slant-eyed girls who darted out of a traffic jam around the corner of the Chinatown telephone exchange. Their sleek hair was marcelled; their gay chatter had not a trace of Chinese inflection. These young ladies were the most modern of modern. They affected a condescending contempt for things Chinese, yet they paused for a long look at the tall young man who was so freakish as to wear a pork pie cap, quilted silk jacket, long gray tunic, and felt-soled shoes.

"Doctor Zeng's awfully handsome, even if he is old-fashioned," said the first.

The other sighed. "I bet he'd look swell in a double-breasted pin stripe."

The two telephone girls would have been amazed could they have known that lovely occidental Ann Carter was saying the same thing to her father, Captain Brian Carter, recently retired from the San Francisco police force. It was because of Ann and her father that Doctor Zeng was hurrying out in search of his peg-legged servant. Guests for dinner, and no food—not even the servant!

1

There were two movie houses in Chinatown, which gave Doctor Zeng's deductive powers a severe test. Chow had seen both the day before. Now, after having spent the early afternoon honing his favorite hatchet to a razor edge, he was gone. And Zeng was seeking him.

AN OLD man who sold candied kumquats and lichi nuts at a corner stand clasped both hands, bowed, and spoke. "I hope you have eaten, Doctor Zeng."

Zeng Tse-Lin had no time for ceremony, but he made a courtly bow, and answered. "May your shadow increase, Honorable Hong. I trust your pious and learned father is well?"

In spite of being a full-blooded white American, Doctor Zeng Tse-Lin—as he was known in Chinatown—was the most ceremonious person in the entire Chinese colony of San Francisco's some thirty thousand inhabitants. At times, however, his patience was sadly tried.

Finally the Honorable Hong said, "If I am not mistaken, your servant is waiting for you at the New Shanghai Theater. He passed by early this afternoon with a basket of groceries, a bottle of *ng ka pay,* and a very fierce expression."

Zeng hurried on, turning down the steep slope toward the theater. He smiled whimsically as he murmured to himself, "There are tigers in the western mountains and there are tigers in the eastern mountains. When Chow is in the Gobi, he steals too many horses. When he is in town, he steals too many hours for the movies."

Zeng just reached the theater in time to hear a hoarse voice roaring in Mongolian. Then he caught the squeal and chatter of the delighted Chinese crowd that was gathering. A basket erupted out of the tangle and a roast duck skated over the cobblestones, then shark fins, and seaweed, and chunks of ginger root.

Two burly cops now ploughed into view. They had blue uniforms and red faces; and their hands were full. Four men would have been comfortably busy giving Lai Hu Chow the bum's rush. The huge Mongol bellowed and suddenly went limp, sagging to the tiles. That threw the cops off balance, physically and mentally. They thought Chow had passed out. "Sure, and how do we carry this big ox?" one grunted. "Clancy, do yez put in a riot call!"

The supposedly helpless Mongol seemed to explode. His wooden leg booted the relaxing Clancy to the curbing. As he bounded upright, the other cop's truncheon cracked down. The blow was wasted on Chow's bullet head; it did not break his even rhythm. He tripped the cop, made an amazing leap to the middle of the street, and sprinted along the slippery cobblestones.

Clancy recovered enough to draw his service .38. "Halt!" he yelled. "Stop or—"

Then he lowered the weapon. The street was packed with cackling spectators, and the Mongol maniac was ducking out of sight beyond a passing truck. "What is the trouble, Officer?" Doctor Zeng asked.

And then the other cop struggled erect, shouting, "Where's the murdering devil?"

The two angry policemen charged up the hill, blowing their whistles.

"What did the big man do?" Zeng asked a chestnut peddler.

"He was throwing knives and hatchets at the screen. We thought this was fun until the police came to arrest him. That was more amusing."

No doubt that Chow had been disappointed when his first hurled weapon failed to make the moving target stop; but Zeng was not sure that this had been merely a test of skill at throwing knives and hatchets. He hurried back to Grant Avenue, toward the big art store whose gilded sign read, ALMOND BLOSSOM HALL OF FRATERNAL ASSOCIATION.

As far as Chinatown knew, Doctor Zeng was a wealthy merchant from Peiping. Few had entered the living quarters on the second floor of the building, and none but Captain Brian Carter and a handful of federal agents had ever seen the laboratory on the top floor.

Doctor Zeng stepped down the alley that separated the ALMOND BLOSSOM HALL from the adjoining WILLOW GARDEN OF MUTUAL PROFIT. Darkness had scarcely hidden him when there was a soft hissing. A cloud of vapor surrounded him. Then came a metallic rustling, and seemingly solid brick swung back on silent hinges.

When the vapors thinned, Doctor Zeng was in one of his secret elevators. If anyone had been spying no eye could have penetrated the opaque fumes or noted which bay of the wall had opened to admit him.

ON THE second floor, the elevator silently stopped. The grilled door folded back so noiselessly that the blond girl who paced up and down the antique palace carpet did not realize the owner of the house had returned.

Ann Carter's lovely face was tense as she twisted a handkerchief.

Zeng stepped silently from behind the embroidered screen that masked the elevator. As he crossed the persimmon red and tawny buff of the rug border, he spoke pleasantly.

"Good evening, Ann. Will you accept my apologies without boring details? I am sorry."

The girl started. "Oh, Lin! How on earth did you—" Then she ran toward him, and caught both his arms. "I'm so sorry, but we can't dine with you, Lin. You'd barely left here when the Police Commissioner phoned. Dad had to leave right away."

Zeng Tse-Lin's bland face became grave. "The Commissioner asked your father to break a dinner engagement?" He edged her toward a bench of teak inlaid with ivory. "Sit down, please. I was hunting that worthless servant, Chow. What has happened?"

"It was hardly ten minutes ago," she said breathlessly. "I couldn't help overhearing because you'd left one of your amplifiers cut in. I got the message when Dad answered the ring in your smoking room. Prince Yuan has been horribly murdered. Some maniac—bit him to death—tore his throat out—with human teeth! The marks are unmistakable."

"Prince Yuan of Mongolia? The one staying at the Saint Francis?"

"Yes, but it happened at Forest Baker's house. It is all so uncanny that the Commissioner wants Dad to handle it, with your help. And I'm afraid of the whole thing, Lin. They were speaking of looting Genghis Khan's grave in central Asia, just before this happened. It's as if some curse, some demon—oh, of course, it's silly, but I hate to think of Dad mixing up in such an outrageous thing! Why can't they let him alone, after thirty years of service? Why can't younger men—"

"No younger man could equal your father, my dear," Zeng Tse-Lin gravely answered, his black eyes resting on her lovely face with an inscrutable expression. "He knows the Chinese colony, and this sounds like a Chinese crime, I am sorry to say. But perhaps I can help him."

"That would be just as bad! I mean—you're a doctor, not a detective!"

Zeng Tse-Lin smiled faintly as he realized that she was concerned about his safety. In spite of her belief that he was Chinese and a person to be regarded as a scholar and not as a man.

He turned to help Ann with her mink coat. The lustrous fur had scarcely settled about her shapely shoulders when Lai Hu Chow *clump-clump-clumped* from the passageway that opened out of the smoking room. He was breathless, his pie-round face battered and his hands bleeding.

"Honorable Master," he said woefully, "two foreign devils beat me with clubs and guns. I lost the stuffed duck and the shark fins and the seaweed and the preserved oranges—"

"As I saw it, you beat and kicked the two foreign devils until they were half dead, and then ran before they could shoot you down," Doctor Zeng interrupted. "What manner of thing is that, throwing knives and hatchets in a movie theater?"

Dr. Zeng Tse Lin

Captain Carter

Nadja Karakho

Lai Hu Chow

Wang Lu

CHOW SHIFTED his weight to his pegleg, grinding it well into the inlaid hardwood of the floor. He grinned amiably now that he realized that Doctor Zeng knew the truth.

"Every time I see the big bearded man shooting at the tall young man who rides the white horse, I do not like it. So this time, I threw knives at the ghost-pictures, each time I hit the dark bearded man's shadow, he will feel ghost knives in that same spot. The foreign devils tried to stop me, so I kicked them both in the stomach. How much will it cost to have a man beaten or jailed in my place? Please take the amount out of my pay, Exalted Master."

Ann, who conducted an English class in Chinatown, understood enough of Chow's dialect to follow. "Does he actually believe those movie stories are true?" she asked.

"Yes," said Dr. Zeng. "And he does not realize that he can't buy a substitute to serve his jail sentences." He turned to Chow: "You have already drawn eleven years' pay in advance to pay fines for brawling, for gambling debts, and for movie tickets. So for the next thirty days, you will not leave the house."

"But the shopping, pious and learned Doctor?"

"I will do that with my own hands."

Chow knelt and knocked his forehead on the floor. "That will disgrace me!" he groaned. "I will lose face. I will be a man of no account."

Zeng considered for a moment. "Well, I'll let one of the clerks do the shopping. But you stay away from movies till further orders, or I'll not only do my own shopping, but I'll cook the stuff myself."

The human mountain was still kneeling in remorse when Ann and Zeng stepped to the screened doorway which led to the exit.

"You have the most unusual methods of discipline, Lin," the girl said.

Doctor Zeng smiled. "Two policemen with clubs hardly made an impression on him, you know. Possibly my way has its good points. But tell me more about Prince Yuan."

"There's nothing more I can add, except that a Russian woman's mixed up in it—Nadja Karakhov—and that every person in the house has a perfect alibi."

"And, doubtless, perfect teeth!"

The elevator made an air-cushioned stop at the ground floor, and Doctor Zeng helped Ann into the long, vermilion sedan waiting there in the underground garage. As the hundred and sixty horsepower engine rumbled, then subsided to a sleepy whisper, he pressed the horn button.

At the double-toned blast, the garage door opened, and Dr. Zeng drove the rakish attractive car up the grade and into the swirling mists.

CHAPTER II

THE UIGHUR SCROLL

F **IFTEEN MINUTES** later Doctor Zeng was in Forest Baker's somber library where the body of Prince Yuan was sprawled in a leather upholstered chair. The dead man was as bulky as Chow, though years younger than Zeng's Mongol servant. His heavy throat was a gory cavern from whence blood had drenched his white shirt and the satin lapels of the dinner coat he had exchanged for the jacket and felt boots of his native country.

His broad, flat face was brought into stark relief by the glow of the hearth fire. His big mouth sagged and his little eyes stared as if he still wondered what had come to tear out his throat. Captain Carter stepped from the group of plainclothes men, photographers and assistant coroners, who were eying Doctor Zeng curiously.

"Look at his hands," he said. "Look at that brandy snifter on the end table. If he'd made any move at all to defend himself, something would have been disturbed."

Captain Carter's close-cropped moustache bristled and his ruddy face tightened into challenging angles as he gestured, his squarish hands turned palms up. He added, "This is a devil of a fix. It's impossible, and still it's up to us to explain it!"

The baffled cops were not discussing business. One muttered to his neighbor, "Where do they get all these big Chinks? If it weren't for his eyes and that dead pan, I wouldn't believe Doctor Zeng was one at all!"

Zeng's ears were far sharper than anyone realized. He turned blandly. "Lectures on anthropology are out of place here, gentlemen, but I might explain. Many of my countrymen are taller then I am, many of them have noses as prominent as yours or mine. China, like these United States, has been a melting pot. In the heart of Asia there are Mongolian men with—"

He pointed to the Captain of Inspectors. "Permit the personal touch, sir. Some have hair as red and eyes as gray as yours."

The Inspector looked confused. "Then what the blazes *is* a Chinaman?" he growled.

"Inspector, what the blazes *is* an American? What is the standard size, color, facial expression, or weight?"

Zeng's answers which implied that he was Chinese were deliberate. Basing them on fact and wide knowledge long ago he had decided that Linwood Lawton, the son of Doctor and Mrs. Hartford Lawton, would become a Chinese scholar.

A bit of simple plastic surgery had given his eyes just enough slant to give his face a Mongolian expression. His cheekbones, a shade on the prominent side, helped the imposture, and the cunning use of a bleach proof dye he had invented while studying chemistry enabled him to put on the finishing touch.

The big query was, would he be equally convincing in China when he went far into the interior to hunt down the criminals who had murdered his father and mother?

All this flashed again through his mind as he stood there calmly explaining to the police that he was Chinese in spite of his size. Then he turned again to the corpse and eyed the savage laceration of the carotid artery. Blood had spurted from it, and was now drying black on the cream-colored hearth tiles and on Yuan's outthrust shoes.

DOCTOR ZENG pointed at the inside pocket of the dinner jacket, indicating the agate knob which tipped the end of a hardwood rod about which was rolled a length of silk damask.

"As we agree that human teeth did mangle Prince Yuan," he said, "let us consider this ancient manuscript in his pocket. Inspector, have you made your fingerprint routine? May I touch it?"

"Help yourself, Doctor. Say, what kind are you, an M.D. or a Ph.D.?"

"Both. Also a Doctor of Science," was the amazing answer as Zeng plucked the roll of silk damask from the dead man's pocket and unwound it. As he read, one eyebrow slowly rose in an ironic arch. "This Uighur manuscript has something to do with treasure, I understand?"

"Yes, and a crazy yarn, too!" Captain Carter supplied. "Genghis Khan's armor, his sword, the horse-tail standard he carried in battle—sacred relics, you might say, plus a few wagonloads of treasure his officers buried with him. But it seems no one could read the manuscript."

Ann came a little nearer. "I am sure Doctor Zeng can read it!"

"I knew many of the Uighur people of Turfan," Zeng said, evasively. Then, to Ann's father, "Captain Carter, I would like to speak to Forest Baker, and to Nadja Karakhov. They told you about the treasure, did they not?"

"They did. They're upstairs in Baker's study."

Carter led the way to the second floor. The coroner's assistants were impatient, but until further orders they had to wait for the corpse. Doctor Zeng was making the most of his Chinese deliberation. Instead of following Captain Carter at once, he joined Ann, and paused for a moment to inspect the rows of leather-bound books, the tall bronze floor lamps, the jade bowls, and the life-sized porcelain Fu dogs. Half-hidden by gilt-encrusted draperies was an old camphor chest, ornately carved; but unlike most of its kind, it had no brass lock and lock plate, nor any metal binding.

"Professor Baker seems to appreciate Chinese art," Zeng murmured.

Ann, impatient as the others, took his arm and demanded, "What are you holding out, Lin? In spite of that horrible sight, you've been smiling to yourself."

"I am sure no one noticed unseemly mirth."

"I did! What does that manuscript say? That started it."

Zeng shook his head. "Better to hear first what they say about the manuscript. Kindly wait below."

He gently disengaged his arm. Leaving her in the vestibule, he went up the stairs, stately in his sleek silken tunic. Captain Carter, pacing and chewing his cigar, was waiting at the door of Baker's study.

"They're a pair of polished liars, Zeng," he whispered. "Better interview them separately. Which will you meet first?"

"By choice, the lovely Slavic lady. But you are unjust, assuming them to be prevaricators. Let me see them together."

Carter barely suppressed a snort; he was annoyed at this upset of a basic principle, that of separating witnesses so that neither could influence the other. But Carter tapped, and a man with a scholarly voice invited them in.

Zeng paused at the threshold, clasped his two hands, and bowed ceremoniously as Captain Carter presented him to Professor Baker and Nadja Karakhov.

"How is your health?" he began. "I trust that your business prospers? And your parents, they are well, I hope?"

Captain Carter's impatience faded when he saw how that formal, old time Chinese litany was confusing the two witnesses, for they had not been prepared for such an approach. But of the two, Nadja Karakhov was the first to meet Zeng on his own ground.

"I hope that your parents are in good health," she countered in that soft, Slavic purr which made her English just a little hard to follow.

NADJA'S BLACK hair was drawn severely back and gathered in a gleaming knot at the nape of her neck. Her gray green eyes had a faint slant, and like Zeng's, her cheek bones were prominent. She was a pale-skinned, lovely woman, with a face angular enough for strength, yet with features sufficiently softened to be wholly feminine. She wore a black gown, snug fitting enough to accentuate her substantial Slavic frame, and for all the warmth of the room, she had a short silver fox wrap about her. One hand held it snug, while the other gestured.

"We were sitting here, Professor Baker and I, when it happened," Nadja answered, once the ceremonial touch was over. She indicated Baker, whose thin face was as expressionless as a totem pole, and not a great deal more amiable. "Prince Yuan had become drunk and a little stupid, so we left him in the library."

"To swill more brandy!" Baker grimaced. "The man fairly drained the decanter after dinner. In spite of cocktails and wine."

"That was old and fragrant brandy," Zeng said. "Very costly."

Baker sat up, pulled his dinner jacket into shape. "It's not that! We'd met to discuss business, and he became swinishly drunk!"

Zeng sighed. "Mongols love hard drink. A racial failing, I might say. It is sad, very sad, that you humored him. But where did Prince Yuan fit into this? I was wondering about that Uighur scroll in his pocket."

"That's a long story. One of Yuan's ancestors was in the burial party of Genghis Khan. On their return, they were to have been ambushed and massacred by the dead Khan's highest officers, so that the site of the grave would remain hidden forever. But Prince Yuan's ancestor had fortunate suspicions, so he slipped from the cavalcade, and thus was the only survivor. He wrote an account of all this, and of his escape. And, a few months ago, Prince Yuan came from Mongolia with the long hidden document."

"Why did he bring it to you?" inquired Zeng keenly.

"Because of my experience in Central Asiatic archeological expeditions," Baker answered. "And because he can't read Uighur. Also, I was going to finance the expedition."

"You never saw the manuscript until tonight?"

"No. Yuan trusted no one. He could not translate it himself. Like many of his kind, he can barely read his own dialect, much less Uighur. Only tradition and nothing else gave him an idea of its actual significance."

Zeng turned to Nadja. "And you, Miss Karakhov? Are you a partner?"

SHE SHOOK her sleek head and sighed.

"No. I knew Prince Yuan in Mongolia. He helped my father years ago when he fled from the Bolsheviki. So when I heard he was in San Francisco, I went to pay my respects, and he invited me to come with him tonight."

This cleared up a few details that Ann had not got when her father had been phoned at Doctor Zeng's quarters. Everything seemed logical, and the two survivors of the trio were each other's alibi. The servant who had served the dinner had left perhaps an hour before the murder.

"We were smoking and drinking a few B-and-Bs," Nadja said, pointing to the cigarette butts in the tray—her own, paper-tipped and rouge-smudged; Baker's, cork-tipped, half-smoked, and ground out.

"Prince Yuan became surly, and refused to surrender the manuscript for discussion, and you had to leave him there?" Zeng summed up.

"Yes. Later, when I went down to persuade him into a happier mood—" Baker gestured. "I found him, as you saw. It was some moments before I could compose myself enough to summon the police."

Zeng nodded sympathetically. "Even shocked as you were, you knew that human teeth had bitten him to death?"

"Eh?" Baker started. "Damn it, could any wild animal have entered the house? Every door was closed."

"I suggested that human teeth had bitten Prince Yuan," Nadja interposed. "We Slavs are superstitious, perhaps, but there was a strong magic about Genghis Khan, and his grave would be protected by a curse. I didn't like this venture, though it was no affair of mine."

Doctor Zeng rose, and included Captain Carter in his announcement.

"I do not see how any Asiatic wizard's spell should strike, for there is nothing in that scroll which concerns Genghis Khan. It is a collection of drinking songs, written by a Uighur poet and dedicated to an Emperor who lived a thousand years before Genghis Khan was born! Now let us have the truth."

There was a moment of silence, then a choking sound. Baker bounded to the door.

"You're crazy!" he shouted, and ran, cursing furiously, toward the stairway.

CHAPTER III

THE WHITE LOTUS

DOCTOR ZENG followed Captain Carter as he raced down the stairs.

Baker was shouting in a cracked voice.

"It's that damned Rayne! He's behind all this!"

Once in the library, Baker seized the manuscript. "The same agate knobs, carved in a lion head." He adjusted his glasses. "Good Lord! You're quite right. Someone did palm this substitute. Yuan would never have known the difference."

"Someone? You mentioned a Mr. Rayne."

Baker flung the scroll into the hearth corner. "A tricky scoundrel! A scholar, but a disgrace to his profession. He was guilty of some hoax in exploration, and resigned from the university faculty some years ago. But he's always had Genghis Khan's tomb on the brain."

"And now you think he committed this murder," Doctor Zeng asked, "and substituted a Uighur manuscript in an attempt to conceal that robbery was the motive?"

Baker shrugged. "I don't know what to say, except that many think the poor chap is a little mad."

"I think we should get Miss Karakhov's ideas," Carter suggested.

"Please do," Zeng answered. "Now, Mr. Baker, where does Mr. Rayne live?"

"I'm sure I wouldn't know. We've never been any too cordial, mainly because our field work at one time conflicted. Since his resignation, he's called on me twice regarding Genghis Khan's grave, and suggested that we bury our differences and pool our resources."

The coroner's assistants carried Prince Yuan's body to the waiting ambulance. The Uighur scroll was included among the exhibits, and Doctor Zeng was requested to appear at the inquest to testify, officially, as to the nature of the document. This routine was interrupted by the hasty return of Captain Carter.

"Harris," he said to the inspector, "I can't find that Karakhov woman! Did she by any chance come down the backstairs?"

Nadja Karakhov had left the house; that soon became clear. Baker's outburst had given her the opportunity to get away unnoticed.

"But why?" Carter demanded. "She wasn't under suspicion. Inspector, have men watch her apartment."

"Please do not disturb her," Zeng requested. "Let me handle this. Her address is on your records, and she would not be silly enough to try to leave town."

"Then what in hell was the idea?" the inspector growled.

"That," Doctor Zeng answered, "remains to be seen."

He bowed to each member of the group, and then went to where Ann had withdrawn to an alcove in the far angle of the somber room. "I am sorry that I shall not be able to drive you home."

"Lin," she said anxiously, "you mustn't try to handle this yourself. That Mongol giant was caught off guard by some horrible maniac, someone he knew, but whose madness he did not have any reason to suspect."

"You mean Baker, or Miss Karakhov?"

"Oh, I don't know! But do be careful."

Doctor Zeng's vermilion sedan swooped out of Saint Francis Wood, and up over Twin Peaks. For a moment, San Francisco was spread out beneath him, long avenues of neon that winked through low-lying mists. The Bay Bridge reached across the water, its vast spans outlined in sodium lights.

He tooled the powerful car over the hump, and down the roller-coaster grades which led to the long curve of the Embarcadero. Presently, he was in a confusion of blind streets.

HE PARKED and snapped off his lights. There was a moment's pause, and when he emerged he was no longer in his conspicuous gray robes. Instead, he wore a black tunic which he had taken from the car's glove compartment. Darting up the flight of steps that made the narrow street passable for pedestrians, he moved with weasel swiftness to the heart of the Telegraph Hill district.

Old frame houses clung to the steep hillsides. Music came from a café, and there was shrill laughter from one of the many studios of San Francisco's Latin Quarter where squalor and gaiety and luxury were strangely jumbled. Finding an address in this section at night would have taken the average person hours, and for all Zeng's knowledge of every part of the city, he lost valuable moments.

Finally he was at a narrow door which seemed to open into the basement level of a cluster of rickety buildings. He fingered the latch, and stepped into a narrow passageway. After thirty feet of darkness he emerged in a small courtyard. In the gloom he could just distinguish stairways which led to balconies overhanging the rubbish-littered back area. Above him, unless he had entirely miscalculated, was Nadja's back door.

In the darkness, he oriented himself. Then he stealthily crept up the swaying stairs which were guarded by a slender railing of gaspipe.

As he ascended, he noted the odors of stale cookery, of sour wine and spaghetti. Then he caught the faint smell of joss sticks; someone who had not long since left a Chinese temple was lurking in this crazy tangle of balconies.

At the end of the flimsily railed back porch Zeng heard a hinge creak, a vague stirring, and then a woman's startled outcry.

"What do you want?" she demanded in Russian.

There was no answer, and no repetition of the question—only a choking sound, the scrape of a chair, a muffled gasp. A man exclaimed in Chinese, "Watch out!"

Glass shattered. A man cursed. There was a moan, and a thump that shook the rickety floor.

All this happened during the moment it took Doctor Zeng to bound to the end of the porch and a screen door there outlined by a light within. His felt-soled shoes made no sound, and he was across the threshold before the four men could turn from their captive.

A silken scarf cut off her protests. One man held her
about the ankles, another held her wrists.

They were dressed in dark suits, their faces masked. Two of them still struggled with Nadja, who for all that solid thump on the floor, had not quit fighting. A silken scarf had cut off her protests, and its folds were now looped about her throat, choking her. One had her about the ankles, and another held her wrists.

"Hurry, tie her!" the leader commanded.

The room was well furnished, which was not surprising in that unpredictable quarter. Much of the light came from a heap of letters which blazed on the hearth.

The leader turned as Zeng bounded into the room and whipped out a straight-bladed knife. The gesture and the flight of steel were little slower than the drawing and firing of a pistol, but Zeng had not barged blindly into an encounter. He had landed poised on both feet, quick eye and quick muscle functioning at once. He twisted, and the knife barely grazed his black tunic. Scarcely checking his advance, he snatched a decanter from an end table, and hurled it.

THE HEAVY missile spattered to fragments against the Chinaman's jaw, knocking him flat. Too certain of impaling the new arrival, the knife thrower had been caught prettily. But the others, having Nadja throttled into semi-consciousness, were now on their feet, and drawing blades.

Zeng sidestepped, caught the wrist of the man nearest him, and twisted. The fellow dropped his knife, yelling with pain from the savage wrench that crippled his wrist. Then Zeng made another dizzying shift, using his disabled opponent as a shield against the other two.

They hesitated, then they separated to attack him from both sides at once. That was what Zeng's maneuver had intended to accomplish. Once again, he was a move ahead. He catapulted his captive crosswise, knocking the two off balance. Working together, they could easily have overpowered Doctor Zeng, but they failed because he had anticipated their reactions to each feint he made.

The knife hurler staggered up, brushing the blood and glass from his forehead, and closed in. Zeng faced the charge, and learned that the leader was more dangerous empty-handed than when armed. The fellow had a deadly collection of wrestling tricks, and for all Zeng's advantage in height and weight, he had his hands full.

For a moment they grappled, vainly shifting from one hold to the next, each testing the other's endurance to the limit, each trying to disable the other. Neither could gain, and the three who had been knocked into a corner during Zeng's first victorious rush were gradually recovering from the shock of crashing against furniture and walls.

Nadja was recovering enough to claw the silk scarf from her throat and mouth. Zeng heard her half-muffled outcry. Breathless himself, he panted, "Grab that knife!"

He spoke in Russian, hoping that Nadja would gain an instant for self-defense. He needed only a split-second's advantage to settle his wiry enemy as the man was weakening from savage punishment.

Then Zeng and his adversary both lost. They lurched over the threshold and against the fragile railing of the balcony. The piping tore from its anchorage. Still grappling, the two crashed to the sloping roof of a low shed.

Above, Nadja screamed. A pistol fired, furniture scraped and thumped, and a door slammed. Zeng and his opponent rolled down to the paving. The shock stunned Zeng, but it was worse for the tough little wrestler. He shuddered, twitched, and lay still, his head lolling at a grotesque angle. His neck was broken; and all Zeng's efforts to take a prisoner for questioning had been wasted.

There was not much chance that anyone would call the police. In this quarter people minded their own business. Recovering from the shock, Zeng went up the stairs as fast as he could. Nadja came running from the front. She had a six-millimeter automatic, which she lowered as she recognized him.

"Where are they?" Zeng demanded

"I did better than pick up the knife," she said, "and they ran. Please sit down, Doctor Zeng."

The letters in the hearth had not only been consumed, but the charred paper had been stirred up beyond reconstruction. Then he noted one envelope, crumpled and browned, which must have been blown from the blaze by a draught. Zeng picked it up.

"Pardon me," he asked, "but were all those letters from Hubert Rayne?"

"So you did come to spy on me?"

"Hubert Rayne," Zeng blandly went on, "is Forest Baker's rival. He seems to have been carrying on a confidential correspondence with you, yet you continue to enjoy Mr. Baker's confidence. In view of tonight's peculiar murder, explanations are in order, Miss Karakhov."

"Indeed!" Mockery and defiance were mingled. "Please continue."

Zeng pointed gravely to an overturned chair. "See that square of red silk, those brass coins—and that one blossom of white lotus?"

"My visitors probably dropped those things while you were knocking their heads together."

"That is my impression," agreed Dr. Zeng dryly. "Those visitors were members of the White Lotus, the *Society of Heaven and Earth*. Their presence tonight tells me that you do not have too long to live."

"What do you mean?" The Russian woman was badly startled.

"I will explain this to you, if you are kind enough to make some things clear to me, such as this friendliness with one Hubert Rayne—and your haste to destroy evidence of it."

CHAPTER IV

THE OPIUM SMOKER

IN GRAPPLING with Nadja's assailants, Doctor Zeng had unexpectedly won an advantage more useful than anything he could have gained from the mere questioning of a prisoner. He settled down to making the most of it.

"This square of silk is a certificate of membership in the White Lotus Society," he said. "You read Chinese?"

She nodded, and he went on, indicating characters with his fingertips.

"Overthrow Tsing and restore Ming. And the Four Excellent Ones, Han Phang, Han Fook, Chang Tien, and Chang Kwok, Guardians of the Gates."

"I don't know why they came after me." Nadja was deeply troubled.

"To me it is quite clear," Doctor Zeng said. "The White Lotus ordered the death of Prince Yuan. Next they sought you. Undoubtedly there will be others."

She leaned forward to lay a trembling hand on his sleeve. "You know? Is that why you came to my apartment?"

"You have not told me about yourself and Hubert Rayne, the man Forest Baker accused of stealing the Uighur manuscript," Dr. Zeng countered.

"Had someone really palmed off a substitute on Prince Yuan? Or were you just bluffing?" the woman pursued. "You Chinese are wily."

"Baker read it after I calmed him down," Zeng answered. "How did you leave, and why?"

"Baker's hysterical outburst distracted the police," Nadja answered. "It was easy for me to leave. I followed a sudden impulse."

Zeng shrugged meaningly. "An impulse, but a rational one. When Baker accused Hubert Rayne, you left because you wanted to destroy every trace of correspondence between you and Baker's rival."

She eyed him for a moment, then slowly nodded. "Yes," she admitted.

Zeng rose, folded his arms, and sighed. "And now the Society of the White Lotus seems to suspect you of having the missing manuscript. Do you? Is that why you left so hurriedly?"

Nadja's face was a pale mask. "I was shaken by that horrible killing. I couldn't stay in that house any longer."

"I can advise the police to search your rooms," Zeng said. "The scroll is evidence pertaining to the murder of Prince Yuan."

"I can't stop you, and I'm grateful to you for having saved me from those four ruffians." She gestured. "You want to use the phone?"

"There is no such hurry, Miss Karakhov. Please sit down and tell me about you and Hubert Rayne." He handed her the half-burned envelope. "And you may have this surviving bit of evidence."

"You're very puzzling," she reflected, taking the scrap. "You could hand this to Forest Baker and convince him that I have been tricking him, secretly working with his rival."

"True, but it does not serve my purpose. Now tell me about Hubert Rayne."

She seated herself and spoke frankly. "I met him in Turfan a few years ago. I was half-starved, the daughter of another Russian refugee. He was and had for years been looking for the sacred relics of Genghis Khan. He was kind to my father and me. In return we gave him bits of gossip we had picked up in our wanderings among the Mongol and Manchu tribes. Later, I met Prince Yuan. And just recently, in San Francisco, I learned that he had come to the United States. Hubert

Rayne told me, asking me to find out what Baker and the prince were planning."

"So you really were spying on them, to help Rayne?"

"Do you still want the police to search my place?"

HE DID not answer. Instead, he stepped to the telephone, and dialed headquarters. When Captain Carter was on the wire, Zeng said:

"Miss Karakhov was attacked in her apartment by four Chinese thugs. May I suggest that plainclothes men be detailed to guard her?... Of course, as a material witness, and, incidentally, to prevent another murder.... No, I can not explain the details over the telephone, but please believe me, this is not a false alarm."

He then said to Nadja, "With that small but efficient pistol, I think you'll be safe enough until they arrive. I shall leave by the back door. Good night, Miss Karakhov."

Once in the court, he played a fountain-pen flashlight about the corner in which he and his opponent had landed. The man with the broken neck was not there.

Zeng smiled, and nodded as if satisfied.

"His comrades came to look, and they found him."

Back at his car, Zeng pressed a button at the left of the starter, and there was a faint humming under the cowl. He had cut in an ultra-short-wave radio set.

"Lai Hu Chow! Lai Hu Chow!" he said to the concealed microphone.

Two receivers would respond to that wave-length. One was concealed in the apartment above the Almond Blossom Hall; the other was in Chow's wooden leg. In a moment the big Mongol was answering: "Yes, Honorable Master?"

"Drive to Berkeley, and watch the house of Hubert Rayne," Zeng ordered, giving the address. He added, "Just watch. Do not take any action unless it is necessary to prevent a killing. If Rayne is in, and should leave, follow him."

Zeng cut the switch and then drove back to Forest Baker's house in Saint Francis Wood. Now that the police had finished their routine it was time for an unofficial look.

Thus far, Zeng had no reason for having Rayne watched, except on the chance that Nadja might try to get in touch with her friend. He reasoned that she would consider herself much more secure from further attack if she left the place which the White Lotus had searched; and Rayne's place would be a logical refuge. Also, she would want to tell Rayne what had happened.

Zeng parked his car and covered the last block on foot. His earlier concentration on the possibility that Nadja had switched scrolls on Prince Yuan was not blinding him to the chance that Baker might have executed such a sleight-of-hand performance himself. Zeng wanted to see what he was doing, now that the police had left the house.

The building stood well back from the street, surrounded and half-hidden by oaks. During the investigation Zeng had noted the layout. He had now his knowledge to serve him, as did the ivy whose luxuriant growth half-hid the bricks of the English manor. But before he began his ascent to the second floor, he paused to consider the peculiar glow that came from the window of the study.

THE LIGHT, dimmed, strengthened again; then there was a moment of absolute darkness.

"Someone is searching the place, using a flashlight," reflected Zeng.

He kicked off his shoes, and tested the ivy whose hundreds of tentacles had won a hold in the crevices of the masonry. Slowly, carefully, he drew himself up, taking every advantage of joints in the masonry, getting toeholds that relieved the ivy of part of his weight. Like a vast black bat, he clung for moments at a time, resting from the strain of combining strength with delicacy of touch. His ascent was rapid, nevertheless, and presently he grasped a sill and found solid support.

The window was unlocked. Zeng had attended to that earlier. From the first, he had decided upon this unofficial search, for the death of Prince Yuan had been too uncanny to be entirely convincing.

The window rose silently. Zeng slipped through and passed into the dark hall. When he reached the door of the study he saw the purpose of the dim light and the cause of its wavering.

A man in a dark suit squatted in the far corner. He had moved a screen to one side, exposing a wall safe. Now he was spinning the dial, and trying the lever that opened the door. He shifted his light, referred to a scrap of paper and renewed his twirling of the dial, cursing under his breath as he began again.

Doctor Zeng waited patiently.

Bit by bit, he got a complete picture of the intruder from each shift of the light that cast a reflection from the burnished metal of the safe. The man was tall, thin and wiry, with a lean, sallow face. He wore woolen socks over his shoes, and on his hands he had white cloth gloves. But most interesting of all was the perceptible reek of opium. He had recently been hitting the pipe.

The man sighed and relaxed. The tumblers slid softly, and the door opened. With trembling hands, he searched the pigeonholes. He pocketed various folded papers, but something apparently was missing.

"Damn it!" he muttered, "Where—"

"Maybe I can help you," Zeng suggested softly.

The man whirled, dropping his light. Zeng closed in, and made a chopping blow with the edge of his hand. The man pitched forward, stunned by the impact against the base of his skull.

Doctor Zeng caught the unconscious intruder, lowered him gently to the carpeted floor. Then he squatted beside him and methodically took the plunder from his pockets.

The papers were closely penned notes on Mongolia, some apparently quotations from ancient records, Mongol and Uighur and Turki, and all of them referring to the burial place of Genghis Khan. But the most interesting thing was the man's identity, which Doctor Zeng learned from the contents of the sallow man's wallet. He was Hubert Rayne, Nadja Karakhov's friend and her accomplice.

The house was still silent, for there had not been enough scuffle to awaken Forest Baker. Zeng closed the door of the study, picked up the memorandum which had guided Rayne in opening the safe, and squatted beside his half-conscious captive.

CHAPTER V

THE SECOND VICTIM

"OPIUM ADDICT ... scholar... apprentice safe cracker," Doctor Zeng said to himself, as he studied the memorandum Hubert Rayne had been using. "Ah! A woman's handwriting."

He saw why Rayne had been fumbling. There were several sets of figures, each varying a little: *"Five right to fifty; four left to thirty-eight; three right to twenty-seven; two left to zero."* Some of the variations were in the number of turns, others were in the digits at which the dial spin was to stop. This suggested that the memorandum had been made by a person who had watched Baker opening his safe and had put down the best possible guesses, as decided from some distance behind him.

Rayne stirred, muttered, opened his eyes. Zeng saw from the contracted pupils that this was indeed an opium addict. When Rayne tried to strike out with his fist, Zeng spoke a gentle warning.

"Be quiet, please. You will awaken Baker, and that would embarrass us both." He smiled reassuringly, and gave the man a hand up. "Like yourself, I am an amateur house breaker."

This approach bewildered the still groggy Rayne. "What is this about?" he muttered. "Who are you?"

"Doctor Zeng Tse-Lin, a person of insatiable curiosity. You, if I am not mistaken, are Hubert Rayne, Fellow of the Royal Geographic Society, and one time authority on Central Asiatic history and archeology."

"One time!" Rayne echoed, voice low and bitter. He cast an apprehensive glance toward the hall. "This is no place to talk."

Zeng smiled. "Then you would leave, and I would wait for the police."

"Eh? Wait for them?" Rayne's face twitched. "What do you mean?"

"If you wish to know, permit me to call them." Zeng gestured toward the extension on the study desk. "They will explain, readily."

Rayne recoiled. "You're a Chinese detective," he accused.

"Rest at ease. Baker's bedroom is some distance from this study, so we are quite safe. Answer a few questions, and I shall not detain you."

Rayne pointed at the safe. "Who are you, what does all this mean? If you're with the police, you can't let me go. See here, are you after the same thing I am?"

"The Uighur scroll that reveals the burial place of Genghis Khan?"

Rayne's face changed. His lips drew back in a snarl that exposed his strong, white teeth. Then his mouth clamped shut. Zeng intently eyed him, and made gestures, a three-fold move with both hands.

He extended his right, with forearm bent, thumb and two fingers straight, and the last two curled back against his palm; his left hand, fingers similarly placed, he put against his heart. Rayne's mouth sagged. He sat there, incredulous and puzzled.

Then Zeng's hands, still in the same position, made a change; forefinger and thumb shaped a circle, and the other three pointed out straight. Rayne, still too confused to speak, half rose from his chair. Zeng's fingers again shifted, middle three bent back against his palm, with two outstretched to shape horns, or the points of a crescent moon.

"You should not be amazed at my making the Threefold Sign of Heaven and Earth. I need not ask if you know the answer. Your recognition of this mystic gesture of the White Lotus Society tells me that you did not waste your time in Asia."

Rayne mopped his forehead. "Doctor Zeng, I've never betrayed any secrets. What do you want?"

"I want information. Tell me about Nadja Karakhov, Forest Baker, and why a man of your caliber loots a safe. I promise not to hinder you when you leave. It is well that you do not have the Uighur scroll, and it will be better if you make it very clear to *everyone*—" he paused at that emphasized word— "that you do not have it. Now relax and speak."

RAYNE BELIEVED, and was reassured. His face twisted a little and he blinked. The succession of shocks had come close to cracking his poise.

"Baker gradually wheedled me into letting him study my notes," he began. "The papers I just took from his safe." He reached to his pocket. "Those papers you have are mine."

"The handwriting told me that. I am sorry, but I must keep them."

Rayne went on in an apprehensive whisper. "Once he had my notes locked up, he would not finance my expedition. There were plausible delays, month after month. But as long as he himself did not fit out an expedition, I was not alarmed. Finally Nadja arrived from China and warned me.

"Then Prince Yuan came from Mongolia and met Baker. I began to realize that I had been played for a fool! Whatever Prince Yuan's Uighur script may contain, my years of study are still valuable, for if the script gave the full secret, so that any scholar could readily use it, why has it not been used during all these centuries?"

Zeng considered during Rayne's pause. "There are many answers to that. But this much is clear. Nadja Karakhov helped you in your attempt to keep Baker from excluding you from the agreement he was making with Prince Yuan."

"Leave her out of this!"

"Very well, but I still believe that she got you the combination to this safe. Prince Yuan was murdered here some hours ago. Do you understand now why I am here?"

"Yuan murdered?" Rayne snapped to his feet. "My God!"

This ended Zeng's control of the opium addict, and he was unprepared for the crazy outburst. Rayne yelled wildly, swept up an ash tray, the tray filled with Nadja's paper tipped cigarette butts, and flung it as he whirled. Though the ashes blinded Zeng, and a rug skidded under his feet, he caught Rayne by the ankle. Rayne toppled. The leather upholstered couch broke his fall, and his frenzied kick smacked Zeng's jaw.

The floor sank beneath Zeng's feet and he
dropped headlong into a glare below.

A metal wastepaper basket clattered against the desk. Rayne lunged headlong through the window. Glass and sash scattered, the pieces tinkling to the ground. He landed with blind luck in a clump of bamboo. Recovering with scarcely a break in his stride, he raced around the corner of the house.

Zeng smiled ruefully. "Four men caused me very little trouble," he said, dusting his hands, "and now one scholar makes a fool of me."

Rayne, if his panic flight took him home, would fall under Chow's catlike vigilance. "Unless," Zeng said to himself wryly, "there is a western movie in the neighborhood!"

The house should by now be in an uproar. But there was no sound to break the unnatural silence.

Zeng snapped on a hall light, and called, "Baker!" He went to the head of the stairs, and repeated the hail. He was still considering the possibility that Baker, poise cracking at last, had taken too many drinks of brandy, and was sleeping off his stupor. After his rigid composure during the police investigation, there might be a reaction. A nervous man would want liquor, and plenty of it.

So Zeng knocked at the bedroom door. There was no answer.

HE TRIED the door. It opened. He snapped on a light. Then he saw why Baker did not answer. He was sprawled in an upholstered chair, clad in a lounge robe that was soggy with the blood which had come from his torn throat.

Blood splashed the counterpane. It drenched the book which Baker had been reading. His posture and the stains indicated that there had not even been any dying struggle. Whether drugged or slugged, Forest Baker, in all probability, had never realized that a monster was about to tear his throat.

There was a fine trail of drops on the cream-colored Chinese carpet. Zeng regarded these, noting their continuation on the hardwood floor.

One had been spread out, as by a shoe sole, the slayer apparently having stepped into the gore dripping from himself.

Zeng followed the trail to the bathroom adjoining the master's suite. There he found a sodden towel on the floor. There were stains in the bathtub.

But there were no footprints on the tiles, and the gleam of the chromium taps convinced him that fingerprints would be lacking.

There was no longer any doubt that a monster in human form had bitten Baker to death.

Zeng wondered where Hubert Rayne had been when the fangs of doom killed Prince Yuan.

As he went back to the study, he said to himself, "Both Rayne and Nadja Karakhov have exceptionally good and strong teeth."

He sat down and dialed Captain Carter's residence.

"Consider this anonymous for the time being," he told the police official. "It is very late, and I am not a relay of men, as you police are. Forest Baker died precisely as Prince Yuan did. I depend on you to release this in a way to keep me from being needlessly detained tonight, for I have much to do."

He hung up, not mentioning Rayne.

CHAPTER VI

ULTIMATUM

DOCTOR ZENG, in spite of pleading fatigue, was far from the end of his endurance, but he wished to meditate on what had happened. He sat in his reception room, his tall frame overshadowed by the carved dragons of the big teak chair. Concealed vapor tubes cast an eerie light unlike the glow of any hour of the day.

"The present is the summation of the past, and an introduction to the future," he reasoned. "The more we consider time, and deal in alibis, the more we are deceived by preconceived opinions as to the time-linkage of events."

So he sat there, considering motives; for motivations do not vary with the hour.

"The unknown, this drinker of blood, killed Yuan and yet left no trace in a house that was searched. Baker, amazed or feigning amazement, was frantic when I told him that Prince Yuan's scroll did not deal with Genghis Khan's grave.

"Nadja left, and the White Lotus overtook her. Fear of further investigation seems to have made her destroy letters from Rayne. No one knows where Rayne was before I caught him rifling Baker's safe."

He considered each statement. He had to find the motive. For, in his own mind, a madman is sane.

"Person crazed by brooding about real or fancied wrong kills Prince Yuan and Forest Baker. Or, Nadja, Rayne's ally, commits this slaying.

Or, the White Lotus is moving against all those who seek the grave of Genghis Khan."

Then he pondered on the ancient terror of Genghis Khan's name; on the uncanny power which had welded the Mongols into a people who had conquered more of the earth's surface than any other had, before or since. Mongols had gone to seed, yet they were still the same hardy nomads, the same blood. The lack of the power kept them from setting all Asia aflame once more.

"The source of power may be buried in the grave of Genghis Khan. Find that symbol, that magnetic talisman, and Mongolia will produce another conqueror."

But thus far, he did not see clearly whether these murders were to prevent the rise of a new Genghis Khan, or whether they were a madman's vengeance.

Zeng let his mind wander. He trusted the subconscious, which has more wisdom than any man's studied effort. He relaxed, making way for that mysterious inflowing of wisdom, opening the road that Occidental education would have blocked had he not in his childhood spent so many years in Central Asia.

Half-reclining in that spacious chair of twining dragons and red silk damask, Zeng slept for a while. Then, refreshed as though he had stretched out on his bed, he stepped into a sound-proofed compartment which a dummy screen concealed. This was his short-wave radio room. Soon the tubes glowed and the transformers hummed.

"Lai Hu Chow! Lai Hu Chow!" he said.

There was no vocal answer, only a curious *click–clack–clock*. Chow's bawling Mongol voice could not be subdued, and this was his way of saying, "I am listening for orders, but I cannot speak."

Zeng said, "Come home and report."

Once more the clacking sound, then silence. Chow had cut the battery power of the tiny set in his wooden leg.

HALF AN hour later, Chow came up from the garage.

"A tall, good-looking Russian girl came to that man's house and entered with a key," he reported. "She acted as though she owned the place. He was not there. She waited, smoking many cigarettes. Finally she stretched out on the lounge and slept, leaving the lights on."

Zeng, waiting for his servant, had with his own hands prepared breakfast. He uncovered bowls of rice, and steaming tea into which butter and barley meal had been stirred.

"Eat, Chow; it has been a cold watch," he said, and picked up long jade chopsticks.

The big Mongol grinned and noisily drank the tea prepared as the men of the steppes drink it, salty and greasy and thick. Between gulps, he spoke.

"Later a man came in, a thin man who smelled of opium. He looked wild, his face was cut. When the woman asked what had happened, he said, 'Damn-damn, I do not find.' Then he pulled the shades. I smelled opium and when the woman tried to make him stop, he said once more, 'Damn-damn,' and then a door closed hard."

"What manner of house is it, and where?"

"Big, but old and badly kept, far out of Berkeley, with many weeds in the yard. He is poor, so he smokes *yen shi.*"

Zeng sighed. It was melancholy, considering the case of a brilliant man who had been reduced to smoking pipe scrapings.

"Go, Chow, and rest while I study these things. Tonight you watch again."

It was past noon when Ann Carter and her father rang for admittance.

"Did you find things as I said?" Zeng asked the grizzled captain.

Carter grimaced. "All too much so!"

"Lin, I've been worried about you, and now this second awful murder!" Ann cried anxiously. "That stealthy lurker must know about you. You'll be next! Why on earth did you risk slipping back into that house?"

"For purposes of observation." Then to Carter, "What did the police laboratory find?"

"That human teeth bit Prince Yuan. That the same teeth settled Forest Baker. It's incredible, but a maniac has killed two men."

Ann shuddered. "And will kill others."

Zeng spread the red silk certificate, the wilted lotus blossom, and the three brass cash on the table. "Perhaps I forgot to mention that the White Lotus Society is involved. I walked in on several ruffians who were attacking Nadja Karakhov, and in the scuffle, one of them must have dropped these."

"The White Lotus? Weren't they outlawed in Singapore?" Carter rose, paced up and down the room. "Now they crop out in San Francisco! I thought we had tongs and criminal organizations whipped, tamed down."

Carter had spent years working for peace between the tongs, but even his broad acquaintance with things Chinese did not include more than a scanty account of the mysterious White Lotus and its bloody deeds in Singapore. Zeng gestured reassuringly.

"It is not as bad as you think. The tongs in themselves were honorable enough, organized for mutual protection and benevolence. Unscrupulous members dealt in drugs and gambling concessions, and hired highbinders to fight rivals in true gangster fashion."

"I know, I know!" The captain was a little impatient.

Zeng smoothly continued. "The White Lotus was originally a splendid fraternal and patriotic organization, much like some of your American lodges. But, unhappily, scoundrels used it for criminal purposes, just as was the case with the warring tongs you finally quieted. Without doubt many chapters of the White Lotus are honorable, useful."

"Where is the local chapter?" Carter demanded. "I've not heard that one exists."

"A raid would be inadvisable," Zeng cautioned. "You do not wish to indict a lodge, you wish to convict an assassin."

CARTER'S RUDDY face darkened.

"Zeng," he snapped, "this is the first time I've felt that you're obstructing justice! I cannot allow you to cover the White Lotus. Damn it, man, much as I hate it, I shall have to—to force your hand."

Zeng knew that the hot-headed captain was threatening to expose his, Zeng's real identity. Ann rose and stood there, tense, wide-eyed.

"Lin! Dad!" she said. "I can't understand this."

For a moment, Zeng was tempted to say, "Force my hand, Captain, and let me abandon my pose. I'd like Ann to know I'm a white man." Then he remembered his mission, and knew that even to win Ann as more than a friend, he could not quit his duty.

"To force my hand would do much harm," he said soberly. "Give me twenty-four hours in which to arrest the guilty person, and the madman who serves him."

Carter's flare of wrath was fading. "Granted, Zeng."

"Do not have me trailed. That would be a death sentence, and you would gain nothing," warned Zeng.

That solemn voice troubled Captain Carter. He picked up his hat and said, gruffly, "Let's go, Ann. If you're going to continue streaking around to watch police work, you'll have to quit that language class!"

Later, Zeng called Chow. "From now on watch Wang Lu's place on Pagoda Lane. I think that he is the Grand Master of the White Lotus."

"Can do," Chow said, testing out his English.

At first glance, it seemed absurd to suppose that the burly Mongol, handicapped with a wooden leg, would be anything but useless in a quest involving stealth, but Zeng knew his man.

Chow grinned, took a hatchet from under his tunic, and tested the edge.

"Boss-man plenty clazy, gettee kill," he said. "My finish White Lotus fella plopa, every damn all."

"I don't intend to get killed, and no matter what happens I don't want you to try to cut down every man in the White Lotus Society. You will only get into a great deal of trouble."

Chow left, honing the hatchet on the palm of his hand.

"Premature vengeance by a loyal servant would embarrass everyone," Zeng reflected. "Haste is indicated."

Then Zeng prepared for a further inspection of the late Forest Baker's home.

CHAPTER VII

MURDERER'S CHEST

IT DID not take Zeng long to coax Captain Carter into a more amiable frame of mind, although Carter still grumbled as they stepped into Baker's library.

"I can't understand why it didn't occur to you in the first place to look for secret closets or cubby holes," he growled.

Zeng ignored the query. He set about patiently tapping the paneled walls, checking every dimension of the room and comparing it against the outside measurements of the house. Outside, men were busy looking for footprints that might have escaped notice when the first lot of moulage had been made. Thus far, they were getting nowhere.

The house was as prosaic as it was large. There were linen closets in which a man could have hidden. There were bins and cabinets in the basement. But there was no disturbed dust to indicate any such taking of cover.

"Note the dust on that Camphor chest," Zeng finally said.

"We fingerprinted that," the captain answered. "What of it?"

"Everything else has a fine film, which is customary when servants care for a bachelor's house. The chest has a heavier coat. This is not reasonable, unless a long-stored chest was carried in after the last house cleaning."

That was what started it. They made a rapid check on the insurance. Every item in the library which was of value comparable to that antique chest was on an inventory, and there were fire and burglary policies. But the dust-coated chest was not listed.

"Why omit it?" Zeng demanded. "Because it is a recent acquisition. Please get in touch with the servants while I examine it."

There was neither hinge nor lock nor any visible joint where the lid fitted on the chest. It was not at once apparent where the cover began, and the metal binding was equally ambiguous. And here was where Zeng's knowledge of things Chinese served him well.

"Puzzle box," he said to the plainclothes men who had come in after completing their second search of the grounds. "No two alike, yet all follow the same principles."

He began tapping, prodding the carved figures, twisting with seeming aimlessness.

"Get a saw!" someone suggested.

That brought a laugh, but Zeng blandly countered, "Not necessary, gentlemen. Look!"

"Huh?" another exclaimed. "I'll be damned, if he ain't gone and done it!"

A panel swung. Zeng plucked at a length of hardwood uncovered by the first motion. He drew up on the tongue of wood and then lifted an inner lid.

"Chinese puzzle, gentlemen, literally that." He pointed into the small space in the center. No wonder the chest was heavy, considering the thick walls needed to contain its ingenious wooden mechanism. "This can also be opened from the inside."

"The hell you say!"

"Recently altered." He indicated chisel and saw marks, showing how the original linkwork had been modified. "For this assassination. I am sure the person who bit Prince Yuan to death was carried here in this chest."

The cops howled that down. "Now, looka here, Doctor Zeng, even a contortionist couldn't double up into that little space!"

The interior was little over three feet long and perhaps a bit less than thirty inches wide. But Zeng had an answer.

"A dwarf, let us say. Very short, but powerful enough to bite a man to death. See there, air holes, recently drilled? Enough to prevent suffocation."

"I guess he could hear, too, when the coast was clear?" said a detective dubiously.

"A dwarf could have enough clearance," Zeng went on, quite unperturbed, "to lift the lid a little, peeping and listening. One move of the inside lever will lift or lock as he desired."

As he spoke, he knelt beside the puzzle chest. He played his flashlight into every corner. "See the coarse black hairs, doubtless rubbed from his head. Note the smell of opium, of joss sticks. See these stains? Possibly blood. So, I shall now look for a Mongolian dwarf."

CAPTAIN CARTER stepped into the room just in time to hear Zeng's concluding words.

"What's that, Zeng? A dwarf?" Carter echoed.

"Yes. Presently I shall explain. But what of the chest, Captain? Any history?"

"A truck brought it here, the handyman says. Forest Baker did not know a thing about it, had made no such purchase, and didn't know what to do with it. But he rather liked it, and decided to keep it until the owner traced it. That was yesterday afternoon, and Yuan was killed that night."

When Captain Carter heard Zeng elaborate on his original terse statements, he began to admit the justice of the deductions.

"That undersized monster was probably there in the chest, waiting for us to clear out so he could escape," he grumbled.

"I would rather say," Zeng corrected, "waiting for his chance at Forest Baker. He may even have managed to put through a telephone call between the time of the first murder, and the time Baker came down to try to wheedle the drunken prince into a better humor."

"You mean, this damn-blasted dwarf took Yuan's Uighur manuscript, and substituted a phony, to throw us off the trail? Not counting, of course, on your noticing the switch?"

Zeng frowned for a moment. "Theorizing makes for confusion. By the way, Captain, will you start my twenty-four hours from now, instead of from the time of our discussion?"

Carter laughed shortly. "Zeng, I still don't know what to make of you. You know very well I could hardly refuse you, and still I ought to clamp down!"

Zeng bowed. "Thank you for the extension. I shall report later."

Zeng's approach to Hubert Rayne's house was open and casual. He expected Rayne and Nadja to be in the weatherbeaten, two-story house in the Berkeley foothills, simply because such a course would be more logical than flight.

Nadja had every reason to fear the White Lotus, and Rayne had been terrified at the thought that Zeng might be an emissary of that sinister society. And since by now Nadja would have told her ally that Zeng had defended her against the White Lotus, they would logically conclude that he was an independent adventurer, taking a hand in the quest for Genghis Khan's relics.

"For all Rayne's comparing notes with Nadja, he could hardly imagine that anyone connected with the police would let an intruder go free," Zeng shrewdly concluded. "So his problem is evading the White Lotus, rather than avoiding the police. And his own house is as good as any place."

He walked through the weed-grown garden and into the deepening shadows of the oaks which half-hid the long-neglected house.

"This is where a splendid mind is buried in poverty, despair, anger, and the fumes of opium. This is a tomb, for nothing lives but the man's body."

AND THEN he pressed the push button, wondering if he might not have to use his lock picks.

His pulse quickened as he heard the *click-clack* of a woman's heels. Nadja Karakhov, breathless as though she had raced downstairs, came to the door. There were dark rings about her splendid eyes, and her face was drawn, weary.

She still wore the black dinner gown.

"I didn't stop to pack a bag, last night," she explained by way of greeting.

"In an hour," Zeng said gravely, "your gown will be quite appropriate. Could we not set the clock forward and put you at ease?"

She laughed, somewhat nervously. "You came to see me?"

"You and Mister Rayne."

Nadja closed the door after Zeng. "I'm sorry, but you can't see him for awhile. He's... asleep. He sat up with a pistol, watching, all night."

Zeng's nostrils flared. "Ah... *asleep*, of course."

"Oh, all right—opium. I thought I'd aired the place out. Poor devil, I might as well admit, I've watched for him!"

She led Zeng into a dusty living-room which, twenty years ago, had been quite fashionable. Zeng seated himself on the lounge, and spoke.

"Let us cease fencing and begin being abrupt. I have just twenty-four hours to arrest the assassin who killed Prince Yuan and then murdered Forest Baker."

The name of the last victim shocked Nadja. Zeng was sure that her amazement and fear were not feigned. He went on.

"Do you see how the fangs of doom bite deep? Already two of those seeking the grave of Genghis Khan have died terribly. It is not accident that you are still alive. It is design, but patterns change swiftly!"

She raised her hands, hiding her tense face for a moment. "Baker— bitten—like Yuan? Oh, my God!"

"This was shortly before Baker's safe was looted, by a person who had a memorandum of the combination, written—*in your hand!*" He was bluffing now.

"You can't prove that," she said, half-heartedly.

Zeng ignored the challenge. "Tell me the truth as you know it, and perhaps I can save you. Who and what are you?"

"I told you." She became stubborn. "I told you all."

"How resolutely they bare their throats to the fangs of doom! It is very clear that you and Baker lied to conceal each other's moves. Yuan was drunk, the autopsy proved that to be true. Baker without doubt did go down and discover the corpse. But some time in the evening, you went down to persuade Yuan. You went first. You exchanged manuscripts, before the assassin bit."

"You're guessing!" she flared.

"What of your swift flight at the first chance, your wearing your coat, so needless in that heated house? You were ready for flight with the true Uighur scroll."

"Why didn't you search me?"

"Because I didn't want to act on suspicion and warn you by a false move. I kept the police off your trail, and went myself to watch you. And the White Lotus was there before I arrived!"

"They were, but what of that?"

"Simple. The slayer was hiding in a chest in the library, watching for his chance to catch one member of the gathering alone. You came down, deftly exchanged manuscripts, and the slayer saw. Though a mad little monster, he need not be without intelligence. Suppose he telephoned, reporting not only his first slaying, but also your bit of juggling?"

Nadja was on her feet, slowly backing away from the smiling Doctor Zeng. He hammered on relentlessly.

"If this was not the case, then it was coincidence that the White Lotus arrived from Pagoda Lane in just a little less time than it took me to follow you from Saint Francis Wood. Coincidence has its limit. The White Lotus and I both came to your apartment for the same reason, and we both failed. You burned letters, as a blind, and used my intervention to get the Uighur scroll out of your possession. Where is it?"

SHE SHRUGGED helplessly.

"You're right, Doctor Zeng. Someone at the house must have set those Chinese on my trail. The scroll? I dropped it out the window while you were grappling, falling. Then I retrieved it, the moment you left, and dropped it in a mail box, and came to tell Hubert Rayne. Now you want to search the house and get the scroll. You're assuming it's Prince Yuan's? Well, you're wrong! We paid—Professor Baker paid—"

"I do not care who paid whom! The White Lotus is determined to keep expeditions from uncovering the sacred relics. Do you think you can outwit them?"

"I'm afraid I can't. Maybe it is well that Hubert is—er—sleeping. I'm sick of all this, Doctor Zeng. I'll get you the scroll. You can give it to the White Lotus, and let peace be declared."

This was better than he had expected. Possession of the scroll would enable him to enter the secret council of the White Lotus, and without the mortal risk of posing as a member. So he followed Nadja into the adjoining room.

She fumbled in a table drawer and found a key and a flashlight. "He locked it in that closet," she said, gesturing.

The panels were solid, old-fashioned; a room with such high ceiling would have high doors, and these would have to be massive, far more so than necessary in rooms of modern style. The door was hung on three hinges instead of two. No doubt that Rayne's most precious things were behind it, for a hasp and solid padlock secured it.

She used the key. "It's never been wired," Nadja explained. "Take this flashlight, and there's a low stepladder."

One end of the large closet was pigeonholed, and scrolls filled it as player piano rolls in a cabinet.

"The top row," Nadja directed.

Zeng played the flashlight, and saw the jade and agate and coral knobs of the rods on which the rolls of paper and damask were wound. He entered the large closet.

Then the door slammed. As he whirled, bounding back, the padlock snapped.

"I could not anticipate your being a fool!" he said. "You are exposing yourself to certain death!"

"I'm sorry to do this, but I have my business, and my risks, just as you have," Nadja answered.

Zeng had counted on the growing menace to force Nadja to good faith; he had not anticipated what he now sensed was a fanatic resolution. Lock picks would do him no good here. And unless he broke out, and quickly, he would be completely discredited with Captain Carter. That would be bad, even though Ann still believed in him.

And if he did escape in time, there was no Uighur scroll to pave his way into the secret circle of assassins. He would have to go as a member, a special envoy just arrived from China. The peril of such an attempt made him shudder for a moment.

Then he began to consider a line of attack.

CHAPTER VIII

SHRINE OF THE WHITE LOTUS

DOCTOR ZENG escaped sooner than he expected. Had it not been for a pen-knife whose blades included one with saw teeth of an alloy steel, it would have taken him hours longer. This blade, little heavier than a jig saw, won him his start. Skillful use of his strength enabled him to complete the jail break.

Zeng snapped on the lights and started on a swift tour of the deserted house. He wanted a clue to Rayne's destination, and Nadja's. And then, upstairs, he found his man.

Rayne was hanging from the bridging of the groined ceiling. He dangled at the end of a new manila rope. His eyes stared sightlessly, his mouth gaped. Near him lay an overturned chair, the varnished seat marred by scratches, indicating that he had kicked it aside.

"Hubert Rayne, destination unknown," Dr. Zeng muttered.

In the fireplace there was a heap of charred paper broken to black bits. On the work table, Zeng noted dustless spaces, exposed by the removal of papers and books. A few unburned bits of paper showed traces of Uighur script, with marginal notes in English. Near the alcove lounge was an opium-smoking layout.

"What poppy dream made him destroy his notes, and hang himself?" Doctor Zeng asked, and then stepped closer to the dangling corpse. He frowned as he eyed the rope, and his expression changed again as he observed the distance between Rayne's feet and the floor.

Doctor Zeng was no longer convinced that this was suicide.

He drove into town and called Captain Carter. "Another man—Hubert Rayne—is dead. Be pleased to get in touch with the Berkeley police, for I am not notifying them. While this is in their jurisdiction, it is really your case."

"Wait, I'll be right over," Carter said.

"I cannot wait," Zeng answered. "I am calling on the Society of the White Lotus. Meanwhile, I suggest an all-car alarm to pick up Nadja Karakhov."

"Wait a second!" Carter exclaimed.

But the line was dead. Doctor Zeng strolled from the drug store. He took the wheel of his sedan and headed for San Francisco.

Carter, meanwhile, was blasting it over the Bay Bridge, Harris, Captain of Inspectors, with him. They wanted first look, and that was what they got. Without siren or red spotlights they approached the desolate house whose lights Zeng had left burning.

Carter said to the inspector, "Damn Zeng's hide, why would he have to run out?"

"I think Zeng knows what he is doing," the inspector answered.

"Of course he knows!" Carter panted a little, racing up the stairs. "But the White Lotus will murder him first and investigate later!"

"Why didn't you have the Chinatown Squad cover the place? You might have given me all the angles, Captain."

"Oh, hell! He convinced me that that would put him in more danger."

The inspector laughed grimly. "You're not staying convinced, Carter."

"Of course I'm not. If Zeng were my own son, I'd not be more worried."

"A swell Chink, all right." The inspector headed down the hall. "Well, here's the corpse."

CARTER HAD brought neither moulage specialists nor photographers with him. But he did have a kit and a camera of his own. Some minutes later he had made a cast of the dead man's teeth.

"For all of Zeng's theories, I still think this is our madman," he explained to the inspector. "A hophead with a grudge. And now, in a lucid moment, the poor devil hangs himself."

The inspector scrutinized the wax matrix, and looked at the dead man's teeth. He whirled about. "You're right, Captain. Look at those incisors! Those canines—their peculiar shape. It's in the bag—Hubert Rayne's teeth and nobody else's bit Prince Yuan and Forest Baker to death! And now Zeng is risking his life for nothing at all!"

Carter groaned. "And I hounded him to it! I hurried him, or he'd have noticed, he'd have suspected. Take over and notify the Berkeley police. I'm going back. I'm doing something about this, regardless!"

Zeng, in the meanwhile, was busy in San Francisco.

There was little chance that the men he had scattered in Nadja's apartment had not identified him. All Chinatown knew the conspicuous Doctor Zeng. Thus, instead of resorting to disguise, he went openly.

He was unarmed. These Chinese were his adopted kinsmen, and Zeng would not declare war. He was acting against criminal individuals, and the less he depended upon armed force the better he would serve justice.

All that Doctor Zeng took with him was his versatile penknife, and a vial of caffeine tablets from his third-floor dispensary. Having seen the recurrence of opium in the background of these weird crimes, he was preparing himself in advance. Already he had swallowed four tablets of the concentrated alkaloid to counteract possible sleepiness.

Zeng threaded his way down the dark alleys that paralleled Grant Avenue. Steep stairways sank from the narrow sidewalks and down into basements. In some of these murky dens, craftsmen and artisans plied their trade, making toys and souvenirs for tourists, shaping dolls, carving images, sawing and soldering metal. In other places, beady-eyed men played main po and fan tan and poker. But for each rendezvous of vice, there were fifty places where yellow men worked overtime, earning a few dollars for the relief of kinsmen in China.

He stopped at the back of the place where Chow should be spying, a narrow shop, unoccupied because of a boycott put on the building. The door was open. Zeng made a chirping sound, like a cricket, but there was no answer. He played his fountain-pen flashlight about the gloom. Chow was not there.

There was no sign of struggle, no trampling of the heap of chestnut shells, and the husks of watermelon seeds where Chow must have squatted, nibbling as he watched. Zeng glanced at his watch. Too much time had passed to allow for inquiry or search. He had to strike at once, for with Hubert Rayne's death the quota of murder was complete, and the assassin might be leaving.

"If Chow is dead, his body would be here," he reasoned. "If he is a prisoner, then he will keep."

Zeng left the deserted post, and went to Wang Lu's place. The narrow shop was lined with shelves containing jars of ginseng roots, mandrake, snake's liver, and dried tigers' hearts—row on row of herbs and seeds and animal substances to cure all ills. A curtain rustled, and an old man stepped from behind its shelter.

HE WAS short and shriveled. He wore a black jacket, black silk trousers, and felt slippers. A skullcap covered his bald head, and his cunning eyes peered through silver-rimmed glasses.

He clasped his hands and bowed as he said, "The Honorable Doctor Zeng is welcome."

"May the Honorable Wang live a thousand years," replied Zeng. Then he made the threefold sign of Heaven and Earth, the succession of gestures which had terrified the late Hubert Rayne.

"Why is your coat so old?" Wang asked.

For twelve hundred years, the answer has been, "It was handed down by Five Ancestors." Zeng made this response, for he was still on firm ground.

The scarcely perceptible stirring of the red curtain with its gold embroidered phoenix seconded the sixth sense which warned Zeng. Hidden eyes were regarding him. His arrival was not a surprise.

"I come to warn you as a man, not as a Brother of the Lotus," he now said. "Do you care to hear what the sons of the wind are whispering?"

A son of the wind meant, in the secret slang of the order, "a police spy, a traitor, an informer."

The Honorable Wang gestured toward an alcove as he drew aside a curtain that concealed it. Opening from the floor was a trap-door with stairs leading underground. Zeng followed the shopkeeper. He had seen Wang press a button, and he was sure that men were being warned, that they in their turn called others.

Doctor Zeng had never fully learned the ritual of the White Lotus. It involved an oath that he would not take, and thus in China, he had declined invitations. But, from studying records seized by the British police in their raids on criminal chapters of the Society, he had learned enough to have a fighting chance.

The underground passage became damp and murky. Finally Wang came to a door which was guarded by two men who wore red masks.

The room beyond was square. Its walls were hung with embroidered banners. There were four painted doorways; symbolic of the cardinal were three archways, arranged in a row, to mark the avenue at whose further end was the carved and gilded points of the compass. In the center shrine of the Five Ancestors.

At one side of the shrine was the statue of smiling Kwan Yin, the goddess of mercy. On the other side was Kwan Ti, the glowering god of war.

Before the door closed behind him Zeng saw four or five masked newcomers join the guards. Then Wang Lu seated himself.

"What news do you bring us?" he asked.

"One of the Lotus Brethren has violated the Fourth Oath, and the Thirty-first."

"To violate an oath is serious. You may be mistaken."

"Let me recite," Zeng proposed. " 'If a member break the laws of the country, he must sustain his own cause, without help from the Brethren.' Because of many violations, the White Lotus is outlawed in Singapore, and in Java. Here, a brother has committed murders. You must not shelter him, for it is not only forbidden, but it will bring evil on the others."

ZENG'S CONTENTION was sound, and Wang knew it, but he countered, "When the Five Ancestors prescribed that oath, they did not refer to the laws of the foreign devils."

"Honorable Wang, it is also written, 'Should a Brother confess a crime, he must not implicate any other Brethren: and whoever does, may he die in the Great Ocean, and the spirits of his ancestors find no rest.' There is one who has betrayed you, and brought evil to all of you. There is one whom you must denounce, one whom you are forbidden to shelter!"

"Who did this thing?" Wang demanded.

"I take a risk in coming here. First you must swear an oath."

Wang was uneasy, for he knew now the manner of swearing that would be proposed, and he had the Chinese fear of that dark invocation. "First, tell me more."

"A dwarf was sent in a chest to murder Forest Baker and Prince Yuan. The law knows of this. Someone has betrayed the White Lotus, by making confessions that implicated others. I come as a friend to advise the surrender of the guilty, that the others may be saved."

But Wang Lu had an answer. "Since you know laws, you know this one: if a member has a dispute with a brother, he must bring his complaint before the council for judgment. Even if you are not one of us, and your lack of credentials makes me suspect you, you may face him with proofs. If he is guilty, he will be surrendered for the good of his fellows."

Wang was stepping into the trap, yet Zeng was uneasy, for he sensed that the crafty fellow was baiting him.

"First guarantee my safety, so that I will not share the traitor's fate, to make silence complete. Suppose that I accuse him, and am cut down the moment I convict him?"

Wang smiled blandly. "I will swear an oath. No one will touch you, except perhaps the man you accuse."

This was trick against trick, but there was no retreat, and Zeng said:

"Let us swear the oath that binds us as you propose!"

CHAPTER IX

THE EXECUTIONER

WANG LU rose and went to the door. He spoke to the guards, and then beckoned to Doctor Zeng, who followed him to the end of the passage. It opened to a small balcony which overhung an airshaft. The guards, except for two who had gone to obey the herb doctor's orders, came after, and stood at both sides of the railed enclosure.

They looked up at the few stars which reached through the skyglow of the city, and they looked down into the blackness which concealed the bare earth. This oath was to be made in full view of gods and demons, and the solemnity of the impending ceremony checked their tongues.

Presently the men returned. One had a lighted taper, two squares of red paper, two brushes, and an inkstand. The second held two white roosters by the legs; in his other hand he carried a pair of short, heavy knives.

Wang Lu and Doctor Zeng took inked brushes and wrote their pledges on the red papers. Then, standing side by side, they thrust the red squares into the flickering taper flame, and let the ash fall into a small bowl.

Narrowed black eyes stared uneasily from blank yellow faces as Wang Lu and Doctor Zeng each reached for a squawking fowl and a chopping knife. This was an awful appeal to the demons of earth and air to destroy whoever broke the oath.

The blades fell. There was a flapping of wings, and both men recited, "If I break this oath, may the earth drink my blood, and may I walk in the lowest hell without a head."

Then, as blood spurted into the bowl which contained the ashes of the burned papers, the witnesses chanted, "May that be our end if we allow an oath breaker to live."

The ancient ritual was completed when rice wine was poured into the bowl of blood and ash. Wang Lu and Doctor Zeng drank, and so did the others. The residue was spilled, so that the spirits of earth and air could taste.

When all this was done, and the awed Brethren had filed back toward the lodge room, Wang dismissed them at the door. He turned to Zeng.

"You and I will wait while they go to get the man who betrayed us. That you know of the dwarf is proof enough that there has been a confession to the police. It will be some time before he arrives, so let us smoke a pipe."

Doctor Zeng could not decline the long-stemmed pipe and the drug which had played such a part in Hubert Rayne's doom. Wang Lu took an opium layout from a cabinet, a weapon on which he counted in making a loophole in the dreadful oath he had sworn. Doctor Zeng was sure of this, but he had to carry on, offering himself as bait.

He could not guess bow the crafty Wang Lu proposed to harm him without incurring the penalties of oath-breaking. He could only hope that he would be equal to the ordeal, that he would be able to reverse the trap.

For a while, the pipes gurgled. Wang Lu, the seasoned smoker, finally roused himself from his languor when a guard entered and announced, "Master, he is waiting."

The old herb seller nudged his guest, shook him gently, waited for him to gain his feet.

"That door ahead," he said. "It is not a ceremonial dummy. Step toward it."

Zeng's attention was focused on the painted panel. He wondered what was ahead. He took a step, and a second.

The floor sank beneath his feet and he dropped headlong into a red glare below, hot air and choking fumes billowed up to meet him. Though the caffeine tablets had to a degree counteracted the effects of the opium, he was still not sufficiently alert to catch the edge.

ZENG CRASHED against a solid floor. There was a momentary suction as the trap above rose and locked into place. The ensuing silence was shocking. It told him how thick the walls must be to shut out the murmur of the city. He was in a sealed room which was quite empty except for the brazier of glowing charcoal and two statues at the farther end.

Dizzy, choked by the dense fumes, Doctor Zeng crawled about the room. It had doors, but one blow told him that they were as solid as those of a cold storage vault. The original purpose must have been to hide fugitives until a police raid was abandoned.

His head was already splitting. The air was dense and sluggish and hot. Carbon dioxide from the glowing charcoal was filling the room. Neither Wang Lu nor any of his men were touching or had touched Doctor Zeng, yet doom spread from that bed of coals. His overburdened heart pounded, distending the veins at his temples.

Kwan Ti, the god on the tall throne, glared triumphantly. Kwan Yin, the merciful goddess, smiled placidly, and made the mystic sign of salvation.

Zeng muffled his fingers with his cap and tipped the brazier. He trampled and beat out the coals before the smouldering floor added to his peril. But this was not enough. He was staggering and red spots danced before his eyes. The invisible fumes already tainting the air would surely kill him even though the source had been extinguished.

His senses began to trick him. The single bulb in the ceiling dimmed and brightened crazily. He wondered why there was any light in that chamber of doom, Kwan Ti's gilded leer seemed to become animate. There was a lifelike gleam in the fierce god's eyes.

Zeng sank to the floor, where the fumes were the worst. Carbon dioxide, much heavier than air, settled and surged over the heavy planks as water would. Which gave him a remote chance. He drew his knife, praying that the slender gimlet would be long enough to reach through the wood. If he could penetrate it, start his tiny saw blade and enlarge the hole, there was the possibility that the fumes would drain out.

Knives seemed to dart through his temples with every agonized heart beat. But for the caffeine that stimulated him, that pipe of opium would have numbed him to his peril, and he would have lain there, yielding to the insidious charcoal fumes. Too late, Zeng saw how cunning Wang Lu had evaded the oath.

He plied the slender saw. Blackness danced about him. Then came a whiff of cold air. He slumped, a sodden heap, for he could not cut a second drain. He lay there, face pressed to the floor, sucking in air.

Zeng did not see Kwan Ti's grin. The gilded face was alive, not carved from wood. The god was descending from his pedestal. His shoulders were very broad, his arms were powerful, though he was only little more than a yard tall. Wang Lu had fulfilled the letter of his oath. Zeng was indeed in the presence of the man he had accused.

A tube, coming up through the painted shrine, had fed the dwarf what fresh air he needed. Thus, seeing his victim collapse, he was preparing for the last move. From behind his pedestal he took a pair of burnished steel tongs whose jaws were set with metal cast in the shape of human teeth, the work of a dental mechanic.

Tracing that work would convict the arch-criminal! The dwarf inhaled noisily from the air tube. Then he waddled swiftly across the room, laid his tongs down and tried to roll his victim face up. Finally succeeding, he set the jaws of the tongs to take a fatal bite from Doctor Zeng's throat.

He had assumed that his victim had succumbed to opium and to suffocation. He did not suspect that the tall man in gray had drunk air from the hurriedly shaped orifice. He yelled hoarsely and tried to jerk back when Zeng snatched the tongs from his grasp and sat up immediately.

"It is useless to run, little man! While I breathe the air that comes to the shrine you filled, you will be suffocating. Unless you tell me who set you to work."

The monster's eyes glared from that fierce, gilded mask. Zeng used the tongs, and caught him by the leg, holding him helpless, stifling in that venomous air. The memory of Prince Yuan's horrible death, and Forest Baker's steeled him to his cruel task.

This stocky dwarf, warped as much in mind as in body, was no more than the tool of some superior. Beyond any doubt, Wang Lu had sent him, so Zeng could not relent.

"Tell me, fool, or smother," he demanded fiercely. "A better death than you planned for me!"

Then Zeng became increasingly aware of a sound he could not quite understand. At first he had mistaken it for his own pulse, drumming in his ears, but now he knew that the walls, thick as they were, quivered and shook. Those were hammer blows, axe blows!

A door swung in.

CHAPTER X

END OF
THE SCROLL

CHOW HAD made good his threat. He had cut away bars and bolts, using an adze instead of his favorite hatchet. His face was slashed and bleeding and his coat was bloody. Behind him, in the dimly lighted passage, two men lay face down in spreading red pools.

Zeng staggered to the door, dragging his choking prisoner with him.

"Where have you been?" he demanded of his huge servant.

"At the movie, just for a little while, Master," Chow answered, chagrined. "To see if my hatchet had hurt the big man. When I came out, someone told me you had passed by. But I could not find you—Wang's door was barred—I knew that I had failed you—so I got an adze and came in through a skylight, and those men—" he pointed at the ones he had cut down—"were waiting here for something to happen. It did."

One of the dead pair was Wang Lu.

"Where are the others?" Zeng demanded.

"They ran when they could not stop me."

"Take this fellow, but don't hurt him."

Much as Zeng wanted to get in touch with the police, he had to search the place and find the Uighur manuscript which had caused this chain of violence. Likewise, he wanted whatever other clues there were, for even during the short time it would take for him to give the alarm, lurking followers of the dead White Lotus chief would return to destroy evidence.

"Men are coming, many men!" Chow cried. "Hear them! Shall I kill this blood-drinker before they can save him?"

"No, you big ox! Wait!" Zeng listened to the tramp of feet, the splintering of wood, the shriek and chatter and squealing of spectators. "That's the police. They're breaking in from every side at once. Did you call them?"

"I didn't have time, master."

Whoever of the White Lotus Brethren might have been preparing to counter-attack after Chow's surprise party would now be scattered.

"There is something odd about the arrival of the police," Zeng said. "Go to meet them, tell them you have searched the place, that all is well with me. That nothing else is to be found. That this dwarf is the killer, and that I will soon explain."

Before his servant could answer, Zeng darted into the farther, gloom of the passage. The sound of Chow dragging his captive up the stairs was muffled by the rumble and roar of the police raid. Zeng found a dark corner behind the compartment in which he had almost been smothered, and listened to the cross-fire of voices.

He was not sure whether he had rightly guessed the origin of the alarm which had brought the police, but his idea was worth following up.

Gradually silence took hold of the building, silence and darkness. Chinese, whether renegade or law abiding, would avoid the locale, lest some enemy report their interest. At last Zeng came from hiding and stealthily ascended the dark stairs which led to the lodge room.

For long moments he waited near the open door.

FINALLY A tiny spot of light blossomed at the far end. The circle of glow moved up and down the pedestal which supported the statue of Kwan Yin. Zeng could distinguish the outline of the searcher.

The light shifted toward the statue of Kwan Ti. There was a suppressed cry of triumph, and the thin, white pencil of light reached for the door.

Zeng already had caught a whiff of familiar perfume, and it confirmed his deduction. He flicked on his own flash, revealing the tense, lovely face of Nadja Karakhov. She cried out, and her hand darted toward the bag tucked under her arm.

"Too late to get your pistol," Zeng said, and seized her wrist.

She recognized his voice. "Doctor Zeng!" she said bitterly.

"Yes, I escaped." He lowered his own light, and saw the Uighur scroll which lay on the floor. "If you will tell the truth, I will say nothing about your efforts to obstruct justice. Otherwise, I shall be compelled to tell how you neglected to report the death of Hubert Rayne. How you locked me up, and then turned in an alarm to get Wang Lu's place raided, so that after the police had thoroughly smashed things, you could slip in and search for this Uighur scroll."

"You know everything, Doctor Zeng," the woman murmured.

"I merely reasoned backward and hindsight is always acute," said Dr. Zeng dryly. "Suppose you fill in the missing parts?"

"I will," she promised. "I've failed at every move, thanks to you!"

"Personally, I am very sorry," Zeng said politely as he led the way through the maze behind the late Wang Lu's herb shop.

The heavy doors which had been hewn or pried from their hinges showed Zeng how much Nadja's strategy had helped him. Chow, dropping through a skylight, had not provided for any quick retreat.

"I shall give you all possible credit for unintentional aid," Zeng said.

Just as they reached the alley a man's voice exclaimed, "There he is now! I knew Chow was lying to us!"

Ann Carter darted out of the shadows. "Lin," she cried, "we've been worried frantic. I made Dad wait here. Oh! You have a prisoner."

"Not a prisoner, but some evidence," Zeng explained, secretly thrilled at Ann's anxiety. "What of Chow and his prisoner? Did the dwarf talk?"

Captain Carter gestured to the car that waited at the corner. "He made a sudden break and Chow threw a hatchet. He missed, and the dwarf ran to the roof where he slipped in jumping to the next building. When we found him, he was beyond talking. I rather think he did it on purpose, judging from what Chow told me."

BUT IT was not until they went to Doctor Zeng's apartment that Captain Carter learned all the details and received full assurance that the case was actually closed, that the dwarf and Wang Lu had been the principal criminals, while the other members of the White Lotus were guilty of no more than loyalty to a misguided leader.

Zeng pointed to the tongs. "It is very simple. The dwarf first slugged his victims, so they could not yell. The circle of death, of course, was to have closed when Rayne died."

"But he committed suicide," Carter protested.

"No, he was hanged. He could not have kicked that chair away, for his feet were further from the floor than the seat on which he was supposed to have stood. Everything else was nicely worked out, but that one detail was wrong. I did not tell you of that simply because I wished you to think, for a while, that the case was closed, while I closed it in my own way."

"But Rayne's teeth very closely matched the bites that killed Prince Yuan and Forest Baker."

Doctor Zeng smiled. "Rayne was an opium addict. During his sodden hours, the White Lotus could easily have made a cast of his teeth, and must have done so. These tongs prove my point. And after one pipe too many, Rayne could very easily be hanged, as if in remorseful suicide.

"Finally, the White Lotus did not know I had already told the police of their final victim's death. Thus, when I worked my way in on a pretext, they attempted to dispose of me by the same murder weapon, and lay the blame on Rayne."

Ann shuddered. "Do you mean that Rayne was killed just to deflect suspicion from the dwarf?"

"No," Zeng answered. "Rayne knew much of the Genghis Khan tradition. Even without the Uighur scroll, he was dangerous. So they eliminated him." He turned toward Nadja. "And now tell us why you went to such great risk to get this scroll."

Zeng unrolled the Uighur manuscript as he awaited the Russian woman's answer.

"The White Lotus as you must have guessed," Nadja explained, "was opposed to anyone's finding the buried treasure and the sacred relics of Genghis Khan. The Mongol and the Manchu have always menaced China."

"As I explained," Zeng said to Ann and her father.

"I am a Soviet Agent," Nadja went on, "and my duty was to prevent the discovery of the great Khan's grave for precisely the same reason. Imagine the predicament of my government if the Mongol power of old times were revived! And you can be sure that no matter who sent an expedition to dig, the surrounding tribes would wait for the success of the excavation and then close in to seize the relics. That was my mission, and I have failed. You have the scroll."

Dr. Zeng studied the Uighur script for a full minute. The silence was becoming oppressive when he raised his eyes to glance at his companions. Ann and her father leaned forward sharply as he arose and approached a great brass brazier with the precious scroll.

"Don't, oh, don't!" Nadja cried out, grasping the meaning of his action.

"Damn it, Zeng," Carter shouted, "that's evidence!"

"Evidence against two dead men," replied Zeng calmly as he struck a light and held the flame to the silk damask. "They have already paid the penalty. Destroying this is more important than prosecuting a society of misguided men who, according to their own lights, did rightly enough. The murderers are dead, Carter. And you have not failed, Nadja. The sword of Genghis Khan, his horse-tail standard—all these things must remain hidden beneath the sands of the Gobi lest they do have the power to incite the Mongols and set all Asia afire."

Slowly the flames licked and ate into the time-stained scroll. Silently all of them watched the brazier become the funeral urn for the ghost of a great secret.

Ann shuddered. "Mongols!" she cried. "How I detest Orientals!" Then she thought of her host, and gasped. She hadn't meant him.

But Zeng was only looking at her with a grave smile about his lips. How deeply he may have been wounded by this involuntary flash of racial prejudice did not show on his features. As far as the world was concerned, he was Chinese—and he couldn't tell Ann any different.

"Oh, Lin!" the girl cried out. "Forgive me. I didn't mean it. I wasn't thinking of you."

"I know," said Dr. Zeng gently. "But I am thinking of you. A courteous host remembers when he has invited guests to dinner, even though they have been delayed. Chow! Lai Hu Chow! Now where can that yellow mountain of flesh have gone!"

"Just serve us some tea and almond cakes, Zeng," yawned Captain Carter lazily. "I'll bet he's gone to a movie."

BLOOD CARGO

CHAPTER I

BULLETS IN
THE DARK

MIDNIGHT FOG eddied around the chunky man, blurring him as he lurched across the steeply tilted street in the heart of San Francisco's Chinatown. His movements seemed laborious, jerky, as if he might be drunk—or badly hurt.

At the middle of the intersection he stopped to listen, although there was little to be heard except the constant drip of moisture from tiled pagoda-style roofs, a rhythmic clanking of cable rollers in the street car slots and the distant moan of foghorns from the bay.

To these sounds the chunky man paid no attention. He appeared to be waiting for something much more important.

Presently it reached his ears: a motor's purr, the whisper of tires on wet asphalt. Far down the slanted block a gray, hearselike automobile was climbing the grade in second gear, its amber fog lights distorted by swirling mist. Nearer, in the black maw of an alley, somebody whistled a signal.

Grunting, the chunky man swiftly adjusted a mask upon his face and fell sprawling on his belly.

Nor was he a moment too soon.

It was a remodeled gray ambulance that came up the hill. Joe Quong was at the wheel. Quong belonged to the newer generation of American-born, college-educated Chinese. His ambition was to become a surgeon, and his job as a Bayside Hospital driver was paying his way through medical school. Soon he would be an intern, like his friend Mike Wingate who sat beside him now.

They made an oddly assorted pair. Quong, the budding master of surgery; Wingate, the lanky Oklahoman with an unerring flair for diagnosis. But they were alike in a desire for careers in the alleviation of human suffering, and this kindred ambition welded their friendship all the closer despite their racial differences. They even planned to set up a partnership practice after graduation.

Joe Quong's thoughts were on this pleasant prospect when his knuckles went suddenly white on the wheel.

"Mike!" he exclaimed. "Good grief, look up there ahead of us!" And he kicked savagely at his brake pedal.

The Oklahoman stared through the windshield.

"A man lying across the car tracks! Lord, we're going to hit him—"

But Joe Quong was already swerving his front wheels, stabbing the brakes alternately on and off as the converted ambulance rocked crazily from side to side. For a moment it seemed the car would go out of control and broadside into that motionless figure ahead.

Then at the last split instant, Quong mastered his careening vehicle, braking it to a shuddering stop less than two feet from the prone man.

"Golly, that was close!" he breathed unsteadily as he cut the ignition. "Come on, Mike. Let's see what's the matter with that guy."

Mike Wingate nodded and they both piled out, made for the fallen man. Then raw chaos erupted from the midnight fog.

THE ATTACK came without warning. First the chunky man in the street rolled over, scrambled upright with an automatic in his fist. Simultaneously, from the side street, two black sedans converged on the remodeled ambulance. More masked men catapulted to the pavement, a pair from each car. Like the chunky one, they too were armed with automatics equipped with bulbous silencers.

The guns were menacingly trained on Joe Quong and Mike Wingate.

"All right, suckers!" a voice growled. "Lift the flippers. This is a hijack."

The words sounded almost fantastic. Hijacking had gone out with prohibition and the dissolving of rum-running mobs, years ago. Liquor was legal now—and besides, there was no cargo of whiskey in the converted ambulance. Its precious freight was far more valuable; priceless, in fact. Because its worth could not be computed in mere dollars and cents any more than one can reckon the cost of human lives.

It was Mike Wingate who broke the sinister silence.

For a minute he glared at the masked, chunky man.

"A trap, eh?" he growled. "I know you. Come on, Joe, let's take these rats! I'm not scared of a punk like Rory Mad—"

The rest of the name never passed his lips, because the effort to speak it cost him his life. Blossoms of saffron flame burgeoned from the bulbous snouts of the automatics—soundless flame, the reports muffled

The mysterious Dr. Zeng Tse-Lin

by the silencers. And Mike Wingate took the full impact of that lethal barrage squarely in the chest.

He staggered and went down under a relentless storm of whispering slugs, dead long before he measured his lanky length on the asphalt. Even after he fell, the killer mob kept shooting at him. Bullet upon bullet tore through his flesh as his corpse writhed a macabre rigadoon in the midnight haze.

The sight of his friend's murder sent uncontrollable frenzy into Joe Quong's heart.

"Blast you!" he bellowed at the top of his lungs. "Blast you for a pack of mongrel curs!"

Fists doubled, eyes blazing, he smashed at the slayers of Mike Wingate.

A slug nicked his thigh but he knew no pain. Rage was an anesthetic dulling him to all feeling, carrying him past mere physical sensation. He bashed a masked mobster in the mouth. The fellow staggered, his lips spurting a gush of crimson. Quong pivoted, struck at another hood.

But the blow never landed. Silenced guns were whispering again, stuttering out hot dosages of death. Joe Quong felt himself jumping and twitching under the bludgeoning smash of bullets that struck him like sledge-hammers. The paving rose toward him. There was a queer salty taste in his mouth—the taste of his own blood.

His throat was afire. His vision was hazed with scarlet swirls of fog. He fell, rolled over and did not get up.

THE CHUNKY man made for the converted ambulance.

"Okay, you mugs. Snap it up! Them dopes is dead and serves 'em right. If that one sap hadn't tabbed me, we coulda let 'em go. But he spotted me and asked for trouble, so he got it. Now we got work to do. Move!"

A masked gunman protested.

"You ain't figurin' to move the stuff outa the ambulance into our jalopies, are you? Why don't we just take the ambulance itself?"

"Because we don't want it anywhere near the hangout, see?" the chunky man snapped. "I know what I'm doin'. You get busy."

With rehearsed precision, the four masked mobsters began swiftly looting the gray machine of its contents. Stacked in the remodeled ambulance were hundreds of glass-lined flasks somewhat resembling thermos bottles, only a great deal heavier. These had to be transferred to the two black sedans, and time was short. The chunky man drove his underlings like slaves. Speed and yet more speed he demanded—and obtained.

At long last the final flask was moved and stowed away.

"That does it," the chunky leader growled with a quick look around. "Now scram, you bums! I'll be seein' you later at the warehouse. Get goin'!"

Motors humming, gears clashing, the two sedans knifed off through the fog. The chunky man waited until he could no longer see crimson tail lights in the soupy mist. Then, removing his own mask, he lumbered away on foot.

The quiet of death settled upon the intersection.

CHAPTER II

DR. ZENG TSE-LIN

TWO BLOCKS distant there stood a curious and ancient building, set slightly apart from its neighbors, although its front faced the street in a line with the other business houses in that area. The main floor was given over to commerce, as was indicated by a sign over the façade.

MANDARIN EMPORIUM

EXCLUSIVE ANTIQUES
ORIENTAL IMPORTATIONS
DR. ZENG TSE-LIN, *Proprietor*

To tourists, the establishment was just another store in Chinatown where objects of art could be bought. But actually it was the House of a Thousand Beatitudes—residence of a man whose life was devoted to the righting of wrongs and the confounding of criminals.

That man was Dr. Zeng Tse-Lin.

Strange stories were whispered about Dr. Zeng. Stories of black magic, of his superhuman strength gained through secret exercises learned while a youthful student in the remote lamaseries of Tibet, of his superlative skill with every known kind of ancient or modern weapon. Scoffers laughed at such tales, but the stories persisted all the same.

It was also said that some of Dr. Zeng's inventions had brought him great wealth; that the experiments he conducted in his mysterious laboratory amazed the most learned professors. And again there were those who disbelieved.

How, they demanded, could a man not more than thirty years old have attained such heights of knowledge? How could so young a person gain the green button of a fifth-examination scholar in China, and at the same time possess degrees in the sciences and arts from Western universities?

Yet even the most dubious outsider was forced to admit that Dr. Zeng Tse-Lin was actually a physician and surgeon of splendid skill, for he had demonstrated his abilities in the care of more than one desperately ill person here in Chinatown. Even so, the full extent of Dr. Zeng's activities could not be guessed, because he kept them well guarded. And the wildest truth of all was the fact that Zeng was not really Chinese. He was a white American whose real name was Robert Charles Lang!

Nobody suspected such a thing, not even the dwellers here in Chinatown, who considered him a sagacious member of their own race. They never knew that his parents had been affluent American missionaries, and that Zeng was born in China and had spent the first twenty years of his life there. But this was so; and it served Dr. Zeng in good stead now, in his assumption of the role of an Oriental.

It was no idle whim that motivated his chosen way of life. Ten years before, while he was in the United States completing his education, bandits incited by Japanese had murdered his parents outside Shanghai. The grim tragedy had seared its mark on Zeng's soul. Since that dark day, he had been a voluntary crusader against crime in all its aspects, masquerading as a Chinese merchant and physician, the better to give battle to the forces of evil.

Bursting with priceless antiques, the Mandarin Emporium was little more than a hobby for Dr. Zeng Tse-Lin. It kept people from guessing his real work—the tracking down of criminals. To the world at large, Zeng's sole interests were the sale of his wares and the healing of the sick.

THIS MORNING the Emporium was still unopened, its windows shuttered to the sunrise. But on the second floor, life was already stirring. Dr. Zeng had risen, bathed and breakfasted. Now, clad in rich mandarin robes, he was prepared for whatever the day might bring.

Even as he glanced toward a far corner of the lavish room, where an ancient Ming dynasty water-clock bespoke the early hour, there came the sound of a mellow gong from below. That was the front doorbell, announcing a caller. From the insistently repeated ringing, Zeng realized that it must be someone driven by an urgent impatience.

Lithely he strode across the thick Kashmiri carpet, a tall hawk of a man, with eyes like black coals glowing in the ascetic mask of his face. He opened the lid of a teakwood box resting on a carved ebony desk. He touched a switch, and on the ground-glass screen within the box there appeared the miniature reflection of a young Chinese girl.

This invention was Zeng's modification of the television principle. A selenium disc lens was concealed in the front door downstairs, its connections running to the receiving set here in the living room. Thus Zeng was able to study all visitors before they were admitted to the House of a Thousand Beatitudes.

Having quickly scrutinized the delicate Asiatic features of the girl at the doorbell, he switched off the current at the moment a towering Mongol servant entered the room.

"A woman comes, my master." The servant bowed. "She—"

"Yes. She is Lotus Loong, daughter of my friend Wu Loong, the dealer in herbs," Dr. Zeng Tse-Lin said, smiling when he saw the Mongol's astonished expression.

Such things always startled this giant Lai Hu Chow, who was under the impression that apparatus such as the television set must be a device of the devil. Not that it mattered to the huge servant, whose round moon face was marked by the scars of a hundred battles.

As far as Lai Hu Chow was concerned, his master could have sported horns and a forked tail and still his servant would have followed him, to the ends of the earth if it were necessary.

There was a bond of friendship between Dr. Zeng and the giant Mongol, a bond sealed by the years they had been together and the perils they had faced side by side.

In fact, Lai Hu Chow was one of the very few who knew the true secret of Zeng's parentage—and of his undercover career as a single-handed fighter against crime.

That unending battle Chow could understand. But he would never comprehend the sorceries of television and the like. Nor did he care. If his master did it, then it must be all right.

Now, munching vigorously on a wad of chewing gum, he blinked at Dr. Zeng.

"You already see visitor?"

"Yes, and you may show her in." Zeng smiled again.

Lai Hu Chow departed with a rolling, rakish gait caused by the fact that he wore an artificial limb from the left knee downward, having lost his leg while fighting the bandits who had slain Dr. Zeng's parents on the outskirts of Shanghai.

PRESENTLY LOTUS LOONG was conducted into the tastefully furnished room. She was dainty and diminutive, her flowerlike face marked by large almond eyes and full red lips. But the eyes were brimming with fear now, and the lips tremulous.

"Dr. Zeng," she began, "I—"

"Welcome, little Lotus. My roof is honored to shelter you. But you are troubled. Tell me just what is wrong?"

"It is—my sweetheart. The man I was to marry. Joe Quong—you remember him?"

"Well do I know him." Zeng nodded. "He is a most estimable young man and will be a great surgeon one day."

The girl's slender shoulders drooped.

"That had been my hope. But now—"

She extended an extra edition of the *Post*. Zeng Tse-Lin took the newspaper and swiftly scanned its banner headlines. A furrow creased his brow as he read:

PLASMA TRUCK HIJACKED!

INTERN KILLED, DRIVER DYING!

En route to the waterfront last night at midnight, a Bayside Hospital truck loaded with blood plasma for shipment to the British Army medical service was held up and robbed of its cargo, its driver mortally wounded and an accompanying intern shot to death.

The intern was Michael Wingate, who would soon have graduated into private practice. He leaves no survivors. The wounded driver is Joe Quong, American Chinese medical student, recently voted the most popular member of his school class.

At a late hour this morning, police were still at a loss to account for the crime. There were no clues that might point to the hijackers, and Joe Quong was unconscious, unable to give any description of the killers.

The truck's cargo consisted of nearly one thousand quarts of blood plasma, all of which was stolen. The plasma, or blood serum, had been obtained from blood donors through a process recently developed, whereby the liquid is separated from the red and white corpuscles, so that it may be used as a universal blood plasma for transfusion into any person.

Use of whole blood in transfusion can cause violent reaction and death, unless the blood types are perfectly matched. This is one drawback of the so-called "blood bank" method of storing whole blood for future transfusions. Such whole blood must be kept separated, classified as to type, and stored in refrigeration.

The new system of eliminating the red and white corpuscles produces a yellowish liquid that can be stored indefinitely at room temperature without deterioration.

When injected, this liquid is mixed with an equal amount of saline solution and helps greatly to restore the patient's strength. The method was originally adopted by the Red Cross for the use of plasma in accident cases and other emergencies, where the lapse of time required for "typing" and finding a suitable donor would result in death.

The plasma cargo which was hijacked last night had been earmarked for shipment to the British Army in the middle east by way of the Suez Canal, and would have been invaluable in saving the lives of wounded Tommies.

The police are working on two possible theories, one of them being that the theft was perpetrated by Nazi agents. Another possibility is that underworld hoodlums are responsible for the hijacking of the priceless cargo, the murder of the intern, Michael Wingate, and the wounding of Joe Quong, driver of the truck.

Greater credence is given to the latter theory, the police believing that the holdup mob may have hoped to sell the plasma back to its owners for a ransom fee. However, as yet, no such demand has been received by hospital authorities.

According to a statement issued at Police Headquarters, Quong will be questioned as soon as he regains consciousness. Meanwhile every law enforcement agency, local, state and Federal, is engaged in a relentless manhunt throughout the San Francisco area for the hijack mob and its loot.

WHEN HE had finished reading all these details, Dr. Zeng Tse-Lin tossed the newspaper aside and stared gravely at the diminutive Chinese girl, Lotus Loong.

"It is written that the lark does not visit the hawk's nest except for good reason," he said soberly. "What is it you seek of me, little Lotus? My surgical skill to save the life of the one you love?"

Her face was a forlorn mask of heartbreak.

"I fear that it is too late for even a skill as splendid as yours, Dr. Zeng," she quavered. "The doctors at the hospital say that he cannot last the day."

"So? Yet I shall examine him all the same, in order to be sure. But there is something else on your mind, O daughter of my respected friend. Perhaps it is that you wish help in obtaining revenge upon those who shot your future mate?"

She held out her small hands imploringly, like trembling ivory flower petals.

"No, not revenge. Justice!"

"Justice?"

"*Aie*, justice for Joe Quong, whom the police have accused of complicity." Tears came into Lotus Loong's almond eyes. "He must be cleared, lest he lose face even in death!"

Dr. Zeng stiffened.

"In what way has he been accused?" he asked.

"Other than himself and his friend Mike Wingate, there were but four hospital officials who knew the exact route the plasma truck would follow on its journey to the waterfront. It was a route kept secret until the final moment, for fear of a possible attack and robbery."

"Yet the attack was made. The robbery occurred."

The girl nodded dolefully.

"It seems to indicate that the truck's route was known in advance by the bandits. But the hospital authorities are above suspicion, and Mike Wingate is dead. Therefore, the police are hinting that Joe Quong was the one who revealed the information to the hijackers."

Zeng's brows drew together in a sharp straight line of jet black.

"But this is fantastic! Quong was riddled with bullets, according to the newspaper account. And would that have happened if he had been in league with the gunmen?"

"The police seem to think so. They say that perhaps Joe sold out to these hijackers, only to be double-crossed and shot to keep him from talking. But I know that is false, Dr. Zeng! Joe is honest. He would not be party to a crime. Please—can you not do something?"

Zeng Tse-Lin fully realized the importance of "face" to a Chinese. Should Joe Quong die from his wounds while under the slightest hint of suspicion, it would bring discredit and disgrace down upon the surviving members of his family—as well as Lotus Loong, this dainty girl who was to have been his bride after graduation.

This alone would have been sufficient motive to induce Zeng to enter the case. But he had an additional reason. His life was dedicated to the tracking down of the lawless, the bringing of criminals to justice. More-over, that precious plasma had been destined for the British Army, a gallant force of men battling against the savagery of the Nazi-Axis dictators.

AMERICA HERSELF now stood in danger of the Axis powers. Loss of the plasma was as ruthless a piece of sabotage as the wrecking of an airplane plant or the disabling of a munitions factory.

Americans, men and women alike, had donated their blood to make that precious serum which had been stolen. Their sacrifice must not be in vain!

Dr. Zeng took Lotus Loong's hand and pressed it.

"Have faith," he said gently. "I shall do my best to exonerate your fiancé and bring the killers to book."

"Thank you, Dr. Zeng!" she breathed. "How soon will you start?"

"At once. Perhaps, at the hospital, we may be able to revive Joe Quong enough that he can tell us what we should know."

Zeng went to a wall panel which concealed a microphone. He spoke a command to the giant Lai Hu Chow downstairs.

"My car," he said. "We have work to do." Then he added mysteriously: "The limb of armaments."

CHAPTER III

COUNCIL OF WAR

S **HORTLY BEFORE** dawn, four serious and worried-looking men had gathered around a polished table in the board room of Bayside Hospital. No sooner did they settle themselves than a newcomer quietly appeared to take the chair usually reserved for the super-intendent.

This newcomer was Captain Brian Carter of the San Francisco Homicide Squad, a compact, muscular Irishman whose ruddy complexion was in sharp contrast to his steel-gray hair and frosty blue eyes. The iciness of those piercing eyes was highly deceptive, for fiery sparks flashed there when the occasion warranted. And the gnarled hands were capable of hardening into fists like hammers.

But at present Captain Carter's manner was easy, his voice silken.

"Good morning, gentlemen," he said.

Soft overhead lights bathed the four men around the table, accentuating the haggard concern scrawled upon their faces. There was wizened little Phillip Fayne, reputed multimillionaire who had financed the hospital in its struggling days, who had been chairman of its governing board ever since, and who recently had subscribed a small fortune for the construction of a new wing.

Next to Fayne sat Wilie Wilke, fat as a well-fed toad, his wrinkled garments belying his status as chief surgeon of Bayside.

From these two men, Captain Carter's glance went toward the other two: Johann Vondrang, the skeleton-thin psychiatrist from Batavia, capital of the Dutch East Indies, who had become San Francisco's top specialist in mental disorders; and Harley Blackton, one-time Canadian lumber baron and scion of a prominent British family. Blackton had won a fortune in Canada, then settled here in the United States to spend it.

Of all the quartette, Captain Brian Carter found the company of Johann Vondrang least pleasant to endure. The tall, skeletal Batavian brain specialist had the eyes of a fanatic, the pallor of a corpse. He was obviously annoyed because he'd been called to a meeting at this early hour. Vexation twisted his bloodless lips to a sardonic grimace of dissatisfaction.

"Omit the formalities, Captain Carter," he said in a voice that rumbled like the threat of thunder. "Whatever you have in mind, let's get on with it!"

"Very good," Carter agreed, his tone a shade grimmer. "You all know who I am. You know why I'm here. Last night at midnight a Bayside truck was hijacked of nearly a thousand quarts of plasma for Britain. One of your interns got killed; the driver was mortally wounded."

"Oh, quite," came the impatient English accents of Harley Blackton, the Canadian. "Since you say we already know these things, suppose you skip the unpleasant details. My point is, why are we here now, y'see?" And he adjusted his impeccable cravat to a jauntier puff.

"I'll make it blunt, then," Carter grunted. "Somebody talked. Somebody spilled the route that that plasma truck was to take. Nobody knew this route except the driver, his intern—and you men."

Philip Fayne leaped to his feet, the wrinkles writhing in his shriveled face.

"Confound you, sir! Are you intimating—"

"I'm not intimating anything. I want to know if any one of you told the truck's route to an outsider. You can answer 'yes' or 'no' and we'll go on from there."

A chorus of growled negatives went around the table. Chief Surgeon Wilie Wilke made fat balls of his pudgy fists and waved them in the air.

"Certainly not!" he wheezed asthmatically. "Don't you think we realized the possibility of robbery? We're not morons, Captain Carter. We took cognizance of the risks involved. There'd already been too much newspaper publicity about the plasma shipment and its priceless value.

"It was like an invitation to thieves! Especially when secret agents of the Axis would be willing to pay almost any amount of money to divert such a cargo to Berlin, for the use of wounded Nazi soldiers.

"Consequently, we tried to shroud the truck's route in secrecy. In fact, we kept the route under cover until practically the last moment, before revealing it to the driver and his intern."

Carter scowled.

"Yet the news leaked out," he reminded them. "One man was murdered and another is dying."

"Then do something about it," Johann Vondrang sneered. "In Batavia the police are efficient. Are you American officers less capable? Perhaps you need a psychiatrist like myself to give you the Binet I.Q. test for intelligence!"

Captain Brian Carter reddened, but held his temper.

"I think we may have intelligence enough to know what to do, Dr. Vondrang. For instance, we have already formulated a theory."

"And that is—"

"The hijacking was carefully planned. But the shooting was incidental; impromptu, you might say. There was a crafty brain behind the job, a brain which understood the seriousness of murder and hoped to avoid it.

"Anybody who had enough imagination to plan such a theft would likewise realize that the chances of possible future punishment would be lessened, if the robbery were managed without a killing."

"But there *was* a killing, old chap!" Harley Blackton protested nasally in his affected British drawl.

"Yes, because probably either the driver or the intern accidentally recognized some member of the stick-up mob," Carter retorted grimly. "I can think of no other plausible excuse for the use of gunplay under the circumstances." Wizened little Phillip Fayne emitted a snort of impatience.

"My time's valuable! Come to the point."

"I'm trying to do just that," the police official answered temperately. "Mike Wingate and Joe Quong were unarmed when they were shot down in cold blood. Therefore, the hijackers need not have feared any physical harm from them at the moment. Then why were Wingate and Quong blasted—unless they might possibly have identified the thieves later?"

DR. VONDRANG lost some of his sneer.

"I retract my doubts as to your intelligence, Captain Carter," he rumbled. "But, granting the truth of this theory of yours, where does it lead us?"

"Everything hinges on the driver of the truck, Joe Quong," came Carter's ready answer. "He's still alive, but slipping fast. There's a chance that he was the one who sold out to the hijack mob—or that he recognized one of them.

"I'm basing all my hopes on the possibility that he'll regain consciousness before he dies. In that case, I may be able to make him tell me what I've got to know."

"You have someone constantly with him now?"

"Yes. I've posted a guard outside his room, and"—Carter's eyes softened a little—"my own niece is by the bedside."

There was pride in the homicide captain's tone when he mentioned his niece, Ann Carter. He had good reason to be proud of her. Despite the fact that she enjoyed an income sufficient for her every need, she was not content to take life easy.

Instead, Ann taught an adult night school class in Chinatown. She knew the Chinese as well as her uncle knew the inside of his pocket. He could not have selected a more intelligent and competent aide.

But the fat surgeon, Wilie Wilke, seemed to be entertaining doubts on this score.

"Why a girl for a job so important?" he demanded abruptly.

Carter's lips narrowed angrily at the implied questioning of his judgment.

"To begin with, I trust her implicitly. In the second place, she speaks the various Chinese dialects like a native. If and when Quong regains consciousness, his mind may be so fogged that he might speak in Chinese rather than English. But whatever he may say, my niece will be able to interpret it. Any objections?"

"Oh, none. None at all." Wilke's puffy cheeks reddened at the undisguised rebuke. "I'm quite sure you know what you're doing, Captain. I was merely curious."

The Dutch psychiatrist shot Wilke an enigmatic look.

"Curiosity, Doctor, can lead to embarrassment—or danger."

Brian Carter scowled, wondering what Vondrang had meant by this remark. The meeting broke up soon afterward.

All four of the board members drifted off, leaving Carter to his official job.

The sun was just rising. In another part of town, Lotus Loong was ringing the front doorbell of Dr. Zeng Tse-Lin.

CHAPTER IV

MISSION OF DEATH

LOUD CLANGOR of a telephone disturbed the empty reaches of a warehouse near the harbor. In the shadows a man stirred, left his companions and lumbered toward the instrument, lifting the receiver with a hand that looked as if it might be more familiar with the knurled butt of an automatic.

"Yeah?" he snarled.

Back came a guarded inquiry.

"Rory Maddern?" it asked.

"Sure. Lay off the monicker. The wire might be tapped."

"That is unlikely." The guarded voice sharpened bitterly. "I must say, you're a fine one to talk about being careful after the mess you made last night, shooting those two men!"

"Heck, Boss, what else could we do? That Wingate dope spotted me from one time he gimme some cough medicine at the free clinic. He'd have fingered me if I didn't bump him!"

"Quite so, my friend. But while you were at it, why didn't you make sure you finished the Chinese driver? But no! You left him alive, and now he's here in the hospital under guard—with Homicide Captain Carter's own niece at the bedside to hear anything he might say if he comes to!"

"Gee, Boss, you think that slant-eye might put the finger on me? But he wasn't the one that tabbed my map. It was the other guy, that Wingate fellow."

"Ah. But did Wingate call your name before you shot him?"

"Well, part of it. But—"

"Then the Chinese may remember it and spill it—unless you stop him first."

"You mean you want me to—"

"I think you understand what I mean, Maddern. You'll find this Joe Quong in Room Two-ten. Now get busy. And by the way, there is one other thing."

"Yeah, Boss?"

"You have that note I prepared before the hold-up. Well, I want you to leave it on Quong's chest after you—er—send him to his ancestors. And remember, if you get caught, you won't live long enough to turn State's evidence against me. I'll make sure of *that*, my friend."

The chunky Maddern shivered.

"Heck, Boss, I ain't gonna do no squealin'!"

"You will never get the opportunity, I assure you. I don't trust you that much. So if you want to save your own skin, you had better not let yourself be captured." With a grim finality, the line clicked dead.

Rory Maddern, the chunky man who had stretched himself in the street the night before to stop the plasma truck, turned on his heel and made for the warehouse exit. He stopped only long enough to procure a silenced automatic and to warn his four hoodlum companions to remain under cover within the abandoned building, where they had holed up since the hijacking.

Six minutes later, Maddern parked his black sedan in front of Bayside Hospital and entered that stately structure on his mission of murder.

Counterfeiting a casual manner, he went to the second floor and strolled, unnoticed, along a silent corridor until he had located the door of Room 210.

Ann Carter leaped into
Dr. Zeng's outstretched arms.

Even though he could not read the numerals from his vantage point
at a right-angle turn in the hallway, Maddern knew this was the room
he wanted—because a plainclothes detective stood stolidly before the

door like a statue in his shiny blue serge, scuffed square-toed brogans and ancient derby hat.

Maddern knew that his first job now would be to get rid of the homicide man. The question was, how?

He could be shot with a silenced bullet, yes. But Maddern had the typical criminal's instinctive aversion to cop-killing. When you croaked a policeman, Maddern knew, you practically assured yourself of a one-way ticket to the California gas chamber. They never let up until they nailed you.

After a moment's thought, the chunky crook hit upon a plan. There was an invalid's wheel-chair standing in the corridor a few feet beyond the plainclothes guard.

Then Rory Maddern drew his silenced gun, took aim. A lance of flame whispered at the wheel-chair, which creaked loudly and began suddenly to move under the bullet's impact.

The Headquarters man, startled, let out a sharp exclamation and turned to look at the rolling chair. That was when Rory Maddern lunged up noiselessly behind him and bludgeoned him over the back of the skull.

The detective collapsed like an empty sack. He would be dead to the world for at least thirty minutes, that was certain; long enough for Maddern to finish his job and make a clean getaway before the alarm could be sounded.

First making sure he hadn't split his victim's skull, Maddern dragged the unconscious homicide man to a broom closet and swiftly stowed him in the restricted space. Then, tense as a stalking animal, he went to the door of Room 210, pushed it open without knocking, strode stealthily over the threshold.

Joe Quong lay on a high, white bed before him, bandaged, his almond eyes closed, his breathing labored and stertorous. There seemed to be nobody else around, which suited Maddern perfectly. Once more his Maxim-silenced automatic came out. He trained it at the unconscious Chinese, and his trigger finger jerked ever so slightly.

There came a subdued gasp from Joe Quong's flaccid lips, a sudden red splotch between his closed eyes. It was finished as easily as that.

Maddern grinned wolfishly with the satisfaction of a job well done. Cautiously he took a sealed envelope out of his pocket, being careful to handle it only by its edges so there would be no condemning fingerprints.

He placed the envelope upon the corpse of the man he had just murdered, knowing that the message was a demand for one hundred thousand dollars' cash, in exchange for the safe return of the stolen plasma—the details to be arranged in a subsequent letter.

Then, on his way to the room's main door, Maddern hesitated. Suppose they discovered the killing before he made his escape from the hospital, he asked himself. Suppose he got nabbed with the death weapon in his possession. That would never do. It would spell the gas chamber for him in short order.

Better get rid of the gun, he told himself. He drew a handkerchief, wiped all trace of prints from the weapon. Next he went to an open window, tossed the automatic as far as he was able to throw it.

A PLEASED look came into Maddern's feral eyes as he saw the blue-steel .38 land in a clump of bushes across the hospital courtyard. But his expression changed abruptly to one of dismay when he heard a sound behind him.

He whirled and saw a door being opened, a door connecting this room to an adjoining one. Somebody was entering, and like a trapped rat Rory Maddern realized that his escape to the main door was being cut off. He could not possibly make it without discovery. To be found here with the body of Joe Quong would mean disaster.

He crouched low, cursing the impulse that had made him toss away his silenced automatic. With it he could have blasted his way to freedom, for he had no regard for human life other than his own. But his oaths did him no good. He was weaponless, and he was on the spot.

Now the newcomer was in full view. She was a girl—a red-haired and very lovely girl, trim and tastefully clad in a green bouclé ensemble that set off her slender figure. Her back was turned to Maddern, and she was approaching Joe Quong's bed with no apparent knowledge that anything was wrong.

This must be the girl they had left here with the Chinese driver, Maddern told himself—the girl who had been waiting to hear anything Quong might spill. She must have stepped from the room for just a moment, only to return before Maddern could make his getaway.

Why in time hadn't she stayed out another couple of seconds? Now she couldn't help seeing the brand-new bullet-hole in Quong's forehead. When she did, Maddern knew, the jig would be up!

In ratlike desperation Rory Maddern acted. Directly to his left was a white enameled table on which stood several bottles, one labeled "Ether." Quick as a ferret he yanked out a handkerchief, grabbed and uncorked the bottle, spilled pungent liquid into wadded cloth. The sound of his movement caused the auburn-haired girl to turn partially around.

Maddern seized her.

Her struggles were futile and of short duration. With the ether-soaked handkerchief pressed against her up-tilted nose and rosebud mouth, she could not avoid inhaling the fumes. A shudder racked her slender form. She went limp.

Maddern started to lower her to the floor, then reconsidered. Maybe the girl had caught a glimpse of his face, he thought. Or perhaps that cursed Chinese had regained consciousness before Maddern made his appearance and had talked to the girl. It was even possible that the girl had been in the adjoining room to telephone such information to the homicide detective.

Any single one of these possibilities would make this redhead dangerous to leave around, that was certain.

"Guess I better bump her," the chunky crook whispered to himself.

But the criminal mind is a warped and twisted mechanism. Not that Maddern had any compunctions about killing a woman. But the thought suddenly struck him that the girl might prove more valuable alive than dead.

For one thing, he was desperately anxious to learn if Joe Quong had revived enough to talk, and if this girl had phoned in anything to the police. She could be forced to tell—but not until she recovered from the effects of the ether. And Maddern couldn't stay in the hospital room that long.

HE CONSIDERED the theft of the plasma. In a way, that had been like a kidnaping. Yeah, kidnaped blood, that's what it was! Blood that was being held for a ransom payoff. So why not hold this girl for ransom, too?

The boss could enforce his demands a lot better with the girl as hostage, Maddern reasoned. Especially since she was Captain Brian Carter's niece. Carter might even be compelled to lay off investigating the case in exchange for her safety—at least until Rory Maddern collected his pay and took it on the run for Mexico and points south!

Having reached this illogical conclusion, Maddern acted on it. Swiftly he stripped a blanket from the bed and wrapped the girl in its folds. Then he lifted her, carried her out of the room

Lai Hu Chow plunged through the burning warehouse.

Just beyond the door stood the wheel-chair at which he had fired a silent bullet to distract the attention of the plainclothes guard a few minutes before. The sight of it gave Maddern a fresh burst of inspiration.

"What a break!" he muttered as he dumped his inert burden into the chair.

Then, as calmly as a hospital orderly taking a convalescent patient out for an airing, Maddern rolled the rubber-tired vehicle forward.

He met nobody on the slanted ramp that led to the ground floor. And nobody stopped him or paid him any attention as he wheeled his unconscious captive out to the street. It was like shooting fish, he chuckled to himself.

Gaining his parked black sedan, he bundled the girl into its spacious tonneau. Then, pulses racing, he slid under the steering wheel and kicked the starter.

The car leaped ahead, careened around the next corner and vanished.

CHAPTER V

THROB OF BLOOD

FOR ALL his wisdom, Dr. Zeng Tse-Lin could not possibly have divined what was taking place at Bayside Hospital while he himself was en route there. But he did feel an intuitive uneasiness as he sat in his own car with Lotus Loong beside him and the giant Lai Hu Chow up front, driving. It was a curious and premonitory sensation, not at all pleasant.

He noticed that Chow slowed the sleek limousine's pace a trifle as they sped past a cheap twenty-four-hour movie theater, whose marquee was emblazoned with posters of the latest wild west picture. If Chow had one failing, it was lurid movies. Whenever the big Mongol got the chance, he would slip off to enjoy the vicarious thrills furnished by two-gun Hollywood cowboys.

"No time for that now, Chow!" Zeng spoke quickly. "There is need for haste. You may look at the pictures another time."

He settled back alongside Lotus Loong as his giant servant-companion fed more gas to purring cylinders. Even so, the added speed was destined to prove fruitless, as Zeng discovered when at last he left Chow with the parked car and took Lotus Loong into Bayside Hospital. The whole building seemed to be in a state of subdued confusion, with nurses and interns scampering aimlessly about corridors swarming with uniformed police.

Lotus began to tremble.

"Dr. Zeng—my heart tells me something has happened—to Joe—"

"It is written that the reed breaks in the wind, but oak is strong. Your father is an oak and you are his daughter. Whatever lies ahead, little Lotus, you must bear up." And Zeng Tse-Lin increased his lithe stride to a partial lope.

Gaining the second floor, he saw a cluster of people clotted around the door of a private room, chattering excitedly. He made for the group with Lotus Loong pattering along behind him. Then he saw someone he knew.

"Brian!" he called. "Captain Carter!"

A heavy-set figure detached itself from the others and came lumbering forward, hand outstretched.

"Zeng Tse-Lin! God, am I glad to see you! I—I—" His thick, gruff voice faltered. Then he regained control of his emotions. "Murder's been done under my very nose—and Ann has been kidnaped!"

The words were so many knives entering Dr. Zeng's heart. This homicide captain was his best friend on earth, barring only Lai Hu Chow. With the single exception of the big Mongol, Carter was the only man in all San Francisco who knew that Dr. Zeng was really a white American.

But it was not the homicide detective's grief alone that stabbed into Zeng Tse-Lin's soul. It was the news that Ann Carter had been abducted—Ann Carter, the captain's niece and the girl Zeng secretly loved!

But he permitted no betraying emotion to cross his impassive masklike face. That would have been un-Oriental, and Zeng was supposed to be a Chinese of the mandarin caste. In consequence, he could only narrow his hotly glowing eyes.

"Tell me the details," he murmured.

"There's little I know to tell—as yet."

CARTER PLUCKED him by the sleeve, led him into the room with Lotus Loong again following. They closed the door and the Chinese girl uttered a wild, sobbing cry.

"Joe—d-dead!"

"The oak does not break," Dr. Zeng reminded her gently.

Then he studied Quong's corpse on the bed, and he knew that murder had struck but recently, for the wound was wet with bright fresh crimson.

From the body of the slain driver, Dr. Zeng's grave gaze lifted to include a group of four men who stood ill at ease on the far side of the room. A raised, interrogatory eyebrow brought perfunctory introductions from Captain Brian Carter.

"These are the members of the hospital's governing board, Dr. Zeng. Chief Surgeon Wilie Wilke. Johann Vondrang, director of psychiatry. Harley Blackton, who organized the drive for plasma to be shipped to the British Army. And Phillip Fayne, one of the original founders. Gentlemen, let me present Dr. Zeng Tse-Lin."

"In his medico-surgical capacity?" came an inquiry from Vondrang, the cadaverous Dutch Batavian psychiatrist.

"No," Carter said. "As an independent investi—"

"A man of medicine, merely," Zeng cut across his friend's words. "I came to learn if I might be of assistance to one who was mortally hurt—the driver, Joe Quong. But I see that I am too late, which is regrettable." He turned casually to Carter. "You were about to tell me what happened?"

"I wish to God I knew!" the homicide official answered bitterly. "Even the detective I left to guard the room can't tell me who knocked him unconscious—because he didn't get to see the fellow's face before the blow was struck."

"And Ann?"

"I'd left her here to catch anything Quong might say if he revived. Meanwhile I held a short meeting with these directors, without learning anything. Twenty minutes later, in the main office, I was informed that Ann had called me on the phone; left a message for me to come upstairs and see her right away."

"Ah," Zeng purred. "Then Quong *had* talked."

"So I assumed. I started for this room, but I was delayed a moment or so—"

"May I inquire what the delay was?" Zeng interposed.

"Dr. Vondrang met me in the hall and asked my personal opinion of the plasma hijacking."

Dr. Zeng looked at the tall, cadaverous psychiatrist.

"Yes, I stopped him," he snapped. "What of it? No harm in a man asking questions, is there?"

"None, sir. It is written that the wise scholar learns by asking, provided he seeks not his knowledge from a fool. And my friend Captain Carter is certainly not that." Zeng again turned to the official.

"You then proceeded upstairs to this room?" he continued.

"Yes—only to find Quong murdered, the guard knocked out and Ann gone. Nobody seems to have noticed anything unusual," Carter's tone held embittered self-condemnation, "yet a killer managed to come here, do his job, leave a message and kidnap my niece.

"Now I don't know what Quong might have told Ann, and she herself is gone, perhaps dead! It's all my fault for exposing her to such a risk!"

ZENG'S FACE betrayed no emotion. "There was a message?"

"A demand for one hundred thousand dollars for the return of the plasma, details to be furnished later. But no hint of a ransom for Ann. Which leads me to believe her abduction was as impromptu as the gunplay last night."

While the detective captain talked, Zeng Tse-Lin's sharp gaze was darting about the room of death. Suddenly his hawklike nose flared at the nostrils and he strode toward a corner, picking up what appeared to be a stenographer's notebook, such as he knew Ann Carter used when teaching a business course at her adult night school class for Chinese.

The book had been partially concealed under a white-enameled metal table, as if it had been dropped there or deliberately thrown.

Captain Carter visibly tensed.

"What's that you've found, Zeng?"

"Something of importance, I think."

Zeng Tse-Lin kept his voice steady, although his heart was thunderously hammering. He flipped the notebook's pages, studied a series of neatly jotted pot-hooks.

"This is Ann's shorthand report of some things that Quong said."

"Can you read it? For God's sake, tell me!" Carter begged.

Zeng nodded, having already translated the regular scrawls. He spoke the words aloud, pretending to be reading from the notebook but actually watching everyone in the room.

"—man lying across car tracks—we stopped the truck to investigate—man wore mask—had gun—more masked men jumped us—Mike Wingate recognized—main hijacker—started to say his name—but was killed before he—could get it out—sounded something like—Rory Mad—Rory Mad—"

As he pronounced the partial name, Dr. Zeng Tse-Lin narrowly inspected the group before him—without their knowledge. He did not watch their faces, however. Experience had taught him that some men, even under great stress, can successfully hide all outward manifestations of emotion.

Zeng himself was a past master at the art of maintaining an immobile demeanor despite his inner feelings, and he knew that he was not alone in this ability.

But there was one thing that no man could control, and that was the rate of heart-beat during excitement or fear. In consequence, Zeng riveted his secret attention upon the throats of the men before him. He watched their jugular veins!

CHAPTER VI

KILLER'S REWARD

DR. ZENG'S unnoticed scrutiny was rewarded—but in a highly puzzling way. To the ordinary, untrained eye there might have been no hint of clue in the attitudes of Phillip Fayne, Harley Blackton, Wilie Wilke and Johann Vondrang. But to Dr. Zeng Tse-Lin, schooled in the observing of almost imperceptible details, there was a sign that could not be misinterpreted; a sign which, for the moment, baffled and bewildered him.

Vondrang, the Dutch Batavian, was the only man of the four whose pulse rate did not increase at mention of the words Rory Mad. The heartbeats of the other three board members had definitely accelerated!

Was it possible that the partial name had been recognized by this trio? The question daggered at Zeng's brain and he did his best to answer it. First, it was difficult to tell about the wizened little millionaire, Phillip Fayne. His pulse possessed an irregular quality symptomatic of a cardiac condition, Zeng realized. An enlarged heart, in all probability; a system loaded with digitalis. This might account for the jerky pulsations at the elderly man's throat.

And as for Wilie Wilke—well, the chief surgeon was so fat that his neck was a bulge of flesh. And what Zeng had assumed to be an increased throbbing of the jugular might easily have been a muscular twitching of fatty flesh. It was impossible to render a positive decision here.

But in the case of Harley Blackton, there was no room for doubt. The Canadian's pulse revealed a hyper-adrenal increase in tempo, the result of some emotion desperately inhibited. A glint of satisfaction leaped into Zeng Tse-Lin's dark eyes.

"Does the name Rory Mad mean anything to any of you gentlemen?" he purred.

Ann Carter

All four board members shook their heads in unison.

"No," they said as one.

Zeng turned to Captain Brian Carter.

"I fear I can be of no further use here, sir. It is obvious that you must conduct your investigation elsewhere. I have work of my own to do. With your permission, I shall take my departure."

Then, politely shaking hands with himself in the accepted Chinese fashion, he left the room and strode along the corridor. He could sense Carter's look of amazement following him, and he regretted a situation that might make the homicide official believe that he had walked out on him. But this could not be helped—at present.

When he gained an alcove, though, Dr. Zeng's manner changed from casual indifference to alert readiness. He stood stock-still, as if waiting.

Presently he saw Captain Carter pass by his hiding place, with Lotus Loong clinging miserably to his arm. Then came the fat surgeon-in-chief, Wilie Wilke. He, too, passed Zeng's alcove without looking in, as did the wizened Phillip Fayne a moment later.

But at the sound of still more footfalls, Zeng Tse-Lin flexed his long, spatulate fingers and chanced a swift glance into the hallway. The Canadian was approaching—the former lumber baron, Harley Blackton.

"Got you!" Zeng breathed.

He darted forward from his place of concealment, seized the dapper millionaire in his steel-hard clasp. Blackton scarcely knew what was happening to him. Before he could attempt to struggle, a thumb found certain nerves at the nape of his neck, nerves which would cause paralysis when properly pressed. Blackton sagged and was yanked into the deep alcove like a sack of grain.

WITHIN THE dank and tomblike depths of a musty waterfront building many blocks distant, Rory Maddern paced nervously. His jumpiness was not caused by the fact that he had put a bullet through Joe Quong's brain a little while ago, but because he had taken a woman captive.

The red-haired girl was still unconscious from the ether she had been compelled to inhale. Now that Maddern had time to think things over, he doubted the wisdom of the course he had taken. Like many another small-caliber crook, he was lacking in the essential quality of initiative. He needed leadership, the kind of leadership furnished at present by the man who had engaged him to hijack that valuable cargo of blood plasma.

Right now Maddern found himself desperately wishing for instructions from his boss. How else was he to know what disposal to make of the kidnaped girl? Maybe he should have killed her outright instead of bringing her here to the hideout, he told himself uncertainly. Maybe he'd catch the devil for doing what he had done—

As if in answer to his unspoken fears, there came a sudden pounding through the dim reaches of the structure—a rhythmic knocking, two raps, then three, then one, spaced with the regularity of a secret code.

Maddern lunged forward to answer the summons. He opened a heavy door and blinked in the early morning sunlight.

"Gee, boss, am I glad to see you!" he whispered.

The newcomer smiled thinly.

"Hello, Maddern. I understand you have a prisoner here."

"Yeah, boss. A jane. I guess trouble's poppin' at the hospital, huh?"

"Rather. In fact, that hardly describes the excitement—thanks to your stupid bungling!"

"Huh, boss? You mean I shouldn't have snatched the wren? But heck, she ankled into that room after I bumped the Chinaman! I had to do somethin' before she spotted me!"

"Quite so, Maddern. But instead of leaving her unconscious like the plainclothes man, you brought her here to the warehouse. Very smart!"

"But boss, I thought—"

"You think too much! My idea was a simple hijacking with no repercussions, no murders. Everything meshed, even to the use of this abandoned building as a hideout. The British would have been glad to ransom the plasma—at no cost to the hospital.

"But *you* had to mess it up! One kill necessitated another. Now you've abducted the niece of the toughest cop in town without even bothering to look around for any message she'd left behind."

"Message?" Maddern paled.

"A shorthand notebook with Joe Quong's statement, including enough of your name to make trouble!"

"Ouch! What are we gonna do?"

"We must move fast. A fellow named Zeng Tse-Lin is interested in the case. There's something about the man that gives me cold chills. If he learns your full name and your connection with this warehouse, a raid is inevitable. They'll recover the plasma, your mob will have to scatter and we won't collect a cent."

"Then let's get the stuff outa here!"

Maddern shivered.

"My idea precisely. Are your men here?"

"Sure, boss."

"Well, go and tell them to load the plasma flasks into the power launch hidden under the end of the wharf. Ferry the flasks to that derelict houseboat in the Tide Flats—the green-painted boat I told you we could use in emergencies. Nobody owns it and nobody will think to look there."

"But listen, boss. The launch ain't quite big enough to hold all them flasks at one time."

"Then tell your boys to make two trips," the other man said impatiently. "Load as many as possible the first time and come back for the rest."

"What about the dame, boss? You want us to take her, too?"

"No. Leave her here. Either the cops will find her or she'll get away by herself, eventually—after the gang clears out. By that time, it won't matter. Now go give your orders and come back here to me."

Maddern moved quickly. Presently he returned.

"The boys is gettin' started, boss. Now what?"

"Only this, Maddern. There's the little matter of your pay-off."

Rory Maddern looked surprised.

"But I thought you couldn't slip me no dough until after you got that hundred grand for the plasma," he said.

"I'm not thinking of a cash pay-off, my friend." The man's voice grew harsh. "You've done a lot of bungling. Too much. You have become dangerous to me. I dislike bunglers. Therefore—"

Maddern's eyes widened in fear when he saw the gun.

"Hey—nix!" he bleated.

Then a great white sheet of flame seemed to erupt inside his brain, consuming his thoughts, leaving black ashes of nothingness.

CHAPTER VII

DEATH'S WAREHOUSE

HAVING SEIZED Harley Blackton at the mouth of that second-floor corridor alcove at Bayside Hospital, Dr. Zeng Tse-Lin drew the Canadian deep into the recessed place and lowered him to a sitting posture, with his back propped against the white-tiled wall.

It would be several minutes before the former lumber baron would regain his senses, Zeng knew. Those minutes were like snails crawling across the clock-face of eternity. He berated himself for the extra pressure he had applied to Blackton's vertebrae. He bent over his captive, as if to revive him by the sheer force of will-power.

"I must be placid," Zeng kept telling himself. "The green-button scholar maintains poise, even as a rock stands against the beating of a surf."

He watched narrowly for the first indications of returning consciousness on Blackton's florid face. It was almost fifteen minutes later when the Canadian's eyelids fluttered. This was the sign for which Zeng had been waiting. It meant the time was ripe for his dangerous experiment.

That this experiment would subject Harley Blackton to peril, perhaps even death, Zeng knew full well. It was a thing he had been taught by an ancient Buddhist wise man in Lhassa years before, and his preceptor had warned him he must never employ it except in direct necessity.

"My son," the ancient one had gravely told him, "I entrust to you a secret which, if misused, could cause irreparable and sometimes fatal injury. Promise me that you will not so misuse it."

Captain Brian Carter

Zeng had promised. In the years since, he had never even considered employing the method in his work. Whether a man be innocent or guilty of crime, no surgeon had the right to endanger that man's life.

But now, for the first and last time in his career, Zeng Tse-Lin prepared without hesitation to risk everything upon the skill of his trained hands. Had there been more time available, he would have sought some means less perilous. But Ann Carter had been kidnaped, might even now be facing some form of ugly death.

Weighing her life against Harley Blackton's, there could only be one decision. The chance must be taken! And if he were to fail, Zeng knew that he himself would stand guilty of murder.

He rallied his courage. He must not fail. He would not! He leaned over the Canadian, and his sensitive fingertips located an almost imperceptible cranial depression under which was located that part of the brain known as Broca's convolution, the center of speech at the posterior section of the third left frontal area.

Anterior to this lay the volition lobe of the lumberman's cerebrum. Sharp pressure here, swift yet carefully measured, caused the retired Canadian's jaw to go slack. He opened his eyes; glassy eyes, vacant as the windows of a tenantless house. He moaned.

Zeng's heart pounded. He had succeeded! He had done his job, and Blackton still lived!

"Listen, Harley Blackton. You will obey me in all things. Do you understand?"

BLACKTON ANSWERED in a voice like that of a dead man, without inflection, robbed of all interest.

"I understand. I obey."

"Good. You will withhold no secrets from me. You will tell me the truth, no matter what I ask."

"Yes, the truth."

Zeng leaned forward.

"Who held up the plasma truck and murdered Wingate? Who killed Joe Quong in his bed this morning, left a message demanding ransom for the plasma, and kidnaped Ann Carter?"

"I do not know."

The answer was unfaltering. Zeng Tse-Lin realized that he was being told the truth. For Blackton, in his present state of suspended will-power, was incapable of giving utterance to a lie.

Inwardly seething, his American instincts for direct action battling against his Oriental training in calmness, Zeng tried another question.

"When part of a name was mentioned a while ago you seemed to recognize it. What was that full name and who is the man?"

"Rory Maddern," came the ready response. "I tried to conceal my knowledge of him because once, in Saskatchewan, I served time for forgery—and Maddern was my cellmate. Recently he came here to San Francisco, threatened to expose my past unless I agreed to help him. Now that he may be mixed up in a murder, I am afraid to admit any connection with him."

"Ah! But you *are* connected. Are you the one who informed him of the plasma truck's route?"

"No. I only got him a job as watchman in an unused warehouse on the waterfront that was inherited by Wilie Wilke not long ago."

Zeng Tse-Lin's throat tightened.

"Wilke—the head surgeon? He owns a warehouse and hired Maddern at your request?"

"Yes."

Zeng stepped back, his eyes glowing like hot coals. The fat, slovenly Wilke might or might not be at the bottom of all this. Owning a warehouse and employing a watchman named Rory Maddern certainly placed him under serious suspicion. But it was written that a man does not leap from a precipice without first measuring the distance of his fall. Zeng knew the wisdom of not fixing Wilie Wilke's guilt until he had obtained more positive proof.

He knew also that he had no time to hunt for the corpulent surgeon now. Ann Carter must first be found, rescued. Everything else must wait.

Again Zeng leaned over Harley Blackton.

"Where is this warehouse?" he demanded. "Give me the address. Quickly!"

The Canadian mumbled a wharf number which Zeng engraved on his memory in figures of fire. Then, lithe as a cat, Zeng whirled and sprang from the alcove into the corridor—where he impacted bruisingly against a skeleton-thin individual whose corpse-white face was alive with sardonic curiosity.

"Dr. Vondrang!" Zeng exclaimed.

The psychiatrist from Batavia smiled mockingly.

"Your methods are most interesting, Dr. Zeng Tse-Lin. I confess admiration—and a lively desire to know which nerves you depressed to render Blackton unconscious, as well as those that paralyzed the centers of volition.

"The process is new to me, obviously much more effective than the so-called truth serum, scopolamine. I think it is a method that you should give to the world for humanity's benefit."

ZENG NARROWED his eyes impatiently.

"Sorry, Doctor. I have no time for eavesdroppers."

"Ah. Then it must be true, what Captain Carter almost admitted about you. That you are an investigator of crime, in addition to your other activities."

Vondrang's lips split in a bloodless smile of amusement.

"Very good," he said. "I wouldn't dare stand in the way of a manhunter." He stepped aside, his expression enigmatic.

Zeng Tse-Lin was already on his way toward the staircase. Like a steady pulse beating within his brain was the name Ann Carter—Ann Carter—Ann Carter! It hammered at his consciousness and drove him like a goad, made him forget everything except the urgent need to find her, save her from jeopardy.

In his churning mind there was little doubt that she had been taken to the warehouse owned by Wilie Wilke. The pattern meshed perfectly. What better hideout could a hijack gang want than such a place? What better cache for the stolen plasma? What better prison for a feminine captive who had been abducted because of what she might know—or guess?

Nor did it occur to Dr. Zeng that he should stop and ask the help of Captain Brian Carter or any other member of the police force. To Zeng Tse-Lin, this was something personal: a task he must accomplish himself, with no other help than Lai Hu Chow, his giant Mongol servant and faithful friend.

But Zeng had a bitter surprise in store. For when he gained the street outside the hospital, he saw nobody but Lotus Loong standing there. Chow was gone and so was Zeng's limousine.

The Chinese girl turned.

"Dr. Zeng—"

He leaped toward her.

"Where is my car? And Chow?"

"I do not know. I came here, thinking to wait for you, but I saw nobody."

Zeng gripped her arm.

"Listen, little Lotus. You recall that motion picture theater we passed on our way here? Where Chow slowed our speed, so that he could look at the posters? Well, I am afraid he has gone there; it is a habit of his. A regrettable habit, at times. And I am in need of him.

"Therefore, you must go to that theater. Find him. Bid him come at once to this waterfront warehouse." Zeng repeated the address which Harley Blackton had given him.

Lotus Loong nodded her understanding.

"But you—how will you reach that place?"

Zeng's eyes had already fastened on a shiny new sedan of expensive make, resplendent in two tones of blue at the curb.

"It is written that the eagle heeds not the wind which bears his flight, so long as he gains his destination," he said.

Then Zeng hurried toward the car he intended to use. He glanced casually at the printed white certificate that was wrapped around the steering wheel column, such as California requires on all automobiles. On the line above the space designated for legal ownership, Zeng read the name of the registered owner.

"Phillip Fayne!" he muttered with a scowl.

WITHOUT QUESTION, the wizened little hospital board chairman would be hopping mad at having his car taken away, with no more by-your-leave than a finance company would grant in a job of repossession.

But Zeng dismissed such thoughts. He had something more important to consider. The sedan's ignition was locked, the key was missing.

No such comparative triviality could stop Zeng Tse-Lin now. His fingers darted under the instrument panel, found certain wires and ripped them loose. He twisted a pair of them together, bridging the electrical system. He knew he had done no genuine damage; for when he heeled the starter a silk-smooth motor responded with warm, purring life. The oil pressure functioned, the generator showed full charge.

Then— "Hey, you! That's Mr. Fayne's car!" somebody shouted asthmatically. "Stop, thief!" And a corpulent figure came down the hospital steps in a bouncing waddle.

It was Wilie Wilke, chief surgeon. Directly behind him ran Phillip Fayne, bristling with anger. But Zeng had no time to parley with the elderly board chairman. Lotus Loong, still at the curb, could explain. Zeng shifted gears, gunned the motor.

Five minutes later he was threading his way through a growing, early-morning clatter of truck traffic in the shipping district. Presently he swerved into a narrow, unused side street which came to a dead end at the waterfront. Brakes squealed in front of the abandoned warehouse Zeng was looking for.

Here there was no traffic, no sign of activity. Zeng slid out of the sedan and loped toward the main door of the structure. A dank smell of seaweed and rotting fish drifted to him from the wharf end of the building, where barnacle-encrusted pilings thrust into the harbor.

Lapping water whispered around those pilings like gossiping tongues, and wisps of fog curled upward in sunshine not yet an hour old as Zeng reached the warehouse entrance.

The heavy, tinder-dry portal was big enough, when opened to accommodate the passage of the largest motor truck. But now it was closed and bolted by means of a huge padlock. There was a smaller door set into the large one, for pedestrian use. But this too was fastened securely, evidently secured from within.

That gave no pause to Dr. Zeng Tse-Lin. Without hesitation he wrapped his spatulate fingers around the padlock's hasp on the big door. He pulled. The sinews of his wrists stood out like cords and sweat formed upon his forehead. Then, under the inexorable leverage of his muscular strength, the entire padlock came away with a rusty shriek, hasp and all.

Zeng shoved the ponderous portal inward and went hurtling over its splintery threshold. Then, as his eyes narrowed catlike in the gloom, he saw something that drew him up short.

There was a silent figure sprawled on the floor to his left, near a pile of refuse and waste paper. It was the body of a chunky man whose skull had been tunneled by a bullet.

CHAPTER VIII

TRAPPED

MURDER HAD come but recently to the chunky man, Dr. Zeng Tse-Lin realized as he made a swift examination of the corpse. There was still warmth in the abdominal region, and the limbs were not yet entirely cold. *Rigor mortis* was absent, giving added proof that the killing had occurred within the past thirty minutes.

Zeng's gaze now fell upon the slain man's belt buckle, a hammered silver bauble with the initials R.M. worked into the metal. The two letters seemed to ring a bell within his mind.

"Rory Maddern?" he whispered. "I wonder!"

Then he heard two sounds which galvanized him into a spurt of activity. The first was an unsteady chuck-*clank*-a-plock, *clank*-a-plock, such as a speedboat's idling motor might make while drifting toward shore, especially if that motor had a defective connecting rod bearing in need of an overhaul. The second sound was a low, whimpering moan—a girl's muffled cry of fear.

"Ann!" Zeng Tse-Lin said intuitively.

He sprinted into the gloomy depths of the warehouse, his hypersensitive ears attuned to catch any repetition of those feminine whimpers.

Presently he heard them again. They seemed to issue from a tiny officelike cubicle to his right, a small room before which lay a neat pile of flasks resembling thermos bottles.

"The plasma flasks!" Zeng breathed.

But there were only a few. What had become of the rest?

He had no time to ponder that problem now. He knew that he had found the hideout of the hijackers, located part of their priceless loot. And he could guess that the major portion of that booty had only recently been spirited to some other hiding place, for fear of discovery here.

What had aroused that fear? The partial mention of Rory Maddern's name in Joe Quong's before-death statement at the hospital, obviously. The criminal behind this desperate game must have realized his jeopardy and had acted to checkmate it. This might also explain the murder of Rory Maddern himself here in the warehouse—if that chunky corpse really was Maddern.

It was but a six-minute drive from the hospital to the waterfront. Among those present in Quong's room at the time Zeng had read Ann Carter's shorthand notes, one individual had seen the jaws of a possible trap closing in.

This man had rushed here to the warehouse to order the plasma removed, at the same time killing Rory Maddern, either for disobedience or bungling. Then, to establish an alibi, the murderer might have returned to the hospital. But who was this individual?

Something kept telling Dr. Zeng that he ought to know the answer, that the essential clue had already been revealed to him. But the solution was elusive. For Zeng could think now only of Ann Carter and her peril. The girl's muffled moans led him onward with nerves taut as the strings of a violin.

Zeng gained the door of the tiny cubicle from which those moans issued. He smashed at the woodwork with his battering weight, burst into the unlighted space to see a vague form huddled on the floor. A reek of ether was sharp pungency in his nostrils as he went to his knees by the girl.

"Ann!" Zeng exclaimed, his voice reverberating in the stillness.

THEN TWO things happened, almost simultaneously. First, the warehouse underpiling shivered slightly at the impact of a boat's hull floating to a mooring. Then a burst of orange flame spewed thunderously at Zeng Tse-Lin from the doorway of the little room in which he had found Captain Brian Carter's niece.

The slug seared a hot furrow of agony across Zeng's scalp, bludgeoning his thoughts to chaos. He toppled across Ann Carter's slender figure. The last thing he heard was a door slamming shut, like the closing of a portal upon his consciousness.

Then his mind blanked out.

The four mobsters in the power launch made their craft fast under the wharf by means of bow and stern lines. Then they went up a rickety ladder, opened a trap-door in the floor of the warehouse and entered the dank, gloomy structure just as the sound of gunfire echoed from up front.

This gun-sound marked an attempt to murder Zeng Tse-Lin. But, of course, the four gangsters could not know that. They knew only that their leader, Rory Maddern, had sent them to ferry a cargo of plasma flasks away from the warehouse, and had not accompanied them on the journey. Now, upon returning for the last small load, they heard a pistol shot. It threw them into incipient panic.

For an instant they froze, contemplating hasty flight. But the firing was not repeated. Hearing nothing but rapidly receding footfalls and the sharp slamming of the front door, one of them decided to investigate.

"Maybe Rory's in trouble. We better go take a gander."

Cautiously they moved through the musty reaches of the structure. Then another of the quartette pointed.

"Look! It's Rory! He's been bumped!"

They all sprang forward to Maddern's corpse, stared at it in puzzled bewilderment. But they had an uglier surprise in store for them, a surprise they discovered when flickering yellow light grew brighter over at the side of the building.

"Fire! The whole joint's afire!"

It was true. Someone had struck a match to several piles of waste paper and refuse rags stacked along dry wooden walls. The tindery woodwork was already crackling, blazing, the flames leaping and spreading across rotten rafters under the whipping draft of breeze that seeped through cracks and interstices. Crimson glow suffused the scene; yellow clots of smoke curled down from the roof like so much poison gas.

Two of the hijack mob lunged desperately toward the barred front door. They never made it. A heavy beam, loosened by walls bulging outward, dropped suddenly upon them, crushing them like bugs under a giant foot. Their death screams echoed weirdly over the rising crescendo of spreading flames.

The remaining pair raced toward the waterfront end of the building.

"A doublecross!" one panted. "The boss croaked Rory and tried to wipe us all out, so he could keep the plasma dough for himself! Nobody else coulda got in here to touch off the joint!"

He gained the trap-door, clawed it frantically open, dropping down the ladder to the moored launch with his companion close behind.

They got the engine going, cast off the bowline and engaged the clutch. Clattering, the boat surged outward—only to halt with a lunging shudder at the end of the fastened stern line, which the two crooks had forgot to cast loose.

Momentum sent one of the pair overboard. His companion, believing the action voluntary, dived after him. Together they stroked desperately toward the safety of the adjoining pier.

CHAPTER IX

INFERNO

A VOICE, PLEADING, sobbing, brought Dr. Zeng Tse-Lin swimming back to dazed consciousness. He blinked, and his eyelids were sticky with the red wetness of his own blood. "Ann!" he choked.

Soft hands touched him, tried to raise his head.

"Zeng— Oh, thank God, you're alive! I—I thought—"

His temple throbbed fiendishly where that bullet had creased the flesh. In his nostrils there was a new, sharp acridity. Not the odor of the ether Ann Carter had inhaled, but the smell of smoke—wood smoke, drifting into the cubicle in an ever-increasing pall.

With the knowledge, Zeng sat upright, fighting the dizziness that assailed him.

"Ann! The warehouse is afire!"

"Y-yes. I know. We—we're done for, Zeng."

She wanted to tell him that it didn't matter, that she was content for it to end this way, as long as they faced death together. For a long time Ann had known that she cared for him, even as she knew he felt the same way about her.

Not that Zeng had ever spoken of his true feelings. But then Ann thought his silence was a natural reticence, because of the racial barrier which separated them.

She was not aware that Zeng Tse-Lin was of her own nationality, and not a Chinese. She could not guess that Zeng hesitated to reveal his love only because his life was dedicated to warfare against crime, that he could not bring himself to ask her to share the dangers involved in that struggle.

To Ann, as to the world at large, Zeng was an Oriental. That was the only thing that kept them apart. And now, with death so imminent, she felt that she could no longer allow it to remain as a barrier.

"Zeng," she whispered as he scrambled off the floor and helped her to her unsteady feet. "Zeng!"

He was staring out of the little room, seeing the surging red holocaust all about them.

"Yes, my dear?"

"Whatever happens, I—I want you to know I—"

Zeng Tse-Lin sensed what she was going to say, and his heart leaped in exultation at the knowledge that she cared for him. But before her words could actually be spoken, there came a startling interruption.

From the street end of the structure a wild, savage cry sounded—a war-cry which Zeng recognized. Then came a shattering noise, as of blazing woodwork being smashed inward. Next through the crackling inferno of flames that leaped and licked up front like a foretaste of doom, a giant figure appeared.

Clothes smoldering, scarred moon-face blistered and jaws vigorously munching a wad of gum, the huge newcomer lumbered toward Zeng Tse-Lin and Ann Carter.

"Lai Hu Chow!" Zeng shouted.

The big Mongol grinned as he spanked sparks from his garments.

"You bet. Lotus Loong give me message in movie show, say Chow meet you here in warehouse. Chow find place on fire. Lots people outside, firemen, cops. Fools try to stop Chow. Chow tell them get quick out of way.

"You say Chow meet you in warehouse, by golly, Chow meet you in warehouse!" Then he looked around. "Bad stuff. Have hard time to get out."

"Not if you obeyed my orders," Zeng snapped. "Remember I reminded you about the limb of armaments?"

"Sure. You say that before we start from House of Thousand Beatitudes, to go to hospital. Chow not forget."

THE GIANT sat down on the floor, drew up his trouser leg—and unfastened his artificial limb.

He had a supply of many such metal legs, each constructed so that it could be used to conceal equipment which his master might need. This particular one was practically a miniature arsenal. It was packed with two .28 automatics, a keen-edged knife and a grenade of Zeng's design.

It was the grenade that Zeng grabbed.

"I'll also take one of the guns. You take the other. Now replace your limb, Chow."

As the giant obeyed, Ann Carter pressed close to Zeng.

"What are you going to do?" she breathed.

"Concussion quenches flame, temporarily," he replied. "It is a method sometimes used in fighting oil well conflagrations. A charge of TNT can stop such flame the way a sword cuts a rope. Down on your faces!"

Zeng pulled the hand grenade's firing pin mechanism, hurled the explosive toward the wharf end of the warehouse.

It struck the blazing rear wall. There was a deafening blast. The wall erupted outward. For a single instant the flames were blown to extinguishment as embers rained from the sagging roof.

In that instant, Zeng Tse-Lin gathered Ann Carter in his arms, raced for safety with Chow at his heels. They gained the wharf proper just as the fire made a closing curtain behind them. Wind-borne sparks seemed to reach out in an effort to drag them back.

Their peril was still acute, Zeng realized. They dared not leap into the harbor, for Ann could not swim. Neither could Chow, impeded as he was by an artificial metal leg.

Then Zeng saw salvation below. A motor launch was bobbing in the water immediately beyond the pier, its propeller churning up sudsy froth but the craft itself making no headway, because its stern line was made fast to a piling.

There was something familiar about the clatter of its engine—chuck-*clank*-a-plock, *clank*-a-plock—as if it had a bad connecting-rod bearing. Where had Zeng heard that sound before?

Suddenly as he scrambled over the dockside and descended a pier support, he remembered. This was the launch that had hit the warehouse pilings just before the shot was fired that had rendered him unconscious. There was no mistaking the queer unrhythmic noise of its power plant.

Zeng was at water level now. He grabbed for the boat's stern line, hauled with all his strength. And as he tugged against the pull of the propeller, he wondered why the launch had been brought here to this wharf. Inch by stubborn inch he drew the craft backward; and just as stubbornly his scalpel-sharp mind attacked the question before him.

A logic as concise as algebra gave Zeng Tse-Lin the answer. There had been but a small number of plasma flasks left in the warehouse. Most of the loot had already been spirited away. This launch, then, must have been the conveyance used for that purpose. Why else had it come to this pier, except to take on a final load of flasks?

The veins stood out like cords on Zeng's temples as he fought to drag the power boat toward him. He had both legs and one arm around the piling, and his task had to be accomplished with a single hand. Above him, Ann Carter and Lai Hu Chow were in danger of being engulfed by wind-whipped flames at any minute. Zeng tugged mightily, summoning the last reserves of his splendid strength, and the launch drew closer.

As he struggled, Zeng Tse-Lin's mind likewise fought with another sort of problem: a problem of reconstruction. Had it been someone from the power boat who had tried to kill him? No; because he remembered hearing the craft grate against the pilings just a few seconds before that shot was fired.

There hadn't been time for a gunman to disembark, come into the warehouse and fire that shot.

Consequently the murder attempt had been perpetrated by someone else—someone already inside the structure. Again Zeng had a feeling that he should know this person's identity; that the essential clue had been revealed to him—

He gave a final tug, and the launch was directly beneath him. He leaped into it, shut off its ignition. The motor clanked to a stop.

"Ann!" he called. "Chow! Jump!"

The girl came first, landing in a heap in Zeng's arms. Then the giant Mongol dropped, just as a section of the blazing warehouse collapsed over the spot where the two of them had been standing on the wharf's upper deck.

CHAPTER X

BLOOD HUNT

IT WAS almost impossible to force a path through the crush of humanity gathered in the dead-end street where the warehouse holocaust raged. The police had established deadlines with taut-stretched ropes, but still the throng pressed forward to hamper the firemen at their work.

Fat lengths of fire hose throbbed with water pressure like so many cobras, under the impulse of pump engines jammed wheel to wheel. A fire tower smashed a blasting stream down upon the burning building's roof.

A concerted gasp went up from the crowd as a portion of the doomed structure collapsed outward, to engulf and demolish a shiny, two-toned blue sedan parked directly in front of the blaze.

Over by a Bayside Hospital ambulance, Dr. Zeng Tse-Lin was impatiently denying any need of medical attention.

"Take care of Miss Carter and Chow," he told an intern. "I assure you that I require no first aid."

This was true enough. For Zeng's magnificent vitality had withstood all the rigors he had undergone, even to piloting a balky launch to the adjoining pier and clambering up a ladder hand over hand, with Ann Carter in his free arm.

Now, standing before the flaming warehouse which had almost become his funeral pyre, Zeng found himself confronted by three of the four members of the hospital board: Johann Vondrang, the cadaverous Dutch Batavian brain specialist; Phillip Fayne, wizened little board chairman; and pudgy Wilie Wilke, chief surgeon as well as owner of the warehouse now blazing like a bonfire.

Only the Canadian, Harley Blackton, was missing. For the very good reason, no doubt, that he had not yet entirely recovered from the effects of the cranial pressure which Zeng had applied upon his lobes of volition. But the presence of the other three men might not have been as strange as it appeared—if the reasons they had already given were to be believed.

Fayne, for instance, claimed that after Lotus Loong informed him of Zeng Tse-Lin's destination, he had angrily hailed a taxi in which to pursue the borrowed sedan, only to find the warehouse already ablaze upon his arrival after a traffic delay.

Wilie Wilke's story was that he had come to see the fire because the structure belonged to him. This sounded plausible enough on the surface, it had to be admitted.

The dour Vondrang maintained that he had merely been actuated by curiosity in coming here.

"After all," he added in his sepulchral voice, "I am rather interested in your activities, Dr. Zeng. Particularly after witnessing a certain experiment you conducted at the hospital—and your behavior afterward."

Zeng permitted himself to smile thinly at this veiled allusion to the ordeal he had forced Harley Blackton to undergo. But the smile was only to conceal a sudden surging elation in his veins. Of the three board members, one was lying. Zeng was sure he knew which one it was.

In brief, he had the answer to his riddle. At long last, he was remembering the one essential clue which had eluded him! He could guess which man had followed him to the warehouse, shot him and then set the place afire.

NOT THAT he could prove it now. Nor did he dare repeat the Blackton experiment, for fear of a possible fatal consequence. Moreover, even if such an experiment proved successful, that kind of testimony under duress would not stand up in court.

To catch his man, Zeng realized that he must bait and set a trap. The springing of this trap would depend entirely upon his own ability to follow a certain clue he had recently noted.

The risk had to be taken, he told himself grimly. Within the hour he had to search for and find a blood cargo—a cache of stolen plasma. Should he fail, the trail would come to a dead end. The plasma would be forever lost; Joe Quong and Mike Wingate would go unavenged.

Zeng Tse-Lin faced the three board members, but addressed his words to Johann Vondrang.

"I appreciate your interest in my methods, Dr. Vondrang. Perhaps some day I may fully elucidate them to you. But now I must beg to be excused. You see, within two hours I think I shall have located the hijacked blood serum—even though the perpetrator of the crime escapes capture."

He turned away. Phillip Fayne and Wilie Wilke tried to stay him, but Zeng waved them aside with no additional explanations.

He made for the Bayside ambulance, where Ann Carter was undergoing first-aid treatment while the giant Chow hovered anxiously nearby. Seeing that Ann was in good hands, Zeng whispered a command to his huge servant.

"Shield me while I commit a theft, Chow. Then be ready to slip away with me quickly. We have a trackless hunt before us, a hunt upon waters where no trail exists!"

Then, concealed by the Mongol's bulk, Zeng Tse-Lin surreptitiously pulled a medicine kit from the ambulance—a black leather bag with Wilie Wilke's name stamped upon it in letters of gilt. It was the typical doctor's medical kit.

From it Zeng abstracted two small vials, which he swiftly put in his pocket before returning the bag to the ambulance. None of this was noticed by the ambulance intern, who was busy attending Ann Carter's needs.

Now, covered by the milling throng, Zeng and his big Mongol shadow quickly left the scene of the warehouse fire and made for the adjoining wharf on the next street. Here they had moored the power launch in which they had escaped the blaze. Zeng lowered himself into the craft. Chow followed. They shoved off.

Over the engine's dissonant clatter, Chow asked a question.

"Where in devil we go now?"

"It is written that wisdom and daring remain when all worldly things have departed. It is likewise written that the beasts of the earth, the birds of the air and the creatures of the sea can make no move without leaving some record of that movement behind them. Observe, please, the woven rope buffer upon the counter of this launch."

CHOW BLINKED and stared.

"Hemp to keep hull from scraping paint when bump something." He munched his gum. "So what?"

"You have failed to notice the flakes and scales of faded green paint adhering to the hemp," Zeng smiled indulgently. "But I saw them when first we employed this craft in escaping the warehouse flames."

As he spoke, he flecked off one of the scales with a fingernail and powdered it between thumb and forefinger.

The Mongol looked puzzled.

"Is old paint."

"Yes. More than that, it is marine paint such as is used for ships in salt water. But it has been exposed to many suns and rains. It comes from a hull long neglected. Perhaps abandoned. A derelict."

"Chow dumb like anything. No catch on."

"We can be fairly positive," Zeng said, "that this launch was used to ferry away the stolen plasma flasks. The scales of green paint tell us that the launch recently contacted some other vessel of ancient vintage—a vessel at one time painted green.

"Now behold another circumstance. There are traces of mud and marsh grass upon our bow, proof that this launch was recently in shallow water while heavily laden. When its cargo was removed, the launch floated higher, leaving those traces fully visible above the water-line."

"You make heads and tails of puzzle?"

"I think I do. I believe the plasma cargo was transshipped to some green-painted derelict resting upon mud bottom in very shallow water. Where do we find such shallows and marsh grass in this region? The Tide Flats! And it is there that we shall seek our goal! More speed, Chow."

Zeng Tse-Lin leaned forward tensely, oblivious to the giant Mongol's amazement at his master's startling powers of deduction.

It was a ten-minute run, perhaps a shade less, to the Flats. With wide-open throttle the launch surged forward, its speed unhampered by heavy cargo. Presently it hove within view of a veritable Sargasso of abandoned hulks careening drunkenly on the mud bottom.

Here were ancient and dismasted windjammers, for the most part, with an occasional barge or splintered scow exposing its wooden bones to the morning sun.

And then Lai Hu Chow extended a pointing, excited finger.

"Is houseboat. Is green—or used to be!"

Zeng shoved the tiller hard over. The launch swept in a lazy half circle into the marshy shallows, and at reduced speed picked its way daintily along a natural winding channel, which led almost to the houseboat in question. A mud bank sucked at the keel of the launch, almost stopped it. But a burst of power freed it of the slippery muck and sent it forward, to touch gently against the rotting houseboat's hull.

Battling his nervous tension, Dr. Zeng flaked a scale of faded green marine paint from the derelict hulk. He compared it with the traces on the hempen buffer of his motorboat.

They matched! There could be no question of it. But there was always the risk of coincidence. More than one abandoned craft might display the same kind of color of paint.

THERE WAS but one way to make sure. A rope dangled over the side of the houseboat. Zeng seized it, swarmed upward. He gained the tilted deck with Chow at his elbow. A weird feeling of loneliness assailed them both, the feeling a man always gets when he boards a vessel long deserted.

The odor of ancient caulking, festering in the heat, arose to mingle with the smells of decayed marsh growth, rotten mussels, the sharp pungency of salt water and the stench of foul bilge.

Cautiously Zeng made for the superstructure and entered a dank main cabin. His eyes were glowing like live coals.

"Look, Chow," he whispered. "The plasma flasks!"

There they were, stacked in disorderly rows, pile after pile of them all around the littered debris of the cabin. And then Zeng knew intuitively that his star was rising, that he had drawn trumps in this perilous game of wits and death.

CHAPTER XI

PLASMA PAY-OFF

LAI HU CHOW chuckled as he saw the flasks.

"Chow catch on! You find stuff. Now we wait for robber to come."

"Right—and wrong," Dr. Zeng corrected his giant companion. "When I voiced my expectation of locating the serum within two hours, it was to warn the criminal that he must move swiftly, if he hoped to forestall me.

"As yet, he does not suspect that I know his identity. And with so much at stake, I think he will appear here very soon, with a plan to move the plasma again to still another hiding place. And I shall be waiting for him. But not you, Chow."

Chow wrinkled his forehead.

"What the devil! You not send Chow away?"

"I must. Your job is to remove the motor launch, lest my quarry notice it when he comes to the houseboat. Seeing the launch, he would know that someone is aboard the derelict. He might leave without coming aboard."

"Is good sense," the Mongol admitted reluctantly. "But Chow no like the idea all the same."

Zeng smiled.

"Be gone. I am competent to take care of myself. Meanwhile, you are to notify Captain Brian Carter of the circumstances. Bid him hover over the bay in an amphibian plane, keeping watch on this houseboat. I shall signal him when I am ready for him to alight and take a hand."

With obvious unwillingness, Chow descended to the launch and headed it away from the scene. Meanwhile, Zeng Tse-Lin busied himself with a certain task.

From one of the two small glass vials he had abstracted out of Wilie Wilke's medical kit, he sprinkled crystals of scale iodine all about the deck of the houseboat. Next, he dampened the flakes with carefully sprinkled droplets of ammonia from the second bottle. The ammonia evaporated quickly. When the job was finished, Zeng retired to concealment inside the cabin.

Moments dragged by endlessly, it seemed to Zeng Tse-Lin. Now that he had time to consider everything, he wondered if he had pursued the proper course. True, he had found the stolen plasma. But suppose the man behind that theft decided it was too dangerous to attempt any further transportation of the flasks. Suppose the clever devil dropped the whole ransom scheme, thereby forever shielding himself from conviction for his crimes.

"No!" Zeng told himself. "He *must* appear!"

Even as his mind whispered the words, he heard the sound of oarlocks. Somebody was approaching in a rowboat!

The small craft grated against the houseboat's hull. A voice drifted up to Zeng.

"Sink this dinghy, pal. We won't want him to get no tip-off that we're aboard and waitin' for him."

"Yeah, I guess you're right," was the growling answer.

Dr. Zeng, waiting in the cabin, felt a sinking sensation in his middle. *Two* men were boarding the derelict houseboat—and neither one of them was the individual he had hoped to snare! He saw his carefully laid plan going awry, and he cursed himself for his failure to take this possibility into consideration.

Without doubt, the newcomers were members of the hijack mob. But they were unimportant by comparison with the man who had schemed the plasma theft from the outset.

Well, it was too late to rearrange the final trap now. Affairs would have to take their course. For it was written, Zeng knew, that the wise man never seeks to alter the inexorable path of fate.

Already the two men were clambering up on deck. Their footfalls sounded on the sun-bleached planking. At once there came a series of sharp, crackling noises, like many small firecrackers exploding.

This was the ammonia-sprayed scale iodine—which detonated in miniature when trodden upon. Zeng had hoped thus to startle the chief criminal, so that he could pounce upon the man with the advantage of surprise.

He considered tackling the two lesser crooks now, for he knew from their startled oaths that they were panicked by those tiny underfoot explosions. But just as he was about to make his move, something stopped him.

One of the men on deck let out a snarl.

"Stand still! I don't know what this crazy stuff is—but it's noisy. And here he comes in a motorboat!"

Purring exhaust-sound came to Zeng inside the cabin as a power launch drew near the houseboat. At the same time, from somewhere overhead, there seemed to come another drone—the steady thrum of an airplane motor. That might be Brian Carter. Chow could just possibly have had time to gain shore and communicate with the homicide official.

Not that it mattered. Zeng Tse-Lin knew that he, and he alone, must handle the situation now. Bungling would cost him his life, he realized. Therefore, he must not fail!

He heard the power craft bump the derelict. He heard someone scrambling up the dangling line. And then he heard the voice of one of the two mobsters.

"Okay, Boss. Lift the flippers," said the voice.

"Why—why—hello, boys! Good thing you're here. We've got to move that plasma again. Fellow named Zeng Tse—"

"Stow it. We ain't helpin' you do nothin' except croak, see? We figure you bumped Rory Maddern and touched off that warehouse to get rid of us, so you could collect all the ransom dough. And the fire got two of the guys—but we made our break. Now comes the pay-off. *Your* pay-off!"

Automatic in hand, Dr. Zeng stepped from the cabin.

"On the contrary," he purred. "It will be a pay-off for all of you. Especially for you—Mr. Phillip Fayne!"

The wizened little board chairman of Bayside Hospital spun around with a squalling snarl of rage and fear.

"You!"

"Quite so," Zeng answered, his black eyes glowing. "I knew you would be the one to come here. You are the man who engaged the hijack mob, the one who informed them of the route to be taken by the plasma truck."

"Why, confound your soul, I—"

"It had to be one of the four board members," Zeng went on relentlessly. "It also had to be the same man who murdered Rory Maddern in the warehouse. Harley Blackton was innocent of that crime. You see, I was conducting an experiment upon his mind at the approximate moment Maddern was being shot. The experiment cleared our Canadian friend, in any case."

"But—but—"

ZENG CUT him off imperturbably.

"Dr. Vondrang was likewise innocent of Maddern's murder," he went on. "Vondrang from the first had eavesdropped upon my experiments with Harley Blackton, beginning with the moment I rendered Blackton unconscious. Hence, Vondrang could not be the man who drove to the warehouse and murdered Maddern."

Fayne grew apoplectic.

"You cursed, meddling—"

"That left Wilie Wilke and yourself," Zeng continued imperturbably. "Wilke might have been the culprit, for he owned the warehouse which was the mob's hideout. He denied knowing Maddern, although in truth he had hired the fellow as a watchman.

"But his denial might have been based upon a desire to stay clear of a nasty mess. And the use of his warehouse could have been your scheme. So that suspicion would fall on Wilke if anything went wrong."

"You can't prove—" Fayne sputtered.

"I already had proof when I borrowed your new sedan," Zeng said. "Although I confess I did not realize its significance until later. Your car itself was the proof.

"Its motor was warm, indicating recent use. The use you made of it in driving the six-minute distance to the warehouse, ordering the plasma removed—and then shooting Maddern. After that you went back to the hospital to establish an alibi, trusting that nobody had noticed your absence."

Fayne choked with rage.

"That's not—" he began.

Zeng smiled without mirth.

"Not conclusive, no. But your registration certificate added certainty to my suspicions, after I remembered it. The certificate listed you as *registered* owner, but a finance corporation as *legal* owner. Therefore, you were either purchasing the car on deferred payments or had borrowed money on it.

"This indicated your lack of funds. A curious circumstance, Fayne, for a reputed millionaire who had subscribed a small fortune for the future construction of a new hospital wing."

"Listen—"

"Consequently," Zeng concluded, "I assumed you to be guilty. Impoverished, unable even to make good your promised gift to the hospital, you saw a chance to recoup your fortunes by extorting one hundred thousand dollars' ransom for the blood plasma.

"You knew Wilie Wilke had a vacant warehouse, with an ex-convict watchman named Rory Maddern in charge. You employed Maddern to round up a hijack mob. Later, you murdered Maddern. Still later, you followed me to the warehouse, shot me, set the place afire.

"Of all the suspects, Fayne, you were the only one with both motive and opportunity. As I told my man, Chow, it is written that wisdom and daring remain when all worldly things have departed. Your worldly wealth had vanished—but you had criminal wisdom and crooked daring. Knowing this, I set my trap for you. And now you're finished."

But Zeng was wrong.

With the desperate fury of a cornered wildcat, Phillip Fayne squealed at the two mobsters beside him.

"It's the gas chamber for all of us unless we do something—make our getaway—"

The gangsters who a moment before had planned Fayne's death now saw that their fortunes lay in battling on his side. Heedless of Zeng Tse-Lin's automatic, they lunged forward. The wizened little ex-millionaire came with them.

TO DR. ZENG, physician and surgeon, the oath of Hippocrates was a way of life, a creed to be observed and maintained at all costs. Healing was his profession, not the meting out of death. Nor was it his duty to act as judge, jury and executioner. He wanted justice done—but legally.

He threw aside his gun. He met his attackers with flailing fists that struck with the swiftness of cobras and the power of hydraulic rams. His knuckles connected with a snarling hoodlum mouth. The fellow moaned through the crimson that spurted from his shattered lips, sagged and went down in an inert heap.

But his gangster companion was already at Zeng's throat as Phillip Fayne hovered close by, gun drawn, seeking an opening to put a bullet through the investigator who had tracked him down. Out of the tail of his eye, Zeng saw this danger even as a savage knee burrowed into his abdomen.

For an instant he gasped as a sickening wave of pain shot into his very soul. The mobster was throttling him now, trying to trip him backward. Zeng's fingers attempted without success to find certain nerves at the nape of his adversary's neck, nerves he could press to render the man unconscious.

The gangster was too slippery, too agile and he outweighed Zeng Tse-Lin a good twenty pounds. He used that weight with cruel viciousness in an effort to slam Zeng to the deck.

Once that happened, Fayne could use his pistol. That would be the end of Dr. Zeng Tse-Lin.

"Let him go!" the wizened board chairman was screeching. "Give me a shot at him!"

Then Zeng remembered his many lessons in judo, that higher branch of ju-jutsu. He allowed his legs to go limber under him. He sagged. His enemy smashed him downward. And then, as Zeng's shoulders crunched on the deck, he uncoiled himself, raising his feet for leverage under the mobster's middle.

"Now!" he breathed.

It was like an explosion, an eruption of superb strength that sent the gangster sailing through the air in a flat trajectory. His big body crashed against Phillip Fayne in a scrambling tangle that smashed both men against the rail. Fayne screamed hideously at the torture of three fractured ribs. He doubled over, sobbing out curses. But his hoodlum henchman did not scream. The man's thick skull had impacted heavily against the planking. He was all washed up.

Zeng Tse-Lin got to his feet, picked up the automatic he had discarded. Not that he needed it. The battle was finished—and it had been won without bullets.

Nearby, an amphibian plane was landing in the shallows and skimming toward the houseboat. From its cabin came Captain Brian Carter's roaring bellow.

"Zeng—are you okay? Zeng! Answer!"

Zeng went to the rail.

"Come and pick up a cargo of rats, my friend. Later you may send for the plasma. Nearly all of it is here, safe."

"But you—what about you?"

THE HOMICIDE official was coming over the side now. His eyes narrowed when they took in the identity of the criminal whom Dr. Zeng had captured: Phillip Fayne.

But Carter asked no questions. If Zeng had made the capture, that was enough for the homicide captain. He knew that his friend did not make mistakes.

"What about you?" he repeated.

Zeng Tse-Lin smiled wearily.

"It is written that the man who fights against the forces of evil is armed with invisible might. I am quite all right, my friend. But I am anxious to return to the House of a Thousand Beatitudes. Perchance a customer will come to purchase a trinket—or a patient, seeking treatment.

"What sort of proprietor is it who will neglect his establishment of business for too long a time?"

And Dr. Zeng calmly lowered himself into Phillip Fayne's motor launch for the journey home.

III

SINISTER HOUSE

CHAPTER I

FLAME-GHOST

FLAMES LICKED like greedy dragon tongues at the night sky over San Francisco's Nob Hill, where a landmark of the city's fabulous past was being destroyed. Through billows of rising smoke and milky swirls of fog the red glare deepened, while an insistent crackle of burning timbers made eerie accompaniment to the throb of pumpers slamming useless tons of water into the conflagration.

Everybody realized that the ugly, old Vorbling mansion was doomed. The firemen knew it as they battled the blaze, and so did the newspaper reporters who watched the unequal fight. Yet nobody was particularly sorry to see it go. For the structure, though it might be a landmark, was an eyesore as well—a rococo and tenantless relic of the ornate Eighties, with all the architectural blunders of that artificial era.

Acrid fire-fumes stung the nostrils of Jimmy Calvin, staff photographer on the *Morning Globe,* as he jockeyed through the crowd for a more favorable position from which to focus on the holocaust. Snapping his Speed Graphic and then making the customary "protection" shot with a minicam, he thought of the mansion's somber history. He recalled the story of the Vorbling family curse, and the legend of the restless Vorbling ghost.

Not that Jimmy Calvin believed in such supernatural tales. But in conjunction with this fire, they would make banner headlines in tomorrow's *Globe.* Especially if his pictures turned out well. That was the thing he had to concentrate on.

He saw an opportunity for an unusual angle shot and seized it. For the moment, nobody stood guard at the base of the fire tower from whose top a smashing stream of water was being aimed into the ill-starred residence. Jumping at the chance, Calvin swarmed up the tower until he was on a level with the third floor of the house. Sparks drifted around him as he triggered a close-up with his press camera.

There was a lance of flame and Jimmy Calvin pitched forward on his face.

And then, when he automatically switched to the minicam for a covering shot, he saw something that brought a choked cry of amazement to his lips. Directly before him was an attic window. And framed in that window he beheld a bearded, haggard face staring out at him with the most agonized expression he had ever seen on a human.

FOR A split instant Jimmy Calvin couldn't believe his own senses. The Vorbling mansion was vacant. It had been vacant for a decade. No one, not even a caretaker, had lived in it since the violent death of the second Pieter Vorbling. Yet there could be no doubt about it—a man was in the attic, looking out hopelessly at the *Globe* photographer.

Even as Jimmy Calvin mechanically clicked his minicam, an angry bellow reached him from the street far below.

"Hey, you! Climb down out of there! Who gave you permission—"

It was a battalion chief roaring through a sawed-off megaphone. But Calvin needed no such irate command to bring him scrambling down the tower. He was already on his way, slipping and sliding in swift descent. He gained the pavement, pivoted to face the furious fire department official.

"Save the harsh words for later, Chief," he panted. "There's somebody up there in the top floor of the house, trapped. I saw him through a window!"

"You're either crazy or plastered, Calvin. Nobody's been in the place for years. Get back past the lines before I call a cop and have you pinched."

Jimmy Calvin stood his ground, obdurately.

"I know what I saw. I'm telling you there's a bearded guy—"

At that very moment, fingers of flame burst through the tindery roof and leaped skyward, swirling, stabbing crimson gashes in the fog and smoke. The roar almost drowned out the sound of Calvin's protests.

The battalion chief made a grim mouth.

"There she goes! The whole works will cave in pretty quick, now. I couldn't send a rescue squad in there even if I believed you. I'd be guilty of murder."

"Murder's the right word!" Calvin snapped, even though he realized the fire official was acting for the best. "You're deliberately letting a man die!"

"Look, Jimmy," the chief said gently. "You've just made an honest mistake. If there were a bearded guy up there, why doesn't he smash the window and call for help? At least we could use the net."

The logic of this left Jimmy Calvin without an answer. But somebody behind him had an explanation ready.

"What you probably saw, young man," a voice quavered, "was the ghost of Pieter Vorbling the First."

For no sane reason, the words tightened Calvin's scalp. He swung around to face the speaker, a gnarled and wrinkled old man whose stooped shoulders were enveloped in a voluminous and ancient opera cape, and whose rheumy eyes held a weird look of fanaticism. He himself had the appearance of a wraith from the past—a ghost talking about a ghost!

His parchment lips made deep seams around a smile as he saw Jimmy Calvin's eyes widen.

"It's quite all right, young man. I didn't mean to startle you. I'm Geoffrey Warren, senior partner in the law firm of Warren, Foxxe and O'Harra."

This didn't mean anything to the newspaper photographer, and his expression said so.

"I've handled the affairs of the Vorbling family through two generations," the oldster continued, "and my father before me was the first Pieter Vorbling's attorney. So I ought to know everything there is to be known about this mansion. And I can assure you it is unoccupied—except by the ghost." He turned to a chunky, younger man standing beside him. "Isn't that right, Michael?"

The chunky man turned and grinned mirthlessly.

"I wouldn't care to be quoted as believing in haunts. But if there is a ghost, I don't envy him. I was in the place a few days ago on a routine checkup—and if ever there was a spooky house, this was it! Certainly there was nothing in it to attract a prowler. It would have been warmer for a tramp to sleep outside than in any of those musty old rooms."

"You made a routine inspection?" Jimmy Calvin asked.

"Yes," the chunky man said. "I am Michael O'Harra. Mr. Warren's junior law partner." He gestured toward the oldster in the opera cape.

Even as he identified himself the roof of the Vorbling mansion collapsed in chaotic flames, sending fountains of sparks spewing upward.

"Well, that's the end of it," the battalion chief growled. "If anybody was in there he's dead now."

Puzzled and uneasy, Jimmy Calvin started down the hill toward where he had parked his car well below the fire lines. He was in a hurry to get to his office, and develop his films. Somehow he could not forget that face he thought he had seen at the attic window. Deep in his mind a vague sense of recognition was stirring, as if at some time in the past he had looked upon those bearded features before—or a picture of them.

He wondered if the old attorney, Geoffrey Warren, might be correct in his claim that the apparition had been the ghost of Pieter Vorbling I. If so, the face would not appear on Calvin's exposed films. He couldn't take pictures of a specter. But if the negatives should reveal that bearded visage, Jimmy Calvin would have irrefutable proof that a living man had been in the doomed residence.

Reaching his car, the *Globe* cameraman shifted his Speed Graphic to his left hand and fumbled for his keys. He was so intent upon opening the locked coupé that he failed to see the two men who furtively trailed him down the Mason Street grade, fixing masks upon their faces as they closed in.

At the last instant, some sixth sense warned Jimmy Calvin and he turned, swinging. He had no chance. A blackjack bludgeoned him across the skull with sickening concussion, drove him to his knees. He tried to support himself on all fours, tried to shove himself upright. Another bruising smash felled him, this time for keeps.

As if from a vast distance away he heard a voice snarling:

"Don't sap him again. Bust the camera and let's get outa here!"

Then a heavy foot crashed down upon Jimmy Calvin's Speed Graphic, reduced it to splinters. Through a surf-like beating of pain that throbbed in his ears, the photographer heard his assailants fading off in the fog, leaving him semi-conscious and too stunned to move or call out for help.

CHAPTER II

UNFINISHED BUSINESS

A **VACANT AND** dismal house, weather-beaten and scabrous
from lack of paint, was across the street from the fire-gutted
Vorbling mansion. And as the flames from the doomed structure died
down, a shadowy figure skulked toward this dilapidated and wretched
residence. He used a key on a rusty side door lock to let himself in.

With a flashlight he probed the gloom, located a steep staircase
leading to the cellar. Scarcely had he descended when a bell jangled
shrilly. From a dusty shelf he lifted a telephone; spoke in guarded tones.

"Did you stop him and destroy his cameras?"

Back came a panting voice, as if the speaker had just walked rapidly
up a steep hill.

"Cameras? There wasn't but one. We fixed that."

"You stupid fools, he used a minicam for protection shots! I saw him.
Go back and finish your job, you blundering idiots!"

From a pay station phone two blocks away, two men presently emerged
and pelted back down Mason Street in chastened haste. But when they
reached the spot where they had attacked Jimmy Calvin, all they saw
was the tail-light of the photographer's coupé vanishing around the
Sutter Street intersection.

Cursing as they realized their quarry had escaped, they hailed a cab
and directed the hacker to take the quickest route to the *Globe* Building,
hoping to intercept the cameraman there. But although they speedily
reached the newspaper office and lurked in front of its entrance more
than an hour, they caught no glimpse of Jimmy Calvin—for he had
decided not to return to the place of his employment.

Instead, he had carried his problem to the only man in San Francisco in whom he had implicit confidence.

That man was Dr. Zeng Tse-Lin.

Deep in the heart of Chinatown lay the headquarters of this mysterious individual, in a building set slightly apart from its neighbors. The
ground floor was a store, above whose entrance a sign proclaimed:

MANDARIN EMPORIUM

EXCLUSIVE ANTIQUES
ORIENTAL IMPORTATIONS
DR. ZENG TSE-LIN, *Proprietor*

But Jimmy Calvin was not interested in objects of Asiatic art. He parked his car on Grant Avenue and walked the short, silent block lined on either side by pagoda-style buildings which, by day, teemed with trade. Now they were dark and deserted, as was the Mandarin Emporium itself when Calvin thumbed the bell button.

He wondered if Dr. Zeng had already retired. The speculation was groundless, for Zeng was a man who did with very little sleep.

Upstairs in the living quarters on the second floor, the tall and hawk-like Zeng Tse-Lin had been reading an ancient Tibetan scroll. Now he looked up at the sound of the deep-throated door gong, his black eyes rapierlike in their intensity.

He arose, his long, lithe body clad in a rich mandarin robe. Crossing the opulently furnished room, he opened the lid of a teakwood box resting on an ebony desk.

Inside was a small reflecting device, blank at present. But when Zeng's clever fingers touched a switch, the ground glass screen glowed to life and disclosed a miniature image of Jimmy Calvin down at the front door.

This was just one of Zeng's many inventions, an adaptation of the television principle which enabled him to study his visitors before admitting them. In Chinatown, the home of Dr. Zeng was known as the "House of a Thousand Beatitudes." But to those who had glimpsed some of its inner mysteries it was more like a house of scientific magic.

SEEING CALVIN and noting the rumpled condition of the photographer's clothing, the bruise above his left temple, Zeng turned and addressed his giant Mongol servant, Lai Hu Chow.

"Go to the door, O friend of my boyhood and my manhood," he instructed. "You will find a newspaper photographer waiting—one Jimmy Calvin. Conduct him to me."

The huge Chinese servitor blinked at his master with the surprise which always showed on his otherwise impassive and moonlike features when Dr. Zeng identified a visitor in advance of actual appearance. Lai Hu Chow knew that Zeng Tse-Lin possessed powers not given to ordinary men. But how these powers operated was a riddle he did not attempt to fathom. Secretly he had a notion—though he never mentioned it—that Dr. Zeng had occasional bargains with the devil.

A bearded face was staring from the attic window,
with an agonized expression.

Not that it mattered. The giant Chow had never known the meaning of fear. The scars of a hundred battles marked him as a warrior. He had even lost a leg as a result of an encounter with the Japanese bandits who had brought death to Zeng's parents, back in China.

Small wonder, then, that there should be a fast bond of friendship between these two men who had faced countless dangers side by side. Small wonder that Chow would have linked arms with Satan himself, had his master commanded it.

As for Zeng, he trusted the huge Mongol as he trusted few other men. In fact, Chow was one of the few persons who knew the truth of Zeng Tse-Lin's parentage—that he was in reality a white American whose baptismal name was Robert Charles Lang!

Even the doctor's Chinese neighbors supposed him to be of their own race. But while it was true that Zeng had been born in China, his mother and father had been affluent American missionaries who had given their lives to the development of that distant land. They had been murdered in their prime by invading Nipponese during a cowardly attack outside Shanghai.

That foul deed had occurred while Zeng himself had been in the United States, finishing his education. Prior to this, he had absorbed everything that the Chinese could teach him. He had studied in the remote lamasery of Central Asia and had been admitted to the secret lores no other white man had ever explored.

Then, in America, he had graduated from the best technological universities and medical schools. As a result, he was a great doctor and a master surgeon; a scientist whose knowledge encompassed myriad fields.

To the wealth inherited from his slain parents he had added another fortune from his amazing discoveries and inventions. The scientific books he had written were standard texts in more than one college, and his methods of gymnastic exercise far outstripped anything taught at home or abroad.

Rich beyond avarice, he had the strength of ten men—and the learning of a hundred. He could have been a leader in any path of life he might have chosen. But because his parents had been killed by criminals he had elected to utilize his vast talents in a never-ending war against crime. This was the grim vengeance he had pledged his murdered father and mother.

The Mandarin Emporium was both a hobby and a shield to conceal his true career. Few realized this. Jimmy Calvin, the man now ringing

Zeng's doorbell, however, was among that few. And Calvin was evidently in need of assistance.

THEREFORE LAI HU CHOW bowed to his master's order and went lumbering from the room, his gait awkward and rolling as a result of the artificial leg he wore. Presently he returned with the *Globe* photographer in tow.

Zeng greeted his guest in Oriental fashion by shaking hands with himself. Calvin had no inkling that he was other than what he appeared to be—a Chinese of the mandarin caste, a scholar entitled to wear the coveted green button despite the obvious fact that he was barely thirty.

"You do my poor dwelling a great honor by gracing it with so illustrious a presence." Zeng's voice was sonorous, resonant. "Be seated, that I may offer you a cup of most inferior tea."

Jimmy Calvin, all his life a San Franciscan, was thoroughly familiar with the Chinese habit of self-disparagement. He knew that Zeng's politeness called for an answer in kind, but he was too excited to indulge in formalities. He waved them aside with an apologetic gesture.

"I've got a problem for you, Zeng. It is one that I'd hesitate to present if I hadn't been at Police Headquarters this afternoon and heard you mention the name Vorbling."

No hint of expression registered on Zeng Tse-Lin's ascetic countenance, for he had schooled himself never to display surprise under any circumstances. Yet Jimmy Calvin's words touched a sentient chord deep within him. It was like the ringing of a hidden and warning bell.

"Yes," he said. "That name was spoken. Captain Brian Carter of the police and I were discussing the strange disaster which overtook the Vorbling yacht. What is your interest in the matter, my friend?"

Calvin quickly told him about the fire on Nob Hill—and the face he had seen at the attic window. He sketched in his conversation with old Geoffrey Warren and the younger Michael O'Harra, including their insistence that nobody could possibly have been in the doomed mansion.

"Except maybe a ghost, according to Old Man Warren," Calvin finished. "And I don't believe that."

Dr. Zeng smiled slightly. "It is written that the wise man does not know what he believes, but that a fool is always positive. And you are no fool, Jimmy."

"Thanks. I suppose you're trying to tell me I shouldn't be too sure it was a real face I saw. All right. Maybe I dreamed it. Then why did two guys trail me to my car, blackjack me and smash my camera—unless they figured I had a picture of that face?"

"Did you have such a picture?" Zeng asked sharply.

"Yes."

"And it was destroyed?"

"The one in the Speed Graphic was. But I always make a protection shot with a minicam, in case of accident. And they overlooked that!"

"Excellent!" Dr. Zeng breathed. "Come."

He led the way upstairs to his own elaborately equipped photographic laboratory. He blacked out the darkroom except for a single ruby light which gleamed like the eye of a dragon. He took Jimmy Calvin's minicam and unloaded it, prepared the spool of negative for dousing in a developer bath.

AS HE worked, he spoke crisply.

"Do you know anything of the Vorbling family history, Jimmy?"

"A little. The first Pieter Vorbling came to California in the gold rush of Forty-nine, didn't he? Struck it rich, I understand."

"There is more to it than that," Zeng replied as he dipped the film in and out of the developing solution. "Vorbling fared as well as most of the early argonauts, but he was not satisfied. Around Eighteen-sixty he turned to hard-rock mining. Employed Chinese labor. He held his coolies in virtual slavery, even to the point of mounting armed guards over them."

"So that's how he founded his fortune!"

"Quite so. Then one of the laborers, an elderly Cantonese, died from a beating Vorbling gave him. Before he passed to his ancestors he called down a curse upon the Vorbling line, even unto the third generation. He predicted that violent death would come to any member of the Vorbling family living under any roof the old man might erect."

Jimmy Calvin felt the short hairs stirring at the nape of his neck.

"So that was the curse. I've always wondered what it might have been. You hear so many garbled versions."

"This one is accurate," Zeng Tse-Lin said quietly, as he worked. "In any event, Pieter Vorbling the First seemed unaffected by the curse. He continued to pile up wealth. But there is one thing we know. Perhaps because he was so busy, so engrossed in other matters, he neither built nor bought a house of his own for years. He was content to raise his family in rented places. Hand me that brown bottle, will you, Jimmy?"

The photographer complied, marveling at the swift sureness of Dr. Zeng's skill as he processed the minicam film.

"Then what happened?" Calvin asked.

"In the early Eighties, the old man joined the trend to Nob Hill and erected, at great expense, the residence which has ever since been known as the Vorbling mansion. But he did not live to enjoy it, for on the first day of his occupancy he fell down the main staircase to his death. Soon there were stories of a ghost haunting those spacious halls."

"The curse was working!"

"Who knows, my friend? Perhaps it was merely coincidence. I doubt that anyone took the legend seriously until Vorbling's son, Pieter Junior, was murdered by a servant who went insane during the stock market collapse of Nineteen-twenty-nine."

"Making two violent deaths," Jimmy Calvin muttered.

"Yes. Will you give me the fixing solution, please? Now we come to the last of the family line, young Pieter Vorbling the Third, a Stanford student when his father was murdered. He ordered the house closed, boarded up, and never entered it again.

"Possibly he feared the curse which stemmed down from his grand-father. Or perhaps he merely disliked the place because it was so old and gloomy."

"It was downright sinister!"

"I agree," Zeng smiled faintly. "It was scarcely the sort of home a gay young fellow like Pieter Vorbling the Third would appreciate. He was the playboy type, a harmless spendthrift whom everybody apparently liked. He spent most of his time on his yacht, which, as you know, regrettably blew up three weeks ago off the northern California coast."

Calvin nodded. "I had the assignment to cover it for my paper. It was pretty bad. Everyone was lost—the crew and nearly a dozen guest passengers."

A QUEER glow lighted Dr. Zeng's eyes for an instant.

"Yes, comprising most of young Vorbling's intimates—college fraternity brothers, many of the girls who had made up numerous house parties at Vorbling's mountain lodge, and one or two business associates in that race-track venture the young man promoted a year ago, which failed."

"You'd almost think the Vorbling curse had widened in scope to touch everybody the kid knew intimately," Jimmy Calvin mused.

"A superstitious person might think so, especially in view of still more recent happenings. Two other men belonging to Pieter Vorbling the Third's limited circle have died during the past ten days under mysterious circumstances, thus reducing that circle to a bare handful of survivors. I should hate to think that even this handful may be marked for death."

"Good Lord!" the *Globe* cameraman whispered. "What d'you suppose it all means, Zeng?" Then he added a shrewd question. "What happens to the Vorbling millions now?"

"Young Vorbling never married. He was too busy having a gay time. In fact, he'd had so much to drink the night the cruise started that he had to be carried aboard the yacht. So his fortune goes into a trust fund devoted to various charities."

"Who's to administer it?"

Zeng Tse-Lin lifted the developed film from its bath.

"Old Geoffrey Warren, the Vorbling lawyer."

"Hm-m-m. The guy who tried to tell me I'd seen a face from the spirit world."

"Perhaps his belief was sincere, Jimmy. Behold." Dr. Zeng snapped on a bright light and held up the strip of minicam negative. "What do you see here?"

Jimmy Calvin stared. "It's that attic window—and there's the bearded man! I guess that proves he wasn't a ghost!"

"It is written that vision is relative. To a man, a stone is insignificant, but to an ant it is a mountain."

"Meaning—"

"Meaning that you are looking upon features identical with those of the first Pieter Vorbling, who died sixty years ago by falling down his mansion staircase!"

CHAPTER III

DEATH AT HEADQUARTERS

JIMMY CALVIN'S throat tightened. Now he understood why the bearded face had seemed vaguely familiar to him, back at that fire on Nob Hill. More than once he had seen newspaper pictures of Pieter Vorbling I, reproduced from old tintypes. Now recognition dawned, full and complete.

"You're right, Zeng!" he choked. "But how could I have made a snapshot of a ghost? It's impossible!"

The tall, hawklike doctor permitted no expression to cross his features, but inwardly he was tense with a potential theory.

"All things have their explanations," he said gravely, "although sometimes the waters of reason are muddied and obscure."

"You mean the face *was* an apparition?"

"I cannot answer you at the moment, my friend. The matter is one that requires further study. For the present, I suggest that you repair to a hotel instead of to your apartment, and maintain a discreet silence concerning what we have seen and discussed."

"Oh, oh! I get it. Ghost or no ghost, you think somebody may take another crack at me."

"As for that," Zeng said, "I merely advise you to be wary. For all those who are touched by the Vorblings seem to die in a mysterious way. Good night, Jimmy. And remember, he who is forewarned wears a protecting armor."

"I'll watch my step," Jimmy Calvin promised as he took his departure.

But with this assurance, Zeng Tse-Lin was not quite satisfied. For his own peace of mind, as well as the safety of his photographer friend, he ordered the giant Lai Hu Chow to follow.

"See that the young man reaches the hotel of his choice unharmed," he bade the big Mongol. "For there is death abroad, and it is written that the night is a time of evil."

When he was at last alone in the House of a Thousand Beatitudes, Dr. Zeng opened a ceramic Buddha and drew forth the telephone it contained. He dialed Police Headquarters and asked for Captain Brian Carter of the Homicide Division.

Presently Carter's rumbling voice answered. "Hello?"

"This is Zeng Tse-Lin. I suggest that you conduct an investigation of the fire which consumed the Vorbling mansion on Nob Hill tonight."

"Investigate? But why, in heaven's name?"

"It has been said that flames destroy, but ashes always remain. I humbly urge that you follow my advice as soon as is feasible, with particular attention to the possibility of arson and the presence of a human corpse."

"Good Lord, man, are you hinting there's been still another murder?"

"I shall explain in the morning at your office, if you will be gracious enough to receive my unworthy visit."

On the screen, Chow dropped his hatchet, stumbled and fell as a blast of flame spewed from the automatic.

Then, with polite expressions of concern for Carter's health, Zeng rang off....

To the men at Headquarters, the tall, robed figure of Dr. Zeng Tse-Lin was a familiar sight. He was known to be a close friend of Captain Brian Carter, and as such he needed no permission to enter the Homicide official's private sanctum.

But no member of the Department suspected the ascetic, keen-eyed man of being as Caucasian as themselves. Nor did they guess that he was secretly joined with them in the war against crime.

IT WAS early morning as he went through Carter's doorway, and if he was surprised to see lovely, red-haired Ann Carter in her uncle's dingy office he gave no sign, no indication of how the girl's presence always unsettled him. Brian Carter arose from his desk, cordially. He liked Zeng, and he was wise enough to realize that this strange, impassive man was far more intelligent than himself. Which was a tribute of no mean proportions, for Carter, a compact and muscular Irishman with ruddy complexion, steel-gray hair and frost-blue eyes, was one of the smartest and shrewdest detectives ever to fight his way to a San Francisco police captaincy.

"Glad to see you, Zeng!" he said warmly. "I hope you won't mind Ann being here. I thought she might help."

This was natural enough, Zeng knew. Because Ann Carter had been a friend of young Pieter Vorbling III at the university. She was one of that group at whom death now seemed to be striking with uncanny regularity.

Zeng smiled at her, and there was a hint of wistfulness in his glowing eyes. The one thing he regretted about his self-imposed Asiatic role was that he dared not tell her he was really of her race. For the good of his cause, however, it was better that she should remain in ignorance of his American parentage. Yet often he deplored the barrier which this raised between them.

"It is a pleasure to behold you again," he said gravely, as for an instant their hands touched and her fine eyes came up to meet his. "There are few whose judgment I would trust as far as I trust yours."

"Thank you," she whispered, a hint of color leaping to her cheeks at the genuineness of the compliment.

Those were no empty words Zeng had spoken, she realized. She understood the Chinese and their manners almost as well as Zeng himself, because she had taught at the Chinatown mission ever since her graduation from Stanford. The dwellers there had come to look upon her as a welcome friend. It was this work which had led to her first meeting with Dr. Zeng, and his subsequent friendship for her police-captain uncle.

And now Brian Carter's cordial manner faded to heavy weariness.

"I've been up all night on that Vorbling thing," he said grimly. "For the life of me, Zeng, I don't see how you guessed so exactly what our investigation would find!"

"Then you did find something?"

"Plenty! First, the fire was incendiary—a touch-off. More than that, there was a corpse in the ruins. A man, burned beyond recognition."

"There has been no identification whatever?"

"Not as yet. I've asked old Geoffrey Warren, the Vorbling attorney, to look at what's left of the body. I don't think he can do us much good, though."

"Perhaps this will help," Zeng Tse-Lin said calmly. Upon Carter's desk he dropped an enlarged print of the film which Jimmy Calvin had snapped with his minicam. Seeing it, Ann Carter uttered a sharp cry of disbelief.

"Why, that's Pieter Vorbling the First, who died in Eighteen-eighty-five! I've seen portraits of him many times! When on earth was this taken?"

"Last night, at the fire."

BOTH BRIAN CARTER and his niece stared at Zeng as if he might be playing some monstrous jest on them. But before either one of them could speak, Carter's phone rang. The Homicide officer lifted the instrument, listened, and hung up. Then he darted a curious glance at Dr. Zeng.

"That was Geoffrey Warren calling from his office, asking me to come right over. He has identified the dead man!"

"Indeed?" Zeng betrayed no emotion. "My car and servant wait outside. I would be honored to transport you in that most miserable conveyance."

Carter smiled shrewdly. "Meaning you'd like to go along."

"If you would not consider it an intrusion."

"On the contrary!" Carter heaved himself from his chair. "I want you to come. You too, Ann."

He held the door for them, and then followed them to the main entrance.

There Zeng paused as he saw a familiar figure standing near his car at the curb, talking to Lai Hu Chow. It was young Jimmy Calvin, and he looked excited.

The photographer turned, recognized Zeng Tse-Lin and ran toward him calling out as he came.

"Zeng! I've been looking for you! Burglars ransacked my apartment last night while I was away from it, and when I phoned my city editor to report it, he said my dark room at the *Globe* had been torn up, and—"

He got no further. A black sedan came roaring up the cable-car tracks. As it passed Police Headquarters there was a sudden barking report, a lance of flame. Jimmy Calvin lurched, threw up both hands and pitched forward on his face as the sedan sped around the nearest corner.

After that, it seemed a dozen things happened at once. First, Zeng catapulted himself at the fallen cameraman and leaned over him for a swift examination. Second, Chow got his motor running and Captain Brian Carter piled in alongside him with drawn gun, while Ann, despite a command to remain behind, hurled herself into the tonneau.

Then, just as the limousine arrowed into motion, Dr. Zeng himself came erect and leaped into the machine with an automatic in his fist as if by magic.

"Speed, Chow, speed!" he said in a taut, deadly voice. "It is our only hope—for there was no license plate on the back of the killers' car!"

Ann intuitively caught the meaning of his words.

"Killers? Then that's why you left that young man lying on the sidewalk! He—He's—"

"Yes," Zeng Tse-Lin's voice vas bleak. "Jimmy Calvin was beyond my poor medical skill. A bullet lodged in his heart."

The ensuing five minutes were a nightmare of blinding and reckless motion. Up front, Chow handled the limousine with consummate and fiendish abandon, oblivious to the chances he took at every intersection. He rounded corner after corner on tires that shrieked raw protest, threading back and forth through an area of ten blocks in a vain search for the sedan from which the shot had been fired.

It was no use. The murderers had escaped as completely as if some cavern had engulfed them. And presently Zeng commanded the giant Mongol to slacken his pace.

"Jackals may go into hiding, but it is written that the tiger shall always be known by his fangs," the hawklike doctor said. "Let us now repair to the offices of Geoffrey Warren, where perhaps we may have better luck."

Chow grumbled, but obeyed. Soon thereafter, Carter and his niece, accompanied by Zeng Tse-Lin, entered the law offices of Warren, Foxxe and O'Harra.

CHAPTER IV

RETURN FROM DEATH

LOCATED ON the second floor of one of the older buildings on Market Street, the musty-smelling suite of the law firm looked almost as senile and decrepit as old Geoffrey Warren himself. The senior partner seemed curiously shrunken behind his battered roll-top desk, and his face had a pinched, bluish appearance that told Zeng's experienced eye that here was a victim of some serious chronic ailment of the heart.

The attorney greeted Carter in a quavering voice and acknowledged the Homicide official's introduction of Zeng and Ann. He then cleared his throat nervously.

"I sent for you, Captain, to admit a grievous error I made last night. Whether it would have made any difference had I taken a different attitude is problematical, since the Vorbling mansion was already enveloped in flames. But the truth is that a newspaper man—I forget his name—claimed to have seen a face at one of the upstairs windows. I ridiculed the idea, as did my partner, Mr. O'Harra. We were so certain the house was empty that we even accused the young man of hallucinations."

Brian Carter made a grim mouth. "It was no hallucination."

"I realize that, now. Because I have identified the charred body which was removed from the ruins. He was my other partner, Roland Foxxe!"

"You're certain?"

"Quite. His watch and two rings removed all doubts. Much as I regret to say it, Foxxe fired the house and killed himself."

"Roland Foxxe killed himself?" Ann Carter burst out. "I can't believe it! I knew him, knew how well he loved life! Why should he do a thing like that? Unless—" Her voice trailed off.

"Unless what, Ann?" her uncle asked.

"Well, he'd been in love with a girl—Lola Martel. She threw him over and became engaged to young Pete Vorbling. Lola was on that yacht cruise. She died with the others. Maybe her death preyed on Roland's mind—"

"The story is less romantic than that, young lady." Warren's tone was thin and tired. "We've gone over Foxxe's accounts, particularly of the Vorbling estate which was in his charge, and we find that he was thousands of dollars short. He was an embezzler. He must have realized, upon the death of young Pieter Vorbling, that his thefts would come to light. So he committed suicide."

"He chose a blamed spectacular method," Captain Carter said sourly. "How much was the shortage?"

"We haven't the exact figures as yet, but the fire insurance on the mansion will unquestionably make it good. He probably realized the insurance would be greater than any sum the property might bring on the open market. So I suppose he reasoned that this extra amount would, in a sense, recompense the estate for what he had stolen. Therefore, what you have called his spectacular method of suicide was both atonement and restitution."

"All the same," Carter persisted stubbornly, "I'll have to be given definite figures for the record."

"My remaining partner, Mr. O'Harra, is working on that," the old lawyer said, pressing a button on his desk.

At once Michael O'Harra came into the room, a chunky young man whose eyes widened when he saw Brian Carter's niece.

"Why— Ann! This is a pleasant surprise!"

HE TOOK her hand and they spoke to each other for a moment. Then, in response to Geoffrey Warren's prompting, he got down to business.

"I suppose Roland thought the Vorbling estate was so large that a hundred thousand dollars or so wouldn't matter. In a way he was right, for there are millions left. And the theft might have remained hidden if Pieter Vorbling the Third hadn't died in that yacht disaster. Naturally that demanded an audit for the probate court, and Roland was faced with exposure. Poor devil, to think he was dying in that house last night and we refused to believe the newspaper photographer!"

For the first time, Zeng spoke. "Did Roland Foxxe sport a beard?"

"Beard?" repeated O'Harra. No, of course not. He was young—about my own age, and as clean-shaven."

"Then it could not have been Foxxe whom the cameraman saw," Dr. Zeng stated impassively.

He produced the enlargement he had previously shown to the Carters. Old Geoffrey Warren affixed his glasses, stared at the print, and went gray about the lips.

"God bless my soul, this is a perfect likeness of the first Pieter Vorbling! I remember him well. I was twenty when he died. But how could—"

Zeng had stepped back a pace, watching everyone in the room. And he caught a fleeting expression of fear on the face of Michael O'Harra, a look which was swiftly erased in favor of a palpably forced smile.

"Absurd!" the younger attorney scoffed. "If that's a picture of the first Vorbling, then the photographer must have got hold of an old print and doctored it into this snapshot for the sake of yellow journalism! May I have this enlargement? I'd like to get an expert's opinion."

"I am sorry, but I prefer not to allow the print out of my possession." Dr. Zeng was polite, but adamant. "However, I can assure you there was no trick photography, for I developed the negative myself."

"Maybe there was a double exposure before the film reached your hands. That cameraman ought to be grilled!"

Zeng Tse-Lin shook his head gravely.

"What you suggest is impossible, sir. The young man is dead. He was murdered just a little while ago."

"Dead!" O'Harra whispered. "Then we have to accept the snapshot as genuine—which means maybe there *is* a ghost. And a Vorbling curse!"

"You seem disturbed, sir," said Dr. Zeng. "May I ask why?"

"You'd be disturbed, too, if you were in my shoes!" O'Harra snapped. "I was one of Pieter Vorbling the Third's friends—which begins to seem like another way of saying I'm a member of a death club, a circle of the doomed!"

From his roll-top desk, Geoffrey Warren quavered:

"Don't say such things, Michael. It's bad for my heart."

Even as he spoke, his telephone rang. He answered it, and evidently he heard something even worse for his heart, because his wrinkled face turned a sickly yellow, and his gnarled knuckles whitened around the receiver.

"Yes…yes…. Oh, my goodness! I can't believe it!…A miracle!…Yes, I'll be here…good-by."

He rang off, and then slumped partially forward in his chair.

INSTINCTIVELY, DR. ZENG knew that death was close to the old man. He could tell by the purplish lips, the fluttering breath, the dulled and stricken eyes. And the doctor's response was an immediate leap to action. He seized Warren and propped him upright while delving accurate fingers into the ancient attorney's pockets.

In the vest he found what he wanted, a small glass ampule enclosed in a tiny wad of cotton.

"Most heart sufferers carry amyl nitrite for emergency use," he stated, as he crushed the ampule under Warren's nostrils.

The old lawyer gasped as he inhaled the pungent fumes. Color slowly returned to his cheeks.

"Thank you, Doctor," he whispered. "You saved my life."

"Yes," Zeng dismissed the incident. "But what is the message which caused you such a nearly fatal shock?"

"The voice of someone I'd thought dead," Geoffrey Warren answered weakly. "That was young Pieter Vorbling the Third on the phone. He's alive, he's in town—and he's coming here to see me!"

The effect was electrifying. An astounded exclamation burst from Michael O'Harra's lips.

"Pete Vorbling—alive? But how can that be possible?"

"He said he owed it all to a surgeon named Hertzig, and that he would explain in person," Warren rejoined in the tone of one who had undergone almost more than a sick man's endurance could stand. "Beyond that, I know nothing. I must wait until he comes here from his hotel before I learn how he escaped the yacht disaster."

Zeng Tse-Lin shook his head. "If you will pardon my unworthy intrusion, sir, as a physician I advise you to put no additional strain upon your heart today. Postpone your meeting with young Mr. Vorbling until tomorrow. For the present, go home and rest."

"But he expects to find me here!"

"Give me the name of his hotel. I shall call him and inform him of your condition. Surely he will understand."

"Well, perhaps, you're right. I *am* worn out. He's at the Sir Francis. Now if you will get a cab for me—"

"I am sure Mr. O'Harra will be glad to drive you home." Dr. Zeng's dark eyes turned to the younger partner. "Am I presuming too much, sir?"

Michael O'Harra seemed only too anxious to be of service. He helped Warren into his voluminous opera cape, supported the old lawyer, and guided his faltering steps to the open door.

When the two men had gone, Zeng spoke rapidly to Brian Carter.

"Take Ann home at once, my friends. And see that she remains there until I contact you at Headquarters, later."

"You've got something up your sleeve, Zeng. What is it?"

"It has been written that the workings of a man's mind sometimes are best clothed in silence. You will forgive me, I hope, if I withhold my answer temporarily."

Carter shrugged in resignation, for he knew it would be useless to attempt to delve into the motives of this strange, enigmatic man.

"Just as you say," he sighed. "Come along, Ann."

The girl gave Zeng a worried smile, then followed her uncle from the office. Zeng immediately lifted the telephone and dialed the Sir Francis. When he got his party he spoke incisively. He then cradled the phone, cast a piercing glance around the room, and departed as quietly as a shadow.

Downstairs, though, a slight hint of impatience crossed his ascetic countenance when he saw his limousine at the curb but no Lai Hu Chow at the wheel.

The giant Mongol had a single failing—the love of lurid Western movies. Frequently at the most inopportune times he would slip away to some cheap theater, perhaps to see a picture he had seen a dozen times before. It was a habit which no amount of argument could break. And now, apparently, he had succumbed to it once more for he was nowhere in sight.

Well, there was no help for it, Zeng concluded. He slid behind the wheel and headed for Chinatown.

CHAPTER V

VISITORS

ONLY AN hour later Dr. Zeng personally admitted a visitor to the House of a Thousand Beatitudes, conducting him upstairs to the luxurious Oriental living room.

"Please forgive my lack of a servitor, Mr. Vorbling," he apologized. "I employ one, but he is sometimes erratic."

"That's okay," the visitor said casually.

He was almost as tall as Zeng himself, and his clothing was impeccably tailored. His face, however, was partially covered with bandages held by adhesive tape, so that only the good-humored mouth and quizzical eyes were revealed.

"I'm curious to know why you phoned me at the hotel and asked me to come here," he observed.

"All in due course, my friend. First, permit me to congratulate you on your miraculous escape from death."

"Miraculous? Well, maybe. Although they say heaven or the devil takes care of drinkers and fools—and I certainly had been having plenty to drink the night my yacht blew up. All I remember of the explosion was an ear-splitting roar. Then I woke up swimming in the water. The sea was running pretty high, and I took quite a beating from the rocks. I had hamburger where my face should have been."

"And?"

"Then came the miracle part. I was washed ashore practically in the front yard of a retired plastic surgeon, a screwy old character named Hertzig. Sort of a recluse; a hermit, you might call him. No chance of my phoning or wiring anybody from that remote spot, of course. I couldn't have, anyhow. I was too bashed up."

"But this Hertzig attended your injuries?"

"Like a master. He hemstitched me until I'll look as good as new—or so he assured me. There'll be some scars, of course. I won't mind them, though. I wasn't too handsome, anyhow." He tacked that latter observation on ruefully.

"It has been said that a handsome man breeds enemies, but a man whose heart is true never lacks friends."

"Friends!" The word was repeated with a tinge of bitterness. "I wish I'd never had any! Look what's happened to almost everybody I cared for. First, ten of them got killed when my yacht exploded—including Lola Martel, the girl I was going to marry. Now I understand two more have died under queer circumstances during the past week or so. And last night Roland Foxxe!"

Zeng made a steeple of his long fingers.

"Would you term Roland Foxxe a friend, after he had embezzled your money?"

"Embezzled? What do you mean?"

"I take it, then, that you have not heard. Well, no matter. I am sure you will be furnished the details by your attorneys. Geoffrey Warren and Michael O'Harra. Which brings me to the actual reason I asked you to visit my miserable establishment. I should like to ask you this: Do you trust those two men?"

"Implicitly!"

"You would suspect neither of them of wrongdoing? Of theft, and perhaps even multiple murder?"

"What rot! Of course I wouldn't suspect them of any such nonsense!"

"Let us hope that your trust is not misplaced, Mr. Vorbling. And now, just one more thing. Can you identify this photo which I mentioned on the phone?"

Zeng produced the enlargement of Jimmy Calvin's snapshot.

"Let's see it. Blast these bandages! They get in my way! But I guess I ought to be thankful I'm not dead along with the others.... Hey, where in thunder did you get this picture? I'd swear it's my grandfather if I didn't know better!"

ZENG TSE-LIN succinctly explained how the snap had been taken.

"Would you say it might be Roland Foxxe wearing make-up?" he asked then.

"Hmm. I don't know. Its possible, of course. But what a nutty thing for him to do when he was killing himself!"

"Perhaps you have spoken more wisely than you know, Mr. Vorbling. There seems to be an insane pattern about many events of the past two weeks, a crazy and deadly rhythm. If you would accept my humble advice, you will do well to guard yourself each moment until the sleeve of mystery is unraveled."

"Thanks, I'll remember that.... I say, *what's that?*"

His exclamation was caused by a sudden rattlesnake buzzing which seemed to emanate from everywhere and nowhere. It was a continuing sound, subdued yet inescapable. The whole house seemed full of it.

As if by some trick of legerdemain there was an automatic in Zeng's hand, suddenly.

"An intruder," he said softly. "Down at my front door. The sound you hear is an alarm of my own contriving, set into operation when the lock is tried by any other key than mine or my servant's, which are of a special electromolecular alloy. Let us look."

As he spoke, Zeng touched a concealed button on the wall. A section of tapestry rustled aside, disclosing what resembled a medium-sized movie screen. This was still another television adaptation, similar to the smaller one he employed to identify visitors at his front door.

In the present case, however, the screen was connected to a battery of electric scanning eyes that were set into the façade of a building opposite the Mandarin Emporium. Zeng secretly owned that building.

By virtue of the installation, the screen on Zeng's living room wall revealed the entire front of the House of a Thousand Beatitudes, as well as a limited section of the block itself, as if seen from across the street. And in the broad light of noon, two men were revealed using a skeleton key on the lock of Zeng's front door. Only their backs could be seen, since they were facing that door as they worked.

And now, as in a motion picture, swift action began. Into the field of vision came a new and giant shape. That was Lai Hu Chow, lumbering along with awkward gait.

Chow spotted the two men just as they succeeded in opening his master's portal. With a speed belied by his ungainliness, he sprang toward the intruders. From the capacious sleeve of his cotton jacket, a glittering hatchet suddenly appeared. The giant Mongol was essentially a man of direct action. His belief was that if a man had an enemy the only thing to do was liquidate him as fast as possible. This was why he enjoyed the Western movies he attended at every chance, and from which he was even now returning.

But as he sprang, his vengeful outcry warned the two intruders. They whirled, and one of them drew a silenced automatic. A blurt of flame spewed from the bulbous excrescence on the muzzle of the weapon. Chow stumbled and went down, his head striking on the curbstone. He lay still.

The two men darted inside the House of a Thousand Beatitudes, leaving their victim sprawled on the sidewalk.

Dr. Zeng's lips compressed, went white.

"Seek cover, Mr. Vorbling," he commanded his bandaged visitor. "I go to greet my uninvited guests."

"Oh, no? I'm joining the party. Something tells me I may be useful."

"Your spirit is commendable, sir, but a welcome has already been arranged for any who dare enter my dwelling unbidden." Zeng opened the door giving access to the staircase. "Halt, O spawn of many vile camels!"

THE TWO men were leaping up the steps, and at Zeng's command they stiffened. The one with the silenced automatic triggered a slanting shot upward.

The slug missed Zeng Tse-Lin but he heard a wincing gasp of pain behind him.

"Mr. Vorbling—you have been hit!" he called.

Then Zeng's foot touched a concealed control in the corridor wainscoting. A startling result ensued. Part of the staircase dropped out of sight like the orifice of a chute. The two oncoming men went plummeting into this yawning aperture, which swallowed them at one gulp.

Then, magically, the staircase became normal again. Dr. Zeng turned.

"How severe is your wound, Mr. Vorbling?"

"It's nothing. Just a sting across the forearm. Didn't even draw blood."

"Then forgive me if I sound inhospitable, but you must take your departure at once. I have work to do."

Zeng ushered him to the front door, then left him and sped toward Lai Hu Chow.

The entire action had consumed less than a minute, from the time of Chow's fall until the present. And since the bullet that had felled him had been noiseless, no crowd had yet gathered.

However, two or three neighboring merchants began to *pad-pad* across the street to determine what was wrong with the huge Mongol. Chow was now staggering upright with an infuriated look on his moonlike countenance and a bruise upon his forehead where it had violently contacted the curbstone.

Zeng waved these neighbors away.

"Chow, my brother!" he said as he reached his huge servitor and friend. "Where did the bullet strike?"

The Mongol, whose grammar was as good as any man's when he was not excited, lapsed into irate pidgin English, preceded by a few unmistakable Western "cuss words."

"Slug hittee me in game leg, knockee me down, makee me conk headee on pavement!" he yammered. "Me gettee plenty even with slomebody, you betcha!"

Zeng breathed a sigh of relief and swung about.

"You will observe, Mr. Vorbling, that no harm has been done. Therefore I beseech you to return to your hotel and guard against any eventuality."

"You mean those two thugs may have been gunning for *me?* You think maybe they followed me here to knock me off?"

"In an insecure world, all things are possible."

"But what about those guys? What happened to them? Shouldn't they be turned over to the cops?"

"It shall be done when I have questioned them. At present I have them safely caged and harmless. I bid you good day, Mr. Vorbling."

When his bandaged guest had driven off, Zeng took Chow's arm. Together they entered the House of a Thousand Beatitudes, where every limping step the Mongol took left a wet stain upon the rich carpeting.

Upstairs, the giant squatted on the floor and removed his bullet-punctured artificial limb. From its hollow interior he ruefully drew the wreckage of a flat glass flask.

"Nuts!" he mourned. "Me forkee out six bits for pint of rice wine and it all leakee before Chow takee one dlink!"

Zeng Tse-Lin's lips curved in an affectionate smile.

"It is written that wine is best for a man when it is spilled upon the ground," he admonished. "Equip yourself with one of your many spare limbs, my incorrigible one. This time see that it contains a gun, not a bottle. Then we shall interview the unwise pair who forced their way into my house."

CHOW OBEYED, and presently they entered a concealed private elevator which lowered them to basement level. Here Zeng made a light, waved the Mongol back, and unlocked the door of what appeared to be a dungeon cell.

He stepped across the threshold and surveyed the two gunmen who had been dumped through the staircase trap-door. One of them drew his silenced pistol, but Zeng was too quick for him. There was a flurry of motion, then Zeng had the weapon and a disarmed thug moaned over a sprained wrist. It did not pay to match either physical or mental strength with Dr. Zeng!

With equal sureness he ascertained that the second evil-doer was gunless. Then he smiled bleakly.

"Your faces are brutish and unintelligent," he addressed them. "But even dolts as stupid as yourselves must realize when you have met your master. Now, will you answer my questions truthfully?"

"We ain't talkin'!"

"You may change your minds. There is but one thing I wish to know. That is the name of the man you work for."

"Try an' find out!"

"That should be comparatively easy," Zeng said. Raising his voice, he called Chow into the barren little room. "These, O my stalwart one, are the unfortunate ones who fired that shot at you. Would you like revenge?"

Chow licked his lips. "How far you lettee me go?"

"Well, they seem reluctant to talk. You might, therefore, remove the silent tongues which they find so useless."

"Hot doggee! The tongues, hanh? Jerkee out by roots!" The big Mongol moved forward, fingers twitching. The nearer thug paled and backed off.

"You're kiddin'!"

"Chow does not know the meaning of the word," Zeng answered. "He only knows obedience to my commands."

Even as he spoke, the giant Asiatic grabbed both gunmen in a grip of steel. They broke into babbling protest.

"Hey—nix! Criminee, the guy means it! We'll spill! Make him turn us loose!"

"Speak, and be quick about it!" Dr. Zeng's tone was resonant, ominous. "You are trying my patience."

CHAPTER VI

DEAD MAN'S NUMBER

VOLUBLE WITH terror, the two thugs gushed information— such as it was. They had been hired a week before by a man whose face they had never seen. He had accosted them in midnight darkness, down near a certain Embarcadero saloon which was their hangout, and he had worn a mask even then.

Subsequently they had driven him on various missions around town whose purpose they could only guess when they saw the next day's newspapers. Those papers had reported murders at the addresses visited.

Then this mysterious masked individual had stationed them on guard outside the old Vorbling mansion on Nob Hill, twenty-four hours a day for a solid week. No reason had been given to them, but last night during the fire they had been instructed to waylay a photographer and smash his cameras.

They had obeyed, only to be told that their victim had a second camera which must be destroyed. In this mission they had failed.

"You were then told to burglarize the *Globe* dark room and the photographer's apartment," Zeng interposed. "But again you failed to locate that second camera. Whereupon your masked employer had you drive him in search of the cameraman this morning. You caught up with your victim in front of police headquarters and shot him down in cold blood."

"Nix, nix! We didn't do no triggerin'! It was the guy in the mask!"

"But you are equally guilty, for you realized by that time that you were working for a murderer. Yet you continued to work for him. You allowed him to send you here to my house, armed. I know the purpose of your visit, so we need not discuss that. It is your employer I seek."

"We don't know nothin' about him, I tell you!"

"How did you contact him when it became necessary?"

The bigger thug narrowed his eyes.

"What's it worth to you?" he whined. "Do we get a chance to lam?"

"Ah! So you think to bargain with Zeng Tse-Lin! There is but one bargain I shall make with you, O son of a turtle. Let your tongue wag within you mouth, or I promise you it will wag upon the palm of Lai Hu Chow!"

The big Mongol flexed his fingers. "Blame toottee!"

"Hey, keep him offa us! Here's the dope you want! It's a phone number—Ballard nine-four-four-three. We was to call it any time anything came up. But it won't do you no good. It's unlisted. We checked on that."

Zeng's eyes glowed. "There are many ways of checking," he intoned somberly.

Then he gestured Chow from the underground room, followed, and locked the door on his prisoners.

Upstairs, he dialed Police Headquarters and got Brian Carter on the line.

"I have tidings," he said, and he told of his captives and the information he had extorted from them.

Carter's response held elation. "Good! Now maybe we'll get somewhere. I'll get busy on that phone number right away. Meanwhile I'll send a squad over to take those rats off your hands. See you soon."

He was as good as his word. Within fifteen minutes police had taken the two hoods from the House of a Thousand Beatitudes. And presently Brian Carter himself arrived. There was no elation in his manner, though.

"I'm afraid we drew a blank," he told Dr. Zeng. "That number on the Ballard exchange is worthless."

"You mean it is listed under a fictitious name?"

"Worse than that," the Homicide official growled. "It's listed to a dead man. The installation is in a hideaway apartment secretly maintained by the late Roland Foxxe!"

ZENG AND Carter looked at each other in heavy silence. Then the police official sank wearily into a chair.

"The whole thing's got me screwy," he said. "I've seen some strange cases in my time, but none like this one! For no reason, a costly yacht blows up and kills a whole group of

Captain Brian Carter

people. Soon, two more persons die mysteriously here in town—both of them belonging to that same general circle. Then a ghost gets its picture taken, and the photographer is killed.

"An embezzler traps himself deliberately in a burning building and goes to spectacular death. Finally Pieter Vorbling the Third returns from the grave, you might say, only to be shot at right here in your house! By heavens, Zeng, I'm beginning, to believe there *is* a curse on the Vorbling family!"

Zeng Tse-Lin bowed his head. "It is written that the ways of Providence are not for the understanding of common mortals. Consider this surgeon, Hertzig, in whose front yard young Vorbling was washed up by the sea."

"What about him?"

"In him, and his being on that particular spot along the coast, you see the workings of the Providence I speak of."

"Call it Providence if you want to. Coincidence seems more like it, to me. I looked up his record, found out he used to be tops in his profession until he got into some trouble with the medical association a year or so ago. Then he gave up his practice, withdrew up north, built himself a shack and cut himself off from the world. He certainly couldn't have known he was to have a wrecked yacht on his doorstep a year later. That was just luck. Good luck for Pieter Vorbling the Third."

"But what sort of luck for Hertzig, I wonder?" Zeng mused.

"An excellent break for him! Young Vorbling will pay him a fat fee for his services, not to mention the publicity he'll get in the newspapers. The story of Vorbling's rescue has made headlines already, in the early afternoon editions. And several reporters have flown north to interview Hertzig personally. Maybe he'll even go back into practice again."

"I wonder," Dr. Zeng said softly.

Carter peered at him narrowly. "Something's hatching under that black hair of yours, Zeng. What is it?"

The tall, hawk-faced man sighed. "Sometimes, my friend, an idea may be so nebulous that it should not be disclosed until it has been proved. I should very much like to talk to this Hertzig surgeon. Would you honor my miserable limousine by making the journey with me? It is but a four-hour drive, and we should gain our destination by nightfall."

Captain Brian Carter stopped the questions which came to his lips. He knew, from Zeng's expression, that such queries would be fruitless. He sighed and got up from the easy chair.

"I'll go along. Maybe the air will do me good."

Fifteen minutes later, with Chow at the wheel, they were speeding northward toward the Golden Gate Bridge....

THE HOUSE which Dr. Josef Hertzig had erected for himself was little more than a ramshackle cabin perched high on a promontory above the rolling surf. The coast was desolate and rugged in the gray dusk as Chow, following instructions he had elicited from a service station miles back, swung off the main highway into what could be termed a side road only by the greatest courtesy.

This deep-rutted pathway skirted the cliff within a few precarious feet of the brink, and there were recent tire marks impressed upon the barren earth. Far below was a ribbon of flat beach, the sand gouged as if by wheels and tail skids where more than one plane had landed. Beyond this beach were clusters of jagged rocks worn sharp by pounding waves.

Brian Carter stared down through a tonneau window of the limousine.

"Br-r-r!" he commented. "Young Vorbling had the devil's own luck to get blown clear of the yacht and then live through those boulders. It's a wonder.... Hey, look! There's a car coming toward us from the shack!"

Up front, Chow increased his speed to gain a turn-out point before meeting the oncoming car where it could not pass. Reaching the wider spot, he swerved expertly. But the other machine, instead of going on by, stopped. An excited, middle-aged man hopped out.

Captain Carter recognized him.

"Aren't you Lew Blake on the Oakland *Ledger?*" he asked.

"Yes. I…. Why, hello, Captain! Man, am I glad to see you! I thought maybe this car would be from some other paper and spoil my scoop. But I know you'll give me a break and let me beat the opposition. I—"

"Stop chattering. What's up?"

"Well, when I tried to charter a plane down in San Francisco to fly me up here so I could interview this Hertzig, the boys from the other dailies had already hired all the available ships. So I had to drive up in my car. That put me a good three hours behind my competition. Everybody had been here and flown away by the time I arrived. I could tell by the signs. But man, what a story it gives me now!"

Carter scowled. "What story?"

The reporter swung to the limousine's running board.

"Drive on ahead. I'll show you."

Chow meshed his gears, sent the car forward, and presently parked it in front of the cabin on the cliff. Then Zeng Tse-Lin and Carter followed the *Ledger* man to the front door of the little building. It was wide open, swinging in the wind.

"See for yourselves." The reporter pointed.

Zeng's piercing eyes penetrated the interior gloom and came to rest upon a stocky, huddled form on the uncarpeted floor. It was Dr. Josef Hertzig. There was a stab wound through his heart. He was dead.

CHAPTER VII

CALL TO THE DEAD

I T WAS eight o'clock at night when Lai Hu Chow finally headed the limousine southward toward San Francisco. During the preceding hours, Brian Carter had been a busy man. He had contacted the local county authorities, notified them of the murder, and then had stood guard pending arrival of the sheriff's men.

As a visiting Homicide expert he had done his best to assist in the preliminary investigation. That had been a task in which Zeng, oddly enough, had offered no hand after his first cursory inspection of the scene of the crime.

Now it was over, and they were speeding homeward down the dark highway. After a few miles, Carter broke the long silence.

"I can't understand it," he muttered. "Hertzig was alive when the last reporters left him and flew back to San Francisco. We know that, because a telephone check has been made by the sheriff. Yet the surgeon was dead when that *Ledger* man arrived by auto."

Zeng emerged from his own enigmatic thoughts.

"I hinted to you, my friend, that Hertzig might never resume his practice."

"You mean you had a hunch he might be killed?"

"The Vorbling touch was upon him, remember."

"Then you *did* suspect he was in danger! That was why you insisted on making this trip. You hoped to warn him!"

"I hoped also to talk with him before it was too late. But I failed, for I neglected to consider the swiftness of airplane travel." Dr. Zeng paused, then added casually: "Do you happen to know if young Pieter Vorbling the Third can pilot a plane?"

"Vorbling? Surely you don't suspect him! Or if you do, I may as well disillusion you. He can't fly a lick."

"You are quite sure?"

"Positive! I remember Ann telling me last year that Vorbling tried to enlist in the Air Service but couldn't make it, even after taking private lessons. Something about balance; some trouble with his middle ear. He couldn't even ride in a passenger airliner without getting deathly sick. And it's a cinch he wouldn't be fool enough to hire a pilot to bring him up here to commit a murder. The pilot would be a witness against him."

"Which clears Vorbling completely."

"You bet it does! Now if you had asked me about that Michael O'Harra fellow—"

Zeng stiffened. "He is a flyer?"

"Yes. Private license and everything. He and Roland Foxxe invested in a plane together—used to go up every week end. He had Ann on many a sightseeing flight. If the killing of Hertzig originated in San Francisco, then Michael O'Harra is the man to think about! And I'm thinking about him—hard."

"Your theory possesses plausibility, at least," Zeng said.

Carter turned toward him.

"What the devil do you know about my theory?"

"It is easy to follow your reasoning. Young O'Harra was also a member of the law firm which managed the Vorbling estate. It is perfectly possible that he, and not Roland Foxxe, embezzled the missing funds. In which case he would have had an excellent motive for murdering Foxxe by trapping him in the mansion and setting it afire. Then Foxxe would appear as a thief who had atoned by committing suicide."

Carter grunted. "You're a clever devil, Zeng. That's my theory exactly! Except that O'Harra might have had an added reason for doing those things. Remember, the estate was to go to charity and the firm would have its management. Old Geoffrey Warren is old and ill, ready for retirement. With Foxxe out of the way, Michael O'Harra would be sole active partner, in control of several million dollars. Many murders are done for less."

"True," Zeng Tse-Lin admitted. "But you are overlooking one factor. The man who died in that fire wore a beard, yet Roland Foxxe was clean-shaven."

"A disguise—perhaps forced on him by O'Harra. It's a thin explanation, but the only one that fits the facts."

"And now young Pieter Vorbling's return from death throws a fresh complication into the case."

CAPTAIN CARTER shrugged impatiently.

"O'Harra couldn't foresee that when he planted a time bomb on Vorbling's yacht."

"Ah. So you even suspect him of that."

"Why not? It would be part of his pattern for covering his embezzlements and gaining control of the estate. There could be a revenge motivation, too. O'Harra, along with Foxxe, had invested in the race-track which young Vorbling promoted. That venture collapsed, you'll recall. Seeing his personal savings wiped out may have caused O'Harra to hate young Vorbling even to the point of murder mania."

"But Vorbling escaped."

"Sure. And that ruined the plans O'Harra had made. Which would account for his hiring a pair of gunsels to kill the kid at your house— another scheme that misfired."

"Now explain the death of Dr. Hertzig," Zeng invited.

"Well, mightn't O'Harra be so infuriated at the saving of Vorbling's life that he would fly up here and murder the surgeon responsible?"

"You could carry it even a step further," Zeng said amiably. "O'Harra might be preparing to deny Vorbling's identity. For after those bandages are removed the young man's appearance may be somewhat altered. In which case, O'Harra might wish to liquidate the unfortunate Hertzig as an identifying witness."

"By heavens, I hadn't thought of that!"

"Then consider it well, my friend, and you will discover it to be completely implausible, along with everything else we have discussed. Logic denies the entire structure of your theory from foundation to conclusion."

"Blast it, Zeng, you mean you've been stringing me along?"

"I would prefer to term it a destruction of all the improbabilities. Which clears the way toward the only possible truth." And the tall, hawklike man fell silent.

It was close to midnight when the limousine finally crossed the Golden Gate Bridge and turned toward the city. Presently it drew up before the darkened Mandarin Emporium. Brian Carter, who had been dozing, awakened with a start.

"Well, here we are," he said grimly. "And in spite of what you've said, my next move will be to give Michael O'Harra a sample of the third degree."

Zeng's answer was sharp, staccato.

"Your next move is to duck—quickly!"

Even as he spoke, he catapulted from the car with a rapier's speed.

Long ago he had realized the advantage of unerring night vision. To aid senses which were already abnormally acute he had included in his daily diet a plentiful supply of the A vitamins that promote sight. As a result of this, he had now discerned a figure lurking in the shadows near his doorway, a man so cloaked in darkness that he might have gone undiscovered by ordinary eyes.

Simultaneously with Zeng's leap from the limousine, the man took a step forward. He hurled a small object at the vehicle.

Zeng Tse-Lin sprang with amazing agility, caught the missile.

"A tear gas bomb!" he whispered.

Then, with a mighty sweeping motion of his arm, he flung the thing far into the night. It landed upon the roof of a three-story building halfway down the block and burst there harmlessly, its fumes dissipating.

THEN ZENG erupted at his assailant before the fellow had an opportunity to turn and run. The ensuing struggle was brief, bewildering, a blurred churning of black shadows. It ended with a significant moan of agony—and Dr. Zeng returned to his companions, dragging with him the inert form of his quarry.

"My back!" the man whimpered. "You busted it... I can't walk!"

"I merely applied pressure to certain spinal nerves, causing temporary paralysis," Zeng retorted with no emotion. "You will walk again, but it will be behind prison walls! Now speak up, and be swift about it. What was your purpose here?"

"I—I was to knock you out with the gas, swipe your keys—get inside your joint and—"

"And steal a certain snapshot negative?"

"Yeah, yeah! How—did you know?"

"Never mind that. Tell me for whom you were working."

"I—dunno. It was a guy—"

"Whose face was masked," Zeng supplied. "A man who gave you a certain telephone number to call in case of emergency. Is that correct?"

"Yeah. Heck! You must be wise to—the whole works!"

"Perhaps I am," Dr. Zeng answered bleakly.

He turned his prisoner over to Carter.

"Since you left your own car parked here at the curb when we journeyed north, Captain," he said, "I suggest that you now transport this unspeakable one to jail."

"You bet I will. I'll sweat him, too, the same as I intend to sweat O'Harra—the man who hired him, whether you believe that or not."

Zeng bowed his ascetic head. "May success be yours, honored friend." And he watched the Homicide officer drive off with the partially paralyzed thug.

As Chow unlocked the door of the House of a Thousand Beatitudes for his master, the giant Mongol asked:

"What you do now to clear up mystery? You have scheme?"

Zeng Tse-Lin ascended the staircase, opened the ceramic Buddha and withdrew its concealed telephone.

"Yes, Chow, I have a scheme. Let us see if we can put through a call to the dead."

CHAPTER VIII

MURDER UNMASKED

WHILE CHOW watched, Dr. Zeng dialed Ballard 9443, the number which he had forced from the two gunmen who had attempted to raid his home twelve hours ago.

From the moment of that noontime fracas to the present midnight hour, many things had transpired. It seemed almost as if a year's action had been crowded into a condensation of time. An ordinary man might have been weary by now. But Dr. Zeng was no ordinary man. His splendid muscles sang with health and his perceptions were scalpel-sharp.

He listened to the repeated sound of the ringing signal, betraying no emotion when it seemed there would be no answer. Infinitely patient, he persisted in his efforts—and at last he was rewarded.

"That you, Jake?" a muffled, querulous voice drifted over the wire. "Did you pull it off? Did you get the picture?"

"If Jake is the man you engaged to put me out of action with a gas bomb," Zeng said almost casually, "then I can report that he failed and is now in a cell. This is Dr. Zeng Tse-Lin."

A startled gasp came to Zeng's ear. Then the muffled voice settled back to its quavering monotone.

"Ah! I might have known you would be too much for a fool like Jake, Doctor. And did you pry this number from him, or from those other two numbskulls I sent to your house earlier? Not that it matters. Perhaps you've already traced the connection and learned that it belonged to a dead man, Roland Foxxe."

"You are bold to admit that much, O my enemy," Zeng said.

"Why shouldn't I admit it? The information won't do you any good. Even if you should raid the apartment where the phone is officially connected, you would find nothing. I'll tell you why. I've got the line tapped, and I'm speaking from another instrument in a far different place. A secret extension, you might call it. And unknown to the phone company, of course."

"Very clever indeed," Zeng Tse-Lin admitted. "But your cleverness rapidly approaches its end."

"Don't be too sure of that, you educated Chinese. I happen to hold higher cards than you know. Now, you listen to me. There's a photograph I want, along with the negative. And it's to be understood there will be no holding back of even a single copy. I expect you to turn it over to me."

"And what leads you to this astonishing belief that I might comply?"

The quavering voice chuckled. "My trump cards, Geoffrey Warren and Ann Carter! I have them both here with me. I'll let you listen to the girl so you'll know I'm not fooling."

At once, Ann could be heard on the line.

"Zeng, it's true! I was kidnaped from my apartment and brought here to some cellar near—" Her words were cut off, as if a palm had been clapped to her lips.

For the first time since he had been drawn into this web of mystery, Dr. Zeng's composure vanished. A wild expression of alarm crossed his countenance, to be replaced by one of sheer savagery. His dark eyes flared with hunger to rend and destroy.

He fought himself back to a semblance of calmness, listened as the voice came back on the wire.

"You see, Doctor? Warren easily responded to my lure, and Miss Carter presented no problem. I simply abducted her. Now the game is mine—and I demand that snapshot. Refuse, and my captives die."

"It is written that the wise man recognizes defeat when it is inevitable," Zeng said somberly. "You shall have the picture and the film. Where must I make delivery?"

"My car shall be sent for you," the voice informed. "Do you accept?"

"I accept, sir. I cannot do otherwise."

THE LINE went dead. Zeng waited an instant, then began dialing a number. While doing this he briefly told Chow of the ultimatum he had received.

The huge Mongol clenched his fists.

"Must work fast!" he exclaimed. "Now you call Captain Carter, eh? Fix for him to follow when car drives you to place of evil one."

"No. For Carter, like yourself, is a believer in direct action. He would wish to raid the killer's lair. And should he succeed, I fear it would spell death to Ann. She would be slain at the first sign of a police attack."

"Then how you save her, O my master?"

"By locating the place where she is held and by going there alone, before our enemy sends his car for me."

"Is good scheme if you find evil one's nest. Surprise assault is mighty weapon. But you do not go alone. Lai Hu Chow will not be left behind!"

Zeng's smile held grateful affection. "Would I go forth into battle without my right arm, O mighty one? But hush, while I inquire about the venerable Geoffrey Warren."

With his last words, there came a response to his dialing. The number he had called was that of the residential apartment hotel where the old attorney lived. He spoke to the desk clerk.

"Can you connect me with Mr. Warren?"

"Sorry, sir. He went out about two hours ago. A phone message got him out of bed and he left in quite a hurry."

"Ah, I see. But tell me something. Since he drives no car of his own, did he take a taxi or did a black sedan come for him?"

"He left in a cab, sir. I called it for him myself."

Zeng Tse-Lin's eyes lighted. "What company, Yellow or Checker?"

"Yellow, from the hack stand just outside."

"Listen closely, my friend. This is very important, a matter of life and death. Will you see if that same driver is back at his stand now?"

Zeng's voice carried even more urgency than the words themselves. The clerk seemed to catch this imperative contagion, for he did Zeng's bidding with no further question. Presently another voice sounded.

"Yeah, this is the driver that rode Mr. Warren. I get his business lotsa times."

"Can you tell me where you took him tonight?"

"Sure. I remember on account I thought it was such a funny place to let him out. The joint looked like nobody hadn't lived in it for years. Upon Nob Hill, it was. A spooky old rat-trap across the street from the house that burned down last night—you know, the Vorbling mansion. So I says to the old gent did he want I should wait for him, and he says no, on account he didn't know how long he was gonna be."

"Thank you, my friend," Zeng cut across this torrent of information. "You have perhaps done a great service for more persons than you think!" And he hung up, turned to Chow. "Come, O my brother. We must make haste."

The command was a welcome one to the big Mongol. With his master at his heels, he clattered downstairs and out to the limousine. Both piled in, and Chow sent the vehicle hurtling ahead.

Presently they halted opposite the ruins of the old Vorbling mansion. Zeng alighted, his giant servitor by his side, and studied the dismally weather-beaten house before him.

Since there were vacant lots flanking it, the hawklike man knew that this must be the place to which Geoffrey Warren had come. There were no other buildings answering the taxi driver's description.

But the house seemed tenantless and long abandoned. Neither lights nor signs of occupancy could be discerned. At last Zeng ventured toward its scabrous front steps.

"Don't make another move, Doctor," a voice from behind him commanded. "You and the big guy are covered!"

Zeng froze, while Chow gave vent to angry mutterings because he had failed to protect his master's rear. This was not the Mongol's fault, however, for the accosting voice came from around the side of the house where the speaker had lurked out of sight. And even Dr. Zeng himself could not see around corners.

But Zeng had more or less anticipated some such situation as the present one. And against this eventuality he had already decided upon a strategy of apparent surrender. At least that would get him inside his enemy's stronghold for the ultimate showdown. The odds might be greatly against him, of course—but Zeng was accustomed to battling against long odds.

He spoke a quiet word to Chow in Chinese, silencing the giant, and ordering him to make no overt move for the present. Then, under the menace of a gun he still could not see, he slowly turned until he was facing the side of the house.

"So you guessed that I might seek you out," he said to the shadows.

"I believe in being prepared," came the muffled rejoinder. "And now you will step this way, both of you. One false move'll earn you a bullet."

ZENG WALKED slowly toward the source of the voice, Chow at his elbow. Then their captor, a formless black blur, got behind them and prodded them through a side doorway into stygian interior darkness.

Here they were commanded to halt momentarily, while deft hands searched them for weapons. Zeng's automatic was confiscated, as well as Chow's sharp tong-hatchet.

Disarmed, they were again forced to move forward. Now a flashlight's ray blazed briefly in the hand of their enemy, disclosing stairs leading steeply downward. They descended, and when they had reached the musty underground room there came the click of a switch. A dim incandescent glowed to life overhead, disclosing a sparsely furnished big place, with odds and ends apparently long discarded. And for the first time, Zeng Tse-Lin got a look at his captor.

The man was enveloped in the voluminous folds of an old-fashioned opera cloak, and his features were completely concealed by a hood-mask covering his entire head from crown to throat. So tightly did this black silk material cling, however, that it disclosed a certain lumpiness of profile which even Lai Hu Chow was able to identify.

"Face bandages under mask!" the huge Asiatic yelped. "It is he who visited you today, my master! It is the young man, Pieter Vorbling the Third!"

Dr. Zeng's lips parted in a cold smile.

"Yes, it is my bandaged visitor. But not Pieter Vorbling the Third. That unfortunate youth is dead. He died in the fire which consumed his family mansion last night."

The masked man's eyes glittered through the slits in the black silk hood. "Since you're so wise, Doctor, suppose you tell me who I really am."

"Very well," Zeng said. "You are the man who wished to make the world believe you committed suicide in the mansion fire. You are Roland Foxxe!"

CHAPTER IX

CRIME PAYS OFF

THE MASKED man tensed. His finger tightened on the trigger of his automatic, and his voice lost its disguising quaver.

"How did you guess?" he demanded.

"It was logic, not guesswork. It began with the yacht explosion, which cost many lives, all of them persons who had been intimates of Pieter Vorbling the Third, including his fiancée. Then two more of his friends died mysteriously, here in the city. Why was the young man's immediate circle thus marked for death?

"A possible purpose was revealed when someone calling himself Pieter Vorbling the Third appeared as the yacht disaster's sole survivor. His first move was a phone call to Geoffrey Warren. To an old man already ill of heart disease, the effect of this call was almost fatal. Had I not happened to be on hand to render medical aid, I am sure Warren would have died. And his death would have been a fiendishly cunning murder, removing another of young Vorbling's intimates."

"And the reason for this?" the masked man purred.

"Well, here was someone claiming to be Pieter Vorbling the Third. He was ready to resume life as a multi-millionaire. Facial surgery had been performed on him, and any alteration of his appearance would be attributed to that surgery.

"But suppose he were an impostor not too sure his surgical disguise would pass muster? In that case he might wish to kill all of the real Vorbling's friends, leaving none to penetrate his imposture. Casual acquaintances would not matter; only close friends.

"Such a wholesale murder plot matched the facts of the yacht explosion, which was obviously the work of a time bomb. Every violent death seemed to fit this impersonation theory. When the last of Vorbling's friends had been liquidated, the impostor could remove his bandages with no fear of detection."

"Clever reasoning," the masked man sneered. "Go on."

"Thank you," Zeng rejoined. "Now consider the impostor. To impersonate Vorbling, he must remove his true self from the scene, for obviously he could not be two men at once. So his original self must die, or at least appear to die. But how?

"A pretended suicide was the answer. And you, Roland Foxxe, had presumably killed yourself in the Vorbling mansion fire after a clumsy embezzlement—which you intended should be discovered, so that your suicide would seem logical. Therefore I began to suspect you, even though you were supposedly dead."

The man nodded his hooded head. "Nice going."

"But you needed a corpse to be identified as yourself by virtue of certain jewelry," Zeng went on. "Who was the victim? The only facts known were that he wore a beard, which you did not, and that he resembled the first Pieter Vorbling. This was brought to light by accident when a newspaper photographer made a snapshot of him in the burning mansion.

"What caused this strange resemblance? And why were repeated efforts made to destroy the picture? The explanation was simple. It is not uncommon for a man to look like his grandfather, and I am convinced our bearded man was the first Pieter Vorbling's grandson. In other words, he was Pieter Vorbling the Third!

"I think he had never gone on his yacht before the ill-starred cruise began. The limp figure which was carried on board, supposedly in a stupor, was probably a dummy. I think you must have kidnaped young Vorbling and imprisoned him in the vacant mansion, where you could study his intimate mannerisms to perfect your forthcoming impersonation. In those three weeks he had no access to a razor, so naturally his beard grew.

"To prevent any chance of his escape, you hired two thugs to watch the house day and night. Toward the end, I think you doped him semiconscious. Then you murdered him by setting fire to the mansion. Thus he served a double purpose. His was the body identified as your own, and his was the life into which you planned to step."

THE MASKED man chuckled. "A smart scheme, eh?"

"Very," Zeng admitted. "And it might have succeeded—except for the accidental snapshot made of young Vorbling when he became conscious and realized his peril. You were afraid that photo might be correctly identified as Vorbling.

"Upon such genuine proof of his death, you would not dare impersonate him. So you went to great lengths to obtain the snapshot. You even killed the photographer who had made it. And when you learned that the film was in my possession, you visited me, hoping somehow to steal it. Your two thugs broke into my house at that same time, for the same purpose. One of them even nicked you with a bullet, not recognizing you as the man he was working for.

"And still your murder mania continued: There was an unethical plastic surgeon named Hertzig whom you had hired to alter your features so that you could pretend to be Vorbling, saved from the sea. When your plans began to misfire, you feared Hertzig might talk. So you flew north and silenced him with a knife. You are a pilot, Mr. Foxxe. You and Michael O'Harra once owned a plane together."

"I was hoping you might suspect O'Harra," the masked one said. "Why didn't you?"

"For many reasons. He was a frightened man, but not a guilty one— and he did not fit the pattern of the previous murders. How, for instance, could he impersonate Vorbling when he still moved about as himself?

"Moreover, the real Pieter Vorbling the Third had been incapable of flying a plane. So again the net of circumstantial evidence was drawn more tightly about yourself. And in conclusion, there were additional motives which only you could have had."

"Name them."

"Gladly," Zeng Tse-Lin said. "You, Roland Foxxe, had been in love with a girl named Lola Martel. She jilted you and became engaged to young Vorbling. Jealousy, therefore, was added to your greed. You wanted her to die in the yacht explosion because she had given her heart to another man. And you wanted that man dead because he had won her from you.

"And finally, you had invested your life savings in a race-track venture promoted by young Vorbling. The promotion collapsed, wiping out your small personal fortune. You deemed Vorbling responsible, and you thirsted for revenge.

"There were your motives. Jealousy, revenge, greed and hatred. Combined, they made a murderous maniac of you. Now you have Ann Carter and Geoffrey Warren here as prisoners, to be killed so that they can never unmask you. Later you will probably eliminate Michael O'Harra. Then you will be safe in your impersonation of Pieter Vorbling the Third. His last close friend will be gone."

The masked man laughed weirdly.

"You are right. Only I won't have to wait to knock O'Harra off. I've got him in this cellar, too. You'll all die together, my clever Dr. Zeng, just as soon as you hand me that photograph and negative."

"Suppose I refuse?"

"You won't dare—unless you'd like to see the girl tortured. I've got four more thugs on tap who'd love that job!"

He pressed another switch, lighting the far end of the subterranean room. There Zeng saw Ann Carter, Geoffrey Warren and Michael O'Harra. The men were trussed and helpless, guarded by a quartette of sullen looking and scowling hoodlums with drawn guns.

The girl was not bound, except for her wrists, and they were held above her head around the neck of a big red, grinning Buddha. She was guarded by a huge Chinese who held her binding ropes wrapped around one hairy fist. He was naked to the waist, bald as a yellow billiard ball, and brassy rings dangled from his long, thick ears.

What Dr. Zeng thought at that sight he did not display by a single facial expression.

He shrugged. "It is written that swift death is easier than prolonged agony," he said. "Therefore I shall give you what you desire, and then I beg of you to make an end of us, quickly."

"Now you're being smart. Let's have the picture."

"My servant has it," Zeng stated. He looked at Chow. "Produce what is necessary from where it is hidden, O mighty one."

CHOW UNDERSTOOD. He squatted on the floor, tugged at his artificial leg and disclosed the hollow space within that member. But it was no snapshot he extracted. It was an automatic, which he suddenly hurled at Zeng.

The hawklike man caught it, and it seemed as if the weapon spat yammering fire while it was still in midair, so swiftly did Zeng go into trigger-action. His first slug smashed at the gun in the masked Roland Foxxe's hand, knocking it from the murderer's grasp.

His next went through the evilly grinning mouth of Ann's captor, just as the huge Chinese snatched a gun from his waist-band and fired—too late. The slug from the Oriental's weapon went wild as he crashed to the floor, dragging Ann and the Buddha along with him.

Then the cellar became a volcano's heart, erupting thunderous explosions and bright flashes of death-flame.

Roland Foxxe's four hired gunsels, after their first instant of stunned surprise, came surging forward in unison, spraying bullets. Zeng went down on his belly, aiming and firing as coolly as if he were on a target range. Two thugs went toppling, and then a third, before Zeng's ammunition ran out.

The remaining hoodlum drew a bead on the prone doctor, like an executioner preparing to do his job. In another second, his slug would end Zeng's career forever, because Zeng had no time to roll toward cover.

Then Chow surged upright on his one good leg. He swung his disconnected artificial limb like a baseball bat; let fly with it. There was a hideous sound of impact as it connected with the gunman's head, braining him.

"Excellent, my giant!" Zeng Tse-Lin said, and scrambled to his feet—just in time to meet the infuriated charge of the maniacal Roland Foxxe.

With a madman's superhuman strength, the masked murderer ripped into the tall, hawklike one who had wrecked his insane plans.

It was no ordinary battle that followed. Zeng doubled over as a kick took him in the groin. Sickened pain flooded him. With a terrific effort he straightened up, smashing his fist into Foxxe's hooded and bandaged features.

Blood spurted from behind the mask as surgical wounds reopened and sutures broke apart. But the crazy man seemed to feel nothing. He charged again, clawing and kicking and punching. Getting in close, he tried to sink his teeth in Zeng's jugular.

"Boss!" Chow bleated. "Knockee devil out of him, quickee! You letee him killee you, me never forgivee you as longee as you live!"

Zeng Tse-Lin grinned and dislodged his squalling enemy. Then, like an uncoiling spring, he catapulted at the madman and wrapped iron arms around his torso. He squeezed.

The sensation was one which he would remember forever. Foxxe's body resisted that tremendous pressure for a moment. But slowly, inexorably, Zeng's strength told. The kill-crazy Foxxe moaned as his breath was driven from his lungs.

Through slits in the mask, his eyes bulged horribly in fear. He squirmed ineffectually, and then there was a crunching of gristle and a splintering of bones as his ribs collapsed.

He went limp, and he died with a curse upon his lips.

By that time, Chow had recovered his artificial leg and attached it. He lumbered toward the prisoners in the cellar, and released them.

Ann Carter was the first to be freed. When she was lifted from the floor she came swaying toward Dr. Zeng Tse-Lin, pallid, shaken. But her eyes were starry with gratitude.

"Zeng!" she whispered. "You saved us all!" For a moment she clung to him, sweetly fragrant and trembling.

He knew that he had other work still to do. Brian Carter must be notified, for the police must come to clean up this scene of carnage. But for the present, Zeng was content merely to hold Ann in an embrace which could not last.

This was his reward. And what better recompense could any fighting man desire?

IV

CAMELBACK KILL

CHAPTER I

FRAME IN THE FOG

DESERTED BY the teeming throngs who daily made it their working place, San Francisco's Embarcadero lay silent in the cloak of night. Gray fog draped the curbside lamp standards, diminishing their circles of radiance so that the side streets which gave upon the waterfront were darker than usual.

And in this darkness a witch broth of crime was brewing.

Far across the bay's restless expanse, the lights of the Oakland Bridge made a glimmering arch not quite obscured by drifting mist. Nearer, the rumble of Market Street traffic sounded faintly as late theatergoers journeyed homeward. None came to the Embarcadero, though, for there were no residences here. This was just a neighborhood of wharves and piers, loft buildings and warehouses; an area peopled only by ghosts from the city's fabulous past—shanghaied sailors and shoddy entertainers and scarlet women walking with silent tread.

Concealed by shadows amidst this spectral and imaginary company there was one spot of life, however. It was a parked sedan, its headlamps doused and its motor idling inaudibly. Two men sat hunched in its front compartment, grim of visage, tense with alertness. The one alongside the driver shifted his position, manifestly impatient.

"I don't like this waitin'," he growled. "How much longer do you s'pose it will be before—"

The driver had started to stretch, but suddenly he lowered his arms and reached for the gear-shift knob. His right foot hovered over the throttle.

"Here comes a truck now!" he whispered huskily. "It looks like it'll do okay. Get ready. Here we go."

He meshed into second, let out the clutch, and sent his sedan surging forward.

THE ONCOMING truck was old, battered, and its engine made a rackety clatter in the night. But despite its age and the fact that he had bought it second-hand, it was a source of pride and satisfaction to its owner.

Steve Conroy had never owned much to be proud of in his thirty years. For him, life had been an endless struggle for his own and his family's bare existence. He was steady-going, a hard worker. But he belonged to that luckless fraternity whose every ambition seems fore-doomed to failure.

Even this truck had proved something of a disappointment. In buying it, he had considered it a step ahead; a move toward ultimate escape from poverty. With the help of his willing wife, he had scrimped and saved to make the down payment. He had gone without tobacco and lunches, even.

He had been wrong, though. As he drove his rattling vehicle forward over the rough pavement, he realized bitterly that in starting out to work for himself he had merely multiplied his worries. Already there was a note overdue on the truck, and although he had worked late every night this week, constant repairs to the old motor had eaten up everything he had gained.

Still, he thought, things soon ought to take a turn for the better. Tonight, for instance, he had finished a tough job of hauling, at good rates. Now, running empty, he foresaw smoother times ahead. He had no premonition of trouble, even when he noticed a black sedan swing from a side street and bear dangerously toward him.

Automatically he sounded his asthmatic horn, thinking perhaps his weak yellow headlights had not been noticed by the driver of the sedan. Fog would account for that, he concluded.

But fog did not explain the other car's continued recklessness. It swung in closer, and Steve Conroy's throat tightened as he realized a collision was coming. His tired muscles responded slowly as he mashed down on the brake pedal.

"Hey!" he yelled.

But the truck's brake linings were worn, the drums scored. A frantic indignation swelled Conroy's chest as he tried to swerve and saw that the sedan was making no similar effort to avoid the impending smash. In fact, it seemed to be deliberately aiming at him.

And it connected, sideswiping him neatly but without too much force. Then Conroy's brakes finally grabbed hold, and he managed to draw up with his right front wheel in the slanted runway of a warehouse drive.

A spasm of pain contorted Conroy's face.

He set his emergency, noting that the offending sedan had also halted a few yards ahead. Dropping down out of his cab, he breathed easier when he saw that the damage to his truck was negligible—a minor dent in a fender already battered shapeless. He turned his attention to the sedan.

It, too, was scarcely hurt, barring a scratch on the glossy black paint. That was a lucky break. A few dollars ought to cover everything, Conroy told himself. Not that he was at fault in the matter, for the blame actually belonged to the other driver. Conroy had no desire to make an issue of this, though. All he wanted at the moment was a chance to go home and rest. He was willing to pay for the privilege.

BUT IT did not work out that way. At least, Steve Conroy was destined not to settle for cash. As he walked toward the sedan, its front doors opened and two men emerged. They advanced at him truculently. The driver, short, barrel-chested, thick of neck, rasped out a torrent of abuse.

"What the devil d'you think you're drivin'—an Army tank?" he demanded. "It's guys like you truckers that make all the traffic accidents! You blasted road-hog!"

Conroy held his temper in rigid check, despite the injustice of this tirade.

"I'm sorry," he said mildly. "I tried to get out of your way but you cut directly into me. It's okay, though. Just to keep you from being sore, I'll settle for whatever you say."

"Cockeyed right you'll settle," the chunky man snarled. "Like this!" And he took a punch at Steve Conroy's head.

Conroy rolled with the blow, mechanically. Then anger flooded him and he charged at his attacker with work-hardened fists. A man was not supposed to stand still and let somebody take a fall out of him, after all. Not when he didn't deserve it.

The only trouble with Steve Conroy was that he forgot the sedan's second occupant—and in forgetting, he left his back unguarded. This was a mistake. The second man closed in on him from behind, swinging a blackjack. It slugged brutally home to Conroy's skull, wielded with vicious power.

Steve Conroy dropped in a crumpled heap not even knowing what had hit him....

How long he remained unconscious, he couldn't guess. But when his senses slowly returned, the Embarcadero was silent and deserted. The black sedan was gone. Of his assailants there was no trace in the eddying fog. The only thing they had left him as a token of the encounter was an aching, swollen bruise at the back of his head; a bruise that throbbed like a pulse.

He arose and staggered to his parked truck. He grew dizzier with every faltering step, and realized he must be suffering the effects of a minor concussion. His one clear idea was to reach the sanctuary of his home, so that his wife could attend his injuries. He was sick. Plenty sick.

Painfully he clambered up behind the truck's steering wheel and heeled the starter. The clattering motor lived, and the transmission gears were no noisier than usual. So he had been correct about the negligible amount of damage his machine had suffered, and he was grateful for it. With luck, he would be home within a few minutes. Home, and in bed.

But his luck did not hold. The first thing he noticed was the truck's heavier riding quality, as if it labored under a burden. And then, before he had traveled half a block, the wail of a police siren cut through damp grayness and a sudden red blaze of spotlight knifed full into Steve Conroy's eyes, blinding him and bathing his features in crimson. Like blood.

Other squad cars were coming from both directions, now. To Conroy's pain-dulled mind it seemed almost as if some of them appeared out of the dark waters of the bay. He pulled over to the curb, without being told, and blinked sluggishly at the blue-uniformed officer who approached him.

"What's the matter, Copper?"

"Don't know yet. An alarm sounded from that warehouse back there."

THE POLICEMAN jerked a thumb toward the loft building in front of which Conroy's truck had been parked a moment before. More police cars were on the scene now, and a dozen bluecoats were rushing inside the structure.

Steve Conroy touched his aching head, gingerly.

"But why hold me?" he protested. "I haven't done anything."

"If you haven't, then you've got nothing to worry about," the patrolman said. "But I better take a look at your driver's license while we're waiting."

Conroy passed it over, willingly enough. The officer examined it, returned it.

"Seems okay. You look like you've been in a fight."

"I was," Conroy said, and told how he had been blackjacked by the two men from the glossy sedan.

Just as he was finishing, a squad sergeant came rushing out of the warehouse and interrupted him.

"Devil's to pay in there!" the sergeant panted grimly to the officer standing by Conroy's truck. "The whole building's looted and a night watchman bumped!... Hey, who's this guy?"

"A trucker, sir. I stopped him on general principles."

"What's he hauling?"

Steve Conroy answered this.

"Nothing. I'm running empty. Just finished a job."

"Oh, yeah? Then what's holding up that tarpaulin? Let's have a look." The sergeant scrambled aboard, lifted the tarp, sprayed light from his pocket torch. "I'll be blowed!"

As he spoke, he pulled out the end of a fat gray coil, thick as a man's forearm but tapering toward the edges—a seemingly inexhaustible length of resilient material that unwound the way a flattened fire hose might be reeled out. Under the tarpaulin were other similar big coils, scores of them, piled knee deep in the body of the truck.

Steve Conroy's mouth dropped open. "Wh-what's that?"

"As if you didn't know!" the sergeant growled heavily. "It's camelback rubber, that's what it is. The stuff they use for recapping and retreading worn tires. Worth almost its weight in gold, these days!"

"But—but where'd it come from? I tell you I was going home, running empty!"

"Save your lies, Bud. It came out of that warehouse and you know it. The place was full of it, frozen there by orders from Washington."

"You—you don't think I—"

"Never mind what I think. The building was full, this afternoon. It's empty now. You add it up."

Conroy's pain-blunted mind was a chaos of swirling apprehension.

"I'm no thief! I didn't steal any rubber!"

"What's the use saying that when you're caught with the goods? Better come clean, Chum. Who hired you to haul these coils away? And where are all the other trucks your mob used? There must have been a whole fleet of them. Speak up!"

"I d-don't know anything about it."

"Sure. The rubber just bounced out by itself and landed here in your truck, hunh? Okay, Pal, have it your way. Let's get going to Headquarters. But remember, that watchman was croaked. This isn't a robbery rap you're up against. It's murder."

CHAPTER II

HOUSE OF MYSTERY

IN THE heart of Chinatown, lights glowed warmly in the windows above a darkened store building set slightly apart from its neighbors. The store itself was tightly shuttered for the night, and a constant drip of fog moisture fell from the lower edge of the gold-lettered sign hanging over the entrance:

MANDARIN EMPORIUM

EXCLUSIVE ANTIQUES
ORIENTAL IMPORTATIONS
DR. ZENG TSE-LIN, *Proprietor*

By day, the Mandarin Emporium was a busy mart of trade, thronged with shoppers, for it was known all over San Francisco that if you wished to purchase Chinese merchandise of superlative quality, this was where to find it.

To Chinatown itself, though, the rooms over the store were far more intriguing than the Emporium proper. For these rooms were the residence of a mysterious individual whose name evoked discussion, comment and speculation wherever it was heard. That man was known as Dr. Zeng Tse-Lin.

In the Chinese language his home was called the "House of a Thousand Beatitudes," but actually it was a house of mystery and a domain of magic. Some there were who whispered that Black Arts were practiced here. But such talk, of course, was idle rumor and guesswork gossip, far from the real scientific truth.

Whispers of this nature were bound to arise concerning a place whose interior had been glimpsed by none but a select few whom Dr. Zeng numbered as his personal friends. Who among the uninformed but could help wondering the source of Zeng's financial wealth when it was obvious that he made little profit on the moderate prices he charged for his Emporium wares and his medical services?

That he possessed a more-than-comfortable fortune was quite obvious. But only a privileged handful of his intimates were aware that he gained this income from his achievements and inventions in realms of science.

Another rumor said that Dr. Zeng never slept; and the lights which burned steadily in his apartment windows seemed to bear this out. Tonight, though, he was not engaged in any of the mysterious experiments that caused his name to be a byword along Grant Avenue and its intersecting alleys which were the nerve centers of Chinatown. Instead of working in his laboratories, he was entertaining a guest.

And his visitor was no less a personage than his old and valued friend, Captain Brian Carter, the dynamic Chief of San Francisco's Homicide Bureau.

They made a strangely assorted pair—Carter, heavy and square and competent in his carefully tailored blue serge, and Dr. Zeng Tse-Lin, tall, austere, hawklike in his rich mandarin robes. A pair, it might be thought, who had nothing whatever in common. But that supposition would be wrong. For in addition to the bond of friendship, a mutual interest engaged them—the study of crime and criminals!

They sat now in Dr. Zeng's tastefully Oriental study, sipping rare and fragrant pearl tea from fragile *chien yao* bowls of finest glazed porcelain while they discussed intricate murder cases of the past—cases which Zeng had helped to solve. And as they talked, Carter felt again the awed admiration which always filled him when he was with this black-haired, keen-eyed man of mystery.

"AMAZING!" HE muttered more than once during their conversation, when Zeng made some especially telling point.

That one word, "amazing," summed up Zeng Tse-Lin perfectly. A physician and surgeon of unequaled skill, despite the fact that he was barely thirty years of age, he likewise possessed master degrees in many other sciences and arts.

He held degrees won from America's finest technological universities after he had absorbed a complete Asiatic education from the ranking colleges in China—not to mention a period he had spent in the remote lamaseries of Tibet as a student of mystic and seldom-revealed depths of Oriental lore.

To these knowledges Zeng had added the wisdom of India, the secrets of the *fakirs* and the exercises of *yoga,* until his body was as steely and supple as a rapier—and as deadly swift. All of which Captain Brian Carter knew. In addition he was aware of one other fact about his host, the most astounding fact of all—which was that Zeng was not really Chinese, but a white American whose true name was Robert Charles Lang!

This would not have been guessed to look at him. Certainly it went unsuspected by his Chinatown neighbors, among whom he daily mingled as an accepted and highly respected member of their own race—a fifth-examination scholar entitled to wear the robes of the mandarin caste and the coveted green button that signified the extent of his learning.

Yet the fact remained that the sagacious Dr. Zeng's parents had been affluent American missionaries in China, and had died there, murdered by marauding Jap bandits.

At the time of that dark tragedy, Zeng himself had been finishing his education in the United States. Upon the slaying of his mother and father, he altered the pathway of his own life. He decided to devote the rest of his days to a relentless war upon crime in all its aspects. That was his way of avenging his murdered parents. In order to further this work, he had established himself in San Francisco, in the guise of a Chinese.

To the world at large, he was a doctor of superlative skill who had become a merchant through hobby. But in actuality, both his medical practice and his Mandarin Emporium were merely twin shields concealing his genuine career as a battler against the forces of evil.

HE SMILED politely now at his guest, Captain Carter.

"Your tea grows cold, O honored friend. Permit me to replenish it with a fresh infusion." And he clapped his hands, twice.

In response, a giant Mongol servitor appeared from one of the rear rooms; a huge, moon-faced man whose impassive features bore many war scars. This was Lai Hu Chow, Zeng's devoted shadow and companion—the only person, barring Brian Carter, who knew the secret of Zeng's parentage.

"Yes, my master?" Chow intoned around a wad of gum that kept his jaws vigorously busy.

"Fetch our visitor a new bowl of this miserably inferior tea, O little one." Zeng's voice held esteem and affection. "And tarry not, lest our poor hospitality seem even poorer."

Chow departed, his gait rolling and rakish due to the fact that he wore an artificial limb, having lost his real leg while fighting the murderers of Zeng's mother and father. Presently he returned with steaming bowls and a plate of almond cakes, which he proffered to the police official.

CARTER HAD just drained the last drop of his tea with obvious enjoyment when he noticed the Ming dynasty water clock in a far corner. He leaped to his feet in dismay.

"Nearly midnight!" he exclaimed ruefully. "I had no idea it was so late! I'll have to be running along, Zeng. Sorry."

Arising and bowing, Dr. Zeng made a graceful gesture.

"It is written that time lags heavily in boredom, but the hours wear wings when devoted to pleasant pursuits. And this night has been most pleasant."

"I've enjoyed it to the hilt, myself." Carter was not to be outdone in compliments. "I always relish these sessions with you, Zeng. Oh, by the way, may I use your phone? I ought to check up with Headquarters before I go home."

"By all means," Zeng Tse-Lin responded.

He pressed a secret button on the side of a contemplative image of Buddha. The statuette opened, disclosing a hollowed aperture in which the telephone instrument rested.

It was a curious-looking telephone, though. The French-type combination transmitter and receiver depended from an oddly shaped hook which jutted out of a small oblong teakwood box, and there was no trace of the usual dial. This puzzled Carter.

Dr. Zeng smiled boyishly. "A new plaything of mine—an experiment," he explained. "Just speak the number you wish to call. A diaphragm picks up the syllables and transforms them to pulsations of energy through a series of electrical relays. In turn, the relays actuate a hidden dial mechanism. Thus you obtain your connection without the necessity of twirling the ordinary manual dial. Rather silly, eh?"

"Silly!" Carter exploded. "Why, man, this may revolutionize the country's telephone system! It's marvelous!"

And he spoke, aloud, the prefix and number of Police Headquarters. A series of quiet clicks rewarded him, and he blinked as his call went unerringly through.

"A robot connection, by golly!" he breathed in astonishment.

A voice from Headquarters floated back over the wire and asked him what in thunder he was talking about.

"Huh? Oh! Skip it. This is Captain Carter. Checking off for the night unless anything's stirring.... What's that you say?" The Homicide officer stiffened. "Heist? Murder? Good gosh! Okay, I'm coming right down. Hold everything!"

He rang off and turned on his heel. Zeng's dark, glowing eyes surveyed him with alert interest.

"Something has happened?" Zeng asked.

"Plenty! Some mob lifted a whole confounded warehouse full of camelback rubber down on the Embarcadero a while ago. Killed an old watchman named Pat Barton while they were at it, the dirty rats!"

Tension gripped Zeng Tse-Lin, although he masked it from his expressionless and ascetic face.

"Pat Barton," he said quietly, but there was more than a hint of grimness in his tone. "I knew him. He was a patient of mine—a nice old man. Two weeks ago he came to me, told me he had an opportunity to get a job as watchman in a rubber warehouse. I wrote a recommendation for him.

"And now you say he's dead. Murdered."

"Yes. But my boys nabbed one of the heist mob, they tell me. A truck driver. Man, will I run him through the wringer!"

"It would be an event I should enjoy seeing," Zeng's voice grew still grimmer. "Would you consider my presence an intrusion, O friend?"

"Not at all. Come along, and welcome. Let's go!"

CHAPTER III

DEATH'S LINE-UP

BRIAN CARTER'S private office was already crowded when the chief and Dr. Zeng arrived there. Zeng entered unobtrusively at his friend's heels, then slipped to a remote corner where he could observe without attracting attention.

The first person on whom his inspection centered was a golden-haired girl, obviously young and, equally obviously, upset, despite her attempts to appear nonchalant. Zeng recognized her at once. He had seen her photograph in the newspapers on many an occasion and against many backgrounds. Cynthia Lancaster had appeared in the public prints far too frequently in her brief twenty-three years of life for her face not to be familiar.

The papers usually referred to her as the "madcap heiress," a word picture ordinarily descriptive of a willful, scatter-brain type of individual. But Zeng's shrewd eyes discerned otherwise. Under this girl's flippantly sophisticated surface, he decided, there was a great deal more intelligence than would be suspected.

She wore a tricky hat, an expensive evening gown and a short cape of silver fox. And at the moment she was smoking a cigarette in a jeweled jade holder of exaggerated length. Under artistically applied make-up her face was already marked by late hours and careless living. In spite of this, though, she was strikingly pretty, with her blond hair coiffed in tight curls clustering about the edge of the little hat.

A pretty girl, indeed! Not the sort that Zeng particularly cared for, but he did not discount her for that reason. His keen mind wondered why a girl like Cynthia Lancaster would come to Police Headquarters at this late hour.

His unspoken question was answered when a dapper and meticulously groomed man of middle age stepped forward and introduced himself to Captain Brian Carter.

"I'm Hal Vondell," he said smoothly. "I am Miss Lancaster's business manager—and her fiancé."

His diction was impeccable, to match his tuxedo. He gave the effect of having studied each gesture, each word, before it was delivered.

Still seeming to weigh every word on mental scales, he went on with his explanation.

"Miss Lancaster owns the warehouse that was robbed. Naturally we came down here as soon as we were notified. A terrible thing. Terrible!" He gave the impression that it wasn't terrible at all, but merely annoying.

Brian Carter nodded. "Thanks for coming." He included both Vondell and Cynthia Lancaster in the remark.

Then he listened as a uniformed sergeant whispered something. When the whispering was finished, Carter peered sharply toward the other people in his office.

"Mr. Nazarian," he said, "will you come forward?"

A wheezing, swarthy little fat man advanced to Carter's desk.

"I am Joe Nazarian," he stated.

There was just a faint touch of Levantine accent in his speech, an oily quality, even as the man himself seemed somehow greasy. Like most Armenians, though, he was politeness personified.

"You owned the camelback rubber stolen from Miss Lancaster's warehouse tonight?" Carter asked him.

"That is correct, sir. I am a rubber importer and processor. My reputation"—he insisted on this for no apparent reason—"is unimpeachable. Ask anybody in San Francisco. Or in the Dutch East Indies, where I do my buying—or rather, where did it until the accursed Japs overran my winter home there."

CARTER MADE a steeple of his fingers, thoughtfully.

"Nobody's trying to impeach your reputation, Mr. Nazarian."

"Quite so, quite so," the swarthy little fat man answered agreeably. "Yet I would not have you think that I am involved in the theft of my own merchandise."

"I hadn't even considered it—yet."

Nazarian smiled. "You will, sir. You undoubtedly will, since that is the way a policeman's mind works. Particularly when you learn that the rubber was fully insured."

Hearing this, Dr. Zeng Tse-Lin frowned. It was written that the man who protests his own honesty is not always to be trusted. Nazarian was making an issue of his integrity.

Why?

At the desk, Captain Brian Carter studied the Armenian.

"You carry insurance, eh? With what outfit?"

"Mine," a new voice answered nervously.

The speaker was a man in the middle forties, balding, closely shaved, and his clothes were good but obviously not tailor-made.

His kind were seen at luncheon clubs, heard making speeches about service to the community, always joining lodges for the sake of establishing new business contacts. They were breezy, full of good fellowship, but quick to worry when things went wrong.

"My name's McKnight—Thomas McKnight," he added. "General agent for Indemnity Underwriters, Incorporated. This is going to hit us hard, Captain. Mighty hard."

"Unless we recover the stolen rubber," Carter rejoined in an effort to reassure him.

From the thin lips of still another man in the background, a cynical snort sounded.

"Small chance!" was the scoffing remark, punctuated with a hiccup.

Zeng peered narrowly at this individual and recognized him as Cynthia Lancaster's dissolute brother. Eric Lancaster bore an amazing resemblance to the blond girl save that his hair was red, unruly, and his eyes green instead of purple-blue. Deep lines of dissipation were etched on his youthful face, accentuating his present tipsy condition, and there was sullenness under the sarcastic leer he gave Captain Carter.

Eric, like his sister, had splashed across the front pages all too often—with the result that he had been disinherited by his father's will and now lived wholly on Cynthia's bounty. As sole heiress to the Lancaster estate, she alone held the purse strings. That was a circumstance bound to stir sullen resentment in so utterly selfish a young man as this.

And Eric's selfishness was betrayed by his bearing, his arrogant manner. Spoiled as a child, pampered and world-traveled in his youth, the bitterness which now marked him was plain. He was hard, though, under the surface. Hard and brainy and competent, like Cynthia herself. And dangerous, too, Zeng concluded as he quietly scrutinized the man. Or at least potential danger lay in his character, easily aroused if someone crossed him.

Having mentally estimated everybody present, Dr. Zeng returned his attention to Brian Carter, who was now addressing the entire gathering.

"Ever since the rubber-freezing order we've been afraid something like this would happen," the Homicide official growled. "I was hoping San Francisco might escape such crimes. But I might as well have wished for the moon."

"So it would seem," Joe Nazarian silkily agreed.

CARTER GLOWERED at the Armenian.

"You should have taken more pains to protect your property until the Army had use for it. You know what tires mean to a public that can't buy them. Honest or otherwise, there are plenty of motorists willing to pay double price for bootleg retreads in the Black Market, no questions asked. It was a temptation to thieves!"

Nazarian spread his hands. "I thought the rubber was safe, I did indeed. I had a good watchman. It never occurred to me that he would be murdered, and a whole fleet of gangster trucks could be driven through the streets without the police stopping them on suspicion."

This oily barb struck home. Carter went brick-red.

"We did stop one of them," he snapped. "Caught the driver with the goods. The Department isn't entirely asleep."

"And has your prisoner confessed, sir?"

"Not yet. He will, though. I'll see to that! He'll lead us to the rest of his mob before I'm done with him." Carter turned to a sergeant standing near his desk. "Where's the guy now?"

"In the line-up room, Captain."

"Good. Bring these people in there. Maybe somebody will recognize him."

Then the Homicide chief motioned for Zeng to join him, and led the way to an adjoining chamber.

This was a good deal larger than Carter's private office, and arranged somewhat in the manner of a small theater. There was a stagelike platform at one end, barren of props but brilliantly lighted by banks of high-powered incandescents across top, bottom and sides. The miniature auditorium itself contained no orchestra seats, though. Standing room only was the watchword here.

And any audience who might stand facing the stage would be practically invisible to those on the platform, for it was almost impossible for human eyes to peer beyond and past the glaring battery of lights. Thus the audience remained in shadowy anonymity, seeing but not seen.

Steve Conroy, the Embarcadero truck driver, stood on the stage now, his features haggard with pain and worry, his eyes dulled by impotent resignation as he blinked across the footlights.

"I don't know anything about that rubber," he was mumbling. "I swear it! I tell you two men ganged up on me, slugged me. And when I woke up, the stuff was in my truck—"

A crisp police voice cut across his pleading.

"That story isn't going to help you, Conroy. You weren't slugged by two unknown men. You got your bruises when you attacked that warehouse watchman. He fought you, so you killed him."

"No! No! I didn't!"

"Better come clean, Conroy, if you don't want to wind up in the gas chamber. Who were the other members of your mob? Where was the loot taken?"

"I don't know!" Conroy answered frantically. "I'd had a job, a late haul. I'd finished it and was going home, empty. I only wanted to make some money to meet my truck payment that's overdue—"

"We know all that," the inquisitorial voice slapped at him. "Sure you were desperate for cash. That's why you joined up with the heist mob. We know you weren't the brains, Conroy. But maybe we'll give you a break if you tell us who that brain guy is. You going to talk?"

"How can I? What can I say that will make you believe…. Wait a minute!"

"Wait for what, Conroy?"

"I just remembered something. Funny it didn't come to me before. The sedan that clipped me—"

"Back at that again, hunh?"

"Yes. Because it's the truth. Maybe I can prove it."

"How?"

"By its license plates. I read the number right after those men sideswiped me. Listen. If I tell you that number will you check on it? Give me that much of a chance to clear myself? Will you?"

The police voice held undisguised disbelief.

"Let's have the number, Conroy. Then we'll see."

Steve Conroy's brow furrowed as he strove to remember.

"It was six-oh-vee-one—"

SOMEBODY AMONG the shadow-swathed audience broke into a fit of coughing. Then, weirdly, a spasm of pain seemed to contort Conroy's face as his open mouth horridly sagged. Drenched in the brilliance of the stage lights, he clutched frantically at his chest. Crimson suffused his features and turned rapidly to a dark purplish hue as his eyes bulged and his lungs labored for air.

He staggered, lurched, seemed to be trying to scream. But no sound issued from his writhing lips. Then, still clawing at the front of his patched jacket, he stumbled and fell headlong, measured his length on the platform's flooring.

Even as Conroy toppled, young Eric Lancaster created a simultaneous commotion in the audience itself.

"That's horrible—I can't watch it—I'm going to be sick!" the youth screamed wildly. "Let me out of here!" And he went plunging toward the exit.

Joe Nazarian's oily voice sounded in the darkness.

"I'll go with you, Mr. Lancaster. Let me help you, sir."

The fat little Armenian waddled with deceptive quickness after the red-haired Eric. Both men gained the door without hindrance. Everybody else in the room seemed too startled to move.

Everybody except Dr. Zeng Tse-Lin.

CHAPTER IV

HOMICIDE DIAGNOSIS

WITH ERIC LANCASTER'S hasty attempt to depart, and Joe Nazarian's quick effort to follow him, Dr. Zeng uncoiled into action.

"Lights!" he shouted.

Then he pressed his lips close to the ear of Captain Carter, standing alongside him in the darkened little auditorium.

"Command everyone to stand still, O my friend. Do not permit a single soul to leave!"

Having thus advised the police official, Zeng seemed to vanish, to melt away in the shadows.

Carter's response was automatic, and couched in the imperative tones of one accustomed to authority, obedience.

"Stand where you are, everybody!" he roared. "No one's to leave this room. Is that understood?"

As he spoke, the main lights were switched on by a sergeant at the rear of the line-up chamber. In this sudden illumination, the small audience was revealed standing spellbound, staring toward the platform where Steve Conroy had crumpled.

That is, everyone was thus staring but three men. Of these, one was Zeng Tse-Lin. By some miracle of catapulting motion, Zeng had hurled himself silently to the room's main exit and now blocked the doorway with his impassive calmness, almost as if he were just entering from the outer corridor.

And in taking up this position, his tall, robed figure effectually blocked Eric Lancaster and Joe Nazarian from rushing out of the rectangular chamber. He had gained the portal a split instant ahead of them.

Nazarian gave vent to a violent protest.

"Stand aside, sir—stand aside! This young man here is sick. He needs air!"

As a matter of truth, young Lancaster looked genuinely nauseated. His dissipated countenance was unhealthily pallid by contrast to the redness of his unruly hair, and his greenish eyes seemed to be sunken in their sockets. He swayed jerkily.

Zeng relinquished his door-guarding post to a policeman who came rushing headlong to relieve him. Satisfied, then, that everyone present would remain in the room, Zeng moved smoothly toward the Lancaster youth.

"I am a doctor," he said gravely. "Permit me to do you a service."

Whereupon his unerringly trained fingers touched certain nerve centers in the region of the young man's diaphragm—the solar plexus area. Even through Lancaster's sporty tweeds, Dr. Zeng had no difficulty in locating those ganglia most intimately connected with the abdominal viscera.

Gently he applied certain mobile pressure there, employing a method he had learned from an ancient Tibetan monk wise in the art of healing. And as Zeng's hand moved, Eric Lancaster lost his unhealthy pallor; stopped his jerky gulping.

"What the devil did you do to me?" he demanded in wonderment. "I—I feel—okay again. I'm not sick any more!"

Zeng nodded benignly. "That was my hope," he said. "I believe the nausea will trouble you no more tonight."

He then turned and made his way toward the miniature stage, where a departmental medical officer was already kneeling over Steve Conroy's motionless form.

Captain Brian Carter hovered close by, making noises in his throat.

"Can't understand it!" he was muttering. "Here a man's on the point of spilling information, and he keels over in a dead faint!"

THE POLICE surgeon looked up grimly.

"Dead, not a faint," he corrected the Homicide chief. "This trucker is past saving."

"*What?*"

"Yes, Captain. Offhand, I'd say he had a bad heart. He must have overtaxed it recently with too much work, and the condition was further aggravated by fear when he was arrested, brought here to Headquarters for grilling."

"You're sure?"

"Practically sure," the medical officer said. "Of course, an autopsy may indicate otherwise."

Dr. Zeng Tse-Lin ventured to interpose himself into the conversation.

"Please pardon my unwarranted intrusion, gentlemen, but I have a curious notion that this was no natural death from failure of the heart. True, the man's dying symptoms seemed reminiscent of angina pectoris—the obvious pain, the clutching at the chest, the contorted face and gasping breath. But observe, now, the indications of asphyxia upon the features—the signs of respiratory paralysis."

"Meaning what?"

"Meaning, perhaps, that Conroy was murdered."

The police surgeon widened his eyes.

"Murdered? By strangulation? Good heavens, man, nobody was near enough to him to choke him! Nobody even touched him until after he fell."

"Quite true. Yet let us examine the body more carefully."

"Why? I've already done that. There's nothing to see except a traumatic abrasion on the back of the skull, a bruise as if from a blackjack blow. Minor concussion, maybe, but certainly not fatal. And not connected with the way he acted when he died."

"No other wounds?" Zeng persisted.

"None," the medical officer snapped, evidently nettled.

"That is what the murderer hoped you would report," Zeng Tse-Lin said impassively. "But behold a slight trace of blood from the mouth. May I borrow your flashlight, Captain Carter? Thank you. Now we shall see. Ah! Just as I suspected!"

"What is it?"

"A wound in the one place where it might possibly go without immediate discovery—within the mouth! See for yourself, at the back of the throat near the soft palate."

Carter peered. "You're right!"

"Yes. A very small missile made this wound, gentlemen. A tiny pellet, traveling with considerable velocity, and aimed with deadly accuracy.

The thug stiffened, in the grip of some horrid paralysis.

Please notice also a few white crystalline granules on the tongue, not yet fully dissolved."

"Granules?" The medical officer tensed.

"Exactly. And unless I am greatly mistaken, I believe it is a substance which your chemical laboratory will identify as aconite, one of the deadliest and swiftest of poisons!"

Brian Carter's jaw jutted. "By Godfrey!"

"To swallow aconite would be fatal enough," Zeng completed his diagnosis. "But in this case it was not only swallowed, but some of it entered the bloodstream through the wound in the mouth as well."

"A poisoned bullet?" Carter breathed.

"A bullet made of poison," Zeng corrected him. "It would be comparatively simple to mix the aconite crystals with dampened sodium chloride—common table salt—and mold the mixture into small pellet form under pressure. Such a pellet could be fired by a powerful air gun, for example. It would kill instantly, leaving little trace."

THE DISCOMFITED police surgeon was generous enough to admit his own earlier error.

"I take my hat off to you, Dr. Zeng. But who the devil would dream up such a fantastic murder method?"

"It is not so fantastic, sir. Aconite, or *bikh,* is widely employed in certain regions of India, where native tribes use it on poisoned slivers from blowguns. Similar usage is found in some of the East Indies islands."

Captain Carter lowered his voice.

"You think somebody here in this room had a blow-gun, Zeng?"

"Or a powerful compressed air pistol, as I mentioned before. It could have been discharged, unnoticed, from the darkened auditorium. You will recall that some person had a spell of coughing. This could have covered the slight noise of the weapon's discharge, I believe."

The Homicide chief hunched his heavy shoulders, drew his thick gray eyebrows together in a bushy line.

"In that case, Conroy may have been telling the truth! The heist gang tried to make him their fall guy by knocking him senseless in front of that warehouse and loading his truck with a small part of the loot. That way, public clamor would be at least partially satisfied. It would look as if we'd made one arrest, even though we didn't nab the rest of the mob!"

"Quite so, O my friend. And, since Conroy was genuinely unable to furnish any information concerning the thieves, they believed they had nothing to fear from him."

"Then why was he murdered now?"

"Because he was about to hurl an unexpected verbal bombshell. He was on the verge of remembering the license number of the sedan which sideswiped him—a sedan belonging to the gang of looters. This made him dangerous, so he was killed under cover of the room's darkness before he could speak."

"A spur-of-the-moment kill!" Carter growled. "Pulled by some person in this very room!"

Zeng Tse-Lin nodded bleakly. "It would seem so."

Then the medical officer broke into the low-voiced conversation.

"It seems strange that the mob would pick some trucker at random, just to make him the goat. Unnecessary, almost."

"On the contrary, it might have been a highly clever bit of scheming," Zeng rejoined. "By framing Conroy in the fog, and then boldly turning up an alarm from the warehouse, the thieves made certain that their crime would be viewed by the police as a daring raid and not an inside job of removing the rubber over a long period of time."

"Inside job?" Captain Carter exclaimed. "You think this whole thing might have been a cover-up to shield the work of somebody connected with the warehouse? The owner of the rubber, maybe? You think Joe Nazarian himself—"

"I offer no concrete theory," Dr. Zeng answered. "I merely suggest possibilities. It is written that a rat's nest has many exits, and the trapper must cover them all."

"They'll be covered," Carter rasped grimly. "We'll start by searching every soul in this room for the weapon."

In Zeng's estimation, the killer was far too crafty to be apprehended by so simple a method. But he kept the opinion to himself, retiring unostentatiously to the background as his friend set the machinery in motion.

Carter faced the little group in the auditorium.

"I'm sorry," he clipped out. "But you'll all have to submit to a search."

THEY STARED at him as if not comprehending the full import of the announcement. It was Hal Vondell, impeccably groomed fiancé of Cynthia Lancaster, who was first to answer.

In the manner of a man who is angry, but who carefully weighs that anger on mental scales, Vondell deliberately let it be known that he objected to any such procedure.

"What right have you to search any of us, Captain? Do you think you'll find the stolen rubber in somebody's pocket?"

Carter's voice was chipped ice. "This is no time for sarcasm, Mister. If you refuse to be searched, I can only conclude that you have something to hide. Let me remind you that a murder has just been committed here, and—"

"Murder?" Vondell paled. "You mean that truck driver is—is dead?"

"I mean exactly that," the Homicide official answered.

A visible stir went through the cluster of persons before him when they realized what had taken place in front of their very eyes. Not until now, apparently, did any one of them understand the significance of Dr. Zeng's low-pitched conversation with Captain Carter and the police surgeon, there on the stage by Steve Conroy's motionless figure.

Vondell's air of righteous indignation vanished.

"My word, I had no idea of such a thing! How was he killed?"

"There will be no statement until after the autopsy," Carter rumbled. "Do you still refuse to be examined?"

"I withdraw my objections," Vondell said hastily. "Help yourself."

Zeng Tse-Lin, watching the faces below him, carefully tabulated the diverse emotions revealed on those various countenances. He noticed a swift look which passed between Vondell and the golden-haired Cynthia Lancaster, like a furtive and wordless message, perhaps a warning. And he saw Eric Lancaster's dissipated features turn pasty at mention of the word "murder."

Joe Nazarian stiffened as he heard the announcement, and then turned to survey his companions with bulging eyes. He moved a step or two sideward, separating himself from the group. Thomas McKnight, the insurance agent, wore a stunned expression that was almost ludicrous when it slowly dawned on him that he was numbered as a possible suspect.

Abruptly, then, they all burst into speech, simultaneously indicating their complete willingness to be searched. Nazarian's oily voice seemed most insistent of all as he demanded that he be given the honor of being first to submit.

"Who else has a greater right to ask precedence?" he asked. "Since I own the stolen rubber, suspicion rests heaviest on me. I claim the privilege of clearing myself."

A hint of theatrical insincerity marked his tone, Zeng decided as he listened. But then he must not be too sure of it, because everything Nazarian said seemed to bear the same quality. A devious man, this Armenian, but not necessarily a guilty one. Time alone would hold the answer to that.

It began to look as if Time must hold the hidden answers to many enigmas, for when the group had been finally searched by deft police fingers, the results were wholly negative. Even Cynthia Lancaster, returning from an adjoining room in custody of the matron who had examined her, proved to be as weaponless as the rest.

IF ANY one of the company had possessed a compressed air gun, that gun was not to be found now.

Captain Carter, nonplussed, drew Zeng aside.

"How the devil can I hold all these people without evidence?" he whispered. "I can't risk half a dozen false arrest suits."

"Then why not release them? It is doubtful that any will attempt to leave the city. The innocent would have no reason to do so, and the guilty man dare not—for two reasons. First, flight would be a confession. Second, he stole a fortune in retread material tonight, but he cannot profit from that theft until the rubber has been sold in its present form or used to recap a vast quantity of worn tires for the Black Market."

"That's true," Carter agreed. "And meantime I can put a tail on every one of the bunch." He turned, raised his voice. "You may all leave, and you have my apology for detaining you."

Then he murmured a command to one of his underlings, who saluted and raced from the room to arrange for plainclothes shadows to follow each suspect.

When the line-up chamber had been cleared, Zeng Tse-Lin commenced thoughtfully pacing back and forth. His hawk-keen eyes held a veiled glitter and his scalpel-sharp mind knifed at the problem confronting him.

Somehow the killer had contrived to dispose of the murder weapon under cover of gloom and confusion. But where had he hidden it?

A sudden fantastic thought struck him. He remembered his own headlong rush toward the exit, when he had barred Eric Lancaster and Joe Nazarian from leaving. He recalled worming his way clear of the audience group, and later rendering aid to the red-haired Lancaster youth for his nausea.

During those instants of swift movement, Zeng realized that he had brushed close to many of the persons in the room, if not all of them.

"I wonder—" he whispered to himself now, pulling up short.

Brian Carter blinked at him. "You wonder what?"

"This," Dr. Zeng said with uncommon harshness.

And he delved a hand into the outer pocket of his own richly brocaded mandarin robe. When the spatulate fingers emerged, they held a queer looking small metal cylinder.

It was the death weapon.

CHAPTER V

TRAP COUNTER-TRAP

A TELEPHONE BELL rang stridently within an abandoned brewery building in the manufacturing district of Oakland. Guided by the rays of a hooded flashlight, a thick-set man hastened to respond. His footfalls echoed hollowly in the vast reaches of the structure, and his beady eyes and barrel chest seemed almost gorilla-like as he shambled forward.

He lifted the receiver. "Yeah?"

The voice that came to him over the wire was high-pitched and falsetto with excitement, anger. It might have been a man's tone, or it might have been a woman's.

"That you, Bennie?"

"Yeah."

"Good. Now listen, you blundering numbskull. You pulled a bad boner on the Embarcadero tonight when you framed that trucker. I told you to daub the sedan's tags with mud so nobody could read the numbers, didn't I?"

"Gosh, I forgot about it!" The thick-set man tensed. "Don't tell me the guy seen my plates and put the finger on me!"

"He started to. I shut him up, permanently."

"You mean you bumped him before he could spill? How didja manage it?"

"I had to do it right there in the line-up room at Headquarters and then stand still for a frisk. They didn't find the air gun on me, though."

"You ditched it?"

"Yes, by slipping it in the pocket of a robe worn by a Chinese doctor who happened to be there. He didn't tumble. Probably doesn't suspect it even now. But he looks like a dangerous customer. If he finds it in his robe, later, there may be trouble."

"That ain't so good, is it?" the heavy-set gorilla grated.

The falsetto voice grimly agreed. "Especially when everybody in the line-up room is being tailed by the cops. Including me. I had sense enough to come straight home, and I think maybe I can get out the back way without my shadow knowing I've left."

"Whatcha figure to do?"

"There's only one thing we *can* do. That's to get the gun off this Dr. Zeng before he finds out he has it."

"You wanna stick him up?"

"Yes. You're to meet me right away at this end of the bridge, see? And this time be sure your tags are smeared. If we're lucky and don't waste time, maybe we can waylay the guy as he goes out of Headquarters. Now step on it."

"I'm on my way," the thick-necked man promised.

He rang off, dashed from the building, hastily daubed grease on the licenses of his glossy black sedan and sent it rolling toward the bridge that led to San Francisco.

Meanwhile, in Captain Brian Carter's office, the Homicide detective and Zeng Tse-Lin were examining the weapon that had dealt death to poor Steve Conroy.

By now they had ruefully ascertained that it bore no fingerprints. The killer either had wiped it clean after using it, or had worn a glove at the time of its discharge.

It was a small, compact black metal cylinder or tube with an outer casing which pumped back and forth to build up compression in its powerful air chamber. Actuated by a spring-release mechanism, this charge of air would pack enough wallop to send a tiny pellet from the barrel with smashing velocity.

STUDYING IT, Carter made a bitter mouth.

"Imagine a man carrying a thing like this around. And loaded with poison!"

Zeng nodded gravely. "It illustrates the type of murderer we must hunt for. The mind that contrived such a weapon is no ordinary one, any more than the gun itself is commonplace. We are dealing with a person both devious and clever; someone who never does things the obvious way, but who is always prepared for any contingency."

"He proved that by killing Conroy," Carter assented gloomily. "He couldn't have known in advance that the trucker had spotted the license number of that black sedan. And yet he was all set to murder the man at an instant's notice."

"Our killer is quick-witted, indeed."

"Quick enough to slip his gun in your pocket," Carter growled. "The one place we wouldn't think to search!"

"That was almost a stroke of genius," Dr. Zeng nodded again. "But in making me his dupe, he miscalculated. Quite likely he believes I will not discover the weapon, at least for a while. And he is wrong, which gives us a slight advantage."

"How so?"

"It is written that chance sometimes opens a gate when other keys fail. We shall try to assist chance a little. I have an idea that our quarry may attempt to regain his gun from me before I find it in my pocket. Very well. If he makes such an effort, I am prepared to apprehend him."

The police official sprang to his feet.

"Not without help!" he objected quickly. "I won't have you using yourself as bait for any such trap unless you're protected."

"If by protection you mean an official escort, I fear that it would defeat my purpose. A criminal might hesitate to waylay me if he saw that I had a bodyguard."

"But suppose something went wrong? What if you stop a slug and the man gets away?"

"It is unlikely." A brief smile flashed across Zeng's mobile lips. "Remember, you have police surveillance on each of the suspects. Once the guilty person makes an incriminating move, I can depend upon his shadow for aid if I require it. Moreover, I shall have Chow close at hand. May I use your phone?"

"Go right ahead," the Homicide chief said dubiously.

Having journeyed to Headquarters with Captain Carter in the chief's car a while ago, Dr. Zeng had left his own limousine at home. Now he dialed the House of a Thousand Beatitudes, where he had likewise left Lai Hu Chow.

"Meet me at once, two blocks north of Police Headquarters," he bade his faithful Mongol servitor when the connection had been established. Then he added a mysterious phrase. "The limb of communications."

Carter peered at him as he rang off.

"The limb of communications. What's that—another false leg gadget?"

The query was shrewdly based on Carter's knowledge of a certain hobby in which Zeng indulged. The hawklike man had created many artificial limbs for the one-legged Chow, each cleverly designed to contain various types of compact equipment—guns, or gas bombs, or knives and ropes in case of need.

Zeng's dark eyes twinkled. "Your thirst for information does you credit, O my friend. Perhaps the answer will be divulged to you soon. At the moment, time presses. I must go."

Shaking hands with himself in courteous Chinese fashion, he bade Carter a sincere good-night and left the building.

THE OUTER darkness was still garbed in fleecy blankets of fog, and there was no traffic, no sound save for the steady clatter of moving cables in the street car slots. But Dr. Zeng was not to be lulled to any false feeling of security. Danger lurked in the drifting mists, he knew, and he was deliberately exposing himself to that jeopardy in order to trap a killer.

He moved north; made no attempt at silence. And as he walked down the street's gentle grade, he heard a sound behind him—a whisper of tires on moist asphalt. That would be a car rolling into motion, lights out, motor dead, its wheels turning merely by the pull of gravity on the incline.

No automobile would move thus unless its driver had some furtive purpose. Zeng's ascetic face was bleak, expressionless, as he realized he had been correct in assuming that he would be attacked!

He gained the next intersection and paused there. Sure enough, a black sedan emerged like a shadowy wraith from the fog. It halted at the opposite curb. From it a thick-set man erupted. He had an automatic in his fist, a mask on his face.

"Stick 'em up!" he snarled at Dr. Zeng. "Make a bleat and I drill you!"

Zeng raised his arms meekly. "If it is money you seek, you will find it in an inner pocket of my coat. Let us have no unnecessary violence, I beg."

The thug shifted his gun, rammed a hand into Zeng's clothes. And then, like lightning striking, Zeng made his move.

As swiftly as a cobra he brought his arms down. One fist impacted upon his assailant's left wrist, deflecting the automatic. The other hand snaked about the man's neck; unerringly located a nerve in the vertebrae. Sharp finger-pressure burrowed at that nerve and the thug screamed wildly as agonizing pain lanced into every fiber of his crooked soul.

He seemed stiffened and helpless in the grip of some horrid paralysis.

"Ar-r-rgh…. Awk…!"

Zeng calmly shook him. "Name me the one who hired you. Quickly, lest I send you shrieking to your ancestors!"

"It—it was—"

The thick-necked thug got no further. From the black sedan a blurt of orange flame burgeoned, even as the car itself got under way with engine roaring, gears whining.

Dr. Zeng felt his captive jerk under the smashing jolt of a well-aimed bullet, then go suddenly limp. Instinct told him that the fellow would never speak again; that he was dead.

And meantime that black sedan was hurtling forward, escaping in the mist with a murderer at the wheel. That killer now had three deaths chalked up against him—Pat Barton, the warehouse watchman; Conroy, the truck driver; and this masked hood.

Hurling the corpse aside, Zeng catapulted across the street, angling. He made a stupendous effort to clutch a hand-hold on the car as it flashed by. His outstretched fingers missed the door handle by the barest fraction of an inch. He grasped again, seeking for the rear bumper.

Something thin and flimsily metallic met his fingers as they closed. With magnificent strength he tried to haul himself up on the speeding machine. But his steely grip on projecting metal was torn loose by the car's surging momentum—or rather, the metal itself came away.

ZENG WENT tumbling to the pavement, and only his superlative muscular coordination saved him from serious injury. As it was, he fell headlong, and the black sedan vanished in misty darkness. The night swallowed it.

As he scrambled upright, Zeng heard rapid, lurching footfalls. Then powerful arms wrapped themselves about him, the arms of Lai Hu Chow, steadying him.

"Thousan' curses!" the big Mongol panted in the pidgin English he used only when excited. "Next time you catchee car, you wait for dliver to stop. You wantee get killed to death?"

"I am unhurt," Zeng reassured him. "And although I failed to capture my prey, I now have a means of learning his identity."

He stared grimly at the grease-smeared metal plate which he had wrenched from the rear of the black sedan.

It was a license tag whose first four digits, *6-0-V-1*, coincided with what Steve Conroy had spoken in the police line-up room just before death struck him!

And now, led by Captain Brian Carter, a cluster of officers came rushing from Headquarters, drawn by the sound of gunfire. Dr. Zeng turned to meet them, and to point out the corpse of the thug who had been slain.

CHAPTER VI

SPECIAL PLEA

THE SUN was barely an hour high the next morning when an inexpensive little coupé drew up before the House of a Thousand Beatitudes. The girl who emerged from it to ring Zeng Tse-Lin's doorbell was dainty, diminutive and altogether feminine from her toeless pumps to the crown of her auburn hair.

For all her fresh and appealing loveliness, though, she carried herself with an air of competence and self-assurance. Looking at her, it would instinctively be recognized that here was a girl of charm and breeding, capable of intelligently directing whatever course she chose to take.

She was Ann Carter—Captain Brian Carter's niece.

This morning, as she stood before Dr. Zeng's residence, she seemed taut and hurried, as if driven by some inner compulsion of considerable magnitude. There was determination in her fine eyes, a set expression upon her tempting red lips. This was not at all like Ann, for ordinarily she permitted nothing to upset her serene nature.

Possessed of an income sufficient to her needs, she had, ever since graduation from college, conducted an adult night school class in Chinatown. It was both hobby and career to her. In addition, she took a lively interest in her uncle's police work. This was the reason for her present call upon Zeng.

She pressed the bell button.

Upstairs, a gong chimed musically. Zeng Tse-Lin, sipping his breakfast tea, set aside the cup and lithely crossed the room. He opened a teakwood box, disclosing a ground glass reflector which glowed to life when a switch was thrown. Upon the screen an image formed—the features of a young, auburn-haired girl.

Dr. Zeng summoned Chow. "Miss Ann Carter comes. Make haste to admit her."

The giant Mongol's jaw dropped as he turned to obey. To him, there was something of sorcery in his master's identification of callers before they entered the house. He could never comprehend the uses of a selenium scanning disk set into the front doorway, an adaptation of the television principle which Zeng employed to behold all visitors in advance. The whole thing was a device of the devil, as far as the huge servitor was concerned.

Not that he cared. If Zeng wanted to have dealings with Satan, that was all right with Chow. In his estimation, his master could do no wrong.

Presently he lumbered back into the room, conducting Ann as if she were a royal princess. And his moonlike countenance broke into a wise smile when he saw the light that leaped into Zeng's eyes as the girl entered.

Chow knew, without being told, that Dr. Zeng was secretly in love with Ann Carter. And the Mongol could never quite understand why his master always masked this feeling. To Chow, a believer in direct action, it seemed that if a man cared for a girl, he ought to tell her so.

But Zeng Tse-Lin thought otherwise. He could not bring himself to ask Ann to share the dangers to which his life as a manhunter exposed him. Therefore, he concealed his true feelings toward her and allowed her to go on thinking he was Chinese. This spurious racial barrier was his mask and his shield.

HE BOWED deeply as she approached.

"My unworthy home takes on the aspect of paradise in the reflection of your presence." His voice was gentle. "I bid you welcome."

"Thank you, Zeng. You make pretty speeches." She flushed at the compliment. "But let's dispense with the polite formalities. I have a favor to ask you."

"If it be in my power, I grant it gladly."

She leaned toward him. "My uncle has told me all about what happened last night. Including how you got that sedan's license tag and turned it over to him."

"And—"

"The tag has been traced. It came from a car belonging to Eric Lancaster."

A glitter leaped into Zeng's hawklike eyes. "So!"

"Please don't jump at conclusions, like my uncle." Ann made an appealing gesture. "Eric wasn't driving that car. It had been stolen several days ago. He reported the theft at the time. It's on the police records, if you want proof."

Zeng felt a sudden pang in his heart, almost like jealousy. Why should Ann be defending young Eric Lancaster, that dissolute and disinherited wastrel? Could it be that she cared for him—wished to shield him?

The girl continued her swift plea.

"My uncle suspects Eric of those three m-murders, and of responsibility for looting the rubber warehouse. He bases his conclusions on the license plates, and on the fact that Eric was the only one last night who managed to elude his police shadow. All the others went to their various homes and stayed there."

"Then your uncle's suspicions are well founded, I fear," Dr. Zeng intoned gravely.

"You mustn't say that! For once, Uncle Brian is wrong! Eric may be wild, dissipated, yes. But he's not a killer or a thief! You've got to believe that—for my sake!"

"For *your* sake, Ann?"

She reddened. "I didn't mean it that way. It's Cynthia Lancaster I'm thinking about. She's a good friend of mine, Zeng. I've known her for years. And Eric is her only brother. When she learned this morning that the police are hunting him, she phoned me and asked me to use my influence to help him."

Zeng Tse-Lin felt a load lifting abruptly from his heart. He smiled wryly at his own jealousy.

"I see. And you probably tried to convince your uncle of Eric's innocence, but got nowhere. Now you wish me to intercede."

"Th-that's right. Will you? Please, Zeng?"

"It is written that a criminal's family is last to suspect his guilt. Naturally Cynthia Lancaster wishes to defend her brother. Naturally she would attempt to work through you. Yet how can we absolve Eric in the face of the evidence against him?"

"Circumstantial evidence!" Ann responded swiftly. "Worthless without real proof. You must help him, Zeng. You *must!*"

Zeng Tse-Lin found it impossible to deny her plea.

"As you wish," he said. "I shall try my best."

Even as she started to thank him, the door gong chimed and in a moment Chow appeared, conducting Captain Brian Carter himself into the room. The Homicide chief looked startled to find his niece already here.

"WHY, ANN!" he exclaimed. Then he turned to Zeng. "Has she told you we've practically got the goods on Eric Lancaster, although we haven't nabbed him as yet?"

Dr. Zeng nodded. "Ann gave me the tidings. But what conclusive evidence have you?"

"Enough," Carter answered grimly. "He gave the slip to his tail last night. It was his car that shot was fired from—the shot that killed the thug you captured. We've identified your murdered prisoner, incidentally. He was a well-known hood, Bennie Burke; had a long criminal record."

Zeng's face was expressionless. "Too bad he did not live to name his employer."

"What difference does it make? Eric Lancaster is our man, the same as it was his sedan that was used earlier in an effort to frame the truck driver, Steve Conroy. It all adds up, even to the fact that Eric is broke and depends on his sister's bounty. The rubber theft was his scheme to grab off a fortune and make himself independent of Cynthia's charity."

"The reasoning is sound, O my friend," Zeng said. "But often a ship of theory will leak when launched upon the sea of facts. Before you are too sure of Eric's guilt, consider the others who were present when Conroy was slain by an aconite pellet."

Carter scowled. "Why bother? Lancaster fits that part of the picture, too. Before he was disinherited, he traveled all over the world. He could easily have picked up information about the poison from the natives who use it."

"Is there no other suspect with a background of travel?"

"We-ell, yes," Carter admitted, uncomfortably. "All of them, as a matter of fact."

"Ah?"

"Cynthia Lancaster herself made a yacht cruise to the Indies three years ago. She spent several months there, studying native customs. Her fiancé, Hal Vondell, was with her. They brought back a collection of blow guns which they turned over to a museum. But Cynthia wouldn't engineer the looting of that rubber when she's already wealthy. Neither would Vondell, when he's going to marry her fortune."

"Don't be too sure about Vondell!" Ann broke into the discussion. "I happen to know Cynthia has had several quarrels with him lately over his management of her estate. Their engagement isn't positive, the way things stand. And he's got a lot of gambling debts. If she jilts him, discharges him, he'll be in a bad fix. That might be motive enough for him to scheme a wholesale rubber theft."

Dr. Zeng spoke quietly. "There are two other persons to consider. McKnight, the insurance agent; and Nazarian, who owns the stolen camelback."

Again Carter looked uncomfortable. "I'll grant McKnight's had business reverses lately. The war has cost him plenty of canceled policies due to rising premium costs. And it seems he was a shipboard radioman before going into the insurance game. Made many a trip to the Orient and the Indies. But it's nonsense to think of him as a big-time criminal. He's not the type."

"And Nazarian?" Zeng said. "We know he formerly lived part of each year in Java. What about his finances?"

"Tied up in rubber stocks and plantations," the police official admitted. "Lost, now that the Japs have taken the islands. It looks like Nazarian's only asset was this warehouse full of camelback. And it was frozen so he couldn't liquidate."

"See?" Ann cried. "He might have planned the theft himself to collect the insurance cash!"

HER UNCLE made a disparaging gesture.

"Nazarian was shadowed to his home last night and stayed there. So did all the rest, except Eric Lancaster. He's the only one who slipped his tail; the only one who could have been in that black sedan. It's so open-and-shut that I'm not even having the others followed any more. Eric's our man, Ann. Sorry. Now will you stop defending him?"

"Not as long as I think he's innocent. For all you know, Nazarian or Vondell could have gone home and then slipped out the back way without your men realizing it. You're concentrating on Eric without just cause."

"You'll think differently when I catch him and sweat him into telling me where the loot was taken," the Homicide chief said grimly, arising. "I'll let you know how I make out, Zeng."

Ann also prepared to leave. But as she accompanied her uncle from the room, she cast a pleading look at Zeng Tse-Lin as if to seek confirmation of his promise to help clear Eric Lancaster. A nod was Zeng's answer.

When his two guests had gone, he went to the phone and made a series of calls. In each case he spoke Chinese. He was beginning to formulate a campaign.

CHAPTER VII

DEATH'S VISITORS

PARTING WITH her uncle in front of the Mandarin Emporium, Ann Carter got into her own little coupé and headed it toward Nob Hill, in which neighborhood Cynthia Lancaster lived.

The residence, old, somber, was a relic of past decades. Even its front doorbell was of the old-fashioned pull-knob type, which set up a clangor within the house as Ann yanked it.

A musty odor emanated from the dark hall when a servant presently responded. Despite the morning sunshine outside, the interior of the residence seemed gloomily foreboding as the servant announced that Cynthia Lancaster was not at home.

Disappointed, Ann turned to depart—and saw an expensive sedan draw to a halt at the curb. It was Cynthia's, and the golden-haired heiress came wearily forward to greet her visitor.

"Ann! What brings you here? Have you any news? Please come in. I—I've got to talk to someone. I'm so worried!"

In the shadowy parlor, Ann sympathetically surveyed her friend.

"Poor dear. You've been out hunting Eric?"

"Yes. But I didn't find him. Oh, Ann, I can't let the police arrest him for a crime he didn't commit!" Cynthia's veneer of sophistication was gone, and haggard lines deepened under her make-up.

"There, there," Ann tried to soothe her. "Since you phoned me this morning, I've been to see a friend of mine who's promised to help. Everything will come out all right."

"If I could only be sure of that!" The blond girl made a bitter mouth. "But you know how wild Eric is. Suppose he were actually g-guilty?"

From the doorway a new voice sounded, suave, restrained, yet holding a hint of anger.

"Cynthia! Get a grip on yourself, dear. Remember you're talking to a police officer's niece!"

The speaker was Hal Vondell, impeccably groomed as always; seeming to weigh each word on mental scales. As Cynthia's intended husband he appeared to assume the right to dictate what she might or might not say.

Turning, the golden-haired girl stared at him in momentary indignation.

"Ann is my friend, Hal."

"Friend! You mean police spy, sent here by her uncle to get a line on your own brother!"

Ann's eyes flashed. All her innate dislike and distrust of the man rose to the surface.

"I think you owe me an apology, Mr. Vondell. How dare you call me a spy?"

"There's no other reason for you to be here—unless you suspected Eric of having come home."

"You—you mean he's in this house? Right now?"

"As if you didn't know," Vondell sneered. Then he turned to Cynthia. "I'm sorry, my dear. I brought your brother home just a little while ago, while you were out. I found him in a barroom. He's upstairs in bed, now. And I suppose this *friend* of yours will immediately inform Headquarters."

The golden-haired Lancaster girl seemed suddenly transformed. One instant she was a sane, civilized person.

The next instant she became a thin-lipped tigress. She opened her handbag, withdrew a small, pearl-handled automatic.

"All right, Ann," she grated. "Blood's thicker than water. I won't let you turn Eric in. I'd kill you first."

"Cynthia!"

"Don't try anything foolish. Move. Upstairs. Hal and I will find some way of taking care of you. Permanently, if you make it necessary."

STUNNED, ANN read the menace glittering in the blond girl's narrowed eyes, caught the sarcastic smile of approval on Hal Vondell's saturnine mouth. The whole scene was like a nightmare, a fantastic impossibility. Yet it was real. Cynthia Lancaster had the look of a potential killer—and already three murders had been committed in the past eight or ten hours.

Could Cynthia have been behind them?

Moving in a daze, Ann was prodded upstairs.

"Stop a minute," the golden-haired girl commanded. "I want to see if Eric is all right." She opened a bedroom door, peered in.

Then a wild cry erupted from her taut throat. *"Eric!"*

Her wastrel brother lay sprawled across a canopied bedstead, and there was an ominous quality to his stillness, a suffused engorgement upon his dissipated face. His red hair was touseled, his collar and tie torn open as if in some desperate struggle to breathe. But he was not breathing now.

Ann Carter, oblivious to the menace of Cynthia's gun, leaped into the room and grasped Eric Lancaster's limber wrist. Then, in horror, she dropped it.

There was no pulse.

"Cynthia!" she whispered. "I—I think he's d-dead."

"No! He can't be! Do something, Ann!" The heiress had apparently forgotten her recent enmity, her savage threats. "*Do* something! Get a doctor—"

That one word, "doctor," triggered Ann into motion. She rushed to the bedroom phone, frantically dialed Zeng Tse-Lin.

And before ten minutes had elapsed, Zeng arrived.

Not that he could do Eric Lancaster any good. As he bent over the recumbent form, he realized that it was too late for even his own superlative medical skill.

Slowly he straightened up, shaking his head in regret.

"Your brother's life has run its course," he said to the trembling Cynthia. "He was murdered."

As he spoke, a shrill bell-clangor sounded downstairs. When a servant responded, two men entered the house.

One was the insurer, Thomas McKnight.

The other was Joe Nazarian.

It seemed a grisly coincidence to Ann Carter that these two men should appear upon the scene at such a time. Or was it coincidence, after all? Could it be that either of them, or both, had some connection with Eric Lancaster's mysterious sudden death and wished to make certain that he had really died?

Ann, together with Dr. Zeng and Hal Vondell, was now in the parlor of the Lancaster residence, confronting the two visitors. Cynthia had remained upstairs, alone with her grief and her brother's body. A phone call had already been put through to Brian Carter at Homicide Headquarters.

It was Thomas McKnight who spoke first. The insurance broker seemed puzzled by the presence of Ann and Zeng, but maintained a businesslike air as he addressed Hal Vondell.

"I've come to see young Mr. Lancaster and pay him his claim for the sedan that was stolen from him a few days ago. The missing car was covered by a policy issued through my office."

"And I, sir," Nazarian said in his oily tone, "happened to encounter Mr. McKnight on his way here, and took the liberty of coming along. Mr. McKnight assures me that I shall collect my insurance on the looted stock of rubber some time today, or tomorrow. Therefore, I wish to pay the arrears of rental on the warehouse, and arrange for cancellation of the lease, since I now have no further need for the building."

BOTH EXPLANATIONS seemed plausible enough. "Glib" was the word Ann Carter thought of, though. Nazarian and McKnight certainly had their stories down pat, she told herself.

Was either man lying, or were they both speaking the truth?

Hal Vondell scowled at the two callers.

"You picked a rotten time to come here and talk business," he rasped. "Eric Lancaster has just passed away, upstairs."

"Good heavens!" the Armenian rubber importer exclaimed unctuously. "How did it happen?"

"This—er—I mean this Chinese doctor here has an idea it was murder. I disagree with him. I found Eric early this morning in an all-night saloon, stupefied from drink. I brought him home, put him to bed. The next time I saw him, he was dead. Acute alcoholism would be my guess. He'd got hold of a fistful of money, I wouldn't know where, and he went on one spree too many."

Zeng Tse-Lin spoke impassively. "Your guess is incorrect, Mr. Vondell. Eric was slain by means of the same drug which was used on that truck driver, Conroy. Aconite."

"Ridiculous! Conroy died the instant the poison hit him. But Eric was okay when I brought him home, barring his being tight. Are you trying to insinuate *I* needled a dose of the stuff in him when I put him to bed?"

"Not at all," Zeng answered mildly. "In Eric's case, I think the drug was administered internally; perhaps in a drink of whiskey. When swallowed, aconite sometimes takes as much as three hours to work its lethal effect. Only when injected does it kill immediately."

"You mean the poison was in him when I found him there in that barroom?"

"Such is my assumption, sir."

Somehow, as he said this, Zeng sensed sudden electrical tension in the parlor. It was a taut aura that seemed to grip everyone present. He had a premonition that by announcing his theory he was laying himself open to danger.

Which was precisely what he intended. It was written that an individual whose conscience is heavy with guilt can sometimes be forced into the open by means of well-chosen words. And Zeng had phrased his theory with deliberate care, as a fencer feints with his foil in order to penetrate an adversary's guard.

Not that he expected any immediately visible result. But he knew he could anticipate a countering move, presently.

As to the nature of that move, time alone held the answer.

Joe Nazarian assumed an oily expression of sympathy.

"Please convey my condolences to Miss Lancaster," he said to Vondell. "I think it best that I leave, now. We can discuss the warehouse at another time. Coming, Mr. McKnight?"

"Yes, of course, of course." The insurer mopped his balding brow. "A terrible thing. Terrible. Makes a man wonder who's going to be struck next." There was a rabbity quality in his voice, his manner; and his eyes held dread.

Zeng Tse-Lin made no attempt to prevent the departure of the two men. To begin with, he had no authority for such an act. In addition, his plan of campaign was based upon each of them being free to move about, without hindrance.

AFTER THEY had left, Hal Vondell remarked that he was going upstairs to see if Cynthia needed him. This left Zeng alone in the parlor with Ann.

"I, too, must depart," he told her. "You wait here for your uncle and inform him of everything that has happened. I shall make contact with him later."

"You've got something in mind? A clue? A plan?"

He nodded. "Even now it is in operation, with the assistance of a group of my Chinese merchant friends. More I cannot say, except that I believe Eric Lancaster was killed because he knew or guessed too much."

"How do you mean?"

"He had come into possession of a large sum of cash, enough to go on a wild spree. Perhaps, somehow, he had guessed the identity of the rubber thief. Perhaps he went to this murderer and demanded hush money, blackmail. The guilty one gave it to him—but later poisoned him to remove the threat of exposure."

"Zeng, I think you're right!" the girl whispered. Her fine eyes probed his own. "Promise me you'll be c-careful."

His heart leaped at this evidence of her concern for his safety, but he masked his feelings.

"Thank you, Ann," he answered in a gentle voice.

Then he turned, left the house, knowing that he walked directly toward peril.

CHAPTER VIII

CAMELBACK TRAIL

OVER IN the manufacturing district of Oakland, humming activity marked the interior of an old brewery building, long since abandoned by its original operators. This was the structure from which the thick-necked thug, Bennie Burke, had departed the previous night in a stolen black sedan to waylay Zeng Tse-Lin.

Bennie's mission had been unsuccessful, ending in his death at the hands of the person he was working for. That man had killed him by a pistol shot from the sedan to keep him from confessing when Dr. Zeng captured him.

The murder of Bennie Burke had not stilled the lawless toil of his fellow criminals, however. A group of them, hoodlums all, were busy now in the abandoned brewery, sorting and classifying and stacking the hundreds of coils of camelback rubber they had stolen from that Embarcadero warehouse owned by Cynthia Lancaster. Hidden in a garage connected to the brewery was the fleet of trucks which had transported the loot.

Another foreman now had Bennie Burke's job of supervision, and as he directed the setting up of certain machinery, the telephone rang, just as it had rung last night to summon Burke out on a task that had proved fatal.

Burke's successor, tall, lanky, squint-eyed, answered.

"Hello?"

"Is that you, Harry?" The voice that came over the wire was pitched to a falsetto register, squeaky, almost womanish. "How's the work coming?"

"It's comin' okay. But look. There's somethin' screwy goin' on. I got some phone tips that don't sound so good."

"Such as?"

The lanky, squint-eyed crook lowered his tone.

"A bunch of Chinese merchants over in Chinatown have been nosin' around, tryin' to buy bootleg tires for their delivery wagons. Seems funny so many of 'em would get the same idea at the same time."

"You're right, Harry!" The womanish voice tensed. "I've got a hunch this is the work of a guy named Zeng. He probably asked a lot of his friends to do it."

"Why?"

"Trying to get a line on us!" the voice snarled. "For some reason, he's butting into the game. I suspected it a while ago, when he called the turn on the death of a certain young jerk who'd put the blackmail bite on me. Now I'm positive!"

"Whatcha gonna do about this Zeng?" the hood named Harry asked.

"Bait a trap for him," the high-pitched voice responded. "Now pay attention while I give you the detail."

Meantime, Dr. Zeng Tse-Lin was departing from the Lancaster residence, leaving Ann Carter there to await the arrival of her uncle, Captain Brian Carter.

And as Zeng made for his limousine parked at the curb, his brow furrowed with annoyance. The giant servitor, Lai Hu Chow, who should have been at the wheel, was nowhere in evidence.

Chow had just one failing. That was a passionate devotion to lurid Western movies. When the mood was on him, it could never be told when he would slip away to some cheap theater and remain there hours on end, watching the same picture over and over. Often he did this when his master needed him most.

Such as now.

There was no use trying to locate him, though. He might have wandered into any one of a dozen downtown movie houses, Dr. Zeng ruefully realized. And he would not return until he had slaked his appetite for blood and thunder.

With a sigh, Zeng drew an extra set of keys from his clothing and unlocked the limousine. Then he headed for Chinatown and his own Mandarin Emporium.

ON HIS arrival, he found the store apparently doing far more trade than the forenoon hour warranted. And all the customers were Chinese, wandering with dignified tread through aisles that were piled high with priceless merchandise.

Zeng Tse-Lin's heart warmed, for these were his neighbors and friends, the men whom he had called by telephone after Ann Carter visited him to ask his help in clearing Eric Lancaster. Honest Chinese business and professional men, these customers were. Only Zeng knew that they were not really customers. They had come to report their findings, in answer to the favor he had requested of them.

At a sign from Zeng, they followed him, one by one, to the stairway leading upward into the House of a Thousand Beatitudes. In his spacious living room he faced them, greeted them with a courteous welcome.

These polite preliminaries finished, he asked the question that burned upon his lips.

"Has any one of you encountered such a person as I seek? A man willing to sell bootleg retread tires without demanding your ration certificates?"

An elderly spokesman stepped forward. "San Francisco's garages, tire shops and automotive accessory stores have been completely combed, O respected Doctor. No dealer volunteered to purvey illegal tires."

Zeng's ascetic face betrayed none of the disappointment he felt.

"There was no hint of a possible Black Market?"

"On the contrary, it would seem that there are no tires of any description available. Even the worn casings, the second-hand and worthless carcasses, have disappeared. Where once they glutted every dealer's shelves because repair materials were unavailable, they have now vanished. As the white man would say, the used tire market has been cornered."

Zeng Tse-Lin bowed formally. "Your services have been of inestimable value. My only request is that you continue your splendid efforts, in the hope that a lead may yet turn up. Meanwhile, permit me to serve all of you with bowls of very inferior tea as a token of my appreciation."

The conventions of Oriental hospitality consumed more than a full hour. When the last guest had departed, Zeng concentrated upon the problem confronting him.

The work of his neighbors had not been entirely in vain. One essential fact had been disclosed—the disappearance of all used tires from the open market. This had deep significance.

It could not be hoped to dispose of a quarter of a million dollars' worth of camelback through ordinary lawless channels. Unprocessed, the coils were practically valueless for clandestine resale. But if it were used to retread vast numbers of outworn tire carcasses, those tires would then have a tremendous monetary worth.

Hence, the unknown head of the warehouse looting mob was undoubtedly engaged in some such gigantic venture, and had established a secret factory for his operations. To locate this plant would be to locate the gang itself, along with its leader.

ZENG REPAIRED to his laboratory and, with swift deftness, improvised a compact apparatus consisting of a small bellows-operated air intake leading through various tubes of chemicals, housed in a portable box. The reagents he selected were those that would react to one certain kind of fumes. In brief, the device was a miniature smoke-analyzer to detect the effluvium of any plant in which rubber was being vulcanized!

It was shortly after noon when he set forth on a lone quest for such a secret factory. Nor was it so strange that he had determined to conduct his search without official help. The matter had become a personal one, for many reasons.

That slain warehouse watchman, elderly Pat Barton, had been Dr. Zeng's patient and friend. His murder demanded avenging. The framing and subsequent killing of poor Steve Conroy, the truckman, had been an equally callous crime; a challenge.

And there was Eric Lancaster's death. Ann Carter had enlisted Zeng's aid in clearing the dissipated youth of suspicion, and Zeng had given his word. He intended to keep that promise, even though Eric was now beyond caring. At least the young man's sister deserved the satisfaction of seeing his name cleared.

Finally, Zeng himself had undergone an attempted assault at the hands of Bennie Burke. And Bennie had been murdered in Zeng's grasp. This definitely must not go unpunished, Zeng told himself darkly.

In the back of his mind, though, a vague thought troubled him. Somehow it seemed that he was already possessed of the one essential clue that would point to the killer's identity. But no matter how often he reviewed all the details, he could not put his finger on it. The thing was obscure, he knew. Still it vexed him that he had failed, thus far, to reason it out.

Mentally he tabulated the original list of suspects, the persons who had been present in the line-up room at Headquarters at the moment of Steve Conroy's slaying. Death had removed Eric Lancaster from this list. The golden-haired Cynthia Lancaster must likewise be crossed off, for it was inconceivable that she would poison her own brother.

Which left McKnight, the insurance agent; Hal Vondell, manager of Cynthia's estate as well as her fiancé; and the devious Joe Nazarian.

Three suspects. And one of them had said, or done, something to incriminate himself—if Zeng Tse-Lin could only remember what it was!

There were two Wild West movies on the double bill, running continuously. Lai Hu Chow sat through three complete showings before his conscience prodded him from the cheap theater to emerge, blinking, into the mid-afternoon sunshine.

Dismayed by the passage of time, the giant Mongol lumbered hastily toward the Lancaster residence on Nob Hill, where he had left his master's limousine. The car was no longer there, though, and Chow fervently cursed himself in several different Chinese dialects as he realized that he had been gone from early morning until three hours past the time of mid-day rice.

Ruefully he turned to trudge in the direction of Chinatown. As he plodded away, the front door of the Lancaster house opened and a girl came down the steps.

"Chow!" she called.

THE HUGE Oriental swung about, his moon-face breaking into a smile when he recognized Ann Carter. Maybe she would offer him a lift to the Mandarin Emporium in her coupé, he thought hopefully. He went toward her.

Ann was only too happy to see him. For several trying hours she had been with Cynthia Lancaster, comforting the grief-stricken heiress, remaining by her side during the preliminary police investigation of Eric's death and the subsequent removal of the body for autopsy.

Nothing more had been said about the bereaved girl's hysterical gun threats earlier in the morning, for Ann was not one to bear a grudge. Nor had the surly Hal Vondell remained in the residence any longer than necessary. Pleading business duties, he had gone downtown soon after the departure of the Homicide detectives, leaving Cynthia alone with Ann.

Now, at last, having given her friend a sedative, Ann felt free to go about her own affairs. And the sight of Chow was like a tonic after the morbid hours she had just experienced. He might even have news of Zeng.

But when she asked him, he merely shook his head.

"Chow no blamee good," he mourned. "Go to movies, forget master. Chow go home now, catch devil."

"I'll take you," Ann volunteered. "Perhaps Zeng will forgive you if I ask him to."

The giant responded with alacrity. But when they reached Dr. Zeng's home they were disappointed to learn that he had gone out, hours ago, and had not yet returned.

At the doorway of the Mandarin Emporium, a Chinese youth loitered, obviously killing time. Catching sight of Ann and Chow, he approached them.

"May I speak to you, Miss Carter?"

She recognized him as a former member of her night school department, the son of a respected dealer in imported foodstuffs. In his turn, the young man knew Ann to be a close friend of Dr. Zeng, frequently working with him when sickness threatened some Chinatown household, and therefore to be trusted.

At her nod, the youth spoke rapidly.

"The doctor asked a number of us to hunt around for somebody who would sell bootleg retread tires. Well, I've found such a person. Now I'm wondering what is to be the next step."

It became suddenly clear to Ann what Zeng had meant when he had told her of a plan he had put into operation, with the help of his Chinese neighbors. Now she understood his method of trying to get a line on the rubber-theft gang.

"Tell me the details of this contact you've made," she said to the youth.

"All I know is, a garage man told me to be on a certain corner, with cash, at four o'clock this afternoon. I thought maybe Dr. Zeng would follow me in another car, but he isn't here. And it's almost time."

Ann's mind worked swiftly. "You go ahead and keep the appointment. Chow and I will trail you."

"Okey-doke!" The youth grinned boyishly. "Just like a G-man story, huh?"

He crossed the street to his stripped-down jalopy and set forth, with Ann and the giant Mongol following in her unostentatious little coupé.

TRAFFIC CONGESTION impeded their progress, but presently the Chinese boy parked south of the Slot and lolled back, waiting. Ann halted farther up the block.

"Watch sharply, Chow."

The big Oriental narrowed his eyes.

"Look! Man stopping in sedan. Speaking to youth. Youth getting into sedan with him. You hurry or we lose them!"

Ann gunned her coupé forward, following the other car at a discreet distance. The trail led straight to the Bay Bridge and across to Oakland, presently ending before what seemed to be a deserted building in the manufacturing district—a rambling old structure of red brick, still bearing the trade-mark of the brewer who once had occupied it.

As the car ahead halted in front of this abandoned brewery, Ann Carter had an abrupt feeling that she had been foolhardy in coming here without first leaving some word for Zeng Tse-Lin or her uncle at Police Headquarters.

The feeling was heightened by her sudden realization that she had driven into a dead-end street, which went no further than the red brick building before her. To get away, she must back out.

And even as she put her gears into reverse, she saw another auto barring the street exit behind her, a car which must have followed her, even as she herself had followed the sedan up forward. Her escape was blocked.

"Chow!" she whispered. "Something tells me we've driven into a trap! Look, ahead! That boy is struggling with the driver of the sedan!"

CHAPTER IX

CRIME'S CAPTIVES

EVEN AS Ann Carter spoke, the Chinese youth in the car ahead sagged under a blackjack blow and the sedan itself rolled forward into what appeared to be a storage garage connected to the abandoned brewery.

Then the car behind Ann's coupé came lancing forward and a pair of sinister-looking men piled out, deploying to either side with drawn guns. Lai Hu Chow yelped a Mongol war cry, opened his door and scrambled out to do battle. His courage was fruitless, for as he emerged from the coupé he was savagely bashed by the clubbed butt of an automatic.

The bludgeoning blow caught him on the back of the skull, its cowardly force felling him like a chopped oak.

On her own side of the little car, Ann faced the second thug. He was tall, squint-eyed, leering.

"Don't you dare touch me!" Ann blazed. "My uncle is Captain Carter of the Police Department, and he will—"

"That's too bad, sister. I don't like cops' relatives, any more than I like cops. Come on."

In spite of herself, Ann shivered as she realized the truth. She and Chow had fallen into the clutches of the rubber thieves. So had the Chinese youth who innocently had led her into this elaborately prepared trap.

It was all too plain that the murder gang must have guessed the details of Dr. Zeng's plan to locate them. In turn, they had deliberately arranged a spurious willingness to sell bootleg retreads to one of Zeng's emissaries—the young Chinese.

Their purpose was clear, now. They had brought the youth to their hideout, knowing that he would be trailed. By capturing anybody who followed him, they would close off this effort to find their headquarters.

The mob's unknown leader had still another purpose, as Ann was soon to discover. Two more hoods came from the brewery, lugged Chow's inert form inside. And herself was hauled into the building, where she stared around in amazement.

The interior was lighted by huge, unshaded incandescents, since the windows themselves admitted no daylight. They had been coated with paint to give the place the appearance of being abandoned.

Scattered all about, amidst long-disused malting vats and brewing apparatus, were dozens of electric molds for vulcanizing new threads on worn carcasses. Stacks of used tires, of all sizes and condition, were piled high on every side. An odor of cooking rubber arose from the circular molds.

Through an open double doorway to an adjoining vaulted chamber, Ann could see vast quantities of coiled gray camelback—the loot from Cynthia Lancaster's warehouse on the Embarcadero. By now, probably, Joe Nazarian had already collected insurance indemnity on that.

Leaving Ann in the grasp of two underlings, the squint-eyed thug who had captured her moved over to a small box fastened on the wall, from which a number of little jack-switches protruded. This was a televox installation, such as many factories employ for interdepartmental communication.

The lanky man thumbed one of the switches, spoke into the device.

"It worked, Boss. We sprung the trap."

A tinny, metallic voice issued back from the box.

"You nail that Chinese doctor?"

"We-ell, no. He wasn't the one that tailed the kid who pretended to need tires. But we grabbed off a great big Chinese man with a map like a full moon. And a jane that says her uncle is a copper named Carter."

THE TINNY voice rasped out an oath. "Zeng Tse-Lin is the guy I wanted nabbed! He's the one I'm scared of. I should have known better than to leave the job to you lugs. I'll have to handle it myself. Until he's out of the way, none of us will be safe!"

"You want I should go with you?"

"No. Stay here and see if you can make the Carter girl talk. Find out from her how much the cops are wise to. There's half a million dollars in this deal for us to split up if it goes right. And the gas chamber for all of us if there's a slip!"

The squint-eyed, lanky man turned away from the televox and approached Ann grimly.

"You heard what the boss just said, sister. Now start spillin'."

At that same moment, Dr. Zeng Tse-Lin was just returning to his Mandarin Emporium. Behind him were wasted hours of searching through the sprawling reaches of San Francisco with his smoke-analyzing device. It had functioned perfectly; too perfectly! A trace of rubber fumes had appeared many times. But in each case, the clue had led to some legitimate plant operated under Government license.

Tomorrow, he concluded, he would try again—but across the bay, in the Oakland district. Meanwhile he entered his store, which was now being closed and shuttered for the evening by the staff of employees.

Zeng summoned his head clerk. "Has Lai Hu Chow returned?"

"Aie. He was here briefly near the hour of four. Miss Carter was with him. She was spoken to by young Wu Shan, son of Wu Ling, the dealer in foodstuffs."

Zeng grew tense, for Wu Shan was one of those whom he had detailed to hunt for a tire bootlegger.

"This young man gave a message to Miss Carter?" he asked.

"So it seemed. He then departed in his car, and Miss Carter followed him in her coupé. She took Chow with her."

An intuitive premonition came to Zeng Tse-Lin. The scene his clerk described could bear but one meaning. Wu Shan must have arranged a Black Market contact and reported it to Ann, who had immediately trailed the youth in the hope of finding a lead to the camelback thieves.

But that had been an hour ago. Ann should have reported her findings by this time, if she had learned anything.

Unless something had happened to her!

Zeng moved swiftly to the Emporium telephone and dialed Police Headquarters. He got Captain Brian Carter on the line.

"Have you had word from Ann, O my friend?"

"Why, no." The Homicide official's voice held surprise. "Is anything wrong?"

"There has been no message received through your police shortwave radio?"

"No. Why should there be? What's eating you, Zeng?"

The tall, hawklike man fought for calm.

"I fear that an evil thing has occurred. Remain by your Headquarters radio until, perchance, a message comes."

He rang off. As he strode through the now-darkened Emporium his mind was geared to supreme effort.

Had his enemy struck at him through Ann? If so, the criminal would not be satisfied with her alone. Zeng himself must be next on the list, for until then, the guilty person would not feel secure. And upon this slender thread of reasoning, Dr. Zeng determined a course of action.

It was a course that required him to seek peril deliberately; to expose himself to death. And even as he made the decision, he remembered the one essential clue which had eluded him all day—the pointing factor that identified the murderous leader of the camelback mob!

FOR ALL the Oriental fatalism he had acquired during his years in China, Zeng Tse-Lin had no wish to die before his time. Therefore, the danger to which he was about to risk himself must be at least partially guarded against. This was only sensible.

No man could be bullet-proof, he realized. There were ways of attaining at least a measure of immunity to injury, though. Quickly he strode toward the rear of the Emporium, peeling off his mandarin robe as he moved. Then, from a display niche, he drew down an antique coat of fine steel Chinese mail, its metal mesh woven so ingeniously as to afford complete freedom of movement even as it armored its wearer against the sharpest sword.

But would it turn a bullet?

Not likely. Yet it might serve to dissipate some of the penetrating force of a slug.

That was all Dr. Zeng asked—a slight shortening of the odds against him. He donned the mail and replaced his robe over it. A casual inspection would not reveal, now, that he wore armor. His head, of course, was still vulnerable, but that was a risk he must assume.

He went quietly to the store's front door, unlocked it, and walked out into the gathering dusk.

Would an attack come at once? For that matter, would it come at all? Or had Zeng miscalculated his enemy's intentions? There was no way of knowing. Either it would happen, or it would not.

Zeng reached his limousine at the curb and climbed in under the wheel. And as he reached forward to switch on his ignition, from an alley across the street there came a curious, explosive, hissing sound, sharp yet faint, like the sudden release of air under high compression.

Almost simultaneously, Dr. Zeng felt a slight stinging sensation in his left shoulder. And he knew instinctively that an air gun had been discharged at him—a gun such as had been employed to murder Steve

Conroy at Police Headquarters. He knew also that he had been struck on the shoulder by its aconite pellet. But he was unpoisoned, for the chain mail had stopped the tiny missile from entering his flesh.

He had two courses open to him. He might leap in pursuit of his assailant, and even capture him. But the murderer might then refuse to divulge what had happened to Ann Carter. If she were a prisoner somewhere, the guilty person could even use her as a hostage, a bargaining price for his own freedom.

Zeng chose the second course; the one which seemed more likely to lead him to the girl he secretly loved.

He grabbed wildly at his shoulder, as if hurt. Then, momentarily, he writhed over the limousine's steering wheel like a man in unendurable agony. He gasped, choked, squirmed. And finally he slumped forward inertly.

As he collapsed, he gambled everything on the killer's curiosity. There was more than a fifty-fifty chance that the murderer would come forward to make sure he had finished his victim. Zeng, therefore, staked everything on this possibility.

By a supreme effort, employing methods he had learned in mysterious Tibet, he deliberately willed his heart to slow its beating until there was no perceptible pulse. Through a system of Oriental auto-hypnosis which had taken him years to perfect, he actually willed himself into a state of suspended animation, a cataleptic coma that had every outward appearance of death!

IN THIS catalepsy, his five external senses no longer functioned. He could not see, nor hear; he was unable to feel anything, or to smell, or taste. Within his brain there was only a flicker of consciousness, like a glowing ember. That ember could only be fanned back to the flame of life by the mightiest effort. And even such an effort might fail.

In which case, Zeng Tse-Lin would die.

He was well aware of this grim possibility, even as he was aware of the identity of the man who had fired the pellet at him. But Zeng took the risk willingly, even eagerly—for he was staking his life to save Ann Carter.

The shadows of pseudo-death claimed him.

CHAPTER X

TEMPORARY CORPSE

SKULKING ACROSS the street, a man peered into the limousine, then grasped Dr. Zeng's lifeless wrist. There was no flicker of pulse.

"Got him!" the man whispered to himself. "Now to get rid of the corpse!"

And he shoved Zeng to the other side of the front compartment, clambered in under the wheel, sent the big car purring forward toward the Oakland Bridge.

Even as the car moved sedately through the streets some deep-seated instinct came alive within the ember which remained dully glowing in Zeng Tse-Lin's mind. Insistently it sparked and grew, demanding that he put forth a supreme effort to awaken. The time had come.

Then began his terrific struggle against the inertia of catalepsy. There was no visible movement of his body, no external sign of the cosmic battle being waged. But with concentrated mental force he willed himself back to life—and life returned slowly, surely, like the seeping of water into an emptied well, drop by healing drop.

Finally, when minutes, an hour, a day, ages had passed, as if from a vast distance away, he heard voices. One was masculine, demanding.

"For the last time, Miss Carter, I'm asking you to talk, to tell me how much that Chinese doctor knew—and how much he informed your uncle."

Thin and threadlike was Ann's response, in a tone from which all hope fled.

"There's no use of my holding out any longer. Now that Zeng's d-dead, nothing m-matters. I'll talk."

"Then begin. Quickly."

Somehow, to Zeng, the voices were louder now. Consciousness was surging back into his mind, his sinews, his blood. His eyes, wide open and sightless an instant before, regained the power to see—dimly at first, then with full vision. He saw that he had been dumped carelessly in a corner of a vast, musty room that smelled of cooking rubber. He saw that his devoted servitor, Chow, lay battered and bound alongside him.

The place was littered with stacks of worn tires, and retreading molds were scattered wherever space permitted between vast, disused brewing vats. The vats themselves, bearing faded trade-mark plates of a brand of beer long since discontinued, informed Zeng that this was a former brewery—and identified its location.

Over on the far side of the room, two thuggish-looking men grasped Ann Carter by the arms. And they were holding her little fists cruelly close to an open recapping mold from which heat arose in visible waves. They had been on the point of closing the mold down with crushing, roasting impact on her dainty fingers, when she whimpered her willingness to talk.

That ugly scene was all Zeng Tse-Lin needed to bring back the last splendid swelling of his strength. He heard the girl pant out a weak phrase.

"Zeng didn't know who was behind the rubber thefts, the m-murders—"

"But I know now!" Dr. Zeng roared in a voice of thunder. He came erect, touching Lai Hu Chow's artificial limb as he moved. "I have you cornered, Thomas McKnight!"

The effect was weird on his listeners. To all intents and purposes, Zeng had been dead. Now he was resurrected, and the men who faced him seemed on the verge of panic, as if he were a ghost.

THERE WERE six or seven hoods in the group, but no one of them was more stunned than McKnight, the insurance agent, as Zeng Tse-Lin marched toward him like an avenging specter.

"You—you—" the man squeaked.

Zeng's voice was a rumble of doom as he took advantage of the consternation he had caused.

"By bringing Ann Carter, Chow and myself here to the old Pilsen Brewery building in Oakland to murder us, you have sealed your own fate."

McKnight stared.

"Even before you fired a poison pellet at me," Zeng thundered, "I knew you were guilty. I realized it the instant I recalled your visit to the Lancaster house this morning with Joe Nazarian—who said you were going to pay his insurance claim on the stolen camelback today."

McKnight made strangling noises in his throat.

"The most inexperienced insurance adjuster would not arrange payment so soon," Zeng stormed. "Why, then, should you approve Nazarian's claim within ten short hours of the theft—unless you knew the rubber would never be recovered? And how could you be certain of that unless you'd engineered the theft yourself?"

The indemnity agent sagged.

"Stolen rubber is all about us," Zeng finished. "Your retreading equipment and the used tires you cornered from the open market will prove you planned a gigantic tire-bootlegging racket. Not only are you a thief and a leader of thieves, but a multiple murderer as well!"

"I—I thought I killed you—"

"You failed to consider that I might be wearing armor."

A change came over McKnight. Instead of fear, sudden anger glowed maliciously in his eyes.

"Armor! And I thought you had some supernatural power!" Abruptly he turned to his dazed henchmen. "Get him, boys! This time we'll make sure he dies!"

Zeng Tse-Lin had been expecting this sooner or later, and he was prepared for it. He eluded the first headlong onslaught with a lithe sideward leap, snagging one thug as he went by. He raised the fellow like a sack of grain and hurled him full at the others. Four or five went tumbling like tenpins, and two did not get up again.

But there were plenty more, including McKnight himself. And now they were whipping out guns. Dr. Zeng pretended to seek refuge by circling around a big vat. He did not go all the way around, though. He halted, waited—and sprang as two hoods caromed after him. He caught them, smashed their heads together before they could cry out. Their two skulls met with a sickening sound of shattering concussion. They dropped.

Ann Carter had plunged across the room to Lai Hu Chow. Desperately she plucked at the giant Mongol's bonds. Zeng, reappearing, saw what she was doing and flashed her swift approval. Then he pitched forward on his face as a volley of shots blasted at him, the thunderous echoes reverberating hollowly in the vaulted old structure.

As he rolled, he grabbed an automatic from the limp hand of one of the crooks he had felled. He took aim, commenced firing. He felt the weapon jump in his fist as he triggered death at his enemies.

But he could not look in all directions at once. And one of McKnight's cutthroats managed to get behind him. The man drew a bead on Zeng's spine.

AT THAT instant, Chow's last fetter came loose. The big Asiatic lunged upright, grabbed two huge truck-tire carcasses from a nearby pile, one in each hand, and hurled them.

"Hey, Boss!" he yelled joyously. "Allee samee like pitchee horseshoes!" And he scored a double ringer over the thug who was about to shoot his beloved master.

The tires settled down around the gunman, pinning his arms to his sides. He yelped, swore—and then Chow slugged him with a knotted fist. The man stopped swearing because he had no more mouth to talk from. Where it had been, there was only a crimson smear of pulped flesh and splintered teeth.

The odds against Zeng and Chow were not so great, now. There were only four more thugs left—and McKnight himself. But the insurance agent was a raging madman as he saw defeat closing in. He fired his automatic wildly until it was empty, then hurled the weapon away from him and whipped out a tiny air gun. He tried to use it, forgetting that it was a single-shot device and that he had emptied its one pellet at Zeng Tse-Lin back in Chinatown.

When its hammer clicked uselessly, he screeched curses, then jumped at Zeng with his bare hands. This was his gravest mistake. Zeng caught him, twisted him as easily as a child would twist a cloth toy.

"Bid your men cease firing, or I shall snap your spine!" the hawklike man commanded grimly.

And then, even before McKnight could scream the order, a terrific series of battering smashes sounded on the main door of the old brewery. The portal splintered inward, and squads of police came surging in like a blue tide. There were Oakland officers and San Francisco patrolmen as well, and they were led by Captain Brian Carter.

"Cops—we're done for!" McKnight wailed. "But how—did they—get here?"

"That's what I'd like to know!" Carter growled, gathering Ann into his arms and then approaching Zeng Tse-Lin, while the remnants of the tire theft mob were being handcuffed.

"How do you explain it, Zeng?" demanded the Homicide chief. "We heard your voice over the police short-wave radio, telling us where to come and what to look for. We moved fast. But how did the broadcast originate?"

Dr. Zeng smiled softly. "The limb of communications," he murmured.

Then Carter understood. "Chow's false leg!"

"That is correct, O my friend. This particular limb contains a compact but powerful transmitter, battery operated, and tuned to the police wave length. It is a device of my own contriving, and quite useful, it would seem."

"Useful to a man smart enough to know what to say after he had switched on the microphone," Captain Carter exclaimed admiringly. "You must have clicked its switch just before you began your accusations."

Zeng smiled again. "Yes. Putting the transmitter into operation was merely a matter of pressing the proper control prior to going into action. Chow himself might have thus summoned help, if he had not been knocked unconscious and then bound so that he could not move. As it was I was forced to trick McKnight into bringing me here so that I could send the message."

"How did you trick him?"

"By making him think he had slain me. He then brought my supposed corpse here for disposal," Zeng explained.

Carter looked about the place.

"He was certainly well equipped for wholesale tire bootlegging."

"Quite so. His insurance agency was no longer profitable, and he must have invested every available dollar in this scheme for reaping a crooked fortune. The indemnity company which he represented would be the only loser. The payment of Joe Nazarian's claim was out of that company's pocket, not McKnight's."

Ann Carter shivered. "I'm g-glad it's over. There'll be n-no more killings now, except in the gas chamber." Then she remembered something, and turned to her uncle. "That young Chinese, Wu Shan! You'll find him tied up in the next room—"

"Unhurt?" Dr. Zeng asked quickly.

"Yes, as far as I know," Ann answered.

"Good!" the hawklike man breathed a sigh of relief. "And now, friend Carter, I suggest that you release him, arrange to send these slain thugs to the morgue and the living to prison. After which, perhaps you and Ann will come home with me to the House of a Thousand Beatitudes for a bowl of very inferior tea."

V

LION'S LOOT

CHAPTER I

SHADOW OF DEATH

THE MAROON sedan moved slowly and erratically, as if the man at the wheel might either have been drinking or was unsure of his course. That was what a casual onlooker might think. But the truth was far more ominous. An invisible passenger was riding in the sedan, keeping clammy company with the driver—and the passenger's name was Death.

When the car emerged from Third Street and crossed Market into Kearny, it veered widely before straightening out. Such jerky progress would have spelled hazard to traffic, except that there was little vehicular congestion at this particular hour of the day. Dusk was settling over San Francisco, and most of the populace had gone home.

Consequently the maroon sedan's curious behavior attracted practically no attention. It turned left into Maiden Lane, then wavered crazily north on Grant Avenue in the direction of Chinatown. Presently it swung in toward the curb; and for an instant the front tires threatened to leap across the sidewalk and crash through the dingy plate glass window of a converted store which bore a sign:

FAR EAST EMPLOYMENT SERVICE

At the last minute, however, the driver regained control of his machine and brought it to a squealing halt. Then he sagged forward, his face gray, his mouth twisted by pain.

"Got to—get—help!" he panted vaguely.

Sweat formed on his forehead, although the evening was cool; and shadows of panic slithered in his eyes.

Within the employment agency, Sally Prescott was covering her typewriter and preparing to close the establishment for the night. In front of her stretched the service room, barren of furnishings except for several long wooden benches used by job-hunters. The benches were empty now, as were the several small interviewing offices that flanked the main room.

Sally was all alone in the place; and soon she, too, would leave. She was tired, for her clerical and stenographic duties were burdensome at best, and today had been especially trying. Since the war had caused all Japanese to be evacuated from the West Coast, the bureau had found it increasingly difficult to meet the needs of its clientele.

FOR ALMOST thirty years the Far East Employment Service had occupied these same quarters on the edge of Chinatown, winning an enviable reputation as a reliable source of Oriental domestic help. Founded by the father of its present owner, the firm had originally specialized in Chinese workers. As time went by and California's Chinese population decreased, this trend gradually shifted to Jap labor.

Now, though, the Japs were no longer available. As a result, the agency's business had sharply dwindled. Sally Prescott realized that her own job might not last many more weeks, the way things were going. In fact, she sometimes wondered how the firm had managed to survive this long.

"Well, I'm not the only one affected by the war," she murmured philosophically.

Then, temporarily dismissing her worries, she left her desk, deftly applied lipstick to her mouth and ran a comb through her shining golden hair. Glancing at her watch, she saw that it was almost six o'clock.

Hal Wilson would pick her up at six sharp, as he always did. Her blue eyes went starry as she thought of Hal, whose ring she wore on the third finger of her left hand. It would not be long until he gave up his present work as a Chinatown tourist guide in favor of an Army uniform. But before that happened there would be a quiet wedding. Then Sally could stop worrying over her employment agency job.

She moved toward the front door, opening her purse to make sure she had her keys. Then the sound of squealing brakes knifed the silence of the street outside.

Startled, the girl stared out through the plate glass window. A maroon sedan seemed about to leap the curb and come smashing into the building, but at the last instant the driver managed to regain control of his wheel. He halted the machine, then slumped forward.

Sally Prescott drew a sharp breath, and a sense of foreboding stole into her heart.

"Andrew McClane!" she whispered uneasily to herself.

She had good cause to feel ill at ease. Andrew McClane had been a major problem to her during the two years she had worked for the Far East Employment Service. A bachelor and the last surviving member of one of San Francisco's oldest families, he lived alone in a gloomy residence not far from Chinatown, stubbornly clinging to a neighborhood which had long since grown unfashionable. Nor did his eccentricity stop at this.

His strangest trait seemed to be a constant dissatisfaction with his domestic help. In less than a year he'd had four different Jap house boys, discharging each one after a few months and engaging another. Curiously enough, he always agreeably furnished excellent references to the servants he dismissed, so they could readily be placed with other families.

None of which had troubled Sally Prescott. What did bother her was McClane's unwarranted interest in herself. He never appeared at the agency without trying to arrange a date with her. Several times, when he had been under the influence of liquor, she'd had real difficulty fending him off.

He seemed to be under the influence now. He lurched out of his sedan and teetered uncertainly on the sidewalk, as if he might fall on his face the next instant. Shambling, swaying, he moved toward the employment bureau.

SALLY'S INSTINCTIVE impulse was to run away. Had there been a rear exit, she would have locked the front door and sped off through the alley. But the building had no back exit, and there wasn't time to escape by the front doorway. McClane was already within a few feet of the entrance, his bleary eyes peering through the glass.

With a resigned sigh, the girl decided to put the best face possible on the situation. Loyalty to her employer kept her from treating McClane as rudely as he deserved. After all, he was a steady client. Therefore, she must be polite to him.

So she opened the door and forced a welcoming smile to her lips.

"Good evening, Mr. McClane." He staggered past her without answering, shuffled to one of the long wooden benches and sank down, shuddering. His flabby cheeks were flushed, his eyes sunken and dilated above pouches of unhealthy fat. With a sort of desperation he buried his face in his hands. When he spoke, the words came through his fingers almost inaudibly.

"Sick—had a few drinks—can't understand—never—felt this way—before—"

He straightened, shaking his head as if to clear it. Then he rolled over on his side, stretching out pudgily on the hard wooden bench.

Sally Prescott stared at him helplessly. She had never seen him like this before, and his stupor frightened her. She made a fluttering gesture with her hands, then pivoted as she heard the front door opening.

"Hal!" she cried as relief flooded through her. "Thank goodness you've come!"

Hal Wilson was tall, lanky, angular, the ruggedness of his face enhanced by deep sun-tan. His smile was good-natured, his eyes merry. But the good humor vanished when he saw the man on the bench.

"McClane!" he growled darkly. "What's he doing here?" And he took an angry step forward.

The girl blocked him, swiftly explaining what had happened.

"So you see we've got to get him out of here, Hal," she finished. "I don't dare lock him in for the night, and yet I can't leave the office open."

"Okay. We'll dump him in his car and let the cops pick him up."

"No, Hal. He's too good a customer. Let's drive him to his home. It isn't far. Then my evening won't be spoiled by feeling responsible for him."

The angular young man started to protest, then broke into a surrendering grin.

"Have it your way, sweet."

He shook McClane, got no response, and lifted the pudgy figure bodily—as easily as he might have handled a baby.

Outside, he deposited his inert burden in the tonneau of the maroon sedan, saw that the ignition key was in the lock and got in under the wheel. Sally settled herself alongside him, turning so that she could keep an eye on the sleeping man.

Hal Wilson started the car, asked the girl for McClane's address and pulled ahead. He was intent on his driving, and Sally's gaze was centered upon the man on the rear seat. Consequently neither one of them noticed that another sedan, which had been parked farther down the street, now got into motion behind them at a discreet distance.

Unaware that he was being followed, Hal Wilson headed for the McClane home and presently stopped in front of the somber old structure.

"Now what?" he asked.

The girl hesitated. "He hasn't got a servant just now. I remember he discharged his last house boy a week ago and we weren't able to find a replacement. So I guess we'll have to carry him inside and leave him."

"Okay. The front door key is probably on this ring with his car key. You open the door and I'll lug him in."

Sally obeyed. By the time her fiancé had carried the fat man up the worn brownstone steps she had the door open. They entered a dark, musty hallway and went into the old-fashioned parlor to the right. Wilson dropped his limp burden onto a moth-eaten sofa and backed away, scowling.

"Now let him sleep it off. We've done all we can."

The girl leaned down. "Hal, look at him! I don't know much about men drinking, but—"

"But what?"

"I'm afraid something's wrong with him. His face has such a funny color. And his breathing seems queer. Maybe he's had a heart attack!"

"Mm-m. You might be right, at that. I guess we'd better get help. Where's the phone?"

"There isn't any. Whenever we want to reach him from the employment agency we have to send a messenger."

The angular young man shrugged. "Let's go, then. We'll hunt up a doctor. I know one near here. He's Chinese, but he's plenty good. His name is Zeng Tse-Lin."

"You get him, Hal. I'll stay with McClane. Maybe I can do something for him while you're gone."

Wilson didn't like the idea of leaving Sally, but even to his untrained eye it was obvious that the fat man was in bad shape.

"All right, sweet," he said, and promised, "I'll be back in less than ten minutes."

He sped from the house, piled into McClane's maroon sedan and sent it roaring forward. He was too preoccupied to notice the car that was parked across the street, nor could he possibly guess the machine had followed him here.

The moment Hal Wilson rounded the far corner, three men came furtively out of the parked sedan and stared at the McClane residence. They held a whispered conference; seemed to come to a decision. One of them got back into the car. The other two scurried over to the opposite sidewalk and made straight for the house in which Wilson had left his golden-haired fiancée.

CHAPTER II

ZENG OF CHINATOWN

IT WAS the hour of evening rice, and little traffic was moving through the narrow streets of Chinatown. Many of the shops were already closed and shuttered for the night. From second-floor balconies came scraps of sing-song conversation or an occasional hint of moon-fiddle music undertoned by the steady clanking of cables in the car-slots.

To Hal Wilson these were all familiar sounds. As a tourist guide he had learned to know the neighborhood intimately, from one end to the other. Its alleys, byways and pagoda-style buildings were second nature to him. And the Chinese who lived here were his valued friends.

Drawing up before a structure set slightly apart from other buildings in the block, he alighted from the maroon sedan and ran toward a recessed door of carved teakwood. Alongside this door there was a store over whose entrance hung a gilt-lettered sign. The lettering proclaimed sedately:

MANDARIN EMPORIUM

Exclusive Antiques
Oriental Importations
DR. ZENG TSE-LIN, *Proprietor*

Hal Wilson had sent many a customer here from his sightseeing parties, for he knew the shop's prices to be fair and the merchandise of excellent quality. In fact, it was common knowledge that the store was merely a hobby for its owner, whose real vocation was the healing of the sick.

As a physician and surgeon, the fame of Dr. Zeng Tse-Lin had spread far beyond the reaches of Chinatown. Uncounted tales were told of the miraculous cures he had wrought, and deep was the respect he commanded, not alone for his medical skill but for his attainments in every other branch of science.

His vast Oriental learning entitled him to the coveted green button of the fifth examination scholar, and he possessed degrees from high-ranking American universities as well. To an inherited fortune he had added still greater wealth by virtue of dozens of scientific discoveries and inventions—yet he had accomplished all these things while he was still barely more than thirty years of age. No wonder, then, that strange stories were whispered of this astounding personage known as Dr. Zeng!

For instance, you might hear of his superhuman strength gained through secret exercise formulas learned while a youthful student in the remote lamaseries of Tibet. Again, rumors might reach you about the sorceries taking place in his private laboratory—things that smacked of black magic. Someone else would speak of his superlative skill with every known type of ancient and modern weapon; his unerring marksmanship with gun or arrow.

There were two facts, though, which you would never hear in connection with Zeng Tse-Lin, for the very good reason that they were completely unknown to the world at large. One fact was that he stood unequaled in the field of criminology, his life secretly dedicated to a battle against lawlessness in all its aspects. The second fact was even more amazing, for Zeng was not actually a member of the Chinese race. He was a white American whose true name was Robert Charles Lang!

His parents had been affluent missionaries to China, where Zeng himself had been born. Later, when he was completing his education in the United States, his mother and father were murdered by Jap bandits near Shanghai. This was the tragedy which had caused Zeng to take up his life work—the tracking down of criminals, the meting out of justice to evil-doers.

TO FURTHER this career, he had hit upon the stratagem of assuming Chinese identity. As a mandarin physician, his secret activities were less likely to be suspected. And his Oriental impersonation was so successful that even his nearest neighbors here in Chinatown never

guessed the truth. They accepted him as one of themselves; respected him as a sagacious member of their own race. To them he was a high-caste Chinese doctor, nothing more.

And it was as a Chinese doctor that Hal Wilson, the tourist guide, knew him. The angular young man alighted from the maroon sedan and made for Zeng's door, seeking medical aid for Andrew McClane.

As Wilson left the car, a brown paper package fell to the gutter. It was a small parcel, carelessly wrapped and of no apparent value, for it had been casually wedged between the front seat and the door. The young guide retrieved it without curiosity, since his mind was on the more important matter of finding Dr. Zeng Tse-Lin. Tucking the package under his arm, he rang Zeng's bell.

The doctor's living quarters occupied the upper floors of the store building and were known in Chinatown as the "House of a Thousand Beatitudes." In a room furnished with tasteful Oriental opulence, Zeng himself was just about to partake of his evening meal when a deep-throated gong chimed mellowly.

The two masked thugs saw that menacing blade
licking at them—and lost their courage.

Clad in rich mandarin robes, Zeng moved lithely to a teakwood box
and opened it; touched a control switch. Within the box there was a
ground glass screen which immediately glowed to life, disclosing a
miniature but perfect image of the man at the door downstairs.

This was Dr. Zeng's adaptation of the television principle—a selenium scanning disk set into the doorway and wired to a receiving set
in the teakwood box. By means of it, he was enabled to study visitors
before admitting them. Now his sharp, hawklike eyes surveyed the
angular young tourist guide.

Satisfied, he closed the lid of the box and clapped his hands twice.

"Chow!" he called.

A giant and ungainly figure lumbered into the room, vigorously
munching a wad of gum. He was Zeng's devoted servitor and companion, Lai Hu Chow, a huge Mongol whose moonlike countenance carried
the scars of many savage battles.

"Yes, my master?"

"Speed thou to the front door and conduct Hal Wilson to me," the tall doctor intoned in a resonant voice. "His face is troubled and he betrays signs of urgent haste, which is unlike him. He may be in need of help."

Chow blinked, turned and departed with a rolling gait caused by the fact that he wore an artificial limb, having lost his real leg while valiantly fighting the murderers of Zeng's parents. As he left the room, he muttered under his breath.

The mutter was one of bewilderment, for Chow could never comprehend the miracle of modern science which enabled his master to identify callers while they were still outside the house. The big Asiatic was firmly convinced that this could only be the work of the devil. At first he had feared for his beloved employer, but as he had seen more and more of Zeng's accomplishments, he began rather to fear for the devil!

He hastened downstairs, opened the door and admitted the impatient tourist guide.

"My master awaits you. Enter."

Wilson was a little startled that Dr. Zeng already knew of his arrival. But he was so worried about leaving Sally Prescott alone in the McClane residence that he gave no thought to the matter. He started to answer Chow with a gesture—and almost dropped the package he was carrying under his arm. For a moment he had forgotten picking it up from the gutter as he got out of the sedan.

Now, thoughtlessly, he placed the parcel on an ebony Manchu dynasty table in the hallway, meaning to retrieve it when he came back downstairs. He followed Chow up to the second floor.

Dr. Zeng Tse-Lin greeted him ceremoniously by shaking hands with himself in Chinese fashion.

"My humble home is honored by your visit, O friend Wilson. May I offer you a bowl of very inferior tea?"

The tourist guide was familiar with the Chinese customs of elaborate politeness, and ordinarily he would have answered with similar courtesy. But time was pressing, so he came at once to the purpose of his visit.

"My fiancée has a sick client on her hands—fellow named Andrew McClane. At first we thought he just had been drinking too heavily, but now it looks as if his condition is really serious. Will you come take a look at him, Doctor?"

Zeng bowed gravely. "The wise physician moves swiftly when illness threatens. We will go immediately."

He sent Chow scurrying for his medicine kit, then went with Wilson out of the house.

Meanwhile, after Hal Wilson left her, Sally Prescott had busied herself by trying to do something for McClane. She got a basin of cold water from the kitchen of the somber old residence, intending to apply cold towels to the pudgy man's forehead. But as she came back through the gloomy hall, she was startled by two men who suddenly appeared before her.

She stopped, thinking for an instant that they were friends of the sick man. But another glance told her that she was wrong. McClane was not the sort who would make friends with men like this pair. They looked like waterfront hoodlums.

"What do you want?" she demanded. "How did you get in here?"

Instead of answering directly, one of the thugs reached out and knocked the basin of water from her grasp. She gasped as the cold wetness splashed her dress, and squirmed angrily as she felt a hard hand seizing her by the wrists.

"Okay, cutie," the hoodlum growled. "Quiet down. What did McClane do with the stuff?"

She kicked, tried to free her hands so she could claw at her captor's ugly face.

"Let me go! How dare you—"

"I said quiet down. We want the junk and we want it now."

She didn't know what he was talking about. But as she stared unflinchingly at him, she realized that she was somehow in danger—and that her one chance to escape would be by sparring for time. Soon Hal Wilson would return with Dr. Zeng. The two of them would be more than a match for these thugs.

THERE COULD be no doubt that the intruders were crooks; that they should be turned over to the police. The trick would be to keep them here until Hal and Zeng arrived. With this in mind, Sally hit upon an impromptu stratagem.

"So you want the stuff," she said evenly.

"Yeah."

"Then ask McClane what he did with it," she snapped. "You'll not get any information from me."

They dragged her into the parlor where the fat man lay inert on the sofa. One of them held the girl while the other searched McClane's clothing urgently. Presently the searcher straightened up.

"He ain't got it on him. But he had it when he was at the café. And the only other place he went was the employment office. This jane must know somethin' she ain't tellin'."

The second hoodlum scowled. "We can make her spill. I'll set fire to a gasper an' burn my initials on—"

"Nix! We ain't got enough time. The jerk that came here with her might come back any minute."

"Then what'll we do?"

"Let's take her along with us an' let the boss talk to her. If he don't get nowheres, we can bust into that employment joint and frisk it. McClane may have stashed the junk there."

With an abrupt movement, Sally Prescott twisted free of the thug who was holding her. Desperately she raced toward the front door of the house.

She didn't make it, though. Both hoods leaped after her. One of them pulled a gun, slapped her over the head with it. Sally toppled forward, unconscious.

CHAPTER III

DAMP CLUE

WHILE ALL this was taking place, Hal Wilson was driving the maroon sedan back toward the McClane residence as fast as it would roll. Behind him came Dr. Zeng's limousine, with Chow at the wheel and the tall doctor in the tonneau.

In his haste, the angular young tourist guide had forgotten to pick up the brown paper parcel he had left in Zeng Tse-Lin's lower hallway, nor did he remember the package now. Moreover, when he finally drew up before Andrew McClane's gloomy house, he saw something that drove the parcel even further out of his thoughts. The front door of the residence was wide open!

"That's funny," he whispered to himself.

He sprinted up the worn steps, followed by Dr. Zeng, and conducted the physician inside. Then he raised his voice.

"Sally!" he called.

There was no answer.

A sinister premonition entered Wilson's heart. He rushed forward to the parlor, saw McClane still lying on the sofa. But there was no sign of Sally Prescott.

"I can't understand it!" The tourist guide's voice was harsh with worry. "She wouldn't go away and leave a sick man. Something must have happened to her!"

He turned and raced through the shadowy hallway; searched room after musty room. But his efforts were fruitless. From attic to cellar he found no trace of the golden-haired girl. At last he returned to the parlor, his face a mask of concern.

"She's gone!" he announced in bewilderment.

Dr. Zeng unbent his tall form, his examination of Andrew McClane finished.

"This gentleman is also gone," he said.

"What d-do you mean?"

"I mean that he is dead—and that we had better notify the police."

Wilson stiffened. "The police? So they can hunt for Sally?"

"Yes," Zeng Tse-Lin's tone was bleak. "And so that they can likewise hunt for the person who poisoned McClane. You see, my friend, this man was murdered."

The blunt statement shocked Hal Wilson temporarily speechless. At last he found a ragged remnant of his voice.

"But—but how can that be? He just seemed tight to me. Maybe too much whiskey stopped his heart."

Dr. Zeng gravely shook his head. "There are poisons which produce external symptoms of apparent alcoholism and this is undoubtedly such a case. Whiskey was not the cause of McClane's death. I repeat that he was murdered."

"Murdered!" the tourist guide whispered. "And Sally vanished! Can there be any connection between these two things?"

The tall, richly robed doctor erased all expression from his impassive features.

"That is a question I am unprepared to answer at this moment. We must contact the Homicide Department without delay. If your beloved has been kidnaped, the sooner it is reported the more likely you are to get her safely back." He then moved swiftly to the front door, with Wilson following him as if fearful of being left alone in this house where death had struck.

Outside, Lai Hu Chow was hunched behind the wheel of Zeng Tse-Lin's limousine, listening with childish delight to a Western serial coming in over the car radio. The huge Mongol looked absurdly disappointed when his master bade him to shut off the set.

"Just getting to exciting part of story!" he bemoaned the interruption. "Guns go *bang-bang*, lots of cowboys killed!"

"We are confronted by a real killing, not a make-believe one," Zeng said gently. "Speed thyself to the nearest telephone and inform the police that they are needed here."

THE MOMENT Chow had driven away on his mission, Dr. Zeng and Hal Wilson reentered the McClane residence for a thorough inspection of all the rooms. Zeng's scrutiny seemed casual, and his ascetic countenance betrayed no hint that he had seen anything of importance. But there was a dark sharpness glowing in his eyes as he finished his tour.

By this time, a radio prowl car pulled up in front of the somber house, followed almost at once by a squad sedan direct from Headquarters. In charge of a beefy Homicide sergeant, the officers clumped inside.

The sergeant took no trouble to hide his impatience while Wilson told all he knew of the matter. As soon as the guide came to the end of his story, the Headquarters detective directed his attention at Zeng.

"Now, then, Doctor," he growled. "You are a doctor, are you?"

Zeng bowed slightly.

"I mean a real doctor," the sergeant persisted. "Not one of these Chinese that sells herbs and such junk."

Hal Wilson started to explode in indignant anger, but Dr. Zeng stopped him with a gesture and answered for himself.

"Yes, Sergeant," he purred softly. "I am a real doctor, as you graciously put it. A graduate of several excellent American universities. Unfortunately I do not carry my diplomas about with me. There are too many."

The Headquarters man was not appeased. He seemed to resent Dr. Zeng's presence on the scene.

"Just what makes you think this man was murdered?" He jerked a thumb toward Andrew McClane's body.

"The evidence," Zeng responded.

"Evidence! Plenty of people die from too much alcohol. And I know this guy's reputation. He was a rounder, a playboy."

The hawklike criminologist nodded. "Very true, sir. But it is written that the untrained eye is sometimes blind. Would you, for instance, recognize the symptoms of atropine?"

"Atropine? What's that?"

"A drug commonly known as belladonna," Zeng Tse-Lin said evenly. "It is not difficult to procure, for oculists have long used it to dilate the pupils of their patient's eyes in order to determine visual defects. Also, up until a few years ago, foolish women employed it to make their eyes appear larger and more beautiful than they really were."

"Oh," the sergeant grunted. "That stuff. Yeah, I've had eye-drops used on me. So what?"

"So I am certain that atropine was the cause of McClane's death," Dr. Zeng answered. "Everything seems to indicate it. The murderer apparently did not wish his victim to die in the place where the drug was administered—for it is a delayed-action poison. Moreover, the killer hoped that anyone seeing McClane would assume him to have too much to drink, instead of being in a dying condition. It was the mistake which both Mr. Wilson and Miss Prescott made. A natural mistake, I might add."

The sergeant's jaw jutted. "I'm not so sure they made a mistake."

"What do you mean by that?" the angular tourist guide demanded swiftly.

"Just this," the Headquarters man barked. "You admitted this McClane had been making passes at your girl. Well, you don't look like the kind of guy who'd stand for that. Maybe you got McClane into the employment agency and slipped him a dose of this bella stuff. Then you hauled him home and got this Chinee doctor friend of yours to come here and front for you."

"Confound you—"

"And that's not all," the sergeant snarled. "The girl's gone. Where is she?"

"I wish I knew!"

"A likely story," the detective said with heavy sarcasm. "I'd say she saw the man dying and lost her nerve. Took it on the lam because she knew she was responsible."

WILSON BALLED his fists, tensed himself to spring at his tormentor. But Zeng restrained him with a touch.

"The wise man knows the virtue of calm silence," he told the guide. "Do you not see that our overzealous sergeant is attempting to goad you into words and actions which you may later have reason to regret?"

Wilson subsided. This seemed to annoy the Headquarters man, who glared at Zeng with unconcealed hostility.

"So you're a lawyer as well as a doctor!"

"No." The tall criminologist was entirely unruffled. "I am not a practicing attorney, although it is true I have passed the bar examinations. Therefore I know of no statute which prevents my giving good advice."

"He'll need more than advice," the sergeant said darkly. "I think I'll send him down to Headquarters."

"But why?" Wilson cried out angrily.

"On suspicion. What did you expect me to do—pin a medal on you for killing this guy?"

The tourist guide lost his head and made a wild break for the door, only to be caught and subdued by two uniformed patrolmen. As his struggles subsided, he turned anguished eyes on Zeng.

"They can't lock me up! They mustn't! Something's happened to Sally. I've got to find her! Make them let me go!"

Dr. Zeng forced himself to ignore the desperate appeal, much as he regretted the necessity. In his own mind he was certain that Hal Wilson was innocent of complicity in McClane's murder, and he felt equally sure that Sally Prescott was likewise without guilt, despite her present unexplained absence.

But he did not wish the Homicide sergeant or any of the other policemen to guess that he was personally interested in the case from a criminologist's standpoint. His status as a manhunter was a secret shared by few persons, and it must continue to remain unrevealed.

Many were the mysterious crimes in San Francisco which would have gone unsolved had it not been for Zeng's undercover work. And if his career was to go forward at peak efficiency he knew he had to keep discreetly silent now.

True, he realized that he need only to communicate with his intimate friend Captain Brian Carter, Chief of the Homicide Division, and this truculent sergeant would be smartly put in his place. But if Zeng used such influence it might give his own game away.

Therefore he dared do nothing to help Hal Wilson now. With a shrug, he watched the angular young guide being led out to the squad car and taken away. After all, it was written that an innocent man may suffer temporarily, but justice always prevails in the end.

Nor was it merely Zeng's friendly feeling toward Wilson that made him certain of the guide's innocence. The tall, hawklike criminologist's discerning eyes had perceived several thing's apparently overlooked by the police. From them he deftly reconstructed what had happened in the gloomy house.

In the first place, there was a wet spot on the hallway carpet, half-way between parlor and kitchen. Near this, another damp splotch appeared on the wallpaper. And on the floor lay an overturned basin, slightly dented.

Then, in the kitchen itself, the cold water faucet of the sink was dripping a little, as if it had not been completely turned off. Yet the porcelain of the sink was not stained, as it would have been if that spigot had leaked for any length of time.

That meant that the drip from the faucet was not the result of a worn washer, but had merely been caught by the spigot-handle closed hastily and incompletely, probably by someone acting in a hurry.

Who had drawn a basin of water and carried it through the shadowy hall? In Zeng's mind, the answer was obviously Sally Prescott. She had evidently tried to help the dying man; had gone for cold water and then, in returning, had overturned the basin.

This would account for the wet place on the carpet. But the damp splotch on the wallpaper added another item to the story. No ordinary accident would have caused such a high splash. Therefore, someone must have knocked the basin of water from the girl's grasp.

In other words, she had been set upon by one or more intruders!

Essentially, then, everything seemed to indicate that she had not left the house willingly, but had been forced to go under duress.

Another factor substantiated this kidnaping theory. In examining Andrew McClane's body for the first time, Dr. Zeng had noticed signs that the murdered man's clothes had been searched—probably by the intruders who later abducted the girl.

Obviously, however, they had not found whatever it was they wanted. Had they been successful, they would not have taken Sally away with them. They might have killed her here in the house, to keep her from subsequently identifying them to the police. Instead, they had kidnaped her.

Why?

Again the answer seemed plain. They wanted to question her, thinking that she might know the location of the object for which they were hunting.

Like a complicated riddle, though, as fast as Zeng untied one puzzling knot he encountered another. Did Sally Prescott really know anything about the object being searched for? What was that object? And where was she being held captive?

Dr. Zeng Tse-Lin frowned thoughtfully as he asked the Homicide sergeant's permission to leave the house. The Headquarters detective granted this permission ungraciously, and Zeng strode out to his limousine—only to find it gone!

CHAPTER IV

ANOTHER KILL

A **NNOYED IMPATIENCE** flashed in the hawklike man's dark eyes as he peered up and down the street. His giant Mongol servitor, Lai Hu Chow, had one failing. That was an ardent devotion to lurid Western movies. At the oddest times, Chow would slip off to some cheap theater and sit through four or five showings of a cowboy picture, entranced by the hard riding and fancy shooting of the actors. The huge fellow from the plains of central Asia could no more resist such entertainment than a child could refuse a candy bar.

Now it looked as if the Mongol had once more succumbed to his innocent vice, and there was no telling when he might return. Zeng's momentary annoyance was replaced by an indulgent smile, for he knew Chow's habit could not be broken. With a philosophical shrug, the tall doctor started walking clown the street in quest of a telephone, intending to summon a cab.

But in this instance he had misjudged his faithful giant. As he neared the corner he saw his sleek limousine approaching with Chow at the wheel. The Mongol halted and opened the car's door for his master. Zeng Tse-Lin slid in beside the big Asiatic.

"What caused you to go away when I have need of you, O foolish one?" he inquired in a tone of gentle reproof.

Chow was unabashed. "Two blocks distant, cars sped by with a wailing as of lost souls. I followed, thinking to see some excitement."

Translated, the Mongol's reference to wailing cars could only mean police machines or ambulances with sirens, Zeng realized.

"And where did these howling vehicles go?"

"To the store which puts men to work," Chow responded.

"The one known as the Far East Employment Service?"

"Yes, my master."

"Drive there in haste!" Zeng Tse-Lin commanded, his interest quickening sharply. "Did you learn why the police cars journeyed to that place?"

"I heard talk. Looters broke in. More I could not discover, for a policeman told me to gettee-the-devil away or he would give me a ticket for blocking traffic. So I departed."

Dr. Zeng scowled. Could it be a coincidence that the employment agency where Sally Prescott worked had been burglarized so soon after Sally's own disappearance? He thought not, for he had little faith in theories of coincidence. There was a hidden connection here somewhere, he felt sure. And he was determined to find that connection.

Originally he had wanted to go to Police Headquarters as rapidly as possible, in order to consult with his friend, Captain Carter of the Homicide Bureau. But the Far East Agency was located on the route to Headquarters, and he would not lose much time by stopping there en route.

Night had fallen when Zeng Tse-Lin alighted from his car and made for the employment agency entrance. Within the bare-looking room lights gleamed brightly down on a score of uniformed officers and plainclothes detectives.

Three men stood near the doorway of a rear office, excitedly talking. One of them, a big, florid man whose clothing was much too flashy, saw Zeng and came forward to greet him.

"Hello, Doctor! What brings you here?"

Zeng smiled politely. "In Chinatown, when a neighbor encounters trouble, his fellow merchants are eager to be of help. I saw the police in your shop as I passed, and I wondered if I might do anything to assist you."

"Nice of you," the florid man said. He was Frank Kempler, owner of the employment bureau, having inherited the business from his father, who had founded it.

PRIOR TO assuming control of the agency, Kempler had been a petty politician and ward heeler. He still looked the part, thanks to his addiction to loud suits and oversized diamonds. A five-carat canary stone glittered in a heavy gold ring on the middle finger of his right hand. Ten more gems, smaller but of equal yellow brilliance, were set into the horseshoe stickpin he wore in his cravat. The effect was flamboyant, matching the man himself.

"Your place of business was burglarized?" Zeng asked him.

"Yeah, but I wouldn't know why. What little money we had on hand was in the safe, and while they cracked the combination, no cash is missing."

"Nothing was stolen, then?"

"Not as far as I can tell, although they certainly messed up our files before they made their getaway. The thing that worries me is what happened to the janitor."

Dr. Zeng's eyes narrowed. "What was that?"

"He must have seen these guys prowl and tried to capture them. So they caved in his skull, the dirty rats. He died before he could be taken to the hospital."

To Zeng Tse-Lin, that was ominous news. It added another murder to the case, provided that this burglary and killing could be linked with the poisoning of Andrew McClane. He had an instinctive conviction that there was such a connection.

The florid Frank Kempler now made a summoning gesture at the two men to whom he had been talking when Zeng first entered. They approached. Kempler spoke perfunctory introductions.

"You know Nick Olson and Lewis LaMarr, don't you, Doctor?"

Zeng shook hands with the pair, expressing courteous pleasure at meeting them again.

Olson was a colorless little individual whose pale blue eyes and strawlike hair betrayed his Scandinavian ancestry. He had a queer way of staring at you without blinking, then shifting his gaze furtively away. In former years he had been a bail bond broker associated in politics with Kempler, and now he managed the employment agency for the florid owner.

Lewis LaMarr, on the other hand, was of a far different cast. Elderly and refined, quietly sedate, obviously of good breeding, he served as the bureau's personnel expert. Early college training had fitted him for this work, and in addition, his social standing gave him entree to most of San Francisco's better homes. Equipped with such connections, he was invaluable in obtaining high-class clientele for the agency.

At the moment, his forehead was creased with worry.

"I suppose you've heard of our misfortune, Dr. Zeng?"

"Mr. Kempler was just telling me."

"To make things worse, our stenographer is missing," LaMarr said unhappily. "Sally Prescott. We've been asked down to Headquarters for a conference. Seems she was involved in the death of one of our clients,

Andrew McClane. Everything happens at once!" He made a disturbed gesture.

"Is there a chance that her disappearance has any bearing upon this burglary?" Zeng ventured casually, watching all three men for untoward reactions. Kempler's florid features grew even redder than usual.

"What a screwy idea! If Sally wanted to rob us, why would she bring in a bunch of thugs? She knew the combination of the safe, realized how little dough was in it. She wouldn't make a thief of herself for a few bucks."

"And even if she did turn crook, she wouldn't cut in no mob of heist guys," the furtive little Olson interjected from a corner of his mouth. "That ain't sensible."

Dr. Zeng nodded his agreement. "However, it is written that many robberies are committed for things other than money."

"You mean there might have been something valuable here that we didn't know about?" LaMarr inquired sedately.

The tall doctor shrugged. "The thieves may have thought so."

Then, politely shaking hands with himself, he left the Far East Employment Service, acutely aware that florid Frank Kempler and colorless Nick Olson were staring after him in shrewd-eyed speculation.

CHAPTER V

MANY QUERIES

CAPTAIN CARTER of the Homicide Squad was a compact and muscular Irishman whose ruddy complexion was in sharp contrast to his steel-gray hair and frosty blue eyes. By sheer, tenacious ability he had risen to his present post, and the efficient manner with which he ran his department was the envy of every other city up and down the Pacific Coast.

This evening he was at his desk when Dr. Zeng Tse-Lin quietly entered his private office at Headquarters. He looked up and gave Zeng a warm smile, for they were intimate friends—so close that Carter was among the select few who were aware of the hawklike man's real status as a white American criminologist of unsurpassed achievements.

"Well, Zeng!" the Homicide official said heartily. "How are you and what brings you here? I know you better than to believe it's just a social call."

"From the eye of the eagle, nothing can be hidden." Dr. Zeng bowed as he delivered the gracious compliment. "It is true that I have a purpose in visiting you. I am interested in the poison murder of a certain Andrew McClane."

Carter leaned back in his battered swivel chair.

"I've been hoping to talk to you about that mess. The sergeant in charge of the case tells me you made a snap diagnosis—and by golly, you were right. As you always are," he added.

"There has been an autopsy so soon?"

"No, just a preliminary medical report. It showed a slug of atropine in McClane's stomach, though. Enough to have killed two or three men. Somebody must have dosed his whiskey."

"And do you suspect anyone except the young tourist guide, Hal Wilson, who was taken into custody?"

Carter shook his head. "Nobody but his girl friend, this Sally Prescott—the one who's disappeared."

"There has been no trace found of her?"

"Not yet. The dragnet's out for her, of course."

"And have you questioned young Wilson?"

"To tell the truth, no," the Homicide chief admitted. "I've been too busy. There was a burglary a little while ago at the employment agency where the Prescott girl works—"

"Yes, I know. The janitor was slain and the murderers made their getaway."

"You certainly get around!" Carter exclaimed. "I'm waiting now to interview the three men who run the employment bureau."

The tall doctor nodded. "That, also, I know. But I fear you will be disappointed in what you get out of them."

"What makes you say that?"

"Intuition, perhaps. But I should like to venture the opinion that the burglary, the death of the janitor, the poisoning of McClane and the disappearance of Miss Prescott are all parts of the same puzzle."

"What?" Carter gasped. Then he leaned forward. "What's your angle on this thing, Zeng?"

"I was drawn into it by circumstance, and now my interest is aroused," Zeng Tse-Lin answered evenly.

The Headquarters official scowled. "I've read my sergeant's report, naturally. According to your statement, the Wilson chap enlisted your medical services for McClane. But when you arrived at the house, McClane was dead and the girl gone."

"True. But she had not departed willingly."

Zeng told of the dripping kitchen faucet, the dented basin and the water stains in the hallway.

"Therefore," he concluded, "I feel positive that she was abducted."

"But why?"

AGAIN ZENG theorized.

"It is quite evident that her kidnapers were searching for something, which they failed to find in McClane's house or upon his body. Perhaps they thought that she could tell them where to locate what they wanted, so they took her with them. Soon after, they ransacked the employment office—still hunting for this missing object."

"I take it, then, that you don't subscribe to my sergeant's ideas about the case. He thinks Wilson and the girl poisoned McClane and she later lost her nerve, ran out."

Dr. Zeng smiled thinly. "The sergeant leaps too quickly at false conclusions. I have known Hal Wilson for several years. I know him to be honorable. He has a temper, yes; and he might desire to settle with any man who made improper advances to Sally Prescott. But he would use his fists, not poison."

"Hm-m-m," Brian Carter mused. Through experience, he had learned that the tall doctor had an uncanny way of putting a long finger directly into the heart of a crime. "You might be right, at that. But what's the next step?"

"Proceed by all means with your interrogation of the employment bureau men. And, if it would not be an intrusion, I should like to remain while you query them."

"Glad to have you," Carter agreed swiftly.

He pressed a button on his desk, and presently three visitors were conducted into the office. They were Frank Kempler, florid and bediamonded owner of the Far East Employment Service; Nick Olson, his colorless and furtive little manager; and Lewis LaMarr, the elderly personnel expert.

They seemed a bit astonished at seeing Zeng in the room, but Carter deftly covered that situation.

"Dr. Zeng is the one who attended Andrew McClane, pronounced him dead and diagnosed the poison which killed him," the police official explained. "For that reason, I've asked him to be here while we discussed the matter."

"What matter?" Kempler demanded, the huge yellow diamond glittering on his hand as he made an impatient gesture. "What has McClane's death got to do with it? I thought you called us in to talk about our burglary."

"There's a possibility that the two crimes fit together," Carter said curtly. Then he slitted his frosty blue eyes. "How well were you gentlemen acquainted with McClane?"

As owner of the employment bureau, Kempler took the lead in responding.

"We all knew him. He hired a lot of help through our office, so we saw him pretty often."

"Were you on intimate terms with him?"

"Not me," Kempler stated flatly. "He was too high-toned for the likes of me."

"Same here," Nick Olson lipped out of the side of his mouth. Then he turned furtively to the elderly personnel expert standing alongside him. "But *you* was pretty thick with the guy, Lew."

Lewis LaMarr looked sedately pained. "I had social contacts with McClane, of course." And he gave the colorless Olson a hurt glance, as if mildly objecting to the way the smaller man had deliberately put him in an embarrassing spot.

Meantime Captain Carter had seized on LaMarr's embarrassment to drive home a sharp question.

"So you had social contacts with McClane, huh? Okay. Do you know any reason why he'd be murdered? Do you know who hated him?"

"Gracious, no!" the elderly man answered in confusion.

Carter swung on Frank Kempler. "How about you?"

THE AGENCY owner toyed nervously with his diamond stickpin.

"Nix, Cap, nix! You know me, pal. I'm no saint. Maybe I got mixed up in some shady deals when I was younger. But poison—oh, no! I get the screaming meemies to think about it."

"Me, too," Nick Olson chimed in like a furtive parrot.

The Homicide chief drummed on his desk. "All right. So nobody knows who poisoned McClane or why. We'll move on to the Prescott girl and her boyfriend, Hal Wilson. What can you tell me about them?"

Information was immediately forthcoming but it proved to be sketchy and of no great value. Sally Prescott had been with the agency two years. She was efficient, pleasant, industrious. She went with Hal Wilson and they planned to be married before that angular young man enlisted in the Army. She'd had some trouble with McClane, but nothing serious.

"That's all we can give you, Cap," Kempler said.

Carter masked his disappointment.

"Very well. Now about your burglary. It's obvious that the thugs who killed your janitor weren't after money. They were looking for something else. Have you any idea what it was?"

"No," the florid man answered. "But as long as you seem to think the heist guys had some connection with the McClane kill, here's an angle for you. Maybe they thought McClane left something in the agency office when he was there."

From his corner, of the office, Dr. Zeng looked sharply at the flashily dressed employment bureau owner. Then a tiny smile touched the tall doctor's lips. This Kempler, for all his flamboyant exterior, had a clever brain; Zeng made a mental note of the fact for future reference.

Presently, Captain Carter dismissed the agency trio. As they trooped out, the Homicide official spread his hands, looking sour.

"We certainly didn't learn much, did we? But then you warned me I'd be disappointed."

"It is written that a wise man finds comfort, even in disappointment; and that a starved tiger stalks his prey all the more warily because of his hunger." Zeng's tone was soft with thought. "Would you be good enough to have one of your men summon Lai Hu Chow here to me? I have just remembered a thing which may prove important."

Carter nodded and pressed a button. Two minutes later the huge, one-legged Mongol servitor lumbered into the office.

"Yes, my master?"

"Think hard," Zeng commanded. "When Hal Wilson entered the House of a Thousand Beatitudes this evening to seek my medical services, he had with him a small brown paper parcel."

"Is so?"

"Yes. I saw it upon the television screen as he stood outside our front door. Yet when he mounted the stairs, he no longer had that package. What became of it?"

Chew blinked, concentrated. "I saw it not."

"Then you cannot tell me if he disposed of it inside, or if he dropped it before entering?"

"No, my master."

Zeng Tse-Lin frowned. "I am positive that the young man did not take the package away with him when he drove ahead of us to the McClane residence. Therefore—"

Brian Carter leaped to his feet. "You mean the parcel may be what those burglars were after at the agency office?"

"It is possible, my friend."

CAPTAIN CARTER'S finger reached for a push button.

"By George, I'll have Wilson up here! I'll sweat the information out of him!"

"Wait." Zeng held up his hand. "I trust the young guide, but in a case of this kind it is better to be sure first than sorry later."

"Meaning what?"

"It has been written that a wise man moves in darkness at a snail's pace while a fool gallops with the speed of a horse. And you are no fool, friend Carter."

"All right. What would you have me do?"

"I suggest that you arrange for Hal Wilson's release and put a competent shadow on him. If he attempts to recover this parcel and meet the girl, we will know that they were involved."

Carter drummed his desk. "Suppose it doesn't work?"

"All alleys have two ends." Zeng smiled. "Meantime, I shall be searching for that package myself. Come, Chow. We have a task before us."

He bowed to Carter, shook hands with himself and departed from the office, with the Homicide official's puzzled gaze following him.

Then, when the tall doctor and his servitor had gone, Brian Carter sighed and set the machinery in motion for turning young Wilson free from custody.

CHAPTER VI

DIAMOND QUEST

THREE MEN were playing poker at a small table, with a greasy deck of cards. On the other side of the frowsy little room there was a lumpy davenport on which lay a golden-haired girl, trussed and gagged. Only her haunted eyes moved as she watched the card players through billowing clouds of cigarette smoke.

A shiver coursed through Sally Prescott when she studied the hard, brutish faces of her captors. Already they had subjected her to vicious indignities and tentative tortures, evidenced by her torn frock and the bruises on her snowy shoulders.

And she realized that she was now enjoying but a temporary respite from their savage attentions. Soon, she knew, they would assail her again in an effort to make her tell what they wanted to know—since they refused to believe her when she denied possessing the information.

She moaned against her gag, wondering why they had momentarily abandoned their efforts to make her talk. Maybe they were awaiting further instructions from the man for whom they worked, she decided. It was the only logical explanation.

As if to corroborate her theory, a phone bell across the room jangled harshly. One of the poker players leaped up to answer the call.

"Hello?" he called guardedly. Then: "Yeah, Boss, this is Sam. Huh? Sure, we got the jane here. But she either don't know nothin' or she's the stubbornest quail I ever seen. We been waitin' to find out whatcha want us to do next."

There was a pause, while the person at the other end of the line apparently asked a question. Then the thug who called himself Sam broke into a blurt of defensive words.

"Look, Boss!" he protested. "We done just like you told us! As soon as you slipped McClane that mickey in the café, we start tailin' him home so we can glom the stuff offa him in his stash where nobody can see. But the poison hits him too soon. He stops his jalopy in front of the agency an' goes inside."

Another pause for another apparent question.

Sam started talking again. "Yeah, Boss. Then the jane an' the Wilson jerk take McClane home. But Wilson goes right out again, see? We figger he's huntin' a doctor, so we barge in the house an' give it a frisk. No dice. This doll catches us an' acts like maybe she knows somethin', so we bring her away with us. On our way, we stop by the agency to see if McClane left the stuff there. I guess you know what happened."

Once more Sam stopped talking to listen.

Presently he resumed. "Huh? You don't say! Sure, Boss, I get whatcha mean. Okay, we'll move right now."

Then he rang off and turned to his two hoodlum companions.

"What's the lay?" one of them asked.

"The doctor that Wilson got for McClane was that tall Chinee we're always seein' around town." Sam growled. "Zeng Tse-Lin. The boss thinks maybe Wilson took the stuff outa McClane's red sedan an' stashed it in Zeng's joint."

"So what?"

"So we're to go to the Chinee's house an' prowl it. Also, the boss got a grapevine from a stoolie at Headquarters. They're gonna turn Wilson loose. We gotta nab him an' try to make him spill. Tony, you stay here with the wren. Come on, Pete. We'll have to move fast."

AT THAT very moment, Dr. Zeng Tse-Lin was entering the House of a Thousand Beatitudes with Lai Hu Chow. Making a light, Zeng moved through the lower hallway with his eyes probing at every corner.

"Young Wilson had the parcel when he arrived," the hawklike man intoned. "He did not have it when he left. Therefore, it must be here." Abruptly he tensed, sprang forward. "Look!"

Chow forgot to chew his wad of gum.

"Goodee gloly!" He lapsed into the pidgin English which he used only when excited. "The package! Sittee on Manchu table as plain as 'leventeen warts on Jap baby's bare backee-sidee!"

Zeng chuckled at the giant Mongol's graphic simile. Then he snatched up the package and ascended the staircase to his living quarters. Here he unwrapped the brown paper, disclosing a thick piece of rolled black velvet.

He unrolled the soft cloth and uttered a muffled exclamation of astonishment when myriad rays of glinting, reflected brilliance flashed into his widened eyes. The velvet roll was literally crammed with diamonds!

In moments more, Dr. Zeng was in his car again and Chow was letting the big limousine roll with all speed back toward Police Headquarters.

Captain Brian Carter looked up from his desk when the two entered his office, surprised to see Dr. Zeng and Chow returning to visit him so soon after their recent departure.

"You must have found that parcel, Zeng," he surmised shrewdly.

In answer, the tall doctor placed the roll of velvet on Carter's desk, revealing its fabulous contents.

"A king's ransom in gems, O my friend. Observe that some of the stones have been roughly pried from their settings, while a great many more still remain in rings and brooches and necklaces. What does this indicate to you?"

"Stolen loot!" Carter exclaimed. He pressed a button.

"Precisely," the ascetic criminologist agreed. "Now we know what the burglars were searching for when they broke into that employment agency and slew the janitor. I should estimate that these stones are roughly worth a quarter of a million dollars—perhaps more."

"And Andrew McClane must have had them when the poison hit him!" Brian Carter rasped. "The stones were in his car. Hal Wilson later used that car to summon you to the dying man. Wilson, for some reason, carried the parcel into your house and left it there."

Zeng nodded. "Which proves Wilson's innocence. He would not have placed the package so carelessly on my hallway table if he had realized its value."

"Not unless he figured that would make a good hiding place," the Homicide chief suggested.

"No, my friend. I am positive the angular young man was unaware of what he carried. I am equally positive that Sally Prescott was kidnaped by men who were hunting these gems in McClane's house—the same men who subsequently turned their attention to the employment bureau office. You see, they were back-tracking McClane's movements."

As Zeng finished speaking, a man entered the room. He was the chief of the robbery detail, a jewel expert as competent in his field as Brian Carter was in matters of homicide.

HAVING BEEN summoned by Carter's push-button signal, the gem expert immediately studied the diamonds glittering on the desk. Presently he looked up.

"I can't be sure about the stones that were pried from their settings," he stated. "But I recognize the others. They're from the series of robberies we had last winter."

Zeng Tse-Lin remembered those burglaries quite well. They had broken all police records for value of loot stolen and number of homes broken into. No arrests had ever been made, but suddenly and for no apparent reason, the crimes had ceased around the early part of May. The unknown gang had not operated since.

Now the hawklike doctor ventured a request.

"Could you get me a list of the houses that were robbed?" he asked Carter.

"Of course!"

When the list came, Zeng carefully scanned it. He was engaged in this when Carter's phone rang. The Homicide official answered, listened, then hung up with a bitter curse.

"Something is wrong?" Zeng asked him.

"Plenty! That was the shadow I'd put on Hal Wilson. He reports that two masked guys jumped the tourist guide on lower Montgomery. Tried to force him into a car. He resisted, and they slugged him with a sap. My man opened fire with his gun and drove them off—but now young Wilson's in the hospital with a concussion. It'll be hours, perhaps days, before we can question him!"

Zeng's face was expressionless, his words carefully weighed.

"Quizzing Wilson would be of no help, I fear. You would learn no more from him than you already know. Obviously those thugs were of the belief that the young man could lead them to the diamonds. Now they have reached a blind alley."

"And so have we!" Carter growled.

"Perhaps not. Matters are developing, O my friend. I shall make contact with you tomorrow morning. It may be that I will have made some progress by that time."

The Homicide chief looked worried. "Better let me give you a body-guard. Suppose that mob guesses Wilson left the swag with you? Then you'll be in danger!"

"I have Chow. He is better than an army with banners."

Zeng smiled. And he silently departed with his Mongol servitor. But Brian Carter's face showed that he had little confidence in Chow's being better than an army.

CHAPTER VII

MASKED VISITORS

S HADOWS DRAPED the quiet side street on which the Mandarin Emporium fronted, and soon there was moisture in the darkness, hinting of a fog that soon would come drifting in from the bay, as Chow stopped the limousine in front of his master's home.

Zeng Tse-Lin alighted, and the big Asiatic started to follow him. But Zeng held up a hand.

"The car will not drive itself to the garage, O foolish one. First put it away, then you may rejoin me."

Grumbling, the giant slid back under the wheel. He could not divorce himself from the habit of considering his master a helpless stripling in need of protection. It made no difference that Zeng could best him in any test of physical stamina. He still regarded himself as indispensable to the doctor's safety.

And in the present case he came very near being right!

As Chow drove the sedan away, Zeng Tse-Lin unlocked the front door of the House of a Thousand Beatitudes and stepped inside, so lost in preoccupation that he gave no thought to possible peril.

He was wondering what could have happened early in May which would account for the sudden stopping of that series of robberies. Knowing the criminal mind, he realized that no successful mob of burglars would quit merely because they had gained enough plunder. There was always a consuming desire to pull just one more job—and then another.

Hence, there must have been some outside reason for the burglaries to cease with such amazing abruptness. What was that reason, Zeng asked himself. He was still turning the problem over in his brain when an arm reached out unexpectedly from the darkness of the hallway and twined about his throat.

The hawklike doctor's reaction was automatic and immediate. Long ago he had discarded the intricacies of ju-jutsu for a far more effective system of his own devising. He moved with the lithe speed of a cobra; used certain leverages. And the unseen attacker went catapulting through space to land with a sickening concussion against the opposite wall.

Zeng's advantage was of short duration, however. Suddenly a light flashed to life and he found himself confronted by another intruder whose face was masked and whose hand clenched a heavy revolver.

"Freeze, wise guy. No more of your Chinee tricks! Hey, Pete—are you okay?"

The first masked marauder dragged himself to his feet, trembling.

"I guess so. Gee, one minute I had him by the gullet an' the next minute lightnin' strikes me!"

"It won't strike no more. Now look, Doc. We ain't got nothin' against you, see? I mean we don't want no trouble. But we lost a package that belongs to us an' we want it back. We got a hunch it was stashed here by that tourist guide jerk, Hal Wilson."

"So?"

"Yeah. We been friskin' this hallway an' the store alongside it, but we didn't find nothin'. So now it's up to you to cough up the stuff."

Dr. Zeng repressed the smile that wanted to curl his ascetic lips. With a little strategy, he could capture this masked pair. And the strategy would be based upon luring them upstairs.

His staircase would do the trick. At the head of the steps a switch was concealed. When pressed, the stair trends tilted and became a long, straight chute-slide ending in a trap-door which would open at the bottom. Thus, anyone caught upon the staircase would go arrowing downward to drop through the yawning trap-door and land in a basement cell, from which there was no escape except when unlocked by Zeng himself.

ALL HE had to do was go upstairs ahead of these men and work the hidden control. Therefore, he pretended to surrender.

"I will lead you to what you want," he said. "Follow me."

They trailed him upstairs, their guns drawn. But Zeng was destined not to capture them by his staircase contrivance. Just as he was halfway up the steps there came a terrific commotion from his front doorway.

It was Chow, roaring a Mongol battle-cry and flourishing a knife that looked as long as a bayonet.

"Halt, sons of camels!" he shouted. "I would see the color of thy livers!"

The two masked thugs wheeled, saw that menacing blade licking at them—and lost their courage. Forgetting their guns, they plunged from the steps and dashed wildly through a side door in the hallway which led into the darkened Mandarin Emporium. There came a crash of splintering glass as they burst out through one of the front show windows.

Even as they fled, Zeng Tse-Lin catapulted downward and tried to pursue. But Chow clumsily got in his way, costing him precious seconds. Then he saw someone else standing behind the yelling giant. The instant he recognized this new figure, he halted and abandoned all thought of capturing the masked men.

"Ann!" he said gravely.

Ann Carter was Captain Brian Carter's niece—a diminutive and dainty red-haired girl whose loveliness always stirred deep longings in Zeng's heart. Nor was it her beauty alone that moved him, for her character was one to arouse any man's admiration.

Despite the fact that she enjoyed an income more than sufficient for her every need, she was not content to take life easy. Instead, she taught an adult night school class in Chinatown, devoting her life to the welfare of its poorer inhabitants.

It was through this mission school that she had first met Dr. Zeng, whose charitable works even surpassed her own. A lasting friendship had sprung up between the girl and the doctor, thanks to their common interest in the underprivileged class of Chinese. It was Ann who had brought Zeng and her uncle together, some years ago. The Homicide official and the hawklike criminologist had since cemented unbreakable bonds of friendship in which Ann shared almost fully.

But although she realized Zeng's accomplishments in the detection of crime, he had never allowed her to learn that he was of her own race. Secretly he cared for her more than he was willing to admit even to himself. Yet he could not bring himself to ask her hand in marriage, for this would mean that she would be compelled to share the many dangers of his career.

Unwilling to expose her to such risks, he had decided to let her go on thinking him an Oriental. In that way, all thoughts of romance would be eliminated from her mind. The decision had been difficult for Zeng to make, but he knew it was for the best. Ann Carter must be protected, even though it cost him many a pang in his heart.

Now she came toward him, arms outstretched.

"Zeng, thank heavens you're safe! I was afraid th-those men might—"

"Your interest in my welfare is more than I deserve," he said gently. "But what drew you into the affair?"

"I worked late at the night class, and on my way home I came by here to say hello to you. Just as I was about to ring your doorbell I heard a crash inside, then voices. I knew something must be wrong, realized you might need help. I ran to find a policeman, and I bumped into Chow at the corner. I told him what I'd heard, and—well, you know the rest."

ZENG THANKED her. She and Chow seemed so proud of having put the masked intruders to flight that he hadn't the heart to tell them that they had actually spoiled his own plans. Had it not been for their untimely appearance he might have captured the thugs and forced some information out of them concerning the man for whom they were working.

Well, other opportunities would come. Meanwhile, Zeng Tse-Lin pressed the girl's hand.

"Will you come upstairs and partake of tea and cakes?"

"I think not, Zeng. It's getting late, and I really must be on my way home. But—are you sure you'll be all right? I mean, are those men likely to come back?"

He smiled gravely. "Have no fear. It is written that a jackal never returns to the scene of a defeat."

His eyes were dark with loneliness as Ann left the house and drove away in her little coupé. Then, repressing a sigh, he turned to Chow.

"Come, O valiant warrior. Prepare thyself, for we now have a visit to repay."

The giant Mongol's moonlike countenance glowed with anticipation.

"Will there be danger, my master?"

"Let us trust not. This mission is one of secrecy. We search for facts, not fighting." Then he added a mysterious command, in words that seemed almost meaningless. "The limb of forcible entry," he said....

The office of the Far East Employment Service was dark and deserted, as was the street on which it fronted. Dr. Zeng observed the building for several minutes before he crossed over to its gloomy entrance.

Making sure that his movements were not spied upon by hidden watchers, he turned to his faithful Chow.

"We will use the glass cutter and putty. It is quickest."

At once the Mongol stooped over and fumbled at his artificial leg, thus revealing what Zeng had meant a while ago when he had mentioned "the limb of forcible entry."

As a useful hobby, Zeng Tse-Lin had constructed many false legs for his crippled servitor. Each one of these legs contained hollow apertures, packed with various devices. For instance, one artificial limb held a miniature but powerful radio transmitter and receiver. Another carried weapons—a small automatic, several bombs both explosive and of the tear-gas type, and a set of wicked knives.

In the present case, Chow's artificial leg was neatly packed with a variety of startling tools designed especially for burglarious entry. He now produced a diamond-sharp glass cutter and a wad of soft putty, which he carefully spread upon the grimy pane of the agency's front door.

Then, with the cutter, he deftly removed a section of the glass itself, pulling it out by means of the putty, so that it would not drop and shatter loudly on the pavement. Next, Zeng reached a capable hand through the resulting hole, located the inner latch and turned it. The door swung open.

The interior was cloaked in almost impenetrable gloom. But Zeng's eyes pierced the darkness, for he had long ago included in his daily diet a plentiful supply of the vitamins which promote night vision. Therefore, he moved forward through the main room without hesitation, Chow following.

IGNORING THE larger office, the tall doctor made unerringly for a small room at the rear. Here he could risk using his flashlight. Its tiny, brilliant ray revealed a bank of filing cabinets before him.

Zeng fell immediately to work upon an inspection of those files. They were in considerable disorder, thanks to the earlier visit of looters who had rummaged through them and disorganized the alphabetical arrangements. Still, though, the oblong cards themselves could be read without trouble.

They represented a list of all the firm's clients, both employers and employees. Zeng compared each one with the mental roster he carried of those families whose homes had been entered and robbed prior to the early part of May. Captain Carter had shown him that list of burglarized houses, and now he checked the list against these file cards.

Presently he stopped for a moment.

"Chow, we have discovered something important."

"Yes, my master?"

"Every home that was robbed had previously obtained servants through this agency. Jap houseboys, in each case."

"Little monkey-men!" Chow said contemptuously.

"I agree. Now, I have here the names of five Jap houseboys. Each Jap worked in one or more of the burglarized homes. And in every case, the Jap had first been employed in the house of Andrew McClane."

The big Mongol blinked. "Is meaning something?"

"I think it means that we are near to the solution of several mysteries. For McClane supplied the references which enabled the five Japs to obtain other employment with families that were subsequently robbed."

Chow started to ask the significance of this. Then he hesitated, his nostrils twitching. Abruptly he broke into excited pidgin English.

"Goshee-gloly, smellee smokee!" he yowled. "Fire! Fire! The whole cussee placee burnee up!"

And he made a wild dash for a corner of the office, where tiny flames were licking at a piled mess of waste paper.

CHAPTER VIII

JAP TRAIL

DR. ZENG followed Chow, overtook and passed him. Should the flame gain headway, the whole structure would blaze to destruction in a twinkling. The building was old, tindery, its woodwork rotten with age. It would be a death-trap for Dr. Zeng and Chow in one more minute!

But the tall criminologist's rapier mind was equal to the peril confronting him. Lightning swift he removed his rich, brocaded robe, blanketed the growing flames. Under that smothering garment the fire smoldered, died down. Chow stamped out the final embers.

As he did, his shoe kicked something which he picked up curiously and extended to his master.

"Look. Is crazy gadget!"

Zeng, examining it, didn't think it was so crazy. It consisted of a small vial of common glycerine stoppered by a make-shift cork of wadded paper which was now damp and soggy. Attached to the neck of the bottle was a tiny metal ashtray containing a burned cone of some material to which a few purple crystals still clung.

"A fire-bug's work!" Dr. Zeng exclaimed softly.

"Somebody try to kill us?"

"No, it was an attempt to burn the building and destroy all records of the agency, I think," the hawklike man answered impassively. "This contrivance here is a simple but effective incendiary bomb."

"How?"

"The bottle's paper cork was bound to soften in a few hours, thus permitting some drops of glycerine to fall upon a mound of potassium permanganate crystals. The chemical reaction is quite interesting. Spontaneous combustion results. With waste-paper on top, the flames were bound to kindle."

"Lucky we here to put out fire," Chow offered.

Dr. Zeng smiled thinly. "But unlucky for a certain criminal whose name I hope soon to know," he said. "Come, our job is finished here. We will go home…."

At nine o'clock the next morning, Zeng appeared at Captain Brian Carter's office just as the Homicide official was beginning his duties for the day. Carter cast a worried look at his caller.

"Ann tells me you had some trouble last night. I warned you to be careful!"

Zeng bowed. "Only a fool refuses to admit that he is wrong. But a wise man profits from experience. I have tidings for you, O my friend."

And he told of the things that had happened last night at the Far East Employment Agency, including his own findings. When he had finished, he looked steadily at Carter. The official scowled thoughtfully.

"An incendiary!" he rumbled. "And what do you make of the Jap houseboy business, Zeng?"

"Well, you had said that the series of burglaries stopped in the early part of May. I wondered why. I also wondered if the employment agency could be involved. Then I hit upon a possible answer which seemed to fit the facts."

"And that answer—"

"In the first two weeks of May, all Japanese were evacuated from this area, including the domestic servants supplied by the Far East Employment Bureau."

CARTER TENSED.

"Here is a list of five Jap houseboys," Zeng continued evenly. "All worked for McClane at one time. All had later gained employment in homes which were subsequently robbed. No suspicion fell on these Japs, for they had moved on again by the time the burglaries took place."

"I get it!" the Homicide chief rasped. "You think the Japs were deliberately planted in those homes. They cased the houses for information concerning jewelry. Maybe they made duplicate keys. Then they would quit their jobs, and later the homes would be entered by an organized mob of burglars!"

Zeng inclined his head. "It is a sound theory. And remember, McClane furnished each Jap with a recommendation, making it easy for those houseboys to be placed with other families. Moreover, McClane had that parcel of stolen diamonds."

"Then he must have been in with the burglary gang!"

"I think so. It would even explain his murder. His confederates poisoned him in order to steal his share of the loot. After all, the game was finished—for the mob could no longer make use of the Japs, who had been evacuated. That is why the burglaries ceased in May."

"You've hit the nail on the head, Zeng!" Carter said admiringly. "It's got to be that way! But our next job is to locate McClane's partners in the mob."

The hawklike man smiled. "Perhaps we can force that information from the five evacuated Japs. I suggest that you find out where they were taken. It was Manzanar, probably. But the Army authorities will tell you for certain. Then you must procure a pass for me to go see them. I speak their tongue fluently, and I think I can make them confess."

"Fine enough. But first I'll seize the employment bureau's records. We may need them in court."

Dr. Zeng started to protest, then reconsidered. He knew danger might exist in Carter's plan, but he also realized the Homicide official's position. Carter couldn't go to the prosecutor's office and ask an indictment on information which Zeng had illegally obtained by burglarizing the agency office.

Therefore, the criminologist said nothing, but went with his friend to the Far East Employment Service.

Their arrival with a squad of uniformed policemen caused considerable excitement. The long benches in the waiting room were occupied by a motley collection of Chinese and Filipino job-hunters who babbled and milled around at sight of the lawmen.

Drawn by this commotion, the firm's furtive little manager, Nick Olson, came scuttling from his private office in the rear. His colorless cheeks grew even paler than usual when he spotted Captain Carter, and he moved angrily forward.

"What's the big idea, copper?" he said from a corner of his mouth. "You act like you was pullin' a raid!"

"Not quite," the Homicide official answered. "Where's your boss?"

"Kempler? He ain't here just now. Now take your flatfeet and beat it. They're disturbin' these Chinese and Filipino boys."

"There's no reason for anybody to be disturbed if they haven't broken any laws." Carter held his rising temper in check, although it cost him an effort. "I've got a requisition warrant here for your files."

"Files?" The furtive man's shifty eyes hardened. "What for?"

"I want them, is all."

"And you can't have them. Not until Frank Kempler says okay. Me, I don't think he'll say okay. He still drags plenty of weight in politics, remember."

Carter blew up. "To thunder with his political drag! No former ward-heeler on earth is going to stop me from doing my duty! Get that straight. Now, where are your files?"

AT THAT moment, the elderly personnel expert, Lewis LaMarr, appeared from another of the small offices. In a sedate tone of puzzlement he asked Olson what was going on.

The furtive little manager profanely explained.

"But really, then," LaMarr said unhappily, "I can't see how we can do anything but give the captain what he wants. After all, he must have a good reason for this. And surely Mr. Kempler will understand when he gets here. He won't hold us responsible."

"Oh, no? That's what you think!" Olson sneered at the personnel man. "Frank ain't gonna stand for these bulls hornin' in on us. We're clean, see? You know that. We don't place no domestics unless they got clean records."

Zeng ventured a quiet question. "Who investigates the people for whom you obtain employment?"

"What's it to you?" Olson snarled suspiciously.

"Forgive me for intruding," Zeng apologized. "But it happens that I am a friend of young Hal Wilson, who is involved in this affair for reasons beyond his control. My interest is even greater, now, for he was seriously injured last night."

"Yeah? I thought he was pinched."

"He was later released, and then attacked by masked thugs," the tall doctor intoned gravely. "I merely seek information that might help unravel the cause of this attack on him."

LEWIS LAMARR tried to pour oil on troubled waters.

"I don't see why we can't answer your question, then. You want to know, who investigates the people that we get jobs for?"

"If you please, sir."

"Well, Sally Prescott did some of that work. And Mr. Kempler, when he had time to spare. Most of the investigations were personally supervised by Nick Olson, here."

The furtive little manager turned on him, snarling.

"And how about yourself, Lew? Don't forget you took care of the Jap situation. A lot of it, anyways."

LaMarr reddened in embarrassment, and Dr. Zeng made a mental note that this made the second time he had seen Nick Olson deliberately place the elderly personnel expert in an awkward spot. The other occasion was when Olson had spoken of LaMarr's social contacts with the murdered Andrew McClane.

Zeng pondered Olson's possible motive for putting Lewis LaMarr in a bad light. And even as he weighed the matter carefully in his mind, the agency's florid owner came in.

"What goes on?" Frank Kempler demanded, waving his bediamonded hand. "What's cooking?"

"This copper's got a warrant to glom our files," Olson answered from the side of his mouth.

"So okay," Kempler said, surprisingly affable. "Let him take 'em. Maybe he'll put them back in order for us. Eh, Cap?"

Grunting, Carter moved to the file room with the others following. The elderly LaMarr opened the file drawers and then grew nervously tense.

"Gone!" he cried. "The cards are all gone!"

And although the police searched the entire building, they learned no more than what Lewis LaMarr had told them. The cards were indeed gone.

Brian Carter swore fervently. "And this means Manzanar is my next best bet!" he growled, and left the agency, trailed by Dr. Zeng and the uniformed detail.

IT WAS far past mid-day, though, before the Homicide official got a pass to visit the Jap reception center at Manzanar and a clearance for a private plane.

All individually owned aircraft had long ago been grounded by orders of the Fourth Interceptor Command.

Pass and clearance took wire-pulling, but Carter managed it. Then, with Zeng Tse-Lin at the ship's controls, they headed southeast at maximum cruising speed.

"It beats me!" the police veteran growled to his tall, hawklike friend. "How did anybody know I was going to sequester the files? Do you suppose there's a pipe-line from Headquarters that tipped somebody off that I was coming?"

"Possibly, my friend. On the other hand, the guilty person is obviously the same one who contrived the delayed-action incendiary bomb. This morning when he saw the fire had been prematurely extinguished, he may have guessed the truth. Therefore, he made off with the files to prevent their use as legal evidence."

With which reconstruction, Zeng fell silent. Nor did he speak again until he had landed his plane in Owens Valley, near the outskirts of the Japanese camp at Manzanar.

CHAPTER IX

SEPPUKU?

BRIAN CARTER and Dr. Zeng were received by the officer in charge of the camp in his private quarters. There, Carter named the five Japs he wished to interview.

"That's strange," the officer exclaimed. "It hasn't been much more than an hour ago that a Federal agent from Oakland flew in here to question those same men, then left again."

Carter's frosty eyes widened. "A Federal agent?"

"Yes. It's queer the Army authorities in San Francisco failed to tell you. Still, perhaps they didn't know it themselves. Maybe I shouldn't have mentioned it. Anyway, no harm done. I'll take you to the Japs you want. They live together in one of the individual houses."

He then led them past a long row of brand-new buildings which gleamed raw—unpainted lumber in the afternoon sun's slanted rays. Presently he stopped before a large cottage and knocked sharply on the door. No answer came.

Frowning, the camp commandant tried the knob. It turned, and he shoved the door open; peered inside.

"Great heavens above!" He recoiled.

Zeng Tse-Lin stared, and although his heart hammered queerly, he betrayed no emotion on his ascetic features. But it took vast will-power to gain such control, for the scene in front of him was like a crimson-spattered nightmare.

Five dead Japs lay sprawled on the cottage floor, disemboweled by the short knives which each one clenched in a lifeless hand. Judging by the coagulated quality of the blood, Dr. Zeng guessed that they had been dead at least an hour.

The camp officer choked.

"I can hardly believe it! Why, they seemed perfectly contented, and they've been here three months! When the camp first opened we had one or two suicides, but nothing like this!"

"Mass hara-kiri!" Carter exclaimed.

Zeng nodded. "Also known as *seppuku.* In Japan, when a man loses face, he often prefers to slay himself rather than live in dishonor."

"Then the whole Jap nation ought to do it," Carter snapped. "Lord knows they dishonored themselves at Pearl Harbor!"

"Your words are wise, O my friend. But in this instance, we are leaping to an incorrect conclusion, I think. In my opinion, these men did not commit *seppuku.* "

The camp commandant stared at him. "Look at the evidence before your eyes, man! In all probability, the Federal agent from Oakland brought them news which caused them to lose face. Therefore they killed themselves."

"Forgive me, sir, if I disagree. What the so-called Federal agent brought them was death."

"What do you mean?" Brian Carter demanded.

"Merely that the visitor was not a government agent. He was a murderer whose purpose in coming here was to slay these Japanese in cold blood, in a manner to resemble hara-kiri."

"But why?"

"To keep us from gaining any information from them," Zeng Tse-Lin answered evenly.

The camp officer snorted. "You think five healthy Japs would stand still while one man knifed them all, one by one? You think they wouldn't have put up a fight?"

DR. ZENG'S sensitive nostrils flared. "There is an odor here which you may not have detected, for most of it has long ago been dissipated. I recognized that odor as the chemical fumes sometimes known as nerve gas."

"Nerve gas?"

"It causes no injury, but it paralyzes its victim temporarily. Long enough for murder to be committed with no answering struggle. And I believe that is what happened here."

"Great grief!" the camp commandant whispered harshly. "What a fool I was to be taken in by that fellow's credentials!"

"What did he look like?"

"Well, he was rather ordinary. Not young. Face a bit flushed, but that might have been from excitement. He wore a lot of diamonds; dressed flashily."

Zeng Tse-Lin plucked at Brian Carter's sleeve.

"Come, O my friend. We must make haste to San Francisco. The long trail is coming to an end."

In this opinion, Carter concurred grimly as he boarded the private plane.

"I'll nab Frank Kempler the minute we're back in town!" he promised. "The description fits him perfectly. Florid face, flashy clothes, too many diamonds. It's open and shut, by golly!"

"So it seems. But I must ask you to do nothing until I lay certain plans."

THE HOMICIDE official's eyes shot icy sparks.

"Why?"

"Because there is a girl to be considered. The employment bureau stenographer, Sally Prescott. She is being held captive, remember. And she must be rescued."

"I'll sweat Kempler until he tells where she is!"

Zeng smiled faintly. "That might be difficult. I think I can find a better way of shedding light upon the darkness." Then he added a curious phrase which seemed to have no meaning. "Black light," he said.

Whereupon he fell silent, now devoting his attention completely to the plane's controls.

Within an hour or so, not long after he had brought the plane to a landing at the airport from which he and Captain Carter had started, Dr. Zeng Tse-Lin was engaged upon a strange task. He was at the telephone, calling up a dozen shady pawnbrokers and asking them guarded questions concerning the prices they might pay for illicit diamonds.

It was evening, and Zeng was making his calls from a crowded restaurant. He seemed utterly oblivious to the three men who were seated at a table just around the pillar from his wall phone. Nor did he keep his voice particularly low.

PRESENTLY HE completed his last call, seemed satisfied with the price quoted, and rang off. Then he made his way from the café, looking neither to right nor left.

At the table near the telephone, the three men gazed after him, then looked at one another. Frank Kempler, beefy and florid, toyed with his diamond stickpin.

"Wasn't that the Chinese doctor?" the employment bureau owner asked his companions.

Furtive little Nick Olson shrugged. "I dunno. I wasn't payin' no attention. Looked like him from the back, though."

"It was Dr. Zeng, all right," Lewis LaMarr agreed in a tone as subdued as his tasteful clothes. "Odd sort of character, that fellow. Did you happen to hear those calls he made?"

Kempler shook his head. "Too blasted noisy in here." He held up a bediamonded hand for the check, paid it, and stood up heavily. "Well, I'll be seeing you guys."

"What's your rush, Boss?" Olson asked.

"Got a date with a chick." The florid man winked significantly. "You know me with dames."

His two associates watched his departure. Presently they, too, left the restaurant and separated without a great deal of palaver. One went north, the other south....

TWENTY MINUTES later the phone rang in an upstairs room of a ramshackle house near Van Ness. Three thuggish-looking hoodlums were playing cards at a small table, and on the far side of the room there was a lumpy davenport.

Sally Prescott still lay on that davenport, bound and gagged. She had been a prisoner for more than twenty-four hours now, and there was numb hopelessness in her blue eyes.

At the sound of the telephone bell, the hood named Sam jumped up to answer the call.

"Yeah, Boss?"

There was a long pause, while the man at the other end of the line spoke rapidly. Then Sam emitted a pleased grunt.

"Okay!" he said. "We'll be there."

He broke the connection; turned to his companions.

"What cooks?" one of them demanded.

"The boss just found out that the Chinee doctor's got them sparklers, after all!"

"Oh, yeah?"

"Yeah. The Chinee is tryin' to fence the rocks."

"So what?" the third crook growled. "I ain't goin' back to prowl that guy's joint no more. Not after the way he batted me around last night!"

Sam chortled. "The boss is gonna glom the ice hisself, see? He ain't lettin' us mess up no second chance. All he wants us to do is wait outside the Chinese feller's door in case of trouble. But we don't move in unless we get a signal. Come on."

"What about this cutie here?"

"She'll keep. The boss wants all three of us." Sam grinned with anticipation. "Guess he figures to split up the swag with us so we can blow town. Maybe he'll let us take the jane along when we lam."

On the sofa, Sally Prescott shivered as she watched the ugly trio leave the room.

Before a half hour had passed, a masked figure broke into the House of a Thousand Beatitudes. Stealthily he stole upstairs, although there was nobody in the building to hear him. Gaining the living quarters of Dr. Zeng, he sprayed the darkness with a beam from his flashlight and began searching.

There was a wall safe on the far side of the living room. He went to it, touched its combination knob. The circular door came open. Within the safe was a roll of black velvet.

The masked man unrolled the cloth, ran his fingers through a pile of glittering jewels.

Furtively he dumped them in his coat pocket, using the black velvet to wipe away any fingerprints he might have left on the unlocked safe.

Then he left the house as silently as he had entered.

Pausing on the sidewalk, he summoned three lurking men to him.

"I got the junk," he whispered. "Go back to the hideout and wait there until I come. We'll divvy up pretty quick now."

The three men scuttled away. Then the masked figure strode rapidly down the street, removing the mask before he reached the next corner.

Lights gleamed in a store window dead ahead, silhouetting the letters which spelled "Far East Employment Service." Apparently somebody was doing some night work there. The man who was no longer masked entered the agency.

"You need any help?" he asked.

He was told to pitch in and assist in making out new index cards for the files, copying them from old ledgers.

CHAPTER X

GUILTY HANDS

O **UTSIDE A** big limousine pulled up before the employment bureau and a tall, robed figure alighted. It was Zeng Tse-Lin. He entered the main room and made for a rear office where the firm's three executives were working.

"Good evening, gentlemen." His greeting included the florid owner, Frank Kempler; the furtive manager, Nick Olson; and the sedate personnel expert, Lewis LaMarr.

Kempler swung around, startled.

"You!" he said heavily. A sullen undertone was in his voice. "What do you want?"

"I wish to do you a favor, sir."

Nick Olson twisted his mouth. "When we need favors off anybody, we'll ask for 'em."

"But surely you can spare me a few moments," Zeng protested courteously. "You must have realized by now that this firm is under suspicion regarding the murder of Andrew McClane and the kidnaping of your stenographer, Miss Prescott."

The diamond glittered on Kempler's hand as he raised it in a challenging gesture.

"So we're under suspicion, eh?"

"Quite so. The police feel sure that one of you is guilty. I wish merely to extend the other two a favor by clearing them—if you will permit me."

All three men eyed him.

"By Harry, you're a cool one!" Olson said crookedly. "How you gonna clear us?"

"With black light," the hawklike man responded.

As he said this, he moved to a wall switch and hovered his hand over it. At the same time, his other hand produced a curious looking contrivance from under his robe.

It resembled a miniature version of an old-fashioned magic lantern; a projector for casting transparent pictures upon some white surface. Operated by self-contained batteries, it had a projecting lens from which no trace of glow could be seen.

Zeng spoke again, calmly.

"A while ago, my home was robbed. The thief thought he was stealing genuine diamonds. Instead, his loot consisted of five-and-ten-cent-store baubles placed there to trap him. Have you gentlemen ever heard of zinc chlorine?"

Three heads wagged a concerted negation.

"It is a chemical—the salts of zinc. When the crystals are dissolved in water, the resulting solution can be used to bathe any object which you desire to make fluorescent."

"Fluorescent?" Frank Kempler yelped nervously.

Dr. Zeng bowed. "That is to say, the objects thus coated will then glow when exposed to the so-called black light which is, in reality, nothing but ultraviolet rays."

"Get to the point!" Nick Olson snapped.

"Very well, sir. Now, I coated the ten-cent-store jewelry with a zinc chloride solution. The person who stole those baubles had to touch them with his hands, naturally. Therefore, some of the zinc chloride would adhere to his skin."

Lewis LaMarr smiled in puzzlement. "And?"

"And the thief, who is also a murderer, will find that his fingers will glow in this black light!" Zeng answered triumphantly as he snapped the wall switch and plunged the office into darkness.

At the same instant he turned on his self-designed portable violet ray device, aiming the lens at the three men in front of him. Five fingers of a single hand glowed weirdly in the gloom. Then that hand vanished for an instant.

IT REAPPEARED just as Zeng turned the room's lights on again. And the hand held a gun.

Lewis LaMarr snarled savagely as he aimed his weapon at Dr. Zeng's heart.

"Okay," he panted. "So you've found me out! So it won't do you any good!"

Bewildered, the sedate personnel expert's two associates stared at him. There was ludicrous disbelief in Frank Kempler's expression, and Nick Olson's furtive eyes held fear.

"Lew!" Kempler cried. "You can't—"

LaMarr shot him through the heart. Then he fired a single bullet at Nick Olson, and the colorless little man toppled lifelessly across the corpse of his employer.

Zeng stood stock-still.

"Why do you not kill me also, O man of no conscience?" he inquired steadily, realizing in advance what the answer would be.

"You know why!" LaMarr rasped. "I want those diamonds—the real ones."

"Ah, yes. They were Andrew McClane's portion of the proceeds of your series of burglaries. You were not content to divide the loot with him. You wanted the lion's share, which means the entire amount. So you poisoned McClane to get them."

The man curled his lip. "McClane was a no-good. He deserved to die!"

"You evidently thought those five Japs deserved to die, too," Dr. Zeng intoned. "You were afraid they might talk, since they had participated in your schemes. Therefore you flew to Manzanar and knifed them. And you wore flashy clothing as well as a number of diamonds. That was to make the authorities believe Frank Kempler was the killer."

LaMarr scowled. "Cut out the chatter. Where are the gems?"

"I am afraid I must refuse to tell you."

"Stubborn, eh? You'll talk when the time comes. I've got men working for me who know all the tricks. Move, now. And if you try anything funny, I'll kill you."

Prodded by the murderer's gun, Zeng Tse-Lin walked slowly to the front doorway and out of the building. His limousine stood at the curb with Chow behind the wheel, and the giant Mongol visibly twitched when he saw his master approaching under such circumstances.

But Zeng's faithful servitor had been well rehearsed in the role he was to play. Instead of fighting, which he would have preferred to do, he broke into an anguished wailing.

"Please!" he cried. "Please do not harm my employer!"

"Shut up and drive!" LaMarr rasped as he forced Zeng into the tonneau, then followed. "Do as I say, or I will shoot your master here and now!"

Feigning cowardice, Chow got the sleek car rolling. And it was not long before Dr. Zeng and his Mongol companion were being prodded into a ramshackle house near Van Ness.

At the head of a flight of stairs, they were finally taken into a shabby room. Zeng's eyes glowed when he beheld a blond girl bound and gagged on a sofa. This, he knew, was Sally Prescott. And the three hard-looking thugs who guarded her were the elderly LaMarr's burglary gang.

Now LaMarr faced the tall, silent doctor.

"Will you tell me where you hid those diamonds?"

"No," Zeng answered quietly.

Cruel anticipation twisted LaMarr's lips.

"I've heard that you high-caste Chinese denote your social position by the length of your fingernails. Well, soon you will have no social position—for your fingernails will be yanked out by the roots. Sam, give me a pair of pliers."

ONE OF the three thugs jumped obediently. He produced the demanded instrument of torture.

Dr. Zeng uttered a resigned sigh as he looked at Lai Hu Chow.

"The time has come when we are out on a limb, O friend of my boyhood. A limb of triumph."

For answer, Chow pressed his good leg against his false one. There was a faint, hissing sound, while the giant and Zeng stopped breathing.

Then, with a swift movement, Zeng Tse-Lin whipped two compact rubber masks from under his robe. One he affixed to his own face. The other he adjusted over Chow's moonlike countenance.

"Now we can breathe, O valiant one!" the hawklike doctor intoned through his rubber mouthpiece.

Curiously enough, Lewis LaMarr made no effort to halt any of these things that were happening. The personnel expert seemed frozen in his tracks—and so did his three henchmen. All of them looked paralyzed, incapable of movement.

Dr. Zeng smiled at them gently. "I know you can hear me, even though you cannot respond. So I shall tell you that I took a leaf from your own book. I equipped Chow's artificial limb with a container of nerve gas."

The criminals merely stared at him, not even able to blink their eyes.

Then Zeng crossed the room and picked up Sally Prescott, who had likewise been rendered helpless by the chemical fumes. As he carried her toward the door, he shot a command at Chow.

"Handcuff those vile scoundrels. Then leave them and quickly follow me. We shall send the police for them later, when the gas has dispersed. Right now I must take Miss Prescott to fresh air." And he bore the girl from the room.

Chow manacled the paralyzed prisoners, who would recover control of their muscles only when it would be too late. Then, with a last merry epithet which he flung at them through his rubber mask, the big Mongol lumbered out.

IN THE House of a Thousand Beatitudes, Zeng Tse-Lin was serving tea to Ann Carter and her uncle. The Homicide official spoke feelingly.

"Yes, Zeng, I admit it ended okay. Sally Prescott is with Hal Wilson in his hospital room right now, and Wilson is recovering nicely. But—"

"But what, O my friend?" The doctor smiled.

"But you shouldn't have taken such chances!" Ann spoke the words which were on her uncle's mind.

"It was necessary," Dr. Zeng assured her gently. "True, I could have trapped LaMarr here when he came to steal the imitation jewels from my safe. But I wanted to have him lead me to his hideout, so that I could rescue Miss Prescott. And so that I could recover LaMarr's own share of the loot."

As he spoke, Zeng produced a parcel. He had found it in the house near Van Ness, and now he revealed its contents. Diamonds glittered in the light—hundreds of them. The lion's loot had been recovered at last.

Brian Carter whispered his amazement. "Zeng, you're simply marvelous!"

From the expression in Ann's eyes, she seemed to think so, too!

VI

BLACKMAIL CLINIC

CHAPTER I

DEATH TO
THE FEDS

THE NIGHT was ominously dark, with just enough fog in the air to veil the stars in shroudlike semi-concealment. All around the bay area, spectral fingers of white glow probed weirdly into low-hanging mists, moving and stabbing and shifting. These were the anti-aircraft searchlights bearing mute witness to the alertness of a nation at war.

It was strange, Steve McCune thought, how San Francisco had changed. Once upon a time its brilliance and light could have been seen for miles, but now the city's glitter was dimmed down to a mere ghost-reflection. This waterfront street, for example, with its electroliers hooded and all neon signs doused by order of the Army Interceptor Command, was like a shadowy gullet waiting to swallow the unwary traveler.

McCune shivered a little and wished for the full power of his small coupé's headlamps instead of the undersized, fender-mounted parking lights which were all the law permitted you to use after nightfall in this neighborhood. He felt worn and weary as he drove slowly home from the shipyard where he was employed; weary, and vaguely uneasy.

IT WAS past midnight, and Steve McCune had good reason to feel tired. In recent months he had been on the swing shift, starting work at four in the afternoon and quitting at twelve. That usually made it around one in the morning before he got home to the old house where he lived with his family.

Sleep was difficult under such conditions. True, he had remodeled the attic into a makeshift bedroom for himself in order to get as far away as possible from daytime traffic noises. But even so, it was hard to obtain the proper amount of rest when everybody else was up and stirring around.

He yawned as he drove; shivered again, although the night was not cold. His sensation of uneasiness persisted, crawling through his marrow

267

like a slithery premonition of impending disaster. His mouth twisted wryly as he thought about his job as foreman of the big shipyard's blueprint department.

It was a good job, an important job, the sort of work which made a man feel that he was valuably contributing to his country's war effort. For the yard was constructing a new and secret type of Q-boat for the Navy, breaking all records in the speedy fabricating of these hush-hush anti-submarine weapons. McCune had thoroughly enjoyed his part in the vast program until a certain thing had happened.

He swore silently, remembering the ugly circumstances that had enmeshed him. Then he glanced at his rear-view mirror and went suddenly tense as he saw the hooded lights of a car behind him. There could be no doubt about it, now. He had suspected it for the past several blocks. He was being followed.

"They're after me!" he whispered.

HE INCREASED his coupé's speed, his palms sweaty on the steering wheel and tiny beads of cold perspiration forming on his forehead. Had the showdown come at last, he wondered? He set his lips grimly as the car jounced ahead over rough paving, and the worry that had been cutting deeper and deeper into his consciousness the last few days was a living, growing cancer gnawing its way into his brain.

He twisted to the right at the next intersection, then right, and left, and left again. He knew these waterfront streets. As a kid he had played through the district. Growing older, he had run errands and then driven trucks for the wholesale markets. He was as familiar with the alleys and byways as he was with his own home.

But turn as he might, the pursuing sedan matched every maneuver. It kept pace with him like a relentless burr. It did more than keep pace—it was gaining on him, coming closer, narrowing the distance with every revolution of its humming tires.

With a sort of dread hopelessness, Steve McCune realized the futility of any attempt to escape. For days he had tried to avoid this decision, but now it had caught up with him.

He was not armed and, in some respects, that fact was a relief. Had he been carrying a gun, he might have been tempted to use it. As it was, he slackened speed and resigned himself to the inevitable.

The trailing car drew abreast, angling McCune toward the curb. A white beam of light cut through the darkness to strike him directly in the face.

"Pull over and stop!" a grim voice called. "No tricks."

Zeng and Don froze in horror as they saw the grotesque dangling body.

He obeyed, braking to a halt and cutting his ignition. The sedan was clamped down alongside, its front door was punched open and a big man in a topcoat swung to the street, a gun glinting in his clenched fist.

"Your name McCune?" he demanded.

"Yes," was the defense worker's answer.

"Steve McCune?"

"That's right."

"Get out," the big man said quietly. McCune complied, instinctively raising his hands as he faced his captor.

Meanwhile the sedan's driver had slid from behind his wheel. Now he loped around to run quick, expert hands over McCune's pockets from behind.

"No gun," he announced, and stepped back a pace.

McCune tried to keep his voice steady.

"What is this?" he demanded.

"You're under arrest," the big man in the topcoat answered bleakly.

He extended his free hand, palm cupped so that the shape of a small gold shield could be made out.

"Department of Justice—the F.B.I.," the big man said, and there was no expression in his tone as he spoke.

McCune's shoulders twitched and his mouth felt dry, his throat tight. It had come! This thing he had been dreading had finally overtaken him. In a way, he was almost glad. At least it ended all the troubled uncertainty which had held him in its grasp.

He was seized with a sudden hysterical impulse to shout, to explain that he had been trying for days to make up his mind to go down to the Federal Building and make a clean breast of the whole rotten business. Which was true enough. He *had* wanted to confess to the authorities, but fear had restrained him.

Now he could talk. Now he could tell what he knew. He would be protected.

He opened his mouth to speak. The words were never uttered, though.

NOISELESSLY AND without lights, a third automobile had drawn abreast of the spot, a black limousine which had coasted to a standstill with a dead motor. A blasting blurt of gunfire pulsed abruptly from this hearse-like vehicle, a yammering thunder of explosions, sharp and staccato as the crack of doom.

Steve McCune's movement was a reflex action. His knees went slack and he dropped to the pavement like a cut rope and rolled under the sheltering bulk of his own coupé. Bullets sang and whined and ricocheted around him, pinging off the sidewalk and the wall of a warehouse beyond. But for the moment, McCune was safe.

The Federal agents were not so lucky. In that first withering rain of slugs the big man in the topcoat had gone down, riddled through the chest.

His companion lurched under the impact of hot lead, but managed to stay on his feet and pull an automatic. He snapped six quick shots at his attackers. Then, like a jackhammer riveting steel, a submachine-gun opened up from the limousine. Steady tongues of flame stuttered out of its muzzle and the second F.B.I. operative doubled over as if he had been chopped in half. He fell sprawling, motionless.

And still the tommy-gun kept up its stammering clatter, pouring a hail of metal into the bodies of the fallen Feds. The two corpses danced a macabre rigadoon as the bullets smashed them.

Then, abruptly, silence settled as the weapon clicked empty. The limousine's motor roared alive and its gears clashed it into forward motion. Like a thunderbolt projectile it surged ahead and vanished around the next corner on tires that screeched soprano protest.

Steve McCune dragged himself from under his coupé and staggered upright. In the chaos of his mind there was no thought of his own troubles, now. He was too stunned, too dazed by the hideous scene he had just witnessed to think of himself. He bent over the two F.B.I. agents where they lay like dark, unmoving blotches in the gutter.

No use calling for medical aid, he realized. Both men were dead.

McCune stood by the riddled bodies, a great riptide of anger smashing through his heart and distorting his judgment. His first impulse was to leap into his coupé and pursue the murder limousine. But even as he whirled and raised one foot to the running board he realized the hopelessness of such pursuit. By now, that death car was long gone. It would be impossible even to guess which way it had headed after disappearing around the first turn.

A new thought blossomed suddenly in McCune's brain, one that made him almost ill. These men, these slain Federal operatives, had been sent to arrest him. Now they were dead—murdered! Maybe he would be accused of the double killing. Maybe a homicide charge would be added to the other thing he had been fearing.

Shakily he got into the coupé, started its motor. His hands trembled as he shifted gears, and his foot was jerky on the clutch pedal. It was torture to be caught between two fires, as he was. On one side loomed the law; on the other side were those enemies who were responsible for McCune's present predicament—enemies who would stop at nothing to gain their evil ends. They had proved that a moment ago with a death-dealing tommy-gun.

McCune was afraid. He admitted it to himself. Nor was he thinking only of his own safety. There was his mother to consider, and his brother Don, and the younger kids. He debated the wisdom of driving straight to the Federal Building right now and giving himself up, telling exactly what had happened, confessing everything he knew about the whole sordid affair.

Would the Government men believe him, though? Would they believe that he'd had nothing to do with the killing of the F.B.I. agents who had been assigned to take him in custody?

"No!" he whispered grimly. "I can't risk it!"

THAT WAS his terror talking, advising him to go home and think it over until morning. Then it would be time enough to surrender. For the present he needed freedom. Freedom to consider all the angles, maybe to warn his family and take them into his confidence, ask them what he ought to do.

That was it. He would go home to the safety of his attic bedroom, where he could think in the bright light of his reading lamp instead of in the depressing, malignant darkness of this dimmed-out waterfront street.

He swerved his coupé across Market, up the hill, and into his own garage. Below him the city fanned out, sinister in its silence. Matching that silence, McCune removed his shoes before he entered the house. He didn't want to awaken anyone now. In solid darkness he edged up the stairway, pausing when a tread creaked under his weight. Sometimes his mother woke up when he came in. Sometimes she would question him about the night's work.

He wanted no questions tonight. He wanted to see nobody. What he needed was to be alone, to ponder the problem confronting him.

He climbed the steep attic steps, fumbled his bedroom door open, stepped over the threshold, closed the door, and turned on the light. There was sanctuary here in these familiar surroundings. He stood still for an instant, breathing deeply of the peace and orderly cleanliness of the place.

So complete was his concentration that he did not hear the small shuffling sound behind him—the rustling noise of a rope being paid out. He did not see the hangman's noose at the end of the peculiarly knotted rope, nor did he guess that he was not alone in the room until the loop was dropped over his head and drawn tight about his gullet.

He tried to turn, then, but it was too late. His hands came up, clawing desperately at the hempen cord which was strangling out his life. His struggles were fruitless. A brutal knee was jammed into the small of his back. The noose cut into his windpipe.

Steve McCune went limp.

CHAPTER II

DR. ZENG TSE-LIN

CHINATOWN, THAT mysterious sector of San Francisco rumored to conceal a thousand secret passages and twice that many weird Oriental customs, was as dimmed-out as the rest of the city. The streets were almost entirely deserted at this late hour, and all shop-window lights had long since been turned off.

The Mandarin Emporium, one of the biggest establishments in the area, was no exception to the rule, its windows, filled with Asiatic objects of art, were tightly shuttered. No trace of illumination could be discerned either downstairs or on the upper floors of the "House of a Thousand Beatitudes" which comprised the residence portion of the building.

But there were lights behind the shrouding curtains of heavy black silk which masked those upstairs windows. For this was the home of that mysterious Chinese physician known as Dr. Zeng Tse-Lin, a man whose vast wealth was exceeded only by his learning. Despite the lateness of the hour, Dr. Zeng was seated in a low teakwood chair, studying the brush marks of an ancient Chinese parchment manuscript.

Zeng was a tall man who looked even taller in his brocaded robe of Oriental silk and his black skullcap with its green button denoting a fifth examination scholar who possessed degrees from the finest Chinese universities. His ascetic face was hawklike, and his dark eyes glowed weirdly with imponderable depths of knowledge.

Through his studies in American as well as Asiatic schools, he had attained mastery of every known science and art. There also were whispered rumors that he sometimes dealt in black magic as well as in medicine and surgery.

Such rumors were bound to surround a man as mystifying as Dr. Zeng Tse-Lin. It was only natural that his Chinatown friends and neighbors should wonder how anybody as young as Zeng could have acquired so many diplomas from so many colleges throughout the world. How could a man scarcely more than thirty be a master surgeon, an internationally famed scientist, an inventor whose patents had already brought him uncounted riches? Surely there must be magic in such a fellow!

In a sense, Zeng actually possessed a magic touch—but it was a magic gained through study of all branches of Oriental and Occidental lore, ancient and modern. That was the true secret of his multifold abilities, just as constant rigorous exercise was the secret of his splendid physical stamina, his superlative strength and his inexhaustible endurance. But of all the rumors which circulated concerning this amazing personage, there was one fact nobody had ever guessed—

Dr. Zeng Tse-Lin was actually a white American whose real name was Robert Charles Lang!

True, Zeng had been born in China. His parents, though, had been affluent American missionaries slain by hoodlum Jap soldiers in the sacking of Shanghai. Zeng himself had been in the United States at that time, completing his education. Upon hearing that Nip thugs had murdered his mother and father, he had vowed his life to vengeance against all wrong-doers, all killers, all criminals.

In consequence, he had made an exhaustive study of the science of detection and had devoted himself to a secret career of bringing law-breakers to justice. Ostensibly he was a Chinese physician of splendid attainments, respected by all who came in contact with him. Outwardly he appeared to be a man who operated the Mandarin Emporium as a sort of hobby. But his medical practice and his Oriental art shop were merely shields to mask his real activities as one of the greatest criminologists the world had ever known.

HE GLANCED up from the faded parchment he had been reading, and smiled at a ponderous individual who lumbered toward him. This was a veritable giant of a man bearing a paper-fragile bowl of steaming, fragrant pearl tea. This towering, moon-faced giant was Dr. Zeng's trusted servitor and friend, a Mongol warrior named Lai Hu Chow.

There was affection and sincere regard in the look which Zeng bestowed upon the approaching Mongol. Chow was a hulking, happy, childlike fellow whose features bore the scars of many hatchet battles, and who walked with the rolling gait of a tipsy sailor.

His rakish stride was not the result of too much rice wine, however. He had lost a leg while fighting the Jap hordes who had murdered Zeng's parents, and now he wore an artificial limb which Dr. Zeng himself had constructed.

Just as this artificial leg was a part of Chow's life, so was Chow a part of Zeng Tse-Lin's existence. In peaceful pursuits or in war against crime, the two men were inseparable companions.

"You stay 'wake too late, you dlink tea to keep from getting sleepy," the giant remarked, offering the steaming bowl. "Is better you go to bed, get some rest."

Zeng sipped the hot infusion.

"You may retire if you wish," he answered in high-caste Mandarin dialect. "As for me, I expect a visitor. A certain young man telephoned me earlier this evening, and he sounded troubled. I invited him to call."

"Somebody sick, got bellyache, maybe?"

"His illness seemed more of the spirit than the body. I can tell you more when I have talked to him. Hark! There is the door chime now!"

Chow grumbled something about foolish persons who chose one o'clock in the morning to pay social calls.

"I go open up," he said.

"No, wait a moment." Zeng closed the ancient parchment and arose from his teakwood chair. "It is written that the wise man looks first before unbarring his portal, lest a tiger enter in the guise of a friend."

As he spoke, the doctor with the hawklike face lifted the ornately carved lid of a large ebony box on the table. Inside this box there was a ground glass screen which grew luminous at the touch of an electrical control. By a series of wires leading down to the front door, connected with special selenium scanning discs, and activated through the grids and plates of electronic tubes, the ground glass screen now reflected the features of a man on the outer steps—the visitor who had pressed the button of the doorbell.

The viewing apparatus was Zeng's personal adaption of the television principle, whereby he could scrutinize all callers before admitting them. In Chow's secret estimation it was a device of Satan rather than science, and he didn't like any part of it. He didn't say anything, though. If such inventions suited Dr. Zeng, then Chow had no objections. He merely refused to look into the machine.

Zeng himself did not peer long at the glass. He saw the night-blurred reflection of a young, freckled, red-haired man whose jaw was rugged and whose eyes were forthright.

"It is truly the one named Don McCune," he murmured. "You may admit him, Chow."

"Don McCune?" asked Chow. "Works at gasoline service station on the corner down street?"

"The same. Make haste to admit him."

PRESENTLY CHOW conducted the broad-shouldered visitor into Zeng's upstairs living room, poured another bowl of tea and bowed himself out. Immediately Dr. Zeng shook hands with himself in the accepted Chinese fashion as he smiled at his caller.

"Welcome to my inferior dwelling, young sir. Partake of my woefully bitter tea and tell me what troubles you."

Don McCune accepted the fragrant cup and tried to mask his worry behind a grin.

"It's good of you to let me come up, Dr. Zeng. I'm probably being a fool, but—"

"It is written that he who knows he is a fool has much wisdom. Speak what is in your heart."

"Well, it—it's my brother, Steve. He works at a shipyard across the bay. I—I don't exactly know how to put it in words, but—well, something's the matter with him. Something serious."

"Such as?"

There was a noticeable hesitation in Don McCune's answer.

"It started with the clinic," he said.

"What clinic?" asked Zeng curiously.

"The one in the old building opposite my gas station. A bunch of doctors and surgeons and dentists organized it two or three months ago as a sort of group insurance health service for folks employed in war industries. Naturally I heard a lot about it, because some of the people from there bought gas and oil from my station. So—well, I persuaded Steve to join it."

"There is nothing wrong in that, if you thought it was a good thing for him."

McCune nodded. "I did think so. Especially when I knew plenty of other shipyard workers had joined. Then, a few weeks ago, Steve had a heavy cold and went to the clinic for treatment."

"And?" Zeng's dark eyes glittered expectantly.

"I noticed a change in him almost right away. I don't mean in his health. He got over the cold soon enough. But he used to be a happy sort of guy—merry, carefree, always joking. Then suddenly he turned sullen—I guess morose is the word I want. Kept to himself, seemed to be worried stiff. We all noticed it—Mom, and the kids, and… well, anyhow, I got to thinking maybe they had given him some medicine at the clinic that wasn't good for him. A bad prescription or something. He's been losing weight, and he don't sleep well, and he can't eat."

Zeng frowned thoughtfully. "Let me understand this. Are you asking me to pay your brother a professional call in my medical capacity? That would be contrary to ethics. One doctor is not supposed to examine another's patient unless the attending physician invites him in for a consultation."

"I know that," Don McCune answered, his eyes straightforward. "I thought you might make an exception in this case, though. Miss Ann Carter suggested it when I spoke to her at the mission school."

CHAPTER III

SPURIOUS SUICIDE

MENTION OF Ann Carter's name turned Zeng's frown into a smile. Ann was the niece of Captain Brian Carter of the San Francisco Homicide Bureau, and Captain Carter was Zeng's closest intimate. They had worked together on many a puzzling crime, and Carter was the only person other than Lai Hu Chow who knew the true secret of Zeng's white parentage.

Moreover, Ann Carter meant a great deal to Dr. Zeng Tse-Lin. Possessed of an income sufficient unto her needs, she devoted her life to a mission school here in Chinatown for underprivileged Chinese children. Zeng admired her for this splendid work, and he admired her even more for her sweet nature, her piquant beauty, her competent self-assurance.

In fact, he never thought of Ann without experiencing a quick surging in his heart. Long ago he might have declared his love for her, except that one fact had always restrained him. His life was consecrated to a never-ending battle against crime, a battle which exposed him to constant peril. He could not bring himself to ask Ann to share that peril, to risk her own safety.

Therefore, he had never let her know how he felt toward her. Instead, he concealed his feelings behind a mask of Oriental reserve, allowing her to believe he was Chinese. This artificial racial barrier served to bar all thoughts of romance.

Just the same, Ann had only to express a wish and Zeng stood ready to obey. So it was now. He peered keenly at Don McCune.

"I am to understand that Miss Carter asked me to take a hand?"

"Yes, sir. You see, this isn't just an independent case. Hundreds of other war workers go to the clinic. If the treatment has the same effect on them that it's had on my brother Steve… well, the damage could be serious in lost man-hours and lowered efficiency."

The tall, sun-bronzed criminologist saw the truth of this, and he reached a swift decision.

"Very well. I shall be happy to talk to Steve. When would it be convenient?"

"Why, right now, I suppose." Don McCune's freckled face showed grateful relief. "He usually gets home from the swing shift around one in the morning. He ought to be there now. That's why I came here at this particular time. I was hoping you might go home with me, get it over with as soon as possible."

Dr. Zeng clapped his hands sharply, and Lai Hu Chow lumbered into the room.

"I eavesdrop at door," the giant said, and grinned engagingly. "You want limousine, eh? I go fetch, chop-chop."

And he went shuffling from the house, chuckling as if at some vast jest. The joke, of course, was his use of pidgin English when he could speak the American language as well as anybody. His master had painstakingly taught him. But he liked to tease Zeng by lapsing into garbled jargon.

"Just like Chinee laundryman when washee dirty shirtee," he said, laughing to himself as he went to get the car.

Fifteen minutes later, the limousine pulled up in front of the house which the McCune family had occupied for years. It was a three-story frame structure on one of the hills west of Van Ness, an old building that had survived the fire and was much the same now as it had been when first built in the early Eighties.

Leaving Chow at the wheel, munching a huge wad of chewing gum, Dr. Zeng followed Don McCune into the house.

"I hope we don't wake Mom," Don whispered. "She's worried enough as it is. Steve's room is in the attic and we'll go right up."

"Very good," Zeng answered. "Lead the way."

They gained the top of the steep attic staircase, and Don tapped lightly on a closed door. There was no response, and a bewildered expression crossed Don's freckled features in the glow from the dimly shaded hall light.

"Strange!" the younger man muttered. "Steve's always home by this time, and he's a light sleeper. Why doesn't he answer?"

"Try the knob," Zeng suggested.

DON OBEYED, and the two men stepped over the threshold, only to freeze in sudden horror. Steve McCune was home, but he was not awake. He would never awaken again. His body dangled grotesquely from a hangman's noose about his neck, a rope which stretched upward to the rafters....

The house was teeming with police within ten minutes. Downstairs, a grief-stricken family huddled numbly and tried to answer official questions as best they could. Up in the attic bedroom, Dr. Zeng conferred with his friend Captain Brian Carter, who had arrived post haste.

Carter was a red-faced, chunky Irishman whose compact form was heavily muscular in its blue serge, and whose jaw jutted to bespeak the efficient courage which had brought him up through the ranks to become the head of the city's Homicide Squad.

"Of course, it was suicide, Zeng," he growled. "Didn't Don just tell me how Steve had been moody and in ill health?"

"Quite so," argued Zeng. "And yet—"

"The thing's open and shut. Steve came home in a depressed mood. He decided to call it quits. He fastened a rope to the rafter, made a noose around his neck, stood on this chair, kicked the chair out from under him, and that was that."

Zeng Tse-Lin's ascetic countenance was impassive.

"Have you any familiarity with the work of a Belgian criminologist named Goddefoy?" he asked quietly. "It was he who first made a scientific study of rope fibers in cases of death by hanging. Assume that a killer wishes to make his victim appear to be a suicide. He loops a noose about the victim's throat, throws the rope over a beam and pulls his man upward, much the same as in the old Wild West necktie parties when a posse of lynchers would string up a cattle rustler."

"Well?"

Zeng shrugged. "In such an event, the rope's fibers will lay in the opposite direction to that of the pulling, due to friction with the beam or rafter. I have casually examined this rope by which Steve McCune's corpse was suspended. The fibers tell an interesting story. I think he was hanged by some other person."

"Poppycock!" Carter scoffed. Then he added apologetically: "Not that I doubt your beliefs, Zeng. You've been right too many times in the past for me to contradict you. All the same, how in thunder could I begin any investigation of a supposed homicide with no clues except the position of some rope fibers? The newspapers would laugh me out of office! And besides, I've already got enough grief on my hands."

"Ah. So?"

Carter made a bitter mouth. "Two F.B.I. agents were murdered by tommy-gun slugs less than an hour ago, down by the waterfront. My hands will be full of that investigation, working with the Federal Bureau. I can't afford to borrow more trouble by considering this Steve McCune case as anything but suicide. Not unless I get more concrete evidence than a length of rope with its fibers rubbed the wrong way."

"You would not object, though, if I were to make an independent survey of the McCune matter?"

"Not at all," Carter answered warmly. "You know I always welcome your help, old friend. Only this time you're off on a false scent, is all."

BOWING AND shaking hands with himself, Dr. Zeng strode downstairs and out of the house. Before joining Chow in the limousine, however, the tall criminologist moved quietly to the rear of the McCune residence and entered its backyard lean-to garage. Here, using his pocket torch, he inspected the dead Steve McCune's little coupé.

The battered car's left rear fender seemed to interest him, particularly where it was marked by a sort of gash across its side. Zeng carefully examined this bright exposure of raw metal and knew that it must be of recent origin, for the salt sea air of San Francisco would have flecked it with rust discolorations within twenty-four hours. What, he wondered, had torn the fender so peculiarly?

In the midst of pondering the problem, he pivoted swiftly as he heard approaching footfalls. Then he saw young Don McCune coming toward the garage, drawn by the will-o'-the-wisp flicker of Zeng's flashlight.

"Oh, it's you," the younger man said wearily. "I came out to walk around and get my mind off—what happened to Steve. I saw your light, and—"

The Chinese doctor nodded. "I understand your sorrow, and it is distasteful for me to intrude upon it. Yet I am glad that you are here, for I wish to ask you a question."

"I'll answer if I can." Don's voice was apathetic.

"Then tell me Steve's usual course of travel from his work to his home. Would it perhaps be along the harbor district?"

"Why, yes. But I don't understand—"

"There are many things which defy explanation at the moment," Zeng said quietly. "Your brother's apparent suicide is one of them."

Don clenched his fists impotently. "I can't understand it, either. Steve was in a jam, I know, but he wasn't the kind of guy who would kill himself."

"Perhaps he didn't," the criminologist intoned.

"You mean—murder?" Horror was in young McCune's voice.

"It is possible."

Don stared. "Do you think those clinic doctors—"

"That remains to be seen," Zeng Tse-Lin answered. Turning then, he strode thoughtfully from the garage.

CHAPTER IV

THE FINGER POINTS

THERE WERE many secret avenues and devious channels through which Zeng obtained information when he so desired. Dawn was filtering across the eastern horizon before he returned to the House of a Thousand Beatitudes in Chinatown. During the intervening hours he had talked to many persons and visited more than one unpleasant place. Now, sending Chow to put the car away, he moved toward his front door with a brown paper parcel tucked under his arm.

The criminologist whirled, brought a lashing uppercut full to the orderly's jaw.

"Zeng!" a feminine voice called to him from the recessed entrance of the shuttered Mandarin Emporium. And then Ann Carter darted into view. "I've been waiting for you!"

His heart leaped, as it always did when Ann was near. From her toeless pumps to her wavy auburn hair she was exquisitely dainty, and her slender curves were subtly emphasized by the tailored sharkskin ensemble she wore. One look at the pert insouciance of her face, the generous fullness of her lips and the steady depths of her fine eyes showed that here was a woman among women—a girl of character and breeding and intelligence, as well as youthful beauty.

With unaffected charm she offered Zeng her hand. He bowed over it.

"I am honored by your presence, which makes the dawn as bright as sunrise. But what brings you to me at such an early hour, Ann?"

"The McCune case," she answered, as he opened the door of his residence and courteously stood aside for her to enter. "Uncle Brian told me some of it, and then I called on the McCunes to see if I could help them in their trouble. Young Don said you'd interested yourself in his brother's so-called suicide, and I thought I'd come over to ask you if you've learned anything."

"I have learned many things," Zeng Tse-Lin said, as he conducted her up to his magnificently furnished living quarters. "And I think I have stumbled into a matter which has ugly ramifications. As yet, however, I cannot guess where the trail will lead."

Ann studied his ascetic countenance. "Would you care to tell me what you've found out thus far?"

"Gladly, if you agree not to repeat what I say. For the present I am reluctant to formulate a theory which would be concrete enough to offer to your uncle."

She smiled softly. "I'll keep mum, Zeng."

"Good." He began unwrapping his brown paper parcel. "To begin with, the unfortunate Steve McCune had charge of the blueprint department of his shipyard's swing shift."

"Yes, I know that."

"Secondly, this shipyard is constructing a new type Q-boat to combat Jap and Nazi submarines."

"I'd heard that, too," Ann said.

"Now we come to secret information. Recently, certain specifications and plans of those Q-boats have fallen into Axis hands. I shall not divulge the source of my information, but at least I can tell you that the F.B.I. has been investigating this leak."

Ann looked startled. "Do they suspect anyone in particular? I mean, somebody on the shipyard payroll? An employee?"

"They do," Zeng said slowly. "In fact, all members of the blueprint department have been under Federal surveillance for several days."

"Including Steve McCune?"

"More than that, Ann. It finally narrowed down until Steve was the only suspect."

HER EYES flashed indignantly. "That's preposterous!" she declared. "Steve was a loyal American! His entire family is above reproach!"

"Nevertheless, the F.B.I. eventually reached the conclusion that Steve was the man who had been selling vital war information to the enemy. Tonight an order was issued for his arrest."

"Government agents were going to pick him up?"

"Yes, for questioning. But the two F.B.I. operatives assigned to the task were murdered on the waterfront. You understand, none of this will ever reach the newspapers. The Department of Justice does not believe in publicity when any of their agents are slain. Just the same, these two men were killed before they had a chance to arrest Steve McCune."

Ann's voice dropped to a whisper. "And then later, Steve was found hanging—as if he had committed suicide to atone for shooting the Federal men!"

"That would be the obvious theory," Zeng Tse-Lin said. "And I grant that it sounds plausible. So plausible, in fact, that this entire case might be closed and considered solved. Yet I cannot quite bring myself to believe it. There is something deeper here, something far more significant which I hope to uncover. And this shall be my first step."

He finished unwrapping the brown paper bundle and withdrew two objects of hardened wax. Ann Carter shuddered slightly when she realized that they were paraffin impressions of human hands.

"What on earth?"

"Among the places I have visited during the past few hours," Zeng told her calmly, "I included the municipal morgue, for an examination of Steve McCune's corpse. I made these paraffin casts of his hands. Come, Ann. Let us go to my laboratory."

She followed him to the next floor above, where three large rooms had been knocked into one. The walls gleamed with white tile, glass shelves, enameled work-benches and a bewildering array of scientific apparatus encompassing electronics, chemistry, photography, physics and lesser-known medical equipment.

Dr. Zeng immediately began a chemical experiment upon the two wax handcasts. Presently he finished the job.

"No trace of nitrate stains," he remarked.

"Meaning what?" Ann asked him breathlessly.

"It proves that Steve McCune discharged no firearms recently. Therefore, he could not have operated the submachine-gun or any other weapon which killed the two F.B.I. men. And yet there were bullet scars on the fender of his coupé, indicating that he was on the scene when the murders took place."

"You think he witnessed the killings?"

"Yes. And perhaps that is why Steve himself was subsequently slain. From the condition of the rope which hanged him, I am convinced that he did not commit suicide."

Ann's eyes narrowed. "He was murdered so he couldn't testify against the ones who shot the G-men! Is that your theory?"

"Partially, yes," Zeng said. "There could have been a secondary motive. Let us assume that he had been working with Axis spies, selling them shipyard secrets. Let us also assume that these spies killed the Federal agents to keep Steve from being arrested."

"It's a horrid thought!" Ann shuddered. "I don't like it."

The criminologist with the hawklike countenance smiled gravely.

"Neither do I," he admitted, "but it may be true. If so, the spies must have realized Steve's usefulness was at an end. The F.B.I. suspected him and tried to arrest him. In brief, Steve was now a marked man. For the safety of the spies, his death was necessary. Therefore, they murdered him and attempted to make it look like suicide."

"You make it sound reasonable," Ann admitted. "But now that Steve is dead, how can you hope to pick up the trail of the spies he was working for?"

Dr. Zeng turned from his laboratory bench.

"I have only one slender clue," he told her. "According to Don McCune's story, Steve's character changed after he had gone to a certain medical clinic for treatment. This clinic is operated exclusively for people employed in war industries. I think I shall investigate the clinic...."

THE RECEPTION accorded Zeng Tse-Lin at the clinic a few hours later would have allayed almost anybody's suspicions. The chief surgeon, Dr. Ormand Tremayne, knew Zeng by medical reputation, and insisted upon taking him on a personally conducted tour of the premises.

Tremayne, a spare, lanky man who sported a bushy black beard and smelled pungently of medicines, seemed genuinely flattered by Zeng's visit.

"It's an honor to have a doctor of your standing show any interest in our work," he said respectfully. "My medical colleagues will be anxious to meet you."

"You seem to have a well-equipped building," the Oriental scientist answered, gazing at his surroundings.

Tremayne's bearded lips parted in a smile.

"We're rather proud of what we've accomplished in such a short time," he confessed. "You see, all of us would have gone into military service, except that each member of the staff is either too old, or suffering some physical disability which makes us unacceptable to the Armed Forces."

"And so you found another means to serve, eh?"

"Yes. Frankly, we were appalled at the conditions surrounding certain war-industry centers. True, there's a shortage of physicians all over the country, but in some localities where thousands of new workers have moved in for essential jobs, the lack of doctors was alarming."

"Therefore you established this clinic," Zeng said.

"Right. Any war worker, or any member of his or her family, can procure medical or surgical treatment as required, for a small monthly sum. I wish we had more with which to work. And I wish there were more doctors willing to follow our lead, opening up similar clinics in other war centers."

As he spoke, the bearded surgeon pressed a buzzer on his desk. A white-jacketed orderly entered the room.

"Yes, Dr. Tremayne?" he murmured, as he came to attention.

"Ah, Lester, will you please ask the staff members to step in here? Thank you."

The orderly made a half-gesture that might have been the beginning of a military salute—or perhaps another sort of salute consisting of an arm raised and outstretched, such as Nazis employ when shouting "Heil Hitler!" Whatever the man had intended to do, though, he arrested the motion before it was well started. But his stride was military as he left the office.

Presently Dr. Tremayne's two medical colleagues entered, clad in the white gowns which they had donned in preparation for the opening hour of the clinic, a few moments away. Tremayne introduced them. The short, tubby one was Dr. Max Ernst, a cherubic and amiably smiling man whose pate was as bald as a peeled Easter egg and whose voice was thickly guttural, heavily accented.

"I haf heard much apoudt you, Dr. Zeng," he declared. "Id iss a bleasure to make your aguaintance."

Zeng bowed politely in acknowledgment, then turned to the second man, Dr. Barton Barryman, a jockey-sized fellow of middle age whose graying hair and sunken eyes betrayed constant devotion to his profession. Barryman spoke tersely, in curt, crisp sentences.

"Honored to have you call, sir. Be glad to have you sit in when I start receiving patients. Welcome your diagnostic advice."

BEFORE ZENG TSE-LIN could either accept or decline this invitation, the bearded Tremayne dismissed his subordinates.

"I won't keep you chaps from your duties," he told them. "I just wanted you to meet Dr. Zeng, and to extend him every courtesy of the clinic."

After they had gone, he smiled at the man in the richly-brocaded Chinese robe.

"You see," he said apologetically, "we have so much to do, and we are so few. We're flooded every day with many more patients than we can handle."

"Then I mustn't interfere." Zeng arose. "Perhaps you'll allow me to return another time."

Tremayne chuckled. "Nothing interferes with our work, Doctor. We don't permit it. But if you'd care to inspect the clinic now, I'll have Hartman show you around. Hartman's our business manager. George Hartman. Wait here and I'll send him in. Meanwhile, if you will excuse me, I have my surgery to look after."

Then the bearded man went from the office, leaving Zeng alone in the room to think about the men he had just met. Could any one of them be linked with Axis espionage activities? Could any one of them be a triple murderer?

CHAPTER V

MYSTERY BOTTLE

EVEN AS Dr. Zeng was considering these questions, the answer, unknown to him, was being enacted in a basement storage room beneath his feet. Down there in that cellar chamber, four men were gathering, four men robed from neck to toe in white surgical gowns, their faces completely concealed behind sterile gauze operating masks, their heads covered by white caps. Shapeless in these disguising costumes, the four were seemingly as alike as quadruplets except that some were tall, some short. Whether they were stout or thin it would be hard to guess. One, apparently, was in command. He spoke tersely.

"Don't like the idea of this Zeng fellow coming here."

"Why not?" another asked. "He's just a Chinese doctor, isn't he?"

"Yes. But did you see this morning's paper? Tells how Steve McCune's body was found hanging. Steve's brother Don made the discovery."

"Well?"

"A Chinese medico named Zeng was with Don at the time," the leader snapped.

"*Gott in Himmel!*" came from behind the gauze mask of another member of the gathering. "Couldt it pe der same man?"

"Must be. No other Dr. Zeng in San Francisco. Mighty funny coincidence he'd come straight here—unless he suspects there's a connection between this clinic and Steve's death. Maybe he's a police stool. Who knows? Point is, I don't trust him. Want him watched every minute he's in the building. Want him tailed when he leaves. Understand?"

Three heads nodded in unison.

"Good," the leader snapped. "Now get to your places. It's one minute of eight."

His underlings faded from the underground chamber as silently as three white-clad ghosts. Not until the last one had departed did the leader make for the door. He glanced at the outer passage, made sure it was empty, then quickly removed his mask and hurried toward a staircase just as a clock somewhere in the upper reaches of the building struck eight deep-throated times, marking the opening of the clinic's day....

George Hartman, the business manager of the enterprise who had been assigned by Dr. Tremayne as Dr. Zeng's escort, was an elderly and affable individual with a hint of brandy on his breath and a tiny network of veins showing beneath the skin of his somewhat bulbous nose. His clothing, while of obviously excellent quality, looked as if it had been slept in.

His eyes held a gratified twinkle as he introduced himself to Zeng Tse-Lin. In a way, he reminded Zeng of the sort of person pictured when the words, "old-time newspaperman" are heard.

Hartman was not a former journalist, though. He was a promoter, a business go-getter, an expert organizer—exactly the type of man needed to direct the manifold activities of an organization such as this clinic. And if he performed his duties efficiently, what did it matter if he liked his breakfast coffee laced with a pony of brandy?

Garrulous, almost naively gabby, he kept up a running fire of chatter as he conducted Zeng through the clinic.

"Great thing, a place of this kind. It brings medicine and surgery down to the low-pay level that workingmen can afford. Health, sir—that's got to be America's watchword today. Keep the workers healthy, I say, and you keep them efficient and productive. Here's our X-ray room. We're mighty proud of it. Everything modern. Just look at this equipment, sir!"

Dr. Zeng smiled politely. "Excellent." But his eyes did not smile. They were busy scanning the Röntgen-ray room for possible clues.

Hartman beamed at his noted visitor's words of approval.

"Glad you like it, sir. Now come this way." He seemed as vain as a circus owner exhibiting a new gorilla. "This is the main operating room. Major surgery. And over here is another, for minor jobs of meat-carving... oops, excuse me. For a minute I forgot you were a doctor yourself. Maybe you don't like your profession to be kidded."

"I don't mind." Zeng smiled again.

"Gosh, thanks. I wouldn't want to hurt your feelings. Now see those three doors over there? That's the doctors' consulting offices where they receive their patients. We won't go in if it's all the same to you. They're all pretty busy this morning. Lots of colds and flu floating around, these days."

Zeng Tse-Lin nodded. "Quite all right. By the way, what are these three alternate doors between the three medical offices?"

"Dispensaries," Hartman said pridefully. "My own idea. Each doctor has one. When we first started, we wasted a lot of time sending what medicines they needed from the main stock-room. Now, for most drugs, each doc can get what he wants from his own dispensary. Here, I'll show you one. Belongs to Dr. Ernst."

"He's the little fellow, bald, speaks with a thick accent?" Zeng asked.

"Yep. Great guy, too. Used to be in some hospital in South America for a big oil company. Came to San Francisco as soon as the war started, ready to do what he could to help."

The Oriental criminologist was listening with only half his attention. His piercing black eyes were busily surveying the little dispensary room with its tiers of shelves containing bottled medicines and drugs.

Zeng possessed the uncanny faculty of being able to photograph a scene with his vision, indelibly engraving it upon the sensitized plates of his memory. One sharp glance was sufficient for his purpose. Years later, he could have accurately named every label on every bottle of the hundreds on these shelves, even specifying their positions.

Now, unknown to Hartman, he performed this amazing visual trick. Then he turned courteously to the clinic's gabby business manager and seemed to devote his entire concentration upon what the man was saying. But in actuality, Zeng was studying his mental photograph of the room, sorting and classifying all the drugs he had briefly seen.

Presently, under the microscopic scrutiny of his superlative memory, he came to one bottle which arrested his thoughts in mid-stream. It was a glass container labeled "Fluid Extract of Ergot," under which designation appeared a chemical formula.

That was a queer thing, he decided. Of what earthly use could ergot be in a clinic of this sort? True, the stuff had recently been used experimentally in the treatment of idiopathic migraine—that is, headaches without apparent causation—but with inconclusive results. The principal use of ergot in medicine was such that it would scarcely be expected to be in use in the treatment of colds and like ailments of war industry workers!

There were two other glaring errors about that bottle. Ergot was a derivative of rye fungus and, therefore, had no chemical formula. Yet this label boasted such a formula, which was absurd under the circumstances. And finally, the substance in the bottle was white, crystalline—not at all what ergot looked like. Therefore the bottle contained something else. Either the label had accidentally been pasted on the wrong bottle, or it was a blind to conceal the nature of the real contents.

WITH A lightning movement, swifter than the cleverest feat of a vaudeville magician, Zeng reached out to the shelf where the bottle stood. He palmed the container, thrusting it up into a capacious sleeve of his brocaded robe—and at that precise instant, two doors opened into the dispensary.

One was the portal of Dr. Max Ernst's adjoining office, and Dr. Ernst himself appeared at the threshold—seeking a bottle of vitamin tonic, he explained. Simultaneously the corridor door opened and the white-jacketed orderly, the man named Lester who had seemed on the verge of giving a Nazi salute a while before, stepped into the room with a message for Hartman.

Zeng repressed a frown; kept his features expressionless. Had either of those two men witnessed his purloining of the fake ergot vial? For that matter, had Hartman himself seen the movement? He couldn't tell. At least, none of the three men gave any indication of knowing what had happened.

A few minutes later, having completed his tour of the clinic, Zeng Tse-Lin followed Hartman into the business manager's own private office. The garrulous Hartman smiled happily.

"Quite a layout, eh, Dr. Zeng?"

"Admirable. But I am curious to know how you handle so many patients and keep their records straight. You must have a marvelous filing system."

Hartman beamed. "We have, sir. I installed it myself. Let me show you."

He conducted his visitor into a connecting room lined with steel filing cabinets crammed with the card-index dossiers of every person the institution had treated. They were arranged alphabetically by names, then cross-indexed according to which attending doctor had given the treatment.

Ostensibly at random, Zeng opened one drawer and casually inspected the file cards. But it was no accident that caused him to select this particular drawer, nor was it coincidence when his long, spatulate fingers sorted out the card belonging to Steve McCune.

He seemed to glance at it for only an instant. But again his photographic memory made a snapshot of the entire record. With rising interest he observed that Steve McCune had been one of Dr. Max Ernst's patients.

Ernst, the physician in whose dispensary Zeng had just found the fake ergot bottle! Ernst, who talked with a German accent!

CHAPTER VI

KIDNAP BREAK

WHEN LAI HU CHOW drove his tall, hawk-countenanced employer back to the House of a Thousand Beatitudes a little later, it was at the top speed permitted by law. Dr. Zeng was in a hurry to get to his laboratory and test the white crystals in the ergot vial, for a fantastic theory was forming in his mind.

But he was prevented from immediately entering his dwelling, because just as Chow parked before the Mandarin Emporium, a loitering figure emerged from the doorway. He was an anxious-looking young man with red hair and an expression of tension on his freckled face—Don McCune. He moved quickly toward Zeng.

"Did you find anything at the clinic?" he asked earnestly. "Have you been there, sir? Have you any news for me about what was wrong with Steve?"

The tall, robe-clad criminologist made a silencing gesture.

"You must be patient," he advised gently. "It is written that the hare's speed sometimes carries him into the snare of his enemies, but a tortoise moves with the slowness of safety."

"Meaning you've nothing to tell me?"

"Very little." Zeng's sonorous voice was compassionate. "I have been to the clinic, yes. I have met the doctors there. More than that I am not yet prepared to say."

The younger man's lips drew into a bitter line. From the depths of his overwrought condition he spoke hotly in growing anger.

"You wouldn't be shielding these doctors, would you?"

"Shield them? Why should I?"

"You know why! You're a physician yourself. Medical men always stick together. I've heard that, more than once. It's the ethics of the profession—one doctor refusing to get another one into trouble!"

The criminologist smiled bleakly. "You misjudge me, Don. You speak without thinking."

"That's where you're wrong. Why shouldn't I be sore at all this delay, with the whole world believing Steve killed himself? I know he was murdered. So do you! I know the clinic was behind his troubles. The police think that's silly, but at least I figured I could count on you for help. Now it looks as if I'd made a mistake. I'm sorry I ever bothered you, Dr. Zeng. Sorry I came to you with my problems. Just forget the whole thing. I'll take care of it myself, in my own way."

With this final outburst, young McCune pivoted and stalked off down the street, oblivious to Zeng's efforts to stay him. Zeng stared after him for a brief moment, then turned to Lai Hu Chow.

"Follow that youth, O Large One," he said in Chow's own native dialect. "Do not interfere with him, but report to me what he does and where he goes."

The giant Mongol nodded and sent the limousine sliding forward. Frowning, Dr. Zeng went into the House of a Thousand Beatitudes and ascended to his third floor laboratory, so preoccupied that for once in his life he forgot to make sure he had latched the front door at street level.

The moment he gained his scientific workshop he produced the bottle with the ergot label. Spilling some of the white crystals into a pyrex beaker, he began adding chemicals, sharply watching the reaction.

The experiment engrossed him, required his undivided concentration. So he was not aware that an intruder had stolen into the laboratory and was skulking up behind him. Only when the muzzle of an automatic bored into Zeng's spine did he realize his jeopardy—and then it was too late.

"Easy, Doc," a voice rasped. "Unless you want me to let you have the big pill right now."

ZENG DID not move. For years he had trained his muscles to perfect coordination, and he had long since ceased to permit himself the privilege of showing surprise.

"What is it you seek?" he said, his voice expressionless.

"You, mainly. And the bottle you stole from the dispensary. Turn around. Slow. And don't give me any lies. Why did you take that bottle? I know you got it. We were watching you."

"Why should I lie? The bottle is in plain view before you, on this bench. I took it because it aroused my curiosity and I wished to identify its contents—just as I can now identify you by your voice, before I have fully faced you. You are the clinic orderly named Lester."

As he said this, Dr. Zeng Tse-Lin turned cautiously and stared into the features of the man who had almost given a Nazi salute in the office of the bearded chief surgeon, Tremayne. No longer clad in a white hospital jacket, Lester looked chunky and solid in his street attire, menacingly muscular, to match the steely blue of his automatic and the gun-metal glitter of his unwinking eyes.

"So you were curious." His lips twisted sardonically. "That's why you stole the bottle."

Dr. Zeng nodded impassively. "And I am still intrigued, now that I have analyzed its crystal contents."

"Ah. Then you know what the stuff really is."

"Yes. Scopolamine—the so-called truth serum. A hypnotic drug used in cases of mania, delirium and insomnia, but in its hydro-bromide form a crystalline sedative. Law enforcement agencies have used it experimentally to extract the truth from suspected liars, for under its influence a man's volition is temporarily suspended so that he cannot tell a falsehood."

Lester grinned unpleasantly. "Boy, are you smart!"

"I am not certain that I agree with you. I am still puzzled by the presence of such a little-used alkaloid in a clinic for war-industry workers. Of course, in view of recent events, perhaps I might hazard a guess. But my theory would be so completely far-fetched and outrageous that I would doubt my own conclusions. For your sake, let us hope that I am wrong."

"It won't matter much whether you're wrong or right, Doc," Lester said significantly. "I think you've stepped in over your depth. In fact, something tells me you won't do any more prying into other people's affairs for a long time to come. Maybe never. That depends on what the head man decides to do about you."

"Head man?" Zeng raised an eyebrow.

"Don't try to pump me. You'll find out soon enough what you're up against. I've got orders to bring you to the boss. Do you come without making trouble, or do I use my own judgment and blow you down right here and now?"

The criminologist's countenance betrayed neither fear nor alarm. He seemed completely without emotion as he answered.

"I seem to be in your hands, my friend. Your gun gives you the privilege of command. Unarmed, I can only obey your orders."

Lester stepped close, explored Dr. Zeng's brocaded robe for possible concealed weapons. Finding none, he backed off and thrust his own automatic into his pocket. But he kept his fist clenched on it so that it made a menacing bulge through the cloth.

"Okay," he grunted. "Let's take a ride."

"As you wish."

Zeng bowed slightly. And he strode toward the staircase with his captor at his heels, watching every move. Down on the second floor, in the living quarters, Zeng cast a veiled glance at a Ming dynasty water clock and was startled by the passage of time. More than an hour had fled since he had dispatched Lai Hu Chow to shadow young Don McCune, an hour that had been spent in chemically analyzing the scopolamine truth-serum crystals.

HOW LONG LESTER, the clinic orderly, had been in the House of a Thousand Beatitudes, silently watching that chemical analysis, the criminologist could not guess. Of only one thing could he be certain—he had left his front door unlatched, and because of this oversight he had fallen into the hands of the enemy.

With the gunman at his side, he strode from the house and perceived a dark limousine parked at the curb, with a pock-faced man seated at its wheel. Pock-Face shot a quick look at Lester.

"Got him, eh? Any trouble?"

"Like taking candy from a kid… get in, Doc."

Zeng started to obey, but at that instant he noticed another limousine roaring in his direction. It was his own car, driven by the giant Chow.

Instinctively Chow seemed to realize that something was wrong. He knew it by Dr. Zeng's attitude, and by the menacing pose of the man named Lester, whose hand was in his pocket clenching a gun. With Chow, such a tableau called for direct action.

With a wild war-cry, the huge Asiatic mashed his throttle wide open and sent his heavy machine yammering toward the kidnap car. Pock-Face, at the wheel of the parked automobile, saw destruction hurtling toward him with the weight of a juggernaut and the speed of a projectile.

It was more than human nerves could take. The driver of the snatch car shouted a hoarse oath of dismay, meshed his gears, and gunned his motor in a frantic effort to avoid the impending smash. He forgot all about Lester standing on the sidewalk with Zeng as a captive. He forgot everything except his own safety, and he sent his limousine screeching away from the curb.

This sudden desertion caused Lester a brief moment of panic—and that was sufficient for Dr. Zeng's needs. The criminologist whirled, brought a lashing uppercut full to the orderly's jaw. The jarring impact felled Lester like a pole-axed steer. He dropped in his tracks, unconscious.

Meanwhile, Lai Hu Chow swerved his oncoming vehicle at the last split instant, so that it barely grazed the kidnap limousine. The shriek of locked tires and squealing brakes made a knifelike din in the morning, and Chow's car swung around in a half circle as he wrestled it under control. This gave the other machine a narrow margin of seconds, and Pock-Face took full advantage of it. He walloped his limousine around the nearby intersection at careening speed; vanished.

Chow should have followed, of course, but he was interested only in the safety of the man he served. Clambering to the street, he lumbered at an ungainly pace to where Zeng stood.

"How'm I doing? I bust up shenanigans quick, huh?"

"You did indeed." Zeng Tse-Lin smiled affectionately.

The big man stared at him. "You okay? Not hurt? You maybe want me to stomp this son of a camel until his face is strawberry pleserves?" He indicated the unconscious Lester.

"No. Merely lift him and carry him into the house before our neighbors are drawn by curiosity. I wish to question him without interference—perhaps by the use of that very truth-drug employed by his unknown chief."

Chow hefted the senseless orderly.

"Truth-drug?" he exclaimed when he had carried his burden indoors.

"Quite so. I shall not try to explain it to you now, O Large One. Soon you will see for yourself how it functions. When our prisoner regains consciousness I shall inject some of it into his arm, hypodermically. Then I think we shall learn many interesting things. For the present, take him down to our cellar and tie him securely."

THE GIANT complied, returning to Zeng and grinning as he reported the prisoner all safely fettered.

"What you want me to do now?" he added.

"You may tell me how it happened that you returned in the nick of time to save me from abduction," the Chinese doctor said. "I thought I ordered you to follow Don McCune."

"Sure. I followed him. That boy is plain fool. He went straight to clinic, started big fight with head surgeon."

Zeng's eyes sharpened. "Tremayne? The bearded one?"

"Aie. McCune collared him in doorway, called him names, said he was the one who had killed his brother, Steve. Bimebye Tremayne get plenty mad, you betcha. He grab McCune, give'm bummee rushee. McCune bounce on sidewalk like golf ball. Oh, boy!"

"Threw the lad out, eh? What did McCune do then?"

"Go for walkee along dockside. I followed him maybe-so for an hour. Nothing happen, so I come home."

"Fortunately for me." Zeng's ascetic lips parted in a faint smile. Then he grew grave. "I think it is time for us to experiment on the man we have captured. Perhaps under the influence of scopolamine he will tell me enough to clear up the riddle."

It took but a moment for the criminologist to go up to his laboratory, prepare a hypodermic and fill it with distilled water in which some crystals had been dissolved. And then, as he turned to descend the staircase, a muffled sound reached him—a sharp, distant report.

It could have been an automobile's motor backfiring, or it could have been a gunshot somewhere in the immediate vicinity. A sudden premonition inched through Zeng Tse-Lin's veins as he raced down to his living quarters.

"Chow! Did you hear that report?"

The giant nodded. "From cellar, seemed like."

In a burst of speed, Zeng descended to the ground floor and then hurtled down the steep steps to the cellar under the House of a Thousand Beatitudes. Dim light filtered from a high, barred window set into the basement wall at street level. This window—a narrow ventilator would be a better term for it—faced the alley at the rear of the building, so that anyone crouching in that alley could peer downward into the cellar.

That was exactly what had happened. Someone *had* peered down— someone with a gun. Someone had seen the unconscious Lester tied helplessly there, and had realized it would be impossible to rescue the prisoner. Therefore, to keep the man from answering any of Zeng's questions, a single bullet had been fired.

The bullet had penetrated Lester's brain, bringing him instant death.

CHAPTER VII

DEATH FOR A DOCTOR

IT WAS well past noon when Don McCune finally tired of his aimless strolling along the Embarcadero and decided to return to his home. In the interim, he'd had time to regret many of his hasty words and actions.

He should not have spoken so harshly to Zeng Tse-Lin, he realized now. And he certainly should not have gone to the clinic and picked a quarrel with Dr. Ormand Tremayne. After the things Don had said to Tremayne, and the threats he had uttered, he scarcely blamed the bearded surgeon for throwing him bodily out of the building.

Maybe it would be a good idea, he concluded, to go back and apologize to Tremayne. And to Dr. Zeng as well. Certainly he had done himself no good by antagonizing them. You caught more flies with honey than with vinegar.

He turned, started walking back in the direction of the clinic. Before he had gone two blocks, though, a police radio patrol car drew up abreast of him.

"Just a minute, chum," a uniformed officer said.

"You mean me?"

"I think I do. Is your name Don McCune?"

"Yes. Why? What's wrong?"

The policeman sprang from the car. Something glittered in his fist. The glittering object was a pair of handcuffs. They clicked around Don's wrists.

"You're under arrest for murder."

"Murder?" The red-haired young man stared. "You must be crazy! I haven't killed anybody!"

"Save it. You admit you had a brawl with Dr. Tremayne a few hours ago, don't you?"

Don felt a sinking sensation in his heart.

"Yes, I—I had words with him. But—"

"So later you went back and caught him in his private office. You shoved a knife in him."

"That's not true!" Don shouted. "I never went anywhere near the clinic after Tremayne threw me out. It's true I threatened him. I suppose there were plenty of witnesses to that. But—"

The cop looked grim. "Maybe you've got an alibi. Can you account for your actions since you left the clinic?"

"N-no. That is, I've been walking along the docks, but I didn't see anyone I knew."

"Then let's go to Headquarters," the officer said....

It was the hour of midday rice, but Dr. Zeng Tse-Lin was too busy to think about lunch. He was compounding some chemicals in his laboratory when he was interrupted by the tinkling of the telephone. He answered, and a warm glow stole through him when he heard Ann Carter's dulcet voice. There was tension in her tone, though.

"Zeng," she asked, "may I come to see you right away?"

His answer was unusually sharp, incisive.

"No! There is danger. I have enemies who might attempt to strike at me through you. You must not come here."

"Enemies?" Ann sounded puzzled. "What do you mean?"

HE DECIDED to tell her enough of the story to convince her she must stay away.

"I am engaged in a certain investigation. Because of an important discovery I made, there was an attempt to kidnap me. With Chow's help, I eluded the trap and captured one of these would-be abductors."

"Zeng! No!"

"It is true. A little while later, my captive was murdered by a shot through a cellar window—a most effective means of preventing his answering any questions I might ask."

"That's terrible!" Ann quavered. "Of course, you've notified the police?"

"Not yet. With all due respects to your uncle, he is an officer who believes in direct action. He might make moves at variance to my own plans. Therefore, I have told him nothing."

"But, Zeng—"

"There were two kidnapers," he continued quickly. "One escaped. Undoubtedly he has reported to his superiors in the organization which I am trying to uncover. The murder of my prisoner proves it. Consequently, these enemies realize that I am still at liberty and am seeking evidence of their identities, their guilt."

"You think they'll make another attempt on your life?"

"Very likely. It is a sort of duel. I am both the hunter and the hunted. So you must not come to my house. I cannot expose you to peril."

She sighed audibly over the phone. "I see. But I'm worried, Zeng—for your sake. I'd hoped to ask your help in another matter, but that's not important now. Nothing's important except for you to be careful. Promise?"

His heart leaped at this expression of her concern for his personal safety.

"I shall take no needless risks," he assured her. "But tell me why you wanted my help."

"It's nothing you can do anything about, now. Don McCune was arrested a while ago for murder. Dr. Tremayne, the head of that war workers' clinic, was found stabbed to death in his office, after Don had quarreled with him. But Don's innocent. I'm sure he wouldn't k-kill anybody!"

The Oriental criminologist scowled. So the bearded Tremayne had been slain after Don McCune had charged him with responsibility for Steve McCune's death! The news meshed into a pattern already forming in Zeng's mind.

Perhaps Don's angry words had aroused Tremayne's suspicions regarding certain aspects of the clinic. Maybe Tremayne had realized he was associated with a murder gang, and had undertaken an independent investigation within the medical group, without asking the aid of other doctors he was certain he could trust. There must be quite a number of such medical men associated with the clinic, in addition to those who had aroused Dr. Zeng's own suspicions.

Possibly Tremayne had stumbled upon some knowledge which made him dangerous to the real culprits. Therefore, they had knifed him to shut him up. And now Don McCune had been arrested for the crime!

"I am sorry to hear of this, Ann," Zeng said evenly. "If I can help Don, I shall. You may hear from me later."

And he rang off and returned to his laboratory work....

IN A building not far away from the Mandarin Emporium, a man with a pock-scarred face sat on a camp stool with earphones clamped to his ugly head. He was that same Pock-Face who had driven the kidnap limousine a few hours before, the man who had deserted the orderly, Lester, after the failure of their scheme to abduct Zeng Tse-Lin.

He reached for a portable lineman's telephone, dialed it. Presently a voice answered him.

"Chief?" he said in a guarded whisper. "This is B-Two reporting. Good thing we tapped that Chinee doctor's line. I just heard him talking to some jane named Ann. She seems to have an uncle on the cops."

"What was the conversation?"

"He told her a little of what's happened, but covered up the details. He also said he hadn't told the police anything yet. I think he's wise to us, though. He savvies the score, even though he don't know who you really are."

"Hm-m-m. Got to stop that Zeng guy. He's dangerous. Slippery, too. But I think I know how to fix him. You say the wren's name was Ann and she's got an uncle on the cops? That means she must be the niece of Captain Brian Carter of the Homicide Squad. Yes—Ann Carter. Okay. Here are your instructions...."

In his laboratory, Zeng was just stoppering several fragile glass vials filled with liquids. He summoned Lai Hu Chow and handed the vials to the giant Mongol.

"The leg of chemicals," he said enigmatically.

The words were no puzzle to Chow, however. He possessed an assortment of artificial legs, designed and constructed by Zeng Tse-Lin in bewildering variety, each created for a special purpose. All were hollow, cunningly contrived to contain various types of equipment. Some held guns, ropes, weapons. Others were the hiding places of bombs, gas throwers, short-wave radio transmitters.

The "leg of chemicals" merely meant a limb fitted with interior niches, lined with plush, in which fragile glass containers could be carried without breakage. Nodding, Chow took the vials and carefully departed with them, to return presently wearing a false leg laden with the thin glass tubes.

"We go smoke somebody out?" he inquired.

His employer smiled. "You speak more truly than you think, O Large One. I wish to inspect the case records of the clinic, and smoke will shield me. Come."

A secret subterranean passage led from Zeng's cellar under a row of store buildings to an exit in a blind byway a block away. The criminologist and his giant Mongol servitor used this underground passage now, for there was a possibility that the main door of the House of a Thousand Beatitudes might be watched by enemies. And Zeng wanted nobody to witness his present actions.

Clouds had gathered, masking the mid-afternoon sunshine and bearing a threat of storm, when he and Chow slipped into an alley behind the clinic building. There were several rear windows in the medical structure, two of them open. Making sure he was not observed, Zeng removed the glass vials from an aperture in Lai Hu Chow's false limb. Deliberately, one by one, he hurled seven fragile containers into the clinic.

The bullet had penetrated Lester's brain, bringing instant death.

The results were startling. Leaping flashes of red and yellow flame seemed to flicker within the building, as if a sudden holocaust had burst into blaze. Actually it was false fire, a chemical trick resembling flames but in reality harmless. Simultaneously, great billows of smoke spread through the clinic and poured from the windows.

ZENG TSE-LIN'S smoke bombs brought panic to the occupants of the building. Patients began streaming out through the big front door, followed by nurses and orderlies and the white-clad doctors themselves—the bald, pudgy Dr. Max Ernst and the jockey-sized Dr. Barton Barryman.

"Der whole blace iss going up!" Ernst shouted wildly, in his thickly guttural accents. "Everding iss lost!"

Barryman's terse, clipped speech cut across the pudgy physician's clamor.

"Sound alarm! Get fire engines. Where's George Hartman?"

"Right here!" The clinic's business manager divorced himself from the crowd of milling patients on the sidewalk. His face was flushed, and the veins on his bulbous nose looked more prominent than usual. "You didn't think I was staying behind to get cooked, did you?"

Barryman bristled like a truculent little bantam rooster.

"I want none of your misplaced humor, Hartman. Don't talk. Act! Get the Fire Department. Don't you realize we stand to lose every dollar of our equipment?"

Reddening, the business manager turned and scuttled toward a fire-alarm box on the diagonally opposite corner. Meanwhile Dr. Zeng, who had been watching this colloquy from the mouth of the alley, whirled and returned to the waiting Chow.

"The time has come for action," he said. "In with you through this rear window. I shall follow."

The giant blinked. "Okay. Me betcha we look like smoked sausage in two minutes bimebye, though!"

"Not at all. Those chemical fumes are bland, harmless. I prepared them so that they would appear thick, but in actuality we can breathe without difficulty."

As he spoke, Zeng leaped to the window, grasped its sill and chinned himself upward by main strength. His movements were so fluently graceful that they made the work of his superb muscles seem like child's play.

Chow followed, more clumsily. Then they were inside the smoke-filled clinic. By unerring instinct, Zeng led the way to the file room which Hartman had shown him earlier that day.

He knew exactly what he hoped to find. The index card on each clinic patient was a record of name, address, medical treatments received, and the doctor who had administered that treatment. Moreover, each patent's war-industry connection was indicated—the plant at which he worked, and the position he held.

Zeng knew these things because he had already superficially examined one drawer of the files this morning, under George Hartman's guidance. Now he wanted to inspect all the drawers, look at every card in the file.

His purpose was to select the names of all patients occupying key positions in war industries—men in charge of blueprints, for instance, or foremen of shops working on secret weapons and armaments. Having abstracted such a list of key men, he then proposed to visit them one by one, interview them and attempt to gain information which might substantiate his theories.

CHAPTER VIII

INJECTION OF TRUTH

UNTROUBLED BY the chemical smoke which billowed around him, Dr. Zeng began his swift scrutiny of the index records. His amazing memory made it unnecessary for him to use pencil and paper when he wished to make a note of any certain name or address. Gradually he acquired a satisfactory list.

Then, presently, he came to the drawer which Hartman had shown him on his first visit here—the file records of all patients who had been treated by the bald, tubby Dr. Max Ernst. The criminologist's expert fingers riffled these cards, his keen vision taking a mental snapshot of each one. Then, abruptly, he frowned.

"There is something wrong here, Chow!" he said shortly.

"Is so? How?"

"This morning, when I looked at these particular cards while hunting Steve McCune's record, there were two more in the file by actual count than there are now. In other words, two cards have been removed since that time. Very clever. Very clever indeed! It would have aroused suspicion if the entire file had been destroyed, but by removing only two individual forms, our master criminal thought he was covering his tracks."

The huge Mongol shook his head.

"Chow dumbee like fun. No savvy."

"It's quite simple," Zeng answered grimly. "The two patients whose cards are missing must obviously be important to the mystery. Perhaps they were enmeshed and victimized in the same way Steve McCune was involved. By removing the index records of these two patients, someone hoped that the men would not be drawn into the investigation."

"Well?"

"The master criminal has made a mistake," Zeng Tse-Lin intoned. "He reckoned without my memorizing ability. In my mind, I will now run through the file as I recall it in its original state. I will 're-see' the two missing cards, read them, and have the information I need!"

As he spoke, he closed his hawk-keen eyes and went into an almost trancelike state of pure concentration which ended only after his superhuman memory had given him the results he demanded. Then he smiled without mirth.

"The end of the trail is in view," he told his giant servitor. "Let us go hastily."

Their departure from the clinic was none too soon, for fire engines were clanging in the outer street and heavy footfalls clumped into the building from the front. That would be the firemen seeking a nonexistent blaze, and a voice seemed to be leading them. It was a curt voice, sharp and terse—the voice of the undersized doctor, Barton Barryman.

"Bad enough our chief surgeon was murdered today. Now this fire—"

Zeng waited to hear no more. He nudged Chow to a rear window, watched the Mongol drop to the alley, then followed and landed as lightly as a cat. Together they sped around a corner and scuttled into an open passageway where stairs led downward to an underground maze—a labyrinth of twisting, turning tunnels which the criminologist knew by heart.

When they emerged above ground a few moments later they were directly beside the garage where Dr. Zeng's limousine was stored. He jumped into the car, gesturing Chow under the steering wheel and gave an address. Chow kicked the starter.

It was but a ten-minute run to the apartment house represented by that street number which Zeng's amazing memory had recalled.

"Stay here, O Large One," the robe-clad criminologist commanded. "I go to interview a man named Dutton, who holds a position of secrecy and importance in a plant which manufactures a new type of anti-tank gun. I shall return soon."

CHOW SETTLED back, munching a fresh wad of chewing gum. He was startled, a moment later, by the reappearance of Zeng.

"You no findee guy?"

"I found him," Zeng said bitterly. "But he could tell me nothing. An empty poison bottle was in his hand, and he was newly dead."

"Killee himself?"

"There are those who would like the police to think so. But I believe he was murdered."

"You callee copper?"

"There is no time for that now. Drive as swiftly as the wind, Chow. We have another man to interview, one whose name is Morrow, and who labors at a factory engaged in making a secret bomb-sight for British aircraft. Speed, Chow, speed! Lest our enemies reach this Morrow ahead of us and slay him as they slew Dutton. For Morrow's was the second card missing from Dr. Ernst's file!"

The Mongol sent his limousine roaring ahead. This time their destination was an old residence on Nob Hill converted into small flats. Nor would Chow allow Dr. Zeng to enter alone.

"I go too. If trouble, I fight like 'leventeen devils!"

There was no trouble, however, when they entered the flat occupied by the man whose name was Morrow. Once again death had outraced Dr. Zeng, for the bomb-sight maker lay sprawled on the rug with a bullet through his brain and a silenced pistol clenched in his stiffening right hand.

Frustrated anger surged in Zeng's heart. Muttering, he noticed a phone across the room, leaped to it and dialed Police Headquarters. In a minute he was connected with Captain Brian Carter. The Homicide official's voice sounded oddly shaken.

"Yes?"

"This is Zeng. Come at once to the address I shall now give you. There has been a murder. Two, in fact."

Within less than a quarter of an hour, Carter came bursting heavily into the room.

"It's too much!" he said harshly. "I'm at the end of my string, Zeng! All these killings, and Ann—"

"What about Ann?" the criminologist asked sharply.

Carter's shoulders sagged in weariness.

"She's vanished. Heaven help me, I'm afraid she's been kidnaped!"

Dusk had fallen like a stormy mantle over San Francisco when Captain Brian Carter finally turned the details of the two new homicides over to his departmental subordinates. Then, harassed and haggard, he consented to accompany Zeng to the House of a Thousand Beatitudes for a conference.

They entered by means of the secret underground passageway and ascended to Dr. Zeng's sumptuous living quarters on the second floor. First making sure the window drapes were tightly closed, Zeng switched on the lights.

"It is now a matter of reviewing what we know," he announced, "and awaiting a message."

"What message?" Carter's tone was dull, tired.

"The message from Ann's abductors," the criminologist answered, without visible emotion. "I feel certain that they will contact me."

"How do you figure that?" Carter's eyes narrowed.

"Because I have the solution to this entire chain of mysteries, beginning with the apparent suicide of Steve McCune and including the murder of Dr. Tremayne, as well as the deaths of those two war-industry workers whose bodies I discovered."

The Homicide captain stared.

"In heaven's name, Zeng, tell me what you know!"

Outside the house, a sudden hissing began. That was the rain, falling at last, drenching the city in an abrupt torrential deluge. Zeng Tse-Lin paced as he talked.

"We shall start with Steve McCune, who was found hanged to an attic rafter. That, my friend, was murder, not suicide."

"I won't argue the point with you," said the Homicide official wearily. "Go ahead."

ZENG BOWED politely. "Steve McCune was on the swing shift of a shipyard in charge of blueprints for a new type Q-boat. Recently he had become morose, ever since receiving medical treatment from a certain clinic for war-industry workers."

"Okay."

"The F.B.I. suspected Steve of selling those Q-boat plans to Axis spies. In an attempt to arrest him, two Federal agents were slain. Steve did not shoot them, however. I made a paraffin test of his hands, after his own corpse was taken to the morgue. That test showed negative."

"The devil you say!"

Zeng nodded. "I believe Steve really was involved with enemy spies. The spies murdered the F.B.I. men to prevent Steve's arrest. They then killed Steve himself, because he was no longer useful."

"But who are the spies?"

"I am coming to that," the criminologist answered. "I interested myself in the case and, at the request of young Don McCune, began investigation. Since Steve McCune's character had changed after he was treated for a cold at the medical clinic, I decided to look into that clinic. I met its staff, and in the dispensary of one doctor named Max Ernst I found a bottle of scopolamine."

Carter scowled. "Scopolamine? Truth serum?"

"Correct."

"But why would a clinic have that stuff?"

"Precisely the question I asked myself. Before I found a possible answer, an effort was made to kidnap me. The men involved were clinic employes. One escaped. I captured the other, an orderly named Lester. I imprisoned him in my basement, but before I could question him, a shot was fired through the window. It killed him. His body is downstairs now. Forgive me for not reporting it, my friend. I had my reasons."

The Homicide captain looked dazed, as he swore fervently.

"Meanwhile," Zeng went on, "Dr. Tremayne, the clinic's chief surgeon, was stabbed to death and you arrested young Don McCune for the crime. But I feel sure Don is innocent. I think Tremayne discovered that some of his staff members were Axis agents and they murdered him before he could talk."

"The clinic is the center of this whole plot, then?"

"I am sure of it," Dr. Zeng responded without hesitation. "I believe they were using the medical organization as a blind which cloaked their real activities. It was more than a blind, in fact. It was the means whereby they obtained information concerning new American secret weapons."

"By bribing key men like Steve McCune?"

The tall criminologist shook his head.

"Steve McCune was too loyal to accept Nazi pay for naval secrets. I think he was an innocent victim of treachery. So were those other men I found dead this afternoon—Dutton, who worked in a plant that manufactured an anti-tank gun, and Morrow, who knew the secret of an aircraft bomb-sight. They gave vital plans to Axis spies, yes; but not voluntarily."

"I don't get it." Carter looked baffled.

"The answer is scopolamine," Zeng said grimly. "You are aware, my friend, that various law-enforcement agencies have employed the drug experimentally to extract the truth from suspected criminals. Under its sedative-hypnotic influence, a man is incapable of telling lies. He answers truthfully to any question asked him."

"You mean—"

Dr. Zeng nodded. "If you were a crook, and someone knew something you wished to learn, would it not be an easy matter to use this truth serum on your victim and then grill him? Especially if you were a clinic doctor pretending to treat a patient for a cold or some similar minor ailment?"

"Good heavens!" Carter muttered. "So that's it! These spies established the clinic for war workers. They chose key men in the various armament industries, injected them with scopolamine and pried military secrets out of them!"

"Quite so. One injection would be sufficient. After a victim had once revealed armament information, he was helpless. The enemy agents could then demand additional data at any time on a basis of blackmail. The war worker would live under a constant threat of having his first act of treachery exposed to the F.B.I. unless he continued to reveal military and naval secrets. That is why Steve McCune's character changed. He knew he had involuntarily betrayed his country, and he feared exposure. When his usefulness ended he was murdered. Today, Morrow and Dutton were likewise slain because my own investigation might lead to them, and the spies were afraid I would make them tell what had happened."

THE HOMICIDE official reached for the telephone.

"We've got to notify the Department of Justice! We—"

"No!" Zeng stopped him sharply. "You are forgetting Ann."

"How can I forget her? She's my only living relative. I think of her as I would my own daughter. But what has she to do with the espionage set-up?"

Hawklike eyes glittering, Zeng Tse-Lin clenched his fists. A bitter vengefulness tinctured his tone as he said:

"Ann means even more to me than she does to you, old friend. And I think these Nazi rats must have learned that fact, perhaps by tapping my phone. In consequence, they kidnaped her, hoping to silence me by using her as a pawn in the game."

"You believe they'll try to strike a bargain? Her safety in exchange for—"

"In exchange for my life," Zeng answered quietly. "They realize I know too much. Now they are gambling on my regard for Ann. It is simply that they seek to lure me into sacrificing myself to save her. Well, I shall play their game."

"You'll risk yourself for Ann's sake?"

"Yes, although I shall have a card up my sleeve. It's an ace which may still win the battle against this master spy who seeks time to cover his tracks and escape."

"But who is he?" Carter erupted savagely.

The criminologist was on the verge of speaking the name of the man he suspected, but at that instant the telephone rang harshly in the room's silence. Long expected and impatiently awaited, the enemy's challenge had come at last.

"Dr. Zeng?" a guarded voice came over the wire.

"Yes"

"Know who this is?"

"I have an idea."

The voice chuckled sardonically. "Very clever. Almost as clever as your smoke bomb at the clinic this afternoon. You didn't learn much, though, did you?"

"I learned enough," Zeng said woodenly.

"And how much have you told the police?"

"Nothing." The criminologist lied for a purpose. "I did not dare, since you have Miss Ann Carter as hostage. Nobody knows the results of my investigation except myself and my servitor, Chow."

"It's a good thing. You probably realize the girl's life won't be worth a plugged *pfennig* if you talk."

"I do realize it," Zeng assented. "I also realize that you wish to offer a trade. You will release Miss Carter only if I give myself into your hands."

Again the voice chuckled. "You and Chow, yes. Are you willing to deal? Excellent. Here are your instructions...."

It took much persuasion to convince Captain Brian Carter that he must not interfere in the forthcoming showdown. As soon as Zeng had finished listening to those telephonic commands, Carter wanted to contact his Homicide Department subordinates and have the criminologist shadowed to the appointed meeting place.

Dr. Zeng refused this offer.

"Ann's life hinges upon my own discretion now, old friend," he said. "If your men follow me, the entire structure of my scheme will collapse.

You must leave now, through that secret passageway by which I brought you here. Henceforward, the fight is my responsibility."

With grumbling reluctance, the police official finally departed. Then, with lightning speed, Zeng Tse-Lin raced up to his third floor laboratory and filled a hypodermic needle with a clear solution. The syringe, of his own special design, he then fitted into one of Lai Hu Chow's artificial legs by means of a swiftly contrived holding apparatus controlled by a small, powerful spring.

Next, Chow detached the false limb he was wearing, and substituted the one with the hypodermic. As he strapped the contrivance in place, his robe-clad master gave him terse orders.

Vigorously chewing a wad of gum, the giant nodded blandly and a smile of anticipation spread across his hatchet-scarred, moonlike countenance.

"Me catchee," he said.

Then he and Dr. Zeng went quietly down to the basement beneath the Mandarin Emporium and made their exit through a deep underground tunnel.

CHAPTER IX

NAZI'S FINISH

BEFORE PEARL HARBOR, many of Chinatown's shops had actually been owned and operated by Japs, their merchandise shoddy and cheap in comparison to the goods purveyed by reputable Chinese. After the cowardly Nip attack on Honolulu, however, all Japanese were removed from the mainland's West Coast and relocated in resettlement centers far from the coastal defense zone. In consequence, many former Jap-operated stores in San Francisco now stood vacant and shuttered, empty of wares.

Over the telephone, that guarded voice had instructed Dr. Zeng to present himself at one of these deserted shops. The address had been twice repeated, together with an admonition of sinister insistence.

"Don't bring anybody with you except your big Chinese pal, understand? Otherwise the Carter girl dies."

Zeng had promised, and he was living up to his word. However, nothing had been said concerning the route he should travel, so he approached his rendezvous with Destiny by a path no enemy would have suspected. In brief, knowing the location of the former Jap store, the criminologist chose to reach it underground!

With the mazes of subterranean tunnels beneath Chinatown, Zeng was as familiar as a tiger in its home cave. Needing no flashlight to guide him, he pressed silently onward through a bewildering series of passages, pausing only occasionally to allow Lai Hu Chow to catch up with him. Before three minutes had passed, the giant Mongol was hopelessly lost.

"Blind like fool bat in coalee holee!" he complained in a whisper.

But Zeng merely hushed him and steered him forward.

Presently Zeng's unerring instinct brought them to a steeply tilted ladder, which they ascended to a trap-door. Opening this without the slightest sound, the criminologist emerged into a vacant store and hauled Chow after him.

A musty smell pervaded the place, and in the dim light from a flickering candle they beheld vast reaches of empty shelves and disused, dusty counters. The candle was on one of these counters, and directly under it there was a chair.

A man sat in that chair, motionless, facing the store front as if watching. He was pudgy, bald, his eyes curiously glassy. Chow took one look and whispered:

"Jumpee jiminy—is fat doctor flom clinic!"

The giant Mongol was right. There could be no mistaking the rotund form and amiable features of Dr. Max Ernst, who had been the physician in attendance upon Steve McCune, Dutton and Morrow—all of whom had since been murdered. Even though Ernst was silent now, it was easy to imagine hearing his thick, guttural Teutonic accent.

Chow crouched. "So he is head of spy ring! I twist his neck likee pretzel!"

"No!" Zeng Tse-Lin clutched his servitor. "Even you, O Large One, cannot kill a man already dead. Do you not behold the stab wound between his shoulder blades?"

"Me great big dope. Need glasses for bum eyesight. Who killee this guy?"

"That is what I hope soon to learn."

As he spoke, Zeng moved toward the front door of the store. Outside, a figure could be seen standing in the entrance, hunched against the driving rain. Unquestionably it was one of the Axis espionage mob, waiting for Dr. Zeng and his huge servant to come along the street. The fellow had a surprise due him, for his expected visitors were already inside the building!

CALMLY ZENG opened the door from within.

"Were you looking for me, by any chance?" he purred.

The man twitched spasmodically, rasped an oath, and pivoted. A Luger automatic appeared in his fist as if by magic, and stunned amazement marred his pitted countenance. He was Pock-Face, the driver of the limousine which had been employed for that unsuccessful effort to kidnap Dr. Zeng.

"How'd you get in here?" he gasped. "Freeze before I blast you!"

Zeng lifted his hands obediently and gestured Chow to do the same.

"We are unarmed, sir. You need have no fear of us. I entered by a secret way."

"I don't get it!" Pock-Face backed his two captives into the rear of the vacant shop. "You could have got the drop on me, but you passed it up. You could have—"

The criminologist smiled bleakly. "It would have done me no good. By coming here through a hidden passage, I hoped to catch your master napping, hoped to rescue Miss Carter. Unfortunately, she is not in sight. Therefore this is not your real hide-out. It is but a blind, a place where I was to surrender myself. As soon as I realized that fact, I knew I must give myself into your waiting hands."

"Yeah," Pock-Face growled. "And you made a wise move."

"Wiser, apparently, than one made by the unfortunate Dr. Ernst." Zeng's gaze went toward the pudgy physician's corpse on the chair.

Pock-Face scowled. "He got nosy. That's what happens to guys who get nosy. Keep that in mind if you want to stay alive a while longer."

"I shall heed your sage advice, sir. And now, if you will conduct me to your employer—"

The gunman sidled to a wall lined with shelves, touched a hidden control and caused an entire section to swing outward on oiled hinges. An aperture was revealed, a secret entrance into the building next door.

The guide gestured Zeng and Chow to walk ahead. He prodded them into an adjoining room which was brightly lighted by an unshaded, dangling incandescent.

In a far corner lay Ann Carter, tied hand and foot, a gag in her mouth and fear in her lovely eyes. The fear turned to hopeless dismay when she saw Dr. Zeng and his giant companion being thrust into view, and realized that they were prisoners like herself.

She was guarded by a thuggish individual who held a Luger in his fist, matching the weapon brandished by Pock-Face. Across the room stood a third man who wore a black silk mask which covered his face from forehead to chin, with slits through which his glittering eyes shone maliciously.

"So you really walked into my trap," he greeted Zeng Tse-Lin in a sardonic, mocking voice.

The criminologist bowed. "I had no alternatives, Mr. George Hartman."

A rasping curse ripped from the masked man's lips.

"You smart Chinese punk!" he snarled, lunging at Zeng. "So you know me, eh?" And he doubled a fist, slugged it home to the mouth of the doctor with the hawklike countenance.

Zeng made no motion to protect himself. But Chow, when he saw blood dribbling down his employer's ascetic face, seemed to go berserk. Squealing a wild Mongol war-cry, the giant lashed out with his artificial leg and kicked at the Nazi agent's shins.

"Asiatic swine!" Hartman yelped as if he had been stuck by a needle.

HE SWUNG on Chow and dealt him a ferocious punch full to the jaw. Chow didn't even blink. Hitting him with knuckles was like striking a rock with a feather. He merely glared. Then, oddly enough, he broke into gargantuan laughter, a merriment that seemed to come from the inner knowledge of some vast secret jest.

Hartman ripped away his black silk mask.

"No need for that any more, since you've guessed my identity," he said, and leered at Dr. Zeng.

No longer did he resemble an affable business manager conducting the financial affairs of a clinic. Even his nose looked less bulbous, and there was no brandy on his breath now. Simple though those disguises had been, when he dropped them his entire personality changed. He emerged in his true character of a Prussian spy, a Junkers militarist, a Nazi fanatic.

"How did you guess me?" he demanded of Zeng.

The criminologist shrugged. "Several things gave you away. Let us call it a process of elimination. The spy master had to be an official of the war workers' clinic. It could not have been the chief surgeon, Tremayne, because he was murdered. That also applies to Dr. Max Ernst, whose corpse is even now in the adjoining vacant store. There was only one other physician—Dr. Barton Barryman. And your own error removed him from consideration."

"My error?"

"Yes. The scopolamine bottle, which you labeled 'Fluid Extract of Ergot.' That was a mistake which no medical man would have made. Scopolamine crystals do not resemble ergot. Any one inspecting the dispensary shelves would have noticed the discrepancy at once. Moreover, there is no chemical formula for ergot yet—you placed a fake formula on the label. And finally, you marked it 'Fluid Extract' but there is no such thing, since ergot is not an exact compound, but varies in manufacture."

Hartman frowned. "I understand. Since no doctor would have used such an obviously spurious label, you assumed that it was done by a non-medical official of the clinic. I was the only man answering that description."

"Quite so, sir."

"You're shrewd," the Nazi granted. "But not shrewd enough. Do you think I intend to release Miss Carter, now that she knows my identity? Do you think you can buy her life with your own?"

"Frankly, no." Zeng admitted calmly. "You never intended to free her. You used her as bait to lure me here, and now you plan to murder us all. Is that not true?"

"It is exactly true!" Hartman grunted.

Dr. Zeng smiled at him, curiously.

"Before you liquidate us, I want you to tell me something. These henchmen of yours—this pock-faced fellow, and the other one whom I have never met before. What do you intend to do with them when you are ready to make your escape from San Francisco?"

A strange expression contorted George Hartman's face, as if he desperately wanted to give a certain answer but found it impossible to utter.

"Why, I'm going to kill them, of course," he blurted in a choked voice. "They are no longer necessary to me. My work is finished here. I shall shoot them down, precisely as I shall shoot you and your servant and the girl."

Pock-Face stiffened when he heard this. So did the other man with a Luger, the one guarding Ann Carter. Pock-Face stared at Hartman.

"Are you kidding, Chief?"

IT WAS Dr. Zeng who said calmly:

"He is telling you the full truth, my misguided friend. You see, Chow had a hypodermic needle full of scopolamine in his artificial leg. The syringe was controlled by a spring. When Chow kicked Hartman a moment ago, he injected the truth serum in your master's ankle."

Pock-Face glared. "So, Hartman! You intend to bump me before you leave, eh? Me and Kroger, here." He indicated his companion in villainy.

"Yes," Hartman's lips formed the word despite his struggles to remain silent. The losing battle he waged against the truth injection brought beads of perspiration to his brow. "I am going to kill you. I don't want you to know it.... *Herr Gott*, what am I saying?"

As he gasped the involuntary admission he pulled a gun. But Pock-Face was already triggering his Luger. The room suddenly roared with a thunder of exploding cordite and reeked with the fumes of those explosions. As swiftly as thought, Zeng Tse-Lin hurled himself toward the corner where Ann lay bound, shielded her with his own body against ricocheting slugs.

Hartman staggered under the impact of bullets from the Luger which Pock-Face aimed at him. As he went down, he got his own weapon into action, he fired, missed Pock-Face, and hit the other man, Kroger, full between the eyes. Kroger dropped in his tracks, dead before he slumped to the floor.

Pock-Face emptied his automatic at Hartman, and Hartman fell backward, moaning, his belly riddled. Then Lai Hu Chow, yelling like a fiend, grabbed Kroger's gun, lunged at Pock-Face, and bludgeoned him over the skull.

The sound of that concussion was sickening. Pock-Face lurched, swayed drunkenly, sagged. Chow blinked at him.

"Him got eggshell head," the Mongol mourned sadly. "Crush to pulpee with first smack. Chow never have no fun!"

Zeng Tse-Lin was not listening to his huge servitor's plaint. The criminologist was too busy unfastening Ann Carter's fetters, tenderly lifting her upright.

"Are you all right, Ann? Did these unspeakable rats harm you?"

She made a wry mouth as if still tasting the gag that had been between her lips. Then, gently, she smiled.

"Hold me, Zeng," she whispered. "Hold me closely. Then I'll know everything's—as it should be!"

His arms enfolded her, for it is written that the embrace of a loved one is more precious than an emperor's ransom. And who was Zeng Tse-Lin to contradict the wisdom of the ancient sages?

CORPSE CARGO

CHAPTER I

FRANTIC CALL

THERE HAD been a heavy fog earlier in the evening. Now, as
the night grew later, this changed to a cold and gusty rain that
slanted across the bay, blanketed the Golden Gate and buffeted San
Francisco with whipping violence. Bloated drops drummed like ghostly
fingers on the grease-filmed front windows of the Consolidated Cab
Company's downtown garage, and a sporadic wind rattled one loose
pane as if patiently seeking to gain entrance.

Within the garage office, Joe Norton shivered a little. He scowled as
he listened to the storm's fury, involuntarily hunched himself over his
desk as if crouching in a foxhole somewhere in the Solomons. That
drenching tempest outside reminded him of the action he had seen in
the South Pacific, and the air's dampness made his chest ache in the
region of the ugly bayonet scar a certain sneaking Jap soldier had given
him on just such a sodden night as this.

The Jap had died screaming, an instant after inflicting the wound.
Joe Norton had attended to that. But for Joe the war had ended at that
moment. The bayonet thrust finished his usefulness to the Marine Corps
and sent him home, invalided out of the Service. Now he was back on
his old civilian job as night despatcher for Consolidated Cab.

He tried to sponge his mind of the battle memories aroused by tonight's storm. The rain was unpleasant, yes; but at least it was good for
business, he told himself. Weather like this kept your cabs rolling
overtime. In fact, Joe had already taken so many phone orders that it
seemed useless to answer when the instrument again jangled angrily.

He picked up the receiver. "Consolidated."

"I've got to have a cab," a man's excited voice raced over the wire.
"Right away!"

"Sorry, sir. Not a chance. There isn't even any use booking you. It
would be hours before I could—"

319

"But it's a matter of life and death!" the excited voice interrupted. "My wife's sick. Got to get her to a hospital. She's scared of ambulances. Her brother died in one. It'd kill her if I made her ride in—in…. Listen, Mac, you got to help me! What am I gonna do? I don't own no car myself."

The keen anguish in the man's tone made Joe Norton hesitate. He glanced up from his desk, peered past the pool of light cast by a shaded, dangling bulb. His gaze focused on the shadowy interior of the garage where there was just one battered cab, a taxi which had skidded into a pole that same afternoon, ripping away a fender and running-board. Because of this mishap, the machine had been laid up for repairs; put out of service. Its engine wasn't damaged, though. It would run okay if it had a driver.

JOE CONSIDERED the situation. He could plug his switchboard lines so that incoming calls would be directly relayed to outlying Consolidated stands. Not that this would do any good, since the branches certainly couldn't handle any more orders than they already had. As long as that condition existed anyhow, Joe wasn't really needed here at the main garage.

There was even a spare Consolidated cap on the hat-rack, left by some forgetful hacker. The headgear helped Norton make his decision. He could wear it and save his own new felt hat. A soothing quality came into his voice as he said to the pleading man at the other end of the wire:

"All right. Let's have the address. I'll help you out."

The frantic customer blurted a number which Joe scrawled on his order pad, noting that it was not far from Grant Avenue and well downtown. At least the haul would be a short one, he mused, as he disconnected. Then he plugged his board, tore off the order form, donned the uniform cap from the hat-rack and moved swiftly to the damaged taxi.

Its motor caught immediately and he drove out the rear ramp, into the rain-lashed alley. His windshield wipers valiantly battled the flood of water which poured down the slanted glass. Visibility was almost zero, in spite of this, and the dimmed-out streets gave him plenty of difficulty in locating the address he wanted.

Presently, however, he found it—a slatternly old residence dating back to the days when this particular street had been one of the city's swankiest. Now all the houses had a decadent look, paintless and shabby, like beggars drenched by the storm. The one Norton was hunting proved even seedier than its fellows. It sagged at the eaves, showed no lights at any of the windows and seemed to have an air of abandonment, desertion.

Still, its number matched what Joe had written on his order pad. He checked to make sure, then alighted and dashed for the rickety front porch. Shaking the rain from his cap, he knocked on the door.

It was opened cautiously, almost furtively.

"Step in a minute, Mac," a husky voice rasped from the solid darkness. "Gimme a hand with her. She's passed out on me."

Norton obeyed, striding over the threshold and wondering why the hallway was unlighted. It was his last conscious thought. A blackjack crashed against his skull and he toppled into a chasm of complete oblivion.

Events marched speedily during the ensuing few minutes. Two brawny men lifted Joe Norton's inert form, silently carried him out to his taxi, dumped him in the front compartment. Then they returned to the house, where another man waited for them. This third man, unseen in the thick gloom of the vestibule, seemed to be in full command.

"You loaded the guy in his cab?" he asked.

"Yeah."

As Norton strode across the threshold a blackjack crashed against his skull.

"Good. Now take out these three stiffs and put them in the hack. Make it snappy."

Obediently the brawny underlings fell to work. Three laborious trips they made from the house to the taxi, each time carrying a limber corpse. Presently the task was done and there were three dead men in the rear of the cab, as well as the senseless Norton up front.

Then, back in the old residence, a conference followed.

"What was the idea glommin' a taxi for this caper when we coulda just as easy hauled them dead Mexicans away in our own jalopy?" one of the heavy-set men said complainingly.

"Our own jalopy, as you call it, happens to be my personal sedan." The voice of the unseen leader was harshly arrogant. "I don't want tattle-tale bloodstains on the upholstery, and those bodies are pretty messy."

"Yeah, Boss, but—"

"Besides, I intend to run the cab into the bay. That's why I used a blackjack instead of a gun. The deaths must appear accidental. Now let's go. You two follow in the sedan. I'll drive the hack. You're to pick me up after I've sent my corpse cargo over a cliff."

CHAPTER II

DR. ZENG

RAIN PELTED against the plate-glass show windows of the Mandarin Emporium, one of Chinatown's most exclusive mercantile establishments. Due to dimout rules, no lights blazed to display the store's costly Oriental treasures. There was a matching darkness at the draped windows of the residential floors above.

The entire structure loomed gloomily forbidding in the tempestuous night, pagoda-style eaves glistening wet, walls slightly detached from the buildings which flanked them. It was a curious, somber place whose very silence seemed eerie.

Nor was that weirdness out of keeping with the reputation of the owner. On the upper floors, known as the House of a Thousand Beatitudes, dwelt this mysterious proprietor—Dr. Zeng Tse-Lin. A physician and surgeon of remarkable attainments, he conducted the Mandarin Emporium as a hobby. He devoted most of his time to a career of healing Chinatown's sick.

But his medical skill was not his sole claim to fame. Along Grant Avenue there were many legends whispered about the strange Dr. Zeng. It was known that he was entitled to wear the green jade button of the fifth-examination scholar even though he was barely thirty; that he possessed diplomas from the best universities of the Orient, Europe and America.

He was a man of wealth, and some said he had gained his riches through black magic and sorcery. Others, less superstitious, guessed more accurately that he had perfected scores of scientific inventions and discoveries, which brought him a princely income.

Regardless of the unnumbered tales told about him, he enjoyed the friendship and respect of his Asiatic neighbors, who accepted him as a cultured and aristocratic member of their own race. And this acceptance was an amazing tribute to Zeng Tse-Lin, for actually he was not Chinese at all. He was a white American and his real name was Robert Charles Lang!

True, he had been born in China of wealthy American missionaries, which accounted for his Oriental education and his ability to masquerade successfully as a Chinese. But the reasons for this imposture went deeper than mere whim. Tragedy lay behind it, and a dark vow of vengeance.

Zeng had been in the United States, completing his studies, when news had reached him that his mother and father had been slain near Shanghai by Jap marauders. That day he had sworn grim revenge upon all forces of evil, dedicated his life to a battle against crime in any form.

In the intervening years he completely mastered the science of criminology; trained his keen mind and athletic body to superlative perfection. Now, although few knew it, Zeng Tse-Lin was one of the world's greatest detectives—a sleuth who, unknown to the public at large, had brought hundreds of criminals to justice.

Disguised as a Chinese physician, with the Mandarin Emporium as an added shield, he was able to pursue his strange double career without arousing the slightest suspicion in the underworld haunts of the lawless.

Tonight, in one of the tastefully-furnished upper rooms of the House of a Thousand Beatitudes, Dr. Zeng was entertaining an old and valued friend—Captain Brian Carter of San Francisco's Homicide Squad. Carter, a compact, gray-haired man who had come up through the ranks by sheer ability and tenacity, knew the true secret of Zeng's parentage. But never, by word or action, would he have betrayed that trust.

At the moment he was sipping pearl tea from a fragile L'ing cup as he reclined in the depths of an easy chair with an exotic Tung Shan cigar between his fingers.

"It's a pleasure to visit you, Zeng," he remarked lazily, a thin stream of fragrant smoke coming from his lips. "I can't remember when I've been so relaxed."

Dr. Zeng's answering smile irradiated his hawklike features and lighted his coal-black eyes. He was tall, and he wore a richly-brocaded mandarin robe which emphasized that tallness.

"It is written that the companionship of friends is like the warm wind of summer," he said, bowing politely. "But your cup is empty. I must replenish it."

He clapped his hands twice, sharply, and a giant entered the room—a huge moon-faced Mongol whose cheeks bore the scars of a dozen battles. He walked with a rolling, rakish gait because he wore an artificial limb, having lost his real leg while fighting in vain against the Jap murderers who slew Zeng Tse-Lin's parents. This tremendous figure of a man was Lai Hu Chow, Zeng's constant companion; his devoted servitor.

"You wantee something, mebbe-so?"

ZENG CHUCKLED indulgently at this pidgin talk. It was one of Chow's mannerisms, a sort of standing jest. Actually the big Mongol could speak excellent American without accent—when he wanted to.

"More tea for our distinguished guest, O Large One." Zeng's voice was pleasantly resonant.

Before the giant could obey, a softly-muffled gong sounded in the room. It was Dr. Zeng Tse-Lin's special telephone bell.

Zeng lifted the instrument from its concealment in a Buddha statue. A moment later, he extended the phone to his visitor.

"For you, Captain Carter."

The Homicide officer frowned as he took the call, for he had instructed Headquarters not to contact him unless he was urgently needed.

"Carter speaking…. What's that? Good grief! All three? Have you notified Washington? Okay, I'll be right down." Ringing off, he faced Zeng. "Trouble," he muttered. "Bad trouble. International complications, maybe."

"Indeed?"

"Yes. Do you remember those three Mexican commercial attachés who made short talks at the Chinatown Rotary Club luncheon today?"

"Of course," Dr. Zeng answered, for he had attended the luncheon with Carter.

The police official clenched his fists.

"I'll let you in on a secret. They weren't commercial attachés."

"Quite so." Zeng Tse-Lin nodded gravely. "I observed their military bearing and assumed them to be Mexican Army officers incognito. Army Intelligence men, perhaps."

Carter looked astonished. "You're absolutely right, although I'm blest if I know how you do it. They *were* Intelligence agents, investigating something mighty big here in San Francisco—something connected with an ugly and new political movement in Mexico."

"The Gray Condors, perhaps?" suggested Zeng.

"What the devil do you know about the Gray Condors?" Carter stared in utter amazement.

Dr. Zeng lifted a shoulder. "It is written that rumors ride upon every breeze. I understand that these Gray Condors are the latest *falange* organization—a Latin-American version of the Nazi order. They are working underground to foment political chaos in Mexico and eventually to establish a dictatorship friendly to the Axis.

"Meanwhile they seek to tear down the present diplomatic accord between Mexico and the United States. They stir up hatred of Americans by lying propaganda, and I have heard of an effort to seize stored rifles from a certain arsenal with which to arm their revolutionaries when the time comes." He made an apologetic mouth. "Forgive me for such a long speech."

"There's nothing to forgive," Carter said worriedly. "You've got the details exactly right. All except one."

"And that?"

"The secret leader of these Gray Condors escaped from Mexico some months ago, and since then has been directing their activities from this country. Nobody knows his name or what he looks like, but there's good reason to think he's operating right here in San Francisco."

Zeng's dark eyes narrowed and his predatory nose pinched in as he drew a deep breath.

"Then those three Mexican Intelligence men were here searching for him?" he asked.

"Yes, with the help of our own F.B.I. and the local Department. But they'll search no more. They're dead."

"Murdered?" Zeng asked sharply.

Carter's scowl was puzzled. "That's the screwy part. It was a taxi accident. They were riding in a cab, and it went off the cliff beyond Seal Beach."

"How long ago?"

"We don't know yet. Some dopy artist who has a shanty down there and likes to walk in the rain discovered the wreckage and reported it. The bodies are at the morgue now."

"I should like to see them." Zeng's tone was taut.

"Then come along," Carter said, and added, "I hope to heaven it was a genuine accident. Murder might make trouble below the Border if the public gets the news that three of their officials were assassinated here in the States. It gives me the shivers."

Dr. Zeng nodded gravely, for he, too, felt a premonition of sinister things ahead. He had a sensation of standing above some yawning abyss where danger lurked, where the slightest misstep would jeopardize not only himself but the government and people of a good-neighbor republic. He turned to Chow.

"The limousine, O Large One. We start upon a perilous journey."

SAN FRANCISCO'S morgue was an unpleasant place, despite its bright lights and dazzling white-tiled walls. There was a smell of formaldehyde in the air; a depressing dampness and a feeling of death as Dr. Zeng and Brian Carter entered to look at the bodies of the three Mexican officers.

Before going into the morgue proper, Carter and Zeng had to pass through a waiting room. Here a group of men sat stiffly in straight chairs, their postures uncomfortable, their faces showing varying degrees of tension. One of them spoke to Carter, as if seeking recognition, but the Homicide captain ignored him except to say gruffly:

"No time for reporters." "Aw, now wait a minute—"

Carter firmly turned his back on the man and followed Zeng, who had already gone on into the chilly chamber where the corpses lay on three marble slabs. Here, in silent concentration, Dr. Zeng Tse-Lin swiftly but expertly examined the dead men.

Presently he looked up. "Odd," he said. "Very odd."

"What is?"

"Each body has a fractured skull, and the fractures are almost identical—as if delivered by a blunt instrument such as a blackjack. If there were only one such injury we might assume it occurred when the taxi crashed over the cliff. But three, all alike.... My friend, we are dealing with murder!"

Carter stiffened. "You're sure?"

"An autopsy will be necessary," said Zeng. "But observe these bruises on the torsos, the arms, the legs. They are characteristic of traumatic injuries received after death. Therefore, the men were killed before the cab fell to its destruction. That taxi bore a cargo of corpses, and the accident was faked."

Worry wrinkles deepened around Carter's eyes. He summoned a morgue attendant.

"Who are those guys outside?" he demanded.

"Identification witnesses, Captain. Your chief deputy rounded them up and brought them here to wait. He thought you'd want everyone present who had met the dead men."

"Good work. Send them in."

A moment later the attendant ushered in the entire group of ill-assorted men from the waiting room. Zeng Tse-Lin's eyes surveyed them covertly, missing no detail, although his outward attitude was one of impassive indifference. Then Brian Carter, annoyed, made a pushing gesture with his hands.

"Here, here!" he called out. "Not all of you at once! I want one at a time. The rest of you go back and come when you're called."

CHAPTER III

MURDER AT THE MORGUE

APOLOGETICALLY THE morgue attendant rectified his error, and after herding the witnesses back to the waiting room he returned with only one of them.

"This man was personal orderly to the Mexican officers, sir," he informed.

Zeng scrutinized the fellow. He was a small, swarthy man who had a soldierly appearance despite his civilian attire. Poorly concealing his grief, the orderly looked at each of the dead men. Then he faced Carter.

"I identify them as my superiors, señor," he said. "Early this evening they left our hotel on an investigation and I did not accompany them. It was the last time I saw them alive."

"Okay. Go sit down in that corner. Next witness."

The morgue attendant conducted another man into the chamber of death. This time it was a tall, black-haired, black-eyed individual whose name was Rodriguez Hernando.

"You may know of me, Captain Carter," he said, as he introduced himself. "I am an importer of Mexican merchandise. My store is on Market Street."

Carter nodded. "You knew these men?"

"Slightly." Hernando's voice sounded somewhat evasive. "As commercial attachés they called at my establishment a few times. More than that I cannot tell you."

"Meaning that you have no further information?" Zeng Tse-Lin said in a dry tone. "Or does discretion make you reluctant to testify in my presence, since I am a stranger to you? I shall be glad to step outside if you have anything more to say to Captain Carter."

"That won't be necessary," Carter snapped. He looked coldly at Hernando. "Dr. Zeng is my trusted friend. He sometimes helps me unofficially in cases requiring specialized medical knowledge. You can speak freely before him."

"I have nothing to add, sir," said Hernando.

"Thanks," the Homicide detective said curtly. "Have a chair. Next," he said to the morgue attendant.

Zeng's ascetic countenance remained impassive as another witness was ushered in, but his interest was tuned to vernier sharpness. The man was one he knew—a refugee Czech professor named Jan Masryllich who recently had been conducting some economic classes at the university across the bay.

Masryllich, elderly, tubby, bald and self-effacing, was something of a mystery. The story of his reputed escape from a Nazi concentration camp was like a piece of fiction. It seemed almost impossible to picture this nervous, emotional man as a person who had killed a dozen Gestapo agents and guards in his successful effort to win freedom. Zeng, studying him, reflected that the aroused rabbit is sometimes endowed with a lion's courage.

For a long moment the meek Czech stared at the three corpses. Then, pointing to one of the bodies, he turned and addressed Carter.

"All I recognize, yess," he said, in a thickly-accented tone. "But this one especially. My friend he was."

"How so?"

The professor's faded blue eyes seemed moist.

"When from Hitler I escaped, no place to go I had. This nation a quota has, so in Mexico I stayed. Because I am from the Nazis a fugitive, and because the Nazis he hated, he into his house took me—and now he in an accident is dead with his brave compatriots."

"Don't be too sure of the accident angle," Carter rasped.

A grim expression darkened his face as he said this. Then the grimness gave way to chagrin, as if he suddenly regretted the remark.

His annoyance was caused by the abrupt intrusion of a jaunty, yellow-haired man who wore loud tweeds with the casual air of a person accustomed to being in the public eye.

"What's that about the accident angle, Captain?" this man demanded, not insolently, but with the brash impetuosity of a frisky, over-friendly pup.

Carter regarded him with disfavor. "Listen. When you braced me in the waiting room a while ago I told you I had no time for reporters."

"Me a reporter? That's hardly flattering, Captain. I always thought a radio commentator was a cut above a newspaperman. Particularly a commentator with more than two hundred thousand listeners." He grinned engagingly. "Remember me? Vandy Lance, head newscaster of KQQQ?"

THE HOMICIDE chief scowled sourly.

"You could be Christopher J. Columbus and you'd still have no business here. Scram."

"Okay, sweetheart, it'll be a pleasure. I didn't want to be here anyhow. I was ordered."

"Ordered?" Carter peered at him suspiciously.

"Sure, by your deputy. He called in everyone who had met the men who were killed in this—er—accident tonight. Have you forgotten that I interviewed them over the radio at the hemisphere solidarity dinner night before last? I'm here as an identification witness if you need me."

"I don't," the Headquarters man snapped. "We've got all the identification necessary. And don't go blatting out your brains on the air about the accident being a possible phony."

"Ah, then do you suspect shenanigans?" murmured Lance.

"I didn't say so," snapped Carter. "I won't know until I talk with the driver of the cab."

"He's alive?"

"Yes. I'm told he's in the hospital, badly injured. Now shut up and beat it. That goes for all of you," Carter addressed the other men in the morgue room. "You may leave, but I'll probably want you at the formal inquest."

Silently they started to file out through a rear door. Then, for the first time in many minutes, Zeng Tse-Lin spoke.

"Pardon me, Captain Carter, but you have overlooked somebody."

"Who?"

Zeng's glance went to the door leading into the waiting room.

"A while ago," he said, "when the entire group entered and you sent them away again, I counted five men. Thus far you have talked to only four—the little orderly, the importer named Hernando, the refugee Czech professor, and Vandy Lance."

Carter beckoned the morgue attendant. "Who's the fifth one out there?"

"The artist, sir. The man who has a shack at the beach, and who discovered the wrecked taxi."

"Send him in."

"Yes, Captain."

The attendant shuffled off. An instant later, his startled cry sounded from the waiting room. "Come quick, Captain Carter! This man is—is—"

The Homicide official sprang forward, but Dr. Zeng was even faster. His mandarin robe flurrying, Zeng hurtled into the other room. Then he drew up short.

Propped stiffly in a chair against the wall sat a lean, sinewy person wearing a floppy slouch hat, threadbare clothing and a flowing black Ascot tie, mark of the Bohemian or the artist. He would paint no more pictures, though, for a knife had been driven between his ribs.

He was dead. Zeng Tse-Lin needed but one look to confirm this.

"Another murder," he said somberly to Carter. "Anybody could have sneaked in here and killed him as he waited."

"Or any of those other witnesses might have done it without being noticed!" Carter breathed excitedly. "Any one of them might have sat beside him and quietly stabbed…. Hey, where are they? Curse it all, I turned them loose!"

He raced toward the morgue's rear exit, but it was too late. His four possible suspects were gone.

Frantically he grabbed a phone. He ordered Headquarters to put out a radio dragnet for Jan Masryllich, Vandy Lance, Rodriguez Hernando and the swarthy little Mexican orderly.

"I'll quiz them until somebody spills!" he raged as he hung up. "We'll find out why this man was knifed!"

"I think the motive is already apparent," Zeng answered levelly.

"Wh-what?"

"Someone feared that this artist may have seen too much of the taxi accident—which was not an accident at all. The knife was used to keep him from talking."

Carter blinked. "Good grief! That proves the three Mexicans really *were* murdered!"

"Quite so. And why were they murdered? Because they had probably come too close to the secret head of that Gray Condor organization. The pattern is beginning to form, my friend. I suggest that we go at once to the hospital and interview the taxi driver. Perhaps he can tell us something about the crash over the cliff, and the Gray Condors who caused it."

The Homicide chief was only too glad to accept this suggestion. But when he and Zeng reached the hospital a little later, a sinister disappointment awaited them. They would not be able to interview the injured hacker now. Somebody had climbed to a window of the unconscious man's room and shot him.

Captain Brian Carter's actions during the next few minutes, after he had spoken hurriedly with Dr. Zeng, must have struck the hospital staff as extremely odd. To begin with, the unconscious taxi driver was not dead. The bullet had merely creased his skull as he lay senseless, the shock sending him into a still deeper coma. Yet Carter insisted upon summoning a hearse for the man.

Queerer still, the hearse, when it arrived, proved to bear the insignia of a Chinatown mortuary. It belonged to a Chinese undertaker and the men with it were Chinese.

Strangest circumstances of all was when Carter released an announcement to the press that the unidentified hacker had died of gunshot wounds. Even Carter himself seemed ill at ease when he made this public statement.

Presently, when he was alone with Dr. Zeng Tse-Lin, he gave voice to his bewilderment.

"I did everything you told me to do, Zeng. But what the devil is the idea? This whole thing is crazy. Including me for taking your screwy advice."

The tall, ascetic criminologist smiled thinly. "It is written that the path of wisdom is often devious and beset with many doubts. Think a minute, my friend. Why should anyone try to murder that cabby?"

"To keep him from telling about the crash, of course."

"Quite so." Zeng nodded. "Now, if it became known that the attempt had failed, the killer might try again. The way things now stand, news has gone out that the cabby died. Our murderer believes he accomplished his purpose, and he will be lulled into a false sense of security. Meanwhile, the hacker is no longer in danger."

"Maybe not," Carter said. "But I'd hate to be in his shoes when he wakes up to find himself in a Chinese undertaking parlor."

Again a thin smile played around the corners of Zeng's sensitive mouth.

"He is in good hands, for I sent Chow along with him to guard him. Moreover, as you know, there are many underground passageways in Chinatown. Perhaps the cellar of the mortuary is connected with my own House of a Thousand Beatitudes." His eyes twinkled.

"So that's it!" Carter exclaimed. "You're going to hide him in your place and take care of him there!"

Zeng neither confirmed nor denied this. Instead, he turned the conversation into a fresh channel.

"Does it not strike you as peculiar, old friend, that the cabby was shot at this particular time?"

"I don't get you."

"Well, it happened shortly after you told those witnesses in the morgue that he had survived the fake accident. Until then, I think none of them knew it. They all seemed somewhat astonished. Soon you dismissed them, and presently, while we were discovering a murder there at the morgue, another murder attempt took place here at the hospital."

Carter clenched his fists. "More and more you're pinning it down to one of those four guys—the orderly, Hernando, Masryllich or Vandy Lance!"

"Yes. But we waste time theorizing when there are matters to be investigated. That hacker, while safe now, is unconscious. He may remain unconscious for hours. We can get no information from him while he is in that condition, so we must seek it in other directions."

"Where, for instance?"

Zeng grew thoughtful. "The wrecked cab was a Consolidated. I think we could check their night despatcher, see if he has any record of the call."

"I've already had that done," Carter said. "There's nobody at the downtown garage. Its switchboard is set so that incoming phone messages are relayed to the branch stands."

"All the same," Zeng insisted, "I wish to see the place for myself." His voice grew deep. "Intuition tells me we must solve these murders swiftly, or there may be trouble in our sister republic to the south. It could be trouble which might be brought to a revolutionary head by the news of those assassinations."

The police captain shrugged. "You have my permission to inspect the garage. Me, I'm going to check my radio dragnet, find out if any of our four suspects have been picked up." He smiled wryly at Zeng. "Good hunting."

"May your own path lead to triumph." The criminologist bowed politely.

Then, shaking hands with himself in courteous Chinese fashion, he went out, alone, to his parked limousine. And as he faced the rainstorm, he felt once more that strange sensation of approaching a yawning abyss where peril dwelt.

CHAPTER IV

BLAST FROM HADES

CONSOLIDATED CAB COMPANY'S main garage proved to be everything that Captain Carter had said—dark, deserted, revealing no clues upon casual inspection. But the methods of Zeng Tse-Lin were far from casual. His keen, hawklike eyes missed nothing and his scalpel-sharp mind perceived facts which would have been unnoticed by ordinary observers.

Using a small, powerful flashlight of his own design, he examined his surroundings. First, on the battered desk, he found a man's hat, almost new, with the initials J.R.N. embossed on the sweatband. Since the storm still raged outdoors, Zeng wondered why any man would go out, hatless, in such weather.

Next he spotted a filing cabinet and, upon opening it, discovered it to contain complete records of the company's employes. He searched for a file card of anyone whose initials were J.R.N. and presently found the listing of a Joseph R. Norton who had worked for Consolidated more than six years until he resigned to enlist in the Marine Corps.

Norton, according to the record, had returned some weeks ago after honorable discharge from military service because of a Jap bayonet wound suffered in the Solomons. He had been reemployed as night despatcher.

In that case, why was he not on duty tonight? Zeng felt certain he knew the answer. The cabby whom he had sent from the hospital in a hearse had a bad chest-scar such as a bayonet might inflict. Therefore, he must be this Joseph R. Norton. In its turn, though, this gave rise to a new question.

Why should a night despatcher be driving a taxi when that was not his job?

Again Zeng found the only logical answer. There must have been an emergency call, something of apparent urgency to which Norton had responded. What was that call?

The tall criminologist bent over the desk, broomed it with his electric torch and discerned an order pad, its top page completely blank. This blankness was deceptive, however. Something had been written on a preceding page which had then been removed. But the writing had been done with a hard pencil, and marks had gone through to the underneath sheet.

Swiftly Zeng ran hypersensitive fingertips over the indentations, his sense of touch reading what the eye could not see—just as a blind man reads Braille. And as he performed the feat, his lips moved silently:

"Seven-ten Romulus Street!"

In another moment he was out in his limousine, heading forward through the pelting rain....

The house at 710 Romulus Street was old and shabby, but the lock on the front door was new, almost pick-proof. To the superlative muscles of Zeng Tse-Lin this offered but a minor problem. He grasped the knob, applied unbelievable pressure. The metal moaned complaint and slowly turned, as if in the grip of some case-hardened steel vise. Suddenly there was a grinding wrench—and the door flew open, forced by the strength of a man's fingers!

Simultaneously, a subdued humming sound began from deep in the darkness of the musty house. It was a noise so faint that ordinary ears would not have detected it. But Dr. Zeng heard it, and a puzzled premonition inched through him.

Cautiously he advanced through the forbidding hallway, stabbing his flashlight beam into the dusty, unfurnished rooms that flanked the passage. In one such room he noticed thick brownish stains on the floor, and his trained surgeon's perception recognized these as blood.

Had the three Mexican officials been murdered here?

If so, why hadn't their corpses been left in the house? Why go to the trouble of hiring a cab, loading the bodies into it, and faking an accidental wreck?

There were two plausible answers. First, the murderer had hoped to make those deaths appear to be the result of an automobile mishap.

Second, the killer probably intended to use this old house again in the future. Therefore, he couldn't well leave dead men lying around.

Zeng's weird sense of impending jeopardy grew stronger, the farther he advanced. He was learning things, piecing bits of the puzzle together, but somehow he felt that he was moving toward doom.

And then, suddenly, that doom erupted.

There were tiny puffing explosions behind him, before him, and to either side of him. *Pop-pop-pop!* they sounded. And, as if by some sinister sorcery, the whole house was abruptly engulfed in roaring flames. They licked upward through the interior, the rotten woodwork blazing as it caught. The heat of Hades swirled through the hallway and thick gouts of yellowish smoke reached toward the robed figure of the criminologist.

Dr. Zeng Tse-Lin was trapped!

FINGERS OF white-hot fire reached at the criminologist's robe, and he retreated before that sweeping inferno. He beat with his hands at the glowing places on his brocaded garment. Turning, seeking escape, he made toward the rear, but a sheet of blinding flame roared at him and drove him away. One after another he tried the side rooms. Each time he was met by new holocausts.

At last there was but one untried chamber left—that forward room where the floor was bloodstained. Here the blaze had not yet gained complete headway. Zeng hurled himself over the threshold, wondering if perhaps there was a window through which he might leap to safety.

There was. At least it was a window, but it was boarded up on the outside, the nailed planks forming a barricade impossible to breach without an axe or some similar instrument. Zeng smashed away the glass pane, but the boards mocked him. Smoke billowed around his face, choked his lungs, put tortured agony into his smarting eyes as he groped for some hand-hold on those outside timbers. But there was nothing he could grasp so that he might exert his magnificent strength.

He peered backward and saw that he could no longer retrace his steps to the hall. A bright curtain of fire roared at the room's doorway, imprisoning him. Once more he felt desperately at the window boards, seeking something at which his fingers could pry. Then, even as he ran his palms over the planks, a thunderous impact smashed at them from outdoors.

Zeng drew away, startled out of his usual stoic calmness. A second blow struck the planking. Splinters flew, and there was a sudden wrenching noise. Abruptly a board came loose, then another, and a third. Framed in this unexpected aperture was a great grinning moon of a face, battle-scarred, the huge jaws vigorously munching a wad of chewing gum.

It was the giant Mongol, Lai Hu Chow.

Like a ponderous one-legged stork, Chow stood braced outside the window. He was using his hard steel artificial limb both as an axe and a crowbar to remove the heavy boards. At last the final one came away.

"You gettee outa there chop-chop or by cussee I have hunk of scorched bacon for master!" he roared.

Then he ducked as Dr. Zeng came scrambling over the sill to drop down beside him.

An instant later Chow had replaced and refastened his false leg. Then he grabbed Zeng's hand, as a father would grasp a recalcitrant child's.

"Let's gettee on our horsee. This place too hottee."

He dragged the criminologist toward the street and unceremoniously shoved him into the parked limousine.

Zeng Tse-Lin's smile was both tolerant and grateful.

"That was a near thing, O Large One. But how did you know that I was in the house?"

As he took the limousine's wheel and put the car in motion, Chow discarded his pidgin English.

"I worried about you," he answered simply. "I circled many blocks in a radius from our own residence, and finally saw our automobile. I guessed that you were in that accursed structure, and then it burst into flames. I saw the blaze sweeping the interior, even though rain prevented it from eating through to the outer walls. When you did not come out, I acted."

"You have my thanks," Zeng said affectionately. "Now park before this drug store. I must use a phone."

The tall doctor entered the all-night pharmacy and called Brian Carter at Headquarters. Swiftly he related the incident of the house on Romulus Street, explaining how he had located it and telling of the sudden fire that had trapped him.

"It was incendiary," he added soberly.

"The devil you say!"

"Yes. I think it was a hideout of the Gray Condor organization, the place where the Mexican secret agents met death. That was the address to which the doomed taxi was summoned."

"But the fire?"

"I heard a humming sound when I first forced the front door. I think it was some mechanical or electrical time-set mechanism which touched off chemical fire. The real occupants of the house, whenever they entered, probably had a way to disconnect the trigger. But if an intruder walked in, as I did, he was caught in a death-trap."

CARTER'S VOICE sounded bewildered as it came over the wire.

"You may be right about that, Zeng, but you were all wrong otherwise. Especially regarding our four suspects. They're innocent."

"What makes you say that?"

"Well, you'll remember I put out a radio dragnet for them, right after we found that artist murdered in the morgue. My Department is plenty efficient, if I do say it myself. In less than five minutes, shadows were fastened on the orderly, on Hernando, on Masryllich, and on Vandy Lance."

"And?" Zeng demanded.

"Not a single one of them went near the hospital. So, obviously, none of them could have shot that hacker. I had all four brought in for questioning, then I let them go. Their alibis were foolproof, because my own dicks had tailed them. Which puts us up against a blank wall."

"Not necessarily," Zeng Tse-Lin exploded a verbal bombshell. "It is possible that one of the four made a phone call to a subordinate, ordering the hospital shooting. The leader of the Gray Condors would surely have underlings ready to do his dirty work for him."

Then the criminologist rang off, cutting short Carter's dismayed exclamation.

Once more in his limousine, Dr. Zeng was struck by a sudden thought.

"Chow!" he said sharply. "You disobeyed me!"

"How so?" the Mongol tried to make his bland features look innocent.

"I sent you from the hospital to accompany the hearse which bore that unconscious taxi man. You were to remove him from the undertaking parlors as soon as you arrived there. You were told to take him through the underground passage to the House of a Thousand Beatitudes and there stand watch over him."

"Sure," Chow agreed innocently.

"Instead," accused Dr. Zeng, "you left him unguarded and came seeking me."

"Good thing, too, or you'd have roasted like a leg of pork," Chow said sagely. Anyhow, I didn't leave the cabby alone. He's in the care of a nurse. Missee Ann Carter."

Hearing that name, Dr. Zeng stiffened. Ann Carter was Brian Carter's lovely niece, a young, beautiful and self-reliant red-haired girl who had a modest personal income and used it to maintain a Chinatown mission school and clinic. There Zeng had first met her. As time had gone on, he had grown to care for her more than he was willing to admit, even to himself.

"How in the world—" he burst out.

"I phoned her," Chow answered placidly.

"You asked her to take charge of my patient? And now she is alone with him in our house, without protection in case of unexpected peril?" The hawklike criminologist made a grim mouth. "I like it not, O Foolish One. Drive. Make haste. We must go home at once to be sure she is in no danger!"

The big Mongol nodded and sent the limousine hurtling on into the storm. In a matter of minutes he parked before the dark store-front of the Mandarin Emporium. Dr. Zeng, alighting, made for his front door.

A tubby figure detached itself from the shadows and accosted him mildly, standing on the sidewalk as if unmindful of the rain that drenched him.

"Dr. Zeng?" the man said meekly. "Hours I have for you been waiting. I must immediately have with you the talk. Of importance it is, for I a clue have."

And Zeng Tse-Lin's eyes narrowed as he recognized the refugee Czech professor, Jan Masryllich.

CHAPTER V

FURLOUGH FROM FEAR

F OR ONCE in his life Dr. Zeng revealed no hint of the courtesy which was usually an innate part of his Chinese masquerade. He did not invite Masryllich into the House of a Thousand Beatitudes, nor was he cordial as he faced the stout little Czech. A hint of asperity tinctured his voice.

"Clues?" he repeated. "Concerning what?"

"My Mexican friends who murdered were," said the Czech.

"Has it been officially announced that the deaths were not accidental, then?"

Masryllich shrugged patiently. "No official announcement do I need. I can recognize the ugly handiwork of Nazis and Falangists."

"Even so, why should you come to me with the clue you claim to possess? I am a doctor, not a policeman."

"Ah, yes. But that Homicide captain, Carter, a good friend of yours is. That I could see. And I thought perhaps you would the message relay to him."

"Why do you not go to Carter personally?" asked Zeng coolly.

The fat man made a bitter mouth. "From a concentration camp in Europe I escaped. I a marked man am. My name I must keep out of any connection with this murder case lest spies of the Axis murder me as a police informer."

"I see," Dr. Zeng said thoughtfully. The Czech's explanation might or might not have convinced him. That could not be told from the expression on the criminologist's lean hawklike face. "What is this clue I am to relay to Captain Carter?"

"A word, incautiously dropped in my presence by my Mexican friends who later killed were. An address it was—a place they to investigate planned. Seven-ten Romulus Street."

Zeng veiled the flame that leaped into his dark eyes. Here, he thought, was a curious turn of affairs. Was Masryllich what he pretended to be, a refugee? Or was he involved in the murder plot, the Gray Condor organization? Had he learned that the Romulus Street house had burned down, and rushed here to allay suspicion against himself by divulging information which, although authentic, no longer had any value?

Holding his tone steady, Zeng said:

"I shall see that this clue reaches the proper authorities. Now you must excuse me. I have work to do."

Dismissing the pudgy little man with a gesture, he turned to the door of the House of a Thousand Beatitudes.

Chow lumbered along behind him. They had entered when, behind them, a sharp cry sounded in the rain. It was a startled sound, freighted with fear, and it seemed to gurgle away into silence as if cut off by throttling fingers.

As fast as a swooping hawk, Zeng Tse-Lin pivoted and hurled himself outdoors. Across the street Jan Masryllich was struggling impotently in the grasp of a tall, black-haired man who had him by the throat and was shaking him savagely with what seemed homicidal intent.

Dr. Zeng gained the far curb and smashed into the Czech's assailant. He seized him and applied pressure to certain spinal nerve ends, a trick he had learned years ago in Tibet. Under his seeking fingers, pain coursed through his captive. The man screamed weirdly and released Masryllich.

Zeng whirled him around.

The giant Mongol made a kicking motion and a blinding
arc of electricity flashed from his toes.

"So!" he intoned. "Rodriguez Hernando, the one who calls himself an importer! And why do you attack this refugee?"

"That fat dog deserves death! Let me finish him. I have been shadowing him for hours!"

"Why?" Zeng reiterated implacably.

"Because I believe him responsible for the murder of my compatriots. He was friendly with them and I am convinced he had a hand in sending them into a deathtrap. Now I find him accosting you, whispering to you. What was his message? Was it the signal you are to transmit to Mexico City for the *falange* uprising to begin? Are you, too, a member of the Gray Condors?"

Zeng Tse-Lin's lips parted in what might have been a smile, although it held no mirth.

"For a supposed merchant," he observed, "you know a great deal. And you suspect even more. This is a most peculiar thing."

"Let me go!" yelled Hernando.

"You claimed to be only briefly acquainted with those slain Mexican officials," Zeng said coldly, "yet now I find you attempting personally to avenge them. I think you were closer to them than you have admitted. Possibly you are a Mexican agent yourself."

Hernando's dark face tensed. "What if I am? My credentials are registered in Washington."

"But they are not licenses to kill."

"Kill, indeed!" Hernando raged bitterly. "While you hold me helpless, Masryllich has escaped!"

THIS WAS true. The fat refugee had scuttled off and vanished in the storm. Zeng was undisturbed.

"That was my intention," he said.

"Then you *are* in league with him and with his Gray Condors!" Hernando exclaimed.

Dr. Zeng had no wish, at this particular moment, to reveal his actual status as an unofficial investigator aiding Captain Brian Carter's homicide investigation. Already he had formulated a certain theory based upon one meager clue, and the theory had been twice shaken—first by the arrival of Jan Masryllich with tardy information, then by Hernando's unprovoked attack upon the Czech. These erratic events muddled the issue, and additional talk would only muddle it further.

Therefore Zeng, instead of denying Hernando's absurd accusation, only shrugged.

"Think what you wish, but do your thinking elsewhere. And remember, if any harm befalls Masryllich I shall hold you accountable."

He released the bogus merchant, who stalked off with his head bent to the rain.

Presently Dr. Zeng returned to his own front door where Lai Hu Chow stood waiting, watching. The giant made astonished noises.

"Me no likee those two fella. Why they come here and raisee holler?"

"It is written that a jackal scents prey from many miles of distance," the criminologist answered obliquely.

"You mean they suspected the presence of the wounded hacker in your house?" Chow demanded in Canton dialect. "They staged a fake fight to draw your attention, hoping a henchman might gain admittance? Was it a trick I foiled by standing guard?"

Zeng smiled. "The ways of men are sometimes obscure. Let us waste no more time in fruitless speculation. I wish to see this injured cabby."

He went into the house and upstairs to a secluded rear room on the second floor. Here he paused at the doorway, his heart secretly leaping as it always did at sight of Ann Carter.

Her blue eyes shining, her red hair reflecting glints of lustrous gold from the light overhead, she came forward.

"Zeng! I'm so glad you're here. Our patient—"

"First I must thank you for looking after him," the criminologist said with grave courtesy. "You have my deepest gratitude. How does he fare?"

"He's regained consciousness, but his memory is gone. Shock, I guess—some form of amnesia. He doesn't even know his name. I can't seem to help him."

Frowning thoughtfully, Zeng approached the bed on the other side of the room where a man lay restlessly, staring with eyes that seemed utterly blank.

"Joe," Zeng said. "Joe Norton."

The injured man displayed no sign of recognition.

Zeng felt his pulse, then turned to Chow and gave a whispered command. The giant left the room, returning a moment later with a cup containing an infusion of aromatic herbs well-known in China but rarely employed in Occidental pharmacology. When the taxi driver had swallowed this pleasant draught he seemed to relax.

"It—tastes—good."

"Yes, and your pain will soon depart," Dr. Zeng assured him gently.

He unwrapped the bandage from his patient's wounded head and expertly touched the hurt places with sensitive fingers. Under soft pres-

Dr. Zeng seized the Czech's assailant and
applied pressure on the spinal nerve.

sure the brain injury responded. The method was a sort of manipulative surgery requiring no scalpels to relieve the tension of fractured bone upon tissue—an amazing demonstration of skill which Zeng Tse-Lin had mastered in the Far East, and which neither American nor European medical schools had ever heard of.

Soon the injured man fell into a semi-coma, almost like an hypnotic trance. He was not asleep, yet he was not truly awake. And while he lay in this curious condition, Zeng began quietly questioning him.

"Joe. Joe Norton. Who was the man who called a cab?"

"I—can't—remember."

"What did he look like?"

"I—can't—remember."

"How did his voice sound?"

"I—can't remember—anything."

Zeng signaled to Ann Carter.

"Hold his wrist," he told her. "Tell me when the pulse accelerates."

As she obeyed, he began speaking in a low monotone, with occasional variations of inflection.

"I want a taxi. I want a cab. I must have a taxi right away. Send me a cab at once. Taxi, please. Can you get me a cab?"

AGAIN AND again he repeated the request, each time altering the phrases, each time pitching his voice differently. It seemed to go on for hours, endlessly, monotonously. And as the words were spoken, Ann's head moved from side to side, indicating that the cabby's pulse showed no change.

After a timeless age, sweat began to bead Dr. Zeng's furrowed forehead. With anxious insistence he kept to his task.

"I've got to have a cab. You've got to help me."

Ann Carter's widened eyes flashed a sudden message. The man on the bed moaned faintly, twitched a little. Zeng had discovered a key phrase!

He stopped, summoned Chow, and whispered to him swiftly.

The huge Mongol lumbered away. When he came back to the room he carried an armload of heavy cooking utensils—metal pans, skillets, stewpots. Impassively he brought them near the bed, while Ann stared in bewilderment.

Zeng Tse-Lin drew a deep breath, knowing that his next move held a human life at stake. But counterbalancing this risk was a whole nation's future safety.

He spoke in the tone of a man in desperate need.

"I've gotta have a cab. You gotta help me!"

Once more the man on the bed stirred fretfully and uttered a weary groan. Simultaneously, at Zeng's signal, Chow dropped his collection of kitchen appliances. They fell with a shatteringly metallic crash. As the noise exploded in the little room the injured hacker sat up wildly.

"Wait!"

Dr. Zeng grabbed at him, gently restrained him.

"You are in no danger, Joe."

"Joe? You—you call me Joe? How do you know my name?"

"You are Joe Norton, are you not?"

"Yes, but—but where am I? What am I doing in this b-bed? How did I get here? I thought I was in a wreck!"

"You were." Dr. Zeng's voice was kind. "Here, drink a little more of this herbal sedative. Your cab went over the cliff near Seal Beach. But first you had been called to a house on Romulus Street. Do you remember?"

"I-I.... *Yes!* Now I remember! I went there and someone slugged me. Everything went black. Later I woke up on the floor of the taxi. A man had been driving it, and—and he was just jumping out. Then I felt the machine falling. There was a terrible crash—"

"Can you give me the name of this man who leaped out?" Zeng asked swiftly. "Can you describe him?"

The answer was a bitter disappointment. "No. I—I never saw his face. I only heard his voice."

CHAPTER VI

ELECTRONIC CLUE

THE RAIN had once more turned to fog, and dawn was streaking the eastern hills when a muffled gong sounded in the depths of the House of a Thousand Beatitudes. Somebody was at the front door, seeking admittance.

Zeng Tse-Lin strode to a teakwood box in his living room and opened its ornately carved lid, disclosing a small ground-glass screen which glowed to life at the touch of a switch. This was Zeng's own adaptation of the television principle, whereby he could scrutinize all visitors before allowing them to enter.

There were selenium scanning discs concealed in the street-level entrance, actuated by black light from the infra-red end of the spectrum. These cells, in turn, were connected by wires to the reception screen in the teakwood box upstairs, so that Zeng saw in the glass reflector a miniature image of the person ringing his doorbell.

Now he glanced at Chow.

"It is Vandy Lance, the news commentator, for whom I have been waiting. Admit him."

A moment later Chow conducted the affable, tweed-clad Lance into the room. The broadcaster carried a rather large package, and his expression was youthfully puzzled.

"Hi, Doc," he said, as he placed his parcel on a Ming dynasty table.

"My humble abode becomes even more inferior in your illustrious presence," Zeng murmured, and bowed formally. "You have brought the apparatus I requested?"

Lance nodded vigorously. "Yep. Captain Carter finally located me and relayed your wishes, although I'll be doggoned if I'm able to understand—"

"It is quite simple, sir," Dr. Zeng replied. "At such an hour, one cannot easily obtain electrical equipment from the ordinary sources. Therefore I thought of you and your connection with Station KQQQ. I was sure you would be willing to assist me."

"Right you are. But what on earth do you want with all this junk? Vacuum tubes, rheostats, fixed and variable condensers, a button microphone, coils, filters. What a list!"

The criminologist smiled. "For a good reason. May I speak in confidence? This is not for a news broadcast as yet."

"Shoot. I'm a clam when necessary. Especially if it means a radio scoop for me later."

Zeng squared his shoulders. "Then here is the picture. That injured cab driver did not die when he was shot at the hospital. He still lives, and through him I hope to assist the police in clearing up the mystery of the three murdered Mexican officials. I have checked the hacker's movements back to the house on Romulus Street where he was originally slugged. I have even broken into that house."

"So you're the one who touched off the fire!" exclaimed Lance. "What the devil are you, a private sleuth or something?"

"Merely an amateur investigator," Zeng replied modestly. "I have no personal motivation except to see justice done."

Lance had an admiring expression in his eyes, mixed with bewilderment.

"But how can you see justice done by using this assortment of electronic stuff I just brought you?" he wondered.

"It is a far-fetched idea of mine," the criminologist said. "The cab driver may recognize the voice of the murderer, the man who slugged him, if he hears it again. Now I have narrowed down the field of suspects to three—Jan Masryllich, Rodriguez Hernando, and the Mexican who acted as orderly to the three slain men. Through science I plan to counterfeit their voices."

"You.... Hunh?"

"Quite so. Perhaps you are familiar with an instrument called a voder, developed in the telephone company laboratories. It is a device into which you can speak and, by adjusting certain controls, have your words issue in different guise—the croak of a frog, the tinkle of a bell, the quack of a duck, the sibilants of a Spaniard, the guttural of a German."

"I've heard of the contraption, yes," said Lance.

Zeng Tse-Lin spread his palms. "I shall construct a voder from the equipment you so kindly loaned to me. Through it, the cabby will hear the simulated speech of our three suspects. He may identify one of them."

"It sounds screwy and brilliant!" Lance said. "But even if it works, how do you figure to put the finger on the guilty guy and make it stick legally?"

"There again I must implore your aid. It is now morning. I believe you broadcast on a Coast-to-Coast hookup some time this afternoon?"

"At four. With a short-wave repeat at five, beamed to the fighting men in the South Pacific."

Dr. Zeng's white teeth flashed. "Excellent! Can you invite the three suspects to your studio, perhaps even ask them to participate in the broadcast? Could you do it without arousing any of their suspicions?"

"Well, I—"

"If you have them all present, I shall also be there. The injured taxi employee with me."

"Maybe I could work it," Lance said, dubiously. "But wait a minute. Won't the guilty one get wise when he sees a lot of cops around?"

"There will be no police. We dare not risk revealing a hint of our plans. Therefore, I must request that you say nothing to Captain Carter or any other official."

THE RADIO commentator chuckled boyishly.

"It's a deal. I'll see you at the studio, five o'clock this evening. Man, oh man! If this thing pans out I'll have a news beat that'll give me a better Crosley rating in one night than it took me six months to reach!"

"Quite so," Zeng agreed, motioning Chow to conduct the visitor to the front door. "And please accept my thanks for aiding me."

For the next several hours, Zeng Tse-Lin's upstairs laboratory hummed with strange activity. During that time the criminologist had at least four phone calls from Brian Carter, to which he responded but briefly and then returned to his task of creating a counterfeit voice machine. It was well into the afternoon when he completed his efforts and carried the result into the bedroom where Joe Norton lay recovering from his hurts. Ann Carter looked up when Zeng entered.

"What in the world is that thing?" she asked.

For answer, Zeng adjusted certain controls, then spoke into the button microphone. But it was not the voice of Dr. Zeng that issued from the contrivance. Far different was the timbre of the words:

"I gotta have a cab—you've gotta help me—step inside a minute, Mac."

Norton sat up from his pillows.

"That's it! That's the one! I'd recognize it anywhere!"

"Good!" Zeng smiled, and there was almost a sinister light in his dark eyes. "I think we are approaching the end of a murder trail."

Lai Hu Chow entered the room.

"The end or the beginning, O Master," he said in high-caste Mandarin dialect. "There is a man loitering across the street, watching this house!"

By a curious circumstance, Ann Carter departed a little later, yet she did not leave the House of a Thousand Beatitudes by its front door, nor did she make her exit through the Mandarin Emporium. There are, according to rumor, many secret subterranean passageways beneath the streets of San Francisco's Chinese quarters. Perhaps this explains why Ann emerged from a café three blocks distant, unobserved by anyone who might have been watching Dr. Zeng's residence.

Still more curious was the fact that Captain Brian Carter subsequently went into that same Chinese restaurant and apparently vanished. At least, he did not come out again, either by the street door or the alley exit.

And, finally, a third strange event took place—this time in the house of Zeng Tse-Lin. Ever since his experiment with a spurious voice from the electronic voder instrument, Zeng had again been busy in his laboratory. Now he came forth with what seemed to be an odd-looking metal device built in the shape of an artificial leg.

He summoned Lai Hu Chow.

"I think you had better wear this limb in place of the one you are now using," he told the giant Mongol. "Make the exchange at once, for the time rapidly comes when you will have need of it."

Chow obeyed without question. He was accustomed to wearing queer false legs of Zeng's design. Often they contained a miniature arsenal of guns and knives. Sometimes they were a receptacle for shortwave radio sets or even gas bombs. In the present instance he listened attentively while his master outlined a terse but comprehensive explanation of the use to which this new leg was to be put.

"I savvee," the hulking servitor said when Zeng had finished talking. Then he added with a note that was half-savage and half-wistful: "Wishee I could usee on nogood who standee across street, watching this building."

Dr. Zeng looked grim. "Be patient. Your chance will come."

CHAPTER VII

CONDOR UNMASKED

JUST A few minutes after four-thirty, the furtive man on the opposite sidewalk looked at his strap-watch, then went nervously into a corner drug store where he made a cautious phone call.

"No sign of 'em comin' out, Boss," was his phoned message.

"Fool!" came an accusing answer. "They probably spotted you and used a secret exit. I might have known you wouldn't get a chance to gun them down."

"What shall I do now, Boss?"

"Get on the job here. We'll use the alternative plan."

Even as this guarded conversation was taking place, an oddly assorted trio emerged from a vacant store on a cross street several blocks away. One of them was the tall, robe-clad figure of Dr. Zeng Tse-Lin. The second was the lumbering giant, Lai Hu Chow. He supported a smaller man whose head and face were bandaged and whose right arm was in a splint.

These three entered Zeng's limousine, which Chow had previously parked at the curb in readiness. The powerful motor purred to life and the sleek car whispered forward, heading toward the broadcasting studios of Station KQQQ. There, a group of suspects were gathered together, among them the murderous leader of Mexico's Nazi-spawned Gray Condor *falange* movement.

It was going on five o'clock, and five o'clock would be pay-off time.

The station's aerial towers were located on the Peninsula. The remote-control studio from which Vandy Lance did his shortwave repeat news broadcast for the South Pacific was in a penthouse structure atop one of the downtown office buildings.

As Dr. Zeng and his companions stepped from the elevator they found the outer chamber deserted, for this was not the main studio where commercial programs originated. It was a special set-up for shortwave purposes such as Lance's summation of the day's events, beamed to American fighting forces. Consequently it lacked the usual guides, flunkies and attendants.

A green light glowed above the door of Studio B, however, indicating that this was where Lance would presently speak into his microphone—at which time the light would turn to red. Zeng led his little party to that door, opened it, and gestured them over the threshold.

Within the room there was a curious, acoustically dead quality resulting from the soundproof texture of the walls, ceiling and heavily-carpeted floor. But even this could not muffle the startled exclamations of three men who were sitting uneasily in the chamber. Rodriguez Hernando, Jan Masryllich and the Mexican orderly stared, astonished, as Zeng entered with his companions.

"What is this?" Hernando demanded.

The criminologist regarded them impassively.

"Myself and my servitor I need not introduce, but perhaps you will be interested in this bandaged gentleman. He is Joe Norton, the driver of the murder cab."

"This—this the driver is?" Masryllich's eyes bulged. "But I thought he killed was!"

"You were deceived," Zeng answered.

"Señor, what means all this?" the swarthy little orderly burst out. "Why was I asked to come here? How does—"

Dr. Zeng waved him silent, then looked across the room to a plate-glass wall behind which lay the studio's control panel and mixing booth. In that glassed-in monitor station stood the newscaster, Vandy Lance, talking to two technicians. Lance waved a greeting through the thick glass, smiled, and came out to welcome the new arrivals.

"Almost afraid you weren't going to make it, Doc," he said affably. "I go on the air in five more minutes."

A harsh, unexpected yell came from the lips of the bandaged man.

"He's the one! That's the voice! It was Vandy Lance who blackjacked me!"

"Yes," Zeng said quietly, "Lance is the murderer, the chief of the Gray Condors."

The smile never left Lance's countenance, but suddenly there was a gun in his steady hand. At the same moment, the two burly mixers crashed out of the monitor room. They also had guns.

Lance chuckled mockingly.

"The pay-off, eh, Doc?"

"Quite so. The pay-off."

LANCE NARROWED his eyes.

"It's funny. When I took you that electronic equipment I figured you were dumb. I thought you'd try to reproduce the voices of Masryllich, Hernando and the orderly. I never guessed you might include mine."

"Then you hoped my efforts would result in a stalemate?"

"I hoped they'd result in your death before you ever reached this studio," Lance said.

"Ah, yes. You had a man posted outside—one of these sound technicians, I believe. But we eluded him."

The broadcaster laughed. "So you did, and then walked into this nice trap I had set for you. Ever since you confided in me about your secret investigations I've been intending to remove you. You suspected too much. And the cabby—he knows too much. As for these others, they'll die, too. They're on the wrong side of the Mexican political fence."

"Do you think yours is the right side?"

"It's the winning side."

"You are an agent of Hitler of course?" Zeng said musingly.

Lance showed his teeth. "That's not hard to guess, is it? I *am* a little puzzled as to how you first came to suspect me, however."

"You have yourself to blame for that," the criminologist answered calmly. "It goes back to the murder of that artist in the morgue. He could not have been stabbed while other witnesses remained in the waiting room. But you and he were the last to stay in that room. You were alone there with him. You were the only one who had an opportunity to knife him, and from opportunity I deduced motive."

"That's pretty thin."

Zeng shrugged. "You also phoned one of your henchmen to go to the hospital and shoot Norton, this hacker here. And finally, when you brought that electrical apparatus to my house, you made a bad blunder. I mentioned the address on Romulus Street, and you said to me. 'So you're the one who touched off the fire!'"

"Well?"

"How could you know that the fire was incendiary, a touch-off, unless you were aware of the fire bombs which had been planted in the house? And if you were aware of them, you must have placed them there yourself."

"Smart enough," Lance admitted. "What else?"

"The rest was simple. I counterfeited your voice with a voder instrument and Joe Norton recognized it. That was the last clue. I realized you were guilty."

The leader of the Gray Condors tinctured his admiring smile with mockery.

"And yet, knowing I was your man, you walked into my trap. Did you think you could startle me and get the drop on me?"

"I hoped to."

"Well, your scheme missed fire. I played along with you just to see how far you'd go. I even brought these other men into the set-up so they could die with you." He indicated Masryllich, Hernando and the orderly. Then he turned to his own brawny subordinates, the two sound technicians. "Start shooting, boys. Gunfire won't get out of this soundproof room."

"The leg of lightning, Chow," Zeng Tse-Lin said softly, almost in a whisper.

What happened in the next instant was almost too fantastic for belief, but those who were in the radio broadcasting chamber believed it, because they actually saw it occur. It was like a blaze of doom bursting from nowhere.

In one corner there was a table, upon which rested a microphone. The instrument was switched off, of course, but its circuit was properly grounded. One of Vandy Lance's underlings was standing near the table, covering the prisoners with his pistol. Directly before him stood Lai Hu Chow.

The giant Mongol made a kicking motion with his false limb, as if momentarily pointing the leg at the gunsel. Then came an abrupt, blinding arc of electricity flashing from the toe of Chow's shoe, a crackling, blue-white knife of spark-spitting intensity.

It issued from a pack of dry cell batteries concealed and insulated in the metal leg. They were miniature batteries of Dr. Zeng's own design, hooked in series to produce twenty-four volts of current—a comparatively low voltage, but achieving tremendous amperage because it flowed through a high-tension coil. This system was much the same as is found in automobiles, which employ a six-volt storage battery and builds up a jolting ignition spark through the use of a similar coil.

IN CHOW'S artificial limb the spark coil was more compact and more powerful, and the released current was cleverly calculated to jump a long gap, to bridge itself between its source and the nearest potential ground. Exactly as Zeng had planned, the table microphone made this ground. It was the thug's misfortune to be standing between the table and Chow's pointing leg.

The result was inevitable. A buzzing, spitting finger of released electricity leaped through the air and slammed with paralyzing force through the gunman's torso. He screamed and tossed away his automatic. He doubled over, with his hands clutching frantically at his stomach.

The unexpected diversion caused Vandy Lance and his remaining hood to whirl, to stare in wide-eyed stupefaction. Then a shot hammered against the room's deadness, a sharp, coughing report from a fantastic source—the splint-encased right hand of the bandaged man.

That one bullet was enough. It nailed the second gunsel full in the chest and smashed him to the floor.

"Boss—look out! The hacker's got a rod!"

"Not the hacker," the bandaged man said.

He ripped off the bindings that had obscured his face. Dr. Zeng Tse-Lin had done an excellent job of disguising his old friend, Captain Brian Carter of the San Francisco Homicide Division.

Vandy Lance pivoted, tried to reach the door. Zeng collared him, swung him around, lifted him high in the air and then hurled him against the wall like a toy. The man moaned in terror as he smashed across the room. Then he impacted sickeningly. He did no more moaning after he fell to the rug....

There were few explanations to be made to Hernando, Masryllich and the swarthy Mexican orderly. They had already heard the boastful confession of Vandy Lance when he had thought himself in control of the situation. They had stood in peril of their lives, faced with murder at the hands of Lance and his henchmen. And in the end they had witnessed an amazing reversal of the tide. They had seen the turning of the tables, thanks to the mysterious individual known as Dr. Zeng Tse-Lin.

But with Oriental modesty the tall, hawklike criminologist backed away from the praises they tried to heap on him. He had done a job, accomplished his purpose. He had wiped out a nest of Naziphiles and solved four murders. Now the episode was ended, the tale told.

He made for the door, tugging Lai Hu Chow along with him.

Brian Carter stopped them.

"I'll be seeing you soon again?" The Homicide officer's eyes twinkled.

"This evening, if you wish," Zeng answered. "When you have cleaned up the details of this monstrous mess. My poor home will be honored by your visit, and Chow will prepare bowls of ceremonial tea."

"I'll be there," Carter promised.

Dr. Zeng's expression was completely blank as he bowed. But there was a hopeful quality in his voice as he suggested:

"Perhaps you will bring your niece?"

"You betcha blingee Missee Ann," Chow chimed in. "By cussee it is litten that no celeblation is complete without plitty girl."

www.ingramcontent.com/pod-product-compliance
Lightning Source LLC
Chambersburg PA
CBHW032227010726
47494CB00002B/378